Michelle Smart's love affair with books started when she was a baby and would cuddle them in her cot. A voracious reader of all genres, she found her love of romance established when she stumbled across her first Mills & Boon book at the age of twelve. She's been reading them—and writing them—ever since. Michelle lives in Northamptonshire, England, with her husband and two young Smarties.

Cathy Williams can remember reading Mills & Boon books as a teenager, and now that she is writing them she remains an avid fan. For her, there is nothing like creating romantic stories and engaging plots, and each and every book is a new adventure. Cathy lives in London. Her three daughters—Charlotte, Olivia and Emma—have always been, and continue to be, the greatest inspirations in her life.

Discover more at millsandboon.co.uk.

MARRIAGE MADE IN BLACKMAIL

MICHELLE SMART

THE ITALIAN'S ONE-NIGHT CONSEQUENCE

CATHY WILLIAMS

MILLS & BOON

First Published in Great Britain 2018
by Mills & Boon, an imprint of HarperCollins*Publishers*
1 London Bridge Street, London, SE1 9GF

Marriage Made in Blackmail © 2018 by Michelle Smart

The Italian's One-Night Consequence © 2018 by Cathy Williams

ISBN: 978-0-263-93543-1

MIX
Paper from
responsible sources
FSC® C007454

This book is produced from independently certified FSC™ paper
to ensure responsible forest management.
For more information visit www.harpercollins.co.uk/green.

Printed and bound in Spain
by CPI, Barcelona

MARRIAGE MADE IN BLACKMAIL

MICHELLE SMART

CHAPTER ONE

LUIS CASILLAS SNATCHED his ringing phone off the table and put it to his ear. *'Sí?'*

'Luis?'

'Sí.'

'It's Chloe.'

That brought him up short. 'Chloe... Chloe Guillem.'

The woman who had spent the past two months treating him as if he were a carrier for a deadly plague?

'Oui. I need your help. My car has broken down on a road on the Sierra de Guadarrama...'

'What are you doing there?'

'Driving. *Was* driving.'

'Have you called for recovery?'

'They can't get to me for two hours. My phone is running out of battery. Please, can you come and rescue me? Please? I don't feel safe.'

Luis looked at his watch and swore under his breath. He was due at the gala he and his twin brother Javier were hosting in half an hour.

'Is there no one else you can call?' Chloe worked for his ballet company in Madrid. In the year the gregarious Frenchwoman had lived in his home city she had made plenty of friends.

'You are the closest. Please, Luis, come and get me.' Her voice dropped to a whisper. 'I'm scared.'

He took a long breath as he did some mental maths. This gala was incredibly important.

Ten years ago Luis and his twin had bought the provincial ballet company their prima ballerina mother had spent her childhood training at. Their aim had been to elevate it into a world-renowned, formidable ballet company. First they had renamed it Compania de Ballet de Casillas, in their mother's memory, then set about attracting the very best dancers and choreographers. Three years ago they had drawn up the plans to move the company out of the crumbling theatre it had called home for decades and into a purpose-built state-of-the art theatre with world-class training facilities and its own ballet school. Those plans had almost reached fruition.

Now they wanted patrons for it, members of the elite to sponsor the ballet school and put it even more firmly on the world's ballet map. Europe's elite and dozens of its press were already gathering at the hotel. Luis *had* to be there.

'Where exactly are you?'

'You will come?'

It was the hope in her voice that did for him. Chloe had the sweetest voice he had ever had the pleasure of listening to. It wasn't girlishly sweet, more melodic, a voice that sang.

He couldn't leave her alone on the mountains.

'*Sí*, I will come and get you, but I need to know where you are.'

'I will send you the co-ordinates but then I will have to turn my phone off to save what is left of my battery.'

'Keep it on,' he ordered. 'Have you got anything to hand you can use as a weapon if you need it?'

'I'm not sure…'

'Find something heavy or sharp. Be vigilant. Send me the co-ordinates now. I'm on my way.'

'*Merci*, Luis. *Merci beaucoup.*'

'I'll be with you as soon as I can.'

Hurrying to his underground garage, he selected the quickest of his fleet of cars, inputted Chloe's co-ordinates into its satnav, then drove it up the ramp. The moment he was clear, he put his foot down, tearing down his long driveway, past the stretched Mercedes with his waiting driver in it.

His clever console, which had calculated the quickest route for him, said he was an hour's drive to her position from his home in the north of Madrid, *if* he kept to the speed limit.

Provided traffic wasn't too heavy this Saturday evening, Luis estimated he could make it in forty, possibly even thirty minutes.

He always kept to the speed limit in built-up areas. The temptation to burn rubber was often irresistible but he always controlled the impulse until on the open road. Today, with thoughts of Chloe stranded in the mountains on his mind, he wove in and out of the traffic ignoring the blast of horns hailing furiously in his wake.

Chloe Guillem. A funny, attention-seeking, pretty child who had grown into a witty, fun-loving, beautiful woman. Truly beautiful.

It had taken him a long time to notice it.

An old family friend, he hadn't seen her for four or five years when she had called him out of the blue.

'*Bonjour*, Luis,' she had said in a sing-song tone that had immediately suggested familiarity. 'It is Chloe Guillem, little sister of your oldest friend, calling to ask you to put friendship ahead of business and give me a job.'

He had burst into laughter. After a short conversation where Chloe had explained that she'd completed her apprenticeship in the costume department of an English ballet company, spent the past two years working for a Parisian ballet company and was now seeking a fresh challenge, he'd given her the name and number of his Head of Costume. Recruitment, he'd explained, was nothing to do with him.

'But you own the company,' she had countered.

'I own it with my brother. We are experts in the construction business. We know nothing of ballet or how to make the costumes our dancers wear. That's what we employ people for.'

'I have references that say I'm very good,' she had cajoled.

'That is good because we only hire the best.'

'Will you put in a good word for me?'

'No, but if you mention that your mother was Clara Casillas's personal costume maker, I am sure that will work in your favour. Provided you are as good as your references say you are.'

'I am!'

'Then you will have no trouble convincing Maria to hire you,' he had laughed.

Luis had thought nothing more of the conversation until around six months later when he'd attended a directors meeting at the old theatre to discuss preparations for the company's move. A galloping gazelle had bounded up to him out of nowhere with a beaming smile and thrown her arms around him.

It had been Chloe, bright and joyous and, she had delightedly told him, loving her time in Madrid. Luis had been pleased to see this face from his past but he'd been too busy to take much notice of his old friend's little sister.

When Luis and Javier had pooled their meagre inheritance to form Casillas Ventures almost two decades ago, they had decided from the start that one of them would always be the 'point man' on each project. This would simplify matters for contractors and suppliers. Luis had taken the role of point man for the construction of the new theatre and facilities. In this venture he had been far more hands on than he would normally be but this was a special project. This was for their mother, a way for the world to see the Casillas name without automatically thinking of Clara Casillas's tragic end at the hands of her husband.

The closer it got to completion, the more hours he needed to put in, overseeing the construction and ensuring Compania de Ballet de Casillas was prepared for the wholesale move to its new premises.

From that embrace on though, whenever Luis visited the old crumbling theatre he somehow always managed to see Chloe.

She always acknowledged his presence, with either a quick wave if working on an intricate costume or a few words exchanged if on a break, her cheeks turning the colour of crimson whatever reception she gave, a little quirk he'd found intriguing but never given much thought to... not until he'd walked past a coffee shop a few months later and caught a glimpse of a raven haired beauty talking animatedly to a group of her peers. Spring had arrived in his home city and she'd been wearing a thin dress that exposed bare, milky-white arms, her thick raven hair loose and spilling over her shoulders.

He would have stopped and stared even if he hadn't recognised her.

How had he not seen it before?

Chloe Guillem *radiated*. Sunlight shone out of her pores, sexiness oozed from her skin. Her smile dazzled.

She must have felt his stare for she had looked up and seen him at the window and the full power of her smile had been unleashed on him and this time it had hit him straight in his loins. He had never in all his thirty-five years experienced a bolt of pure, undiluted, unfiltered lust as he had at that moment.

He'd taken her out to dinner that very night. It had been the most fun and invigorating evening he could remember. Chloe was funny, full of self-deprecating wit, a raucous laugh never far from her voluminous lips. And she was sexy.

Dios, was she sexy. He had been unable to tear his eyes away, greedily soaking up everything about her, all the glorious parts he'd been oblivious to. It was incredible to think he'd been blind to it for so long.

And the desire was mutual. Luis knew when a woman wanted him and Chloe's body language had needed little interpretation.

But when they had left the restaurant she had rebuffed his offer of a nightcap by hailing a taxi.

He had never been rejected before. It had intrigued rather than discouraged him.

'If not a nightcap how about a goodnight kiss?' he'd asked before she could escape into the cab, taking her face into his hands and gently rubbing his nose to hers. Her scent had filled his senses, reminding him of English strawberries and cream.

Her eyes had been stark on his, the flirtatious glimmer that had been prevalent the whole evening suddenly gone, her beautiful plump lips drawing together.

'Next time, *bonita*,' he had whispered, inhaling her scent again.

All the confusion on her face had broken into a smile that had shone straight into his chest. She had stepped back and nodded. 'Yes. Next time.'

'You will let me kiss you?'

The smile had widened, baby-blue eyes glittering with promise. 'Yes, I will let you kiss me.'

But there had been no next time and no kiss. Two days

later everything had gone to hell with her brother. Chloe had cancelled their planned date and stopped accepting his calls. When he visited the ballet company she kept her head down and pretended not to see him.

They hadn't exchanged two words in almost as many months.

Why the hell he was tearing down roads at an average speed of a hundred miles an hour to rescue a woman who had dropped him like a hot brick he could not fathom, and especially on this night of all nights.

A curse flew from his lips when, thirty-four minutes after leaving his home, he reached the co-ordinates Chloe had given him.

It was a passing place on the winding road, with a flat grassy area for day-trippers to enjoy the spectacular view over a picnic. There was no one there. And no broken-down car.

He brought the car to a stop and grabbed his phone from the passenger seat. In his haste to get to her he'd forgotten to turn the ringtone up and only now did he see he had three missed calls from his brother.

He called Chloe. It went straight to voicemail.

Getting out of the car to search for her, he called Javier back.

'Where are you?' his brother snapped, picking up on the first ring.

'Don't ask. I'll be there as soon as I can.'

'I'm grounded in Florence.'

'What?' Javier was supposed to be at the gala already. In Madrid. Not Florence.

'My plane's been grounded on a technicality. It passed all the safety checks this morning. Not a single issue of concern. Something's not right.'

Luis disconnected the call, a real sense of disquiet racing through him. The sun was descending over Madrid in the far distance but the orange glow it emitted did nothing to stave off the chill that had settled in his bones.

His brother was grounded in Florence and suspected sabotage.

Luis had been lured to the middle of nowhere in the Sierra de Guadarrama in his dinner jacket, on a rescue mission where the damsel in distress had disappeared.

He checked the co-ordinates again.

This was definitely the right place.

So where the hell was she? And why was his sense of disquiet growing by the second?

Chloe Guillem took a seat in the first-class lounge at Madrid-Barajas airport and removed her phone from her carry-on bag.

She had six missed calls and seven text messages, all from the same number. She deleted the messages without reading them and fired off a message to her brother.

Mission accomplished. Waiting to board flight. x.

The glass of champagne she'd asked for when entering the lounge was brought to her table and she took a large sip of it at the moment her phone rang.

Cursing to herself, she switched it to silent and threw it down.

Two minutes later it vibrated in a dance over the table.

She had a new voicemail.

Her gut told her in the strongest possible terms not to listen to it.

She pressed play.

Luis Casillas's deep, playful voice echoed into her ear. 'Good evening, Chloe. I hope you are safe wherever you are and have not been kidnapped by a gang of marauding youths. You might wish you had been though because I *will* find you. And when I do…' Here, he chuckled malevolently. 'You will wish you had never crossed me. Sleep well, *bonita*.'

It was the emphasis on his final word rather than the implied threat that lifted the hairs on her arms.

Bonita.

The first time he had called her that she had thought she would never stop smiling.

Now she was overcome with the urge to cry.

He was not worth her tears, the two-faced, treacherous, conniving, evil bastard.

Thank goodness she'd had the sense to resist his offer of a nightcap…

Chloe downed the rest of her champagne and grimaced.

It hadn't been sense that had stopped her accepting his offer or his goodnight kiss. It had been fear.

Her date with Luis had given her a sense of joy she hadn't felt since her early childhood where she had spent innocent, happy days climbing trees and running around with friends, cocooned with love, blissfully unaware life could be anything other than wonderful. Luis was tied up in those memories.

Once upon a time she had been smitten with him.

She'd wanted to be sure his feelings for her were genuine and that he wasn't looking at her only as a potential conquest. As hard as it was, she'd wanted to trust him. She'd wanted his respect.

At the end of their date when his nose had rubbed against hers and every ounce of her being had strained on an invisible leash to escape her brain and *kiss* him, she had almost given in. She'd spent their entire date imagining him naked, something she'd blamed on the erotic dream she'd had of him the night before but which she'd known, deep down, was her own hidden sexuality breaking free for this man who'd stolen into her teenage heart and now demanded to be heard.

What had she been *thinking*?

Luis had no respect.

He had made a mockery of her brother's trust in him and by extension made a mockery of her and her dead mother. He was as bad, no, *worse*, than her pathetic father.

She knew his brother was equally culpable for ripping her brother off but Javier hadn't been the one to embrace her tightly at her mother's funeral and promise that one day the pain would get better. That had been Luis. Witty, sexy, fun-loving Luis, the only man who had ever captured her feminine attention. The only man in her twenty-five years she had ever dreamed of.

Whatever Benjamin had planned for him could not come soon enough.

The board on the wall with the constantly updated list of all departures and arrivals showed her own flight was now boarding.

Hurrying to her feet, Chloe made her way to the departure gate.

Now she knew what Luis Casillas was capable of she had to take his threat to hunt her down seriously.

Only when she looked out of the window of her first-class seat on the flight paid for by her brother and watched Madrid shrink from view did her lungs loosen enough to breathe easily.

Luis thought he'd be able to find her? Well, good luck to him. She would be the needle to his haystack.

The Grand Bahaman suburb of Lucaya was, Chloe could not stop thinking, a paradise. Her brother had set her up in a villa in an exclusive complex where all her needs and whims were taken care of and all she had to worry about was keeping her sun lotion topped up.

She had spent her first six days there doing nothing but lazing by the swimming pool and refreshing her social media feeds, her worries slowly evaporating under the blazing sun. As far as boltholes went, this was the best. It had exclusivity but also, should Luis carry out his threat to hunt her down, the comfort of safety in numbers.

She doubted he was sparing her a moment of his thoughts. The fallout in Madrid and the rest of Europe was growing in intensity. Chloe read all the news and gossip torn between glee and heartbreak.

It should never have come to this. Luis and Javier should have done the right thing and paid her brother the money they owed him, all two hundred and twenty-five million euros of it.

Seven years ago, on the day Chloe and her brother were told their mother's cancer was terminal, Luis had called Benjamin for his help, dressing it up as an investment opportunity.

The Casillas brothers had paid a large deposit on some prime real-estate in Paris that they intended to build a skyscraper on that would eclipse all others. The owner of the land had suddenly demanded they pay the balance immediately or he would sell to another interested party. He'd given them until midnight. The Casillas brothers did not have the money. Benjamin did.

He gave them the cash, which amounted to twenty per cent of the total asking price. It was an eye-watering sum.

Tour Mont Blanc, as the skyscraper became known, took seven years to complete. Two months ago, Benjamin had received his copy of the final accounts. That was when he realised he'd been duped. The contract he'd signed, which he'd believed stated his profit share to be twenty per cent as had been verbally agreed between him and the Casillas brothers, had, unbeknown to him, been altered before he signed. He was entitled to only five per cent of the profit.

His oldest, closest friends had ripped him off. They'd taken advantage of him at his lowest point. They'd abused his trust.

When they'd refused to accept any wrongdoing Benjamin had taken them to court. Not only had he lost but the brothers had rubbed salt in the wound by hitting him with an injunction that forbade him from speaking out about any aspect of it.

Chloe would never have believed Luis could be so cold. Javier, absolutely, the man was colder than an ice sculpture, but Luis had always been warm.

Now the press was alive with speculation. Benjamin whisking Javier's prima ballerina fiancée away from the Casillas brothers' gala and marrying her days later had the rumour mill circling like an amphetamine-fed hamster on a wheel. An intrepid American journalist had discovered the existence of the injunction and now that injunction was backfiring. So far only the injunction itself was known about but a frenzy of speculation had broken out about the cause of it, none of it casting the Casillas brothers in a favourable light.

Let them be the ones to deal with it, Chloe thought defiantly, shoving her beach bag over her shoulder and slipping on her sparkly flip-flops. She was safe here in the Bahamas and her brother was safely cocooned with Freya in his chateau.

Leaving the tranquillity of the complex for only the third time since her arrival a week ago, she spent an enjoyable fifteen minutes strolling in the early-morning sun to Port

Lucaya, very much looking forward to a day of island hop-ping on the complex owner's yacht.

The invitation had been hand delivered by the manager the evening before, the man explaining it was an excursion the owner provided for favoured guests whenever she visited. A guest had been taken ill so the invitation was Chloe's if she wanted it. Thinking she couldn't come to much harm if it was a woman hosting the event—she'd read too many horror stories about young women and rich men on yachts to have been comfortable with it being run by a rich male stranger—she had been delighted to accept. She couldn't spend a fortnight in the Bahamas hiding away.

Chloe liked to keep busy. She liked to be with people. Being alone with only her thoughts for company meant too much time to think. Better to let the past stay where it was by always looking forward and keeping her mind busy and her life full.

She found the port easily, the pristine yachts lined up in the small bay an excellent giveaway. Opposite it was the Port Lucaya Marketplace she'd heard so much about and which she had promised herself a visit to. Looking at the quaint colourful tourist trap bustling with life and exotic scents brought a big smile to her face. She would go there tomorrow.

Turning her attention back to the yachts, Chloe scanned them carefully, looking for the one named *Marietta*. Her excitement rose when she finally located it. At least four decks high, the *Marietta* was the biggest and most luxuri-ous-looking of the lot. Not quite cruise-ship size, it looked big enough to accommodate dozens of guests with room to spare.

But where was everyone? The metal walkway for pas-sengers to board had been lowered but she saw and heard none of the sounds and sights you would expect of a large party going off on an all-inclusive day trip.

As she hesitated over whether to step onto the walkway, a figure wearing what she assumed was captain attire appeared on deck.

'Good morning,' he said, approaching her with a welcoming smile. 'Miss Guillem?'

She nodded.

'I am Captain Andrew Brand. Let me show you in. I'll give you the mandatory safety talk as we go.'

Chloe joined him on the gleaming yacht with a grin that only got wider as he showed off the magnificent vessel, pointing out the bar, swimming pool and hot tub on the next deck up, then taking her inside.

This yacht had *everything*, she thought in awe as she tried her hardest to pay attention to what she was being shown and told.

After showing her the Finnish sauna that had a window looking straight out to sea, he took her to the top deck to what was appropriately named 'the sky lounge' and left her with a young woman with tightly curled hair who made her a cocktail of coconut blended with mango and rum and served it in the coconut shell with a straw. This stretched Chloe's smile so wide her mouth must have reached her ears. She enjoyed it so much she readily accepted a second, then took a seat on one of the plentiful cappuccino-coloured leather seats encircling the lounge.

She gazed out of one of the many windows, imagining the spectacular view of the stars at night from this wonderful vantage point, and hoped she would be lucky enough to experience it for herself. The estimated finish time of the day's excursion had been vague.

Which reminded her that she still seemed to be the only guest.

And where had the barwoman gone?

Unease crawling through her, Chloe opened her beach bag to search for her phone.

Just as her fingers closed on it, a tall figure stepped into the lounge.

Although the figure was only in the periphery of her vision, it was enough for her stomach to roil and ice to plunge into her veins.

Feeling very much like a teenager watching a horror movie and wishing she could cover her eyes to hide from the scary bit, she slowly turned her head.

And there he stood, filling the space around him like a dark, menacing shadow, a grim smile on his face.

Luis.

'Hello, *bonita*. It is a pleasure to see you again.'

CHAPTER TWO

LUIS FELT IMMENSE satisfaction to read the horror in Chloe's baby-blue eyes.

'Nothing to say?' he taunted. 'I have travelled a long way to see you, *bonita*. I would have thought that deserved an enthusiastic welcome.'

Those wonderful pillowy lips he'd fantasised about kissing parted then snapped shut as she swallowed, shock clearly rendering her dumb.

'You're not normally this shy.' He folded his arms across his chest and stroked his jaw. 'Is it delight at seeing me that has struck you mute?'

Her wonderfully graceful throat moved, colour creeping over her cheeks. 'What...? How...?'

'Is that the best you can come up with?' He shook his head with mock incredulity.

She blinked rapidly and blew in and out. 'I've been set up.'

'The sun hasn't damaged your observation skills, I see.'

The baby-blue eyes stared straight into his. 'You bastard.'

'If we are moving straight to the name-calling, I have a select number of insults I can apply to you. Which shall I start with?'

'Forget it.' Hooking her large bag over her shoulder, she

got to her feet. 'Let's not waste time. Say what you need to say. I have a holiday to enjoy.'

He gazed at the long legs now fully on display, only the top half of her supple thighs covered by the tight blue denim shorts she wore. *Dios*, for a She-Devil she had the most amazing body. Beauty, heavy breasts covered in a red T-shirt, a slim waist and a pert bottom…he defied any red-blooded heterosexual man out there not to fantasise about bedding her.

'My apologies,' he said sardonically. 'I didn't realise you were on a holiday. I thought you had run away.'

'No, it's definitely a holiday. Sun, sea, pina coladas and hot men.' She smiled as she listed the latter, a jibe he knew perfectly well was intended to cut at him. 'Getting far away from you was an added incentive but not the main consideration.'

'Would your brother have paid for you to holiday in the Bahamas if you hadn't agreed to do his dirty work?' The booking for her flights and villa had been paid for personally by Benjamin.

'*Au contraire,*' she said, switching from English to her native French. Between them they spoke each other's languages and English fluently. 'I didn't agree to do his dirty work. I insisted on it.' The smile she now cast him was pure beatific. 'Your gallantry at rescuing a damsel in distress does you credit. Knowing you were on those mountain roads searching for me is a thought I will cherish for ever.'

The rage that had simmered in his veins since he and Javier had pieced all the parts of the jigsaw together flashed through his skin.

Luis hadn't expected contrition from her but her triumph was something else.

Chloe had sent him on a wild goose chase so he would be late for the gala. Her brother had conspired to ground

Javier's flight to Madrid so he too would be late for the gala. With both Casillas brothers out of the way and the world's media present, Benjamin had pounced, stealing Javier's fiancée away and taking her to his secure chateau in Provence. And then he had proceeded to blackmail them: Javier's fiancée in exchange for the money he claimed they owed him. If the money wasn't forthcoming he would marry her himself.

Luis could not remember the last time his brother had been so coldly furious. Javier had dug his heels in and refused to pay. For Javier it was a matter of principle. They had done nothing illegal and a court of law agreed with them. They didn't owe Benjamin a cent.

For Luis, Benjamin's actions were a declaration of war. All the guilt he'd felt and his plans to put things right between them had been discarded in an instant.

The press photographs of Freya leaving the gala hand in hand with Benjamin had captured a certain *something* between the pair of them that had made Luis wince for his brother. Whether Javier's fiancée was an unwitting tool in the plot or a willing supplicant was irrelevant. Those pictures had shown his brother's fiancée gazing into his enemy's eyes with a look of rapture on her face. Javier would rather starve than take her back.

His brother had been right not to take her back. Their enemy had married Freya two days ago, barely five days after stealing her away. The fallout against the Casillas brothers had accelerated.

Chloe had willingly played her part in this. She would find herself playing a role to end it and whether that was willingly, he could not care less.

'Cherish those memories, *bonita*,' he said, hiding his anger with a beatific smile of his own. 'You earned them. You have proven yourself to be a fabulous actress.'

She fluttered her long black eyelashes at him. 'Were you worried about me? How touching.'

Remembering the burst of raw panic that had grabbed him to find her car missing from the place he had expected it to be… Worried, Luis concluded grimly, did not begin to cover it.

It was only because he had known her since she was in her mother's stomach, he told himself. For the first three years of Chloe's life he, Javier and Benjamin, all ten years older, had been her chief babysitters. None of them had been enthusiastic about the job, especially when she'd entered toddlerhood and turned into a pint-sized She-Devil.

More fool him for being so blown away by her adult beauty that he'd failed to see behind the fun-loving façade to the fully grown She-Devil beneath the milky skin.

'I would not be human if I hadn't been concerned,' he said blithely.

'I think it's debatable whether you and your brother are human at all.'

He spread his arms out and winked. 'Oh, I am *very* human, *bonita,* as I am more than happy for you to discover for yourself.'

A tinge of colour slashed her pretty rounded cheeks. She scowled at him and pulled her bag even closer into her side. 'Are we done yet? Have you finished with your fun?'

'Finished? *Bonita*, my fun with you has only just begun.'

Indeed, this was already much more fun than he had envisaged. Chloe's belligerent discomfort and outrage were things of beauty, acting like salve to his rabid anger.

'Yes, well, *my* fun is over. I'm going.'

'Going where?' he asked as she stomped to the door, giving him an extremely wide berth as she moved.

'Back to my villa.'

'How?'

It was the way he said that one word that made Chloe pause and her heart accelerate even faster and the sick feeling in her stomach swirl harder.

It didn't matter that Luis had found her, she kept telling herself. It had been inevitable that their paths would cross again one day. At least it was done with and she could stop worrying about it.

'Have you been so enraptured by my presence that you failed to notice we're no longer at port?' he mocked.

She turned her head to look out of the window to her left. Then she turned it to the right.

Then she spun round to face the front, curses flying through her head.

The captain had set the *Marietta* to sail and she hadn't even noticed.

'Get this thing turned around right now!' she demanded, eying him squarely.

He rubbed his chin. 'No, I don't think I will.'

'The captain will turn it round.' She took three quick paces to the door and pressed the green button beside it.

'That won't work,' he commented idly. 'The crew have been instructed to leave us alone until further notice.'

'Take me back to port right now or I'm calling the police.'

He strode to the bar and laughed. It had a cruel, mocking tinge to it. 'Why ruin this wonderful reunion with talk of the police?'

She could have easily stamped her feet. 'Because you're holding me here against my will.'

He turned his back on her to study the rows of spirits, liqueurs and mixers lined up on the bar. 'Drink?'

'*What?*'

'I need a drink. Do you want one?'

'I want you to take me back to port. This game has gone on long enough.'

'This is no game, *bonita.*'

'Stop *calling* me that.'

He looked at her and winked. 'I remember when it made you blush.'

'That was before I knew what kind of a man you really are, you unscrupulous jerk. And stop winking at me. If this isn't a game, stop acting like it is.'

'If I am acting like it's a game, you conniving witch, it's to stop myself from grabbing you by the shoulders and shaking you until your teeth fall out.' He flashed his perfectly white and perfectly straight teeth at her. 'Or from taking the kiss you owe me.'

She sucked in a sharp breath.

His threat didn't bother her because she instinctively knew Luis would never lay a finger on her in anger.

But the mention of the kiss she owed him...

Chloe spent her days surrounded by dancers. The male ones had the most amazing physiques and they worked hard to maintain them, the look they strove for lean and strong. To her eyes they were beautiful sculptures but not sexy.

Luis was a hulk of a man, burly and rugged, a man for whom chest waxing would be considered a joke. If he had any vanity she'd never seen it. Even his dark hair, which he kept long on top and flopped either side of his forehead, never looked as if he did more to it than run his fingers through it when he remembered.

Square jawed, his hazel eyes surrounded with laughter lines, his nose broad, cheekbones high, lips full but firm, the outbreak of stubble never far beneath his skin.

In a world of metrosexual men, Luis was a man who drank testosterone for breakfast and made no apologies for it. He would be as comfortable chopping wood with an axe as he would holding a meeting in a boardroom and she found him *very* sexy.

She'd dreamed of kissing him when she was seventeen years old, dreams that had faded to a hazy memory over the years but then re-awoken with a vengeance when she had started work at Compania de Ballet de Casillas. Months after she'd joined the company Luis had turned up. She had been delighted to see him, had spontaneously thrown her arms around him and been completely unprepared for the surge of heat that had bathed her upon finding herself pressed against his hard bulk in that fleeting moment.

That heated feeling had been with her ever since. All she'd needed was one glimpse of him and her heart would pound. She would smile and try to act nonchalant but had been painfully aware of her face resembling a tomato.

That heat was there now too, vibrating inside her. Not even the knowledge of his treachery had dimmed it. She hated herself for that.

He looked up from the bottle of black vodka he was examining and smiled unpleasantly. 'The insults hurt, don't they?'

'You deserve yours and more for what you did to my brother.' And to me, she refrained from adding.

Learning how deeply he'd betrayed her brother had cut her like a knife. The more she and Benjamin had put the pieces together, the deeper the cut had gone, all the way back to her earliest memories.

Had Luis and Javier always had contempt for her family? Or had the damage done by their mother's horrific murder at the hands of their father been the root cause of it?

Their mothers had been closer than sisters. As far back as Chloe could remember Luis and Javier had been a part of their lives. They would come and stay with them for weeks at a time in the school holidays then, when she had reached eight and them eighteen and they had snubbed university to set out on their own path, they would still drop in for visits whenever they were in Paris.

Their visits had always made her mother so happy. When she'd been diagnosed with lung cancer they had been there for all of them. Luis had visited her mother so many times in hospital the staff had assumed he was one of her children.

Had the supposed feelings he'd had for her family all been a lie? If not, then how could he have tricked her brother into signing that contract on the day their mother's condition was diagnosed as terminal?

Luis replaced the bottle of vodka in his hand with a bottle of rum, twisted the cap off and sniffed it. 'Whatever we did to your brother he has repaid with fire. He has gone too far and so have you. Thanks to you and your brother conspiring against me and *my* brother, our names are mud.'

'Good. You deserve it.' She hated the quiver in her voice. Hated that being so close to him evoked all those awful feelings again that should never have sprung to life in the first place.

Her heart shouldn't beat so wildly for this man.

She swallowed before adding, 'You took advantage of him when our mother was dying. I hope the journalist investigating the injunction unveils your treachery to the world and that everyone learns what lying, cheating scumbags the Casillas brothers are.'

Hazel eyes suddenly snapped onto hers, a nitrogen-cold stare that sent a snake of ice coiling up her spine. 'We did not cheat your brother.'

'Yes, you did. I don't care what that court said. You ripped him off and you know it.'

His nostrils flared before he stretched out a hand to the row of cocktail mixers. 'I am going to tell you something, *bonita*. I had sympathy for Benjamin's position.'

'Of course you did,' she scorned with a shake of her hair.

'The terms of profit were reduced from twenty per cent to five per cent under the advice of our lawyer. Your brother's contribution to the project was a portion of the funding whereas Javier and I would be doing all the work.'

Luis remembered that conversation well. It was one of only a few clear recollections from a day that had flown by at warp speed as he and Javier had battled to salvage the deal they had put so much time and money into.

'You agreed on twenty per cent. That was a verbal agreement.'

He added crushed ice to the concoction he'd put in the cocktail shaker. 'Benjamin was sent a copy of the contract to read five hours before we all signed it. He didn't read it.'

Javier had been the point man on the Tour Mont Blanc project and emailed the contract to Benjamin. Luis had been unaware of his twin's failure to mention the change in the profit terms in that email. When they had gone to his apartment to sign it, the atmosphere had been heavy, the news of Benjamin's mother overshadowing everything.

Luis had only discovered three months later, at Louise Guillem's funeral of all days, that Benjamin still thought he would be receiving twenty per cent of the profit. It had been a passing comment during the wake, Benjamin nursing a bottle of Scotch and staring out of his chateau's window saying he didn't know how long he would have to keep the wolves from the door and ruefully adding that, if only the Tour Mont Blanc project could be speeded up and he had his twenty per cent profit now, all his money troubles would be over.

Luis had had many arguments with his brother through the years but that had been the closest they had ever come to physical blows. Javier had been immovable: Benjamin should have read the contract.

His twin was completely hard-nosed when it came to business. Luis was generally hard-hearted when it came to business too. They weren't running a charity, they were in the business of making money and at the time their bank balance had been perilously close to zero.

But Benjamin had been their oldest friend and Luis had been very much aware that Benjamin's frame of mind on the day of the signing had been anywhere but on the contract.

With Javier digging his heels in, Luis had decided that it would only cause bad feeling and acrimony if he told Benjamin the truth. It had been better for everyone that Luis wait for Tour Mont Blanc, a project that would take years, to be completed and for all the money to be in the bank before speaking to Benjamin man-to-man about it and forging a private agreement on the matter.

'He didn't read it because he was cut up about our mother. He *trusted* you. He had no idea the terms had been changed. He signed that contract in good faith.' Chloe's eyes were fixed on his, ringed with loathing. 'He gave you the last of his cash savings. That investment meant he couldn't afford to buy the chateau outright and he had to get a huge mortgage to pay for it so our mother could end her days there. He almost lost everything in the aftermath. You took his money then watched him struggle to stop himself from drowning.'

'We were not in a position to help him. It gives me no pleasure to admit this but we were in as dire a financial situation as Benjamin was. We'd grown too big too soon and over-extended massively. The difference between us and Benjamin was that Benjamin saw no shame in admitting it. We did, and I am only sharing this with you so you understand that I'm not the treacherous bastard you think I am. At that time we were *all* trying to save ourselves from drowning. I'd always had it in the back of my mind that when the Tour Mont Blanc project was complete I would come to a private agreement with Benjamin and pay him the extra profit he felt he was due...'

'You didn't do that though, did you? The first he knew of it was when he saw the final accounts!'

'I'd been overseeing a project in Brazil. Javier sent the accounts before I had the chance to talk to Benjamin about it. I flew back for Javier's engagement party and your brother came in all guns blazing firing libellous accusations at us. Call it human nature, call it bull-headedness but when someone threatens me my instinct is to fight back. I admit, ugly words were exchanged that day—we were all on the defensive, all of us, your brother included. He would not discuss things reasonably...'

'Why should he have?' She stared at him like a beautiful, proudly defiant elfin princess, arms folded belligerently across her ample chest, as sexy a creature as could be imagined.

Luis still struggled to comprehend how he'd been oblivious to her beauty for all those months or how he could be standing there with the woman who had conspired against him and his twin and find his blood still pumping wildly for her. He didn't know which need he wanted to satisfy the most: the need to avenge himself or the need to throw her onto the nearest soft furnishing and take that delectable body as his own.

Soon he would do both. He would screw her over in more ways than one.

'Humans respond better to reason. Fight or flight, *bonita*. Benjamin made threats, we dug our heels in, then he hit us with the lawsuit and we had no choice but to defend ourselves. But I still had sympathy for his position. In truth it is something that hadn't sat well with me for many years.

I'd hoped to speak to him privately and come to an agreement once the litigation was over with and tempers had cooled and we could speak as rational men. Legally, I had nothing to prove. Javier and I had done nothing wrong and that's been vindicated in a court of law.'

'If you really believed that, why take the injunction out on him?'

'Because there has been enough rubbish in the past two decades about my family. Do you have any idea how hard it is being Yuri Abramova and Clara Casillas's sons?' Luis downed his cocktail and grimaced at the bitter taste that perfectly matched his mood.

He tipped the glass he'd filled for Chloe down the bar's sink and reached for a fresh cocktail shaker.

'We are the sons of a famous wife killer,' he continued as he set about making a more palatable cocktail, one that would hopefully wash away the bile lodged in his throat. 'It is one of the most infamous murders in the past century. There have been documentaries made about it, books and endless newspaper articles. A Hollywood studio wanted to make a movie about it. Can you imagine that? They wanted to turn my mother's death at the hands of my father into entertainment.'

Chloe tried her hardest not to allow sympathy to creep through her but it was hard. Luis's past was something that never failed to make her heart twist and tears burn her eyes. She blinked them back now as she imagined the vulnerable thirteen-year-old he would have been.

She had been only three when Luis's mother had been murdered, far too young to have any memories of it.

But she *had* been there.

Clara had been performing in London on the night of her murder in a production of *Romeo & Juliet*. Yuri, a ballet dancer who had defected from the old USSR in the seventies and whose career had gone into freefall, had watched the performance convinced his wife was having a real-life affair with Romeo. When the performance had ended, Yuri had locked Clara in her dressing room, preventing dancers and backstage staff from entering when the screams and shouts had first rung out.

By the time they'd smashed the door open, Clara was dead, Yuri's hands still around her throat.

Luis and Javier had been in the hotel across the road from the theatre babysitting Chloe with Benjamin.

Chloe and Benjamin's mother, Louise, who had loved the twins fiercely, had been the one to break the terrible news to them.

He poured the fresh cocktail into two clean glasses. 'Imagine what it has been like for us growing up with that as our marker. We are hugely successful and rich beyond our wildest dreams but still people look at us and their first thought is our parents. You see it in their eyes, curiosity and fear.'

He pushed one of the glasses towards her and put the other to his lips. He took a sip and pulled a musing face. 'Not too bad. Better than the last one but I think I'll stick to construction and property developing.' He took another sip. 'As I was saying. My parents. A legacy we have tried hard to escape from while still honouring our mother.'

'Is that why you took her surname?' The question came before she could hold it back. It was something she'd been intensely curious about for years.

'We took it because neither of us could endure living with our father's name. We have worked hard to disassociate ourselves from that man and to make our mother's name synonymous with the beauty of her dance and not the horror of her death, but now everything has been dredged up again and *you* are partly responsible. Our lives are back under the media's lens and again we find the world wondering how much of our father's murderous blood lives in our veins.' He inhaled deeply. 'We took out the injunction to stop this very thing from happening because we knew Benjamin was an explosive primed to detonate. We are close to signing a deal to build a new shopping complex in Canada. Our partner in this venture has stopped returning our calls.'

'Then he's a smart man who knows he will be ripped off.'

The flash of anger that rippled from Luis's eyes was enough to make her quail.

'We did *not* rip him off and if anyone says otherwise we will sue the clothes off their back.'

'You ripped my brother off,' she said defiantly. 'Feel free to sue me. I would love my day in court.'

'I have a much better way of dealing with *you*, *bonita*, but as for your brother, I will not say this again—we did not rip him off. I was going to get the gala out of the way and then call him but, instead, Benjamin stole Freya and tried to blackmail us. All my sympathy left me then. As far as I'm concerned, your brother can go to hell. The press speculation his actions have wrought are untenable. My assistant found comments on a newspaper website querying whether Freya ran off with Benjamin because she feared she would end up like my mother.'

Chloe winced. She had many issues with Luis and Javier but they could no more help their parentage than she could help hers. 'That's disgusting.'

'I'm glad you think so because you are going to help put things right. If you hadn't called with your tale of terror I would have been at the gala before Benjamin stepped foot inside it. None of this would have happened.'

'He believed you owed him two hundred and twenty-five

million euros,' she spat, her fleeting compassion overridden by anger. 'Did you expect him to roll over and accept that? Did you expect *me* to? I was there with him at the hospital when you made that call begging for his help and his money.'

She'd been there, at the first turn of the wheel of the whole mess.

Chloe had been sitting on a bench in the hospital garden with her big brother, both of them dazed; her crying, he ashen, both struggling to comprehend the mother they loved so much was going to die. That was when Benjamin had received the call from Luis asking for his financial help.

'If you felt Javier had been cheated would you sit there meekly and allow it to go unchallenged when there was something practical you could do to help?'

'Probably not.' He shrugged. 'But would I have conspired to kidnap a woman and hold her to ransom…? No, I would not have gone that far if the first throw of the dice had not already been rolled.'

'I did not conspire to kidnap Freya! I helped whisk her away from a potential marriage made in hell and…'

'Is that how you justify it to yourself? I must remember to dress my actions up in a similar fashion when I tell you that you won't be returning to port until you have married me.'

CHAPTER THREE

FOR A MOMENT there was an intense buzzing in Chloe's ears. She shook her head to clear it, being careful not to take her eyes from Luis, who was now leaning forward with his elbows on the bar.

'What are you talking about?'

His eyes were intense on hers. 'I've not kidnapped you, I've borrowed you. Would that be how it's said? Is that how I can justify it?'

'No, what was that rubbish about marrying me?'

'That? That's the next stage. If you want to go home you have to marry me first. But let us not call it blackmail. By your logic it will be…an incentive? How does that sound?'

'It sounds like your cocktail has gone straight to your head.'

'And you haven't drunk yours yet. Try it. You might surprise yourself—and me—and like it.'

'Not if it makes me as drunk as *you* clearly are.'

'Regretfully, I am not drunk but I *am* serious.'

The hairs on her arms lifted, coldness creeping up her spine and into her veins. She hugged her bag closer to her. 'Okay, this game stops now. I'm sorry for my part in the affair. Is that what you want to hear? Okay then, how about this? I was wrong, I apologise. I'm sorry…*je suis desolée… lo siento…mi dispiace…*'

Amusement flickered in his hazel eyes. 'Can you apologise in Chinese too?'

'If that's what you want I'll teach myself it and say it to you, just *let me go*.'

The spacious windowed walls of the lounge were closing in on her. Suddenly it felt imperative to get off this yacht. She needed dry land and space to run as far and as fast as she could. Luis's defence of himself, his hulking presence, his magnetism…it was all too much.

It had always been too much but it had never scared her before, not like this.

She had such awareness for this man. She remembered all the visits he'd made to the theatre when she'd been working there, how she would sense his presence in the building long before she caught sight of him, almost as if she had an internal antenna tuned to his frequency. That antenna was as alert now as it had ever been and vibrating like the motor of a seismograph recording an earthquake.

She needed to find safety before the ground opened up and swallowed her whole.

He studied her silently, the brief amusement disappearing into seriousness. 'I warned you in my message that I would find you and that you would live to regret crossing me,' he told her slowly. 'You have known me long enough to know I am not a man to make idle threats.'

'Believe me, right now I am regretting it.'

'You're only regretting that I found you, not your actions.'

She opened her mouth to lie and deny it. His denials about not being party to Benjamin signing the contract under false pretences and that he'd wanted to put things right had sounded so sincere that there had been a few moments when she'd wondered if he might be speaking the truth.

His threats to marry her made her glad she hadn't swallowed those lies.

It would never happen. *He* could go to hell first. Hell was where he belonged, him and his cold monster of a brother.

'I can see the truth in your eyes, *bonita*,' Luis said grimly before she could speak. 'You don't believe me and you don't regret your actions. In many respects I commend you for your loyalty to your brother.'

It was a loyalty he understood.

Luis and Javier had always been loyal to each other. Though far removed from the other in looks and personality, they had grown and developed in the same womb and the bond that bound them together was unbreakable, tightened by the tragedy of their lives.

'Benjamin's own sister marrying me will kill the rumours and stop people believing that Javier and I are the devil's spawn. It's the only way to repair the damage.'

'I would rather swim to shore than marry you,' she spat, not caring at that moment that she'd never even mastered a basic doggy paddle.

'It will be the only way you get home if you don't agree to it.' He placed his chin on his knuckles. 'But have no worries, *bonita*. I am happy to wait for as long as is needed for you to come to the correct decision.'

'Then we will sail these seas for ever because I will never, ever, marry you and there is nothing you can do to make me.' She smiled tremulously. 'You can't threaten to fire me—I've already quit.'

It didn't escape his attention that she was inching her way to the door. Any moment she would bolt on those long gazelle-like legs.

Let her run. Chloe would soon discover there was no escape.

He returned the smile. 'You have not worked your notice period. I can sue you for that and I can sue you for breach of contract.'

'What have I breached?'

'You passed on confidential information about one of our dancers to your brother.'

'Freya's not an asset, she's a person.'

'She's a company asset. You acted as a spy against our interests.'

'You would have to prove it. Look at their wedding photo. It's obvious they're in love with each other.' Her beautiful smile widened but there was a growing wildness in her eyes. 'See? My instincts were right. Benjamin took her to punish Javier but he already wanted her for himself and she wanted him. You can sue me for whatever you want but if you won it wouldn't matter; Benjamin would pay any fine.'

'I could make sure you never work in the ballet world again.'

'I'm sure you could and without much effort but I don't care. I survived on an apprentice's salary, I'll cope. I don't care what job I do. I'll wait tables or clean bathrooms.'

'You would throw your career away?'

Her heart-shaped chin lifted. 'Some things are more important. I knew the risk I was taking when I made the call to you.'

'Interesting,' he mused. 'You will be pleased to know I have no wish to destroy you. Your brother? *Sí.* I would gladly destroy him but the feud can end here and now—call it an additional incentive. All you have to do is marry me and all the bad blood will be over.'

'You call that an incentive?' she said disdainfully. 'There is nothing more you can do to hurt him than you have already done.'

'Any hurt caused was not deliberate,' he asserted through gritted teeth.

'You would say that. You wanted me to feel guilty

enough that I agreed to your nefarious plan. Well, it hasn't worked. I don't believe you ever intended to give him any of the profit you denied him and I regret nothing. I will never marry you.'

The last of Luis's patience snapped.

He'd only been prepared to make up the profit shortfall because Benjamin was his oldest friend. In truth, despite his bulging contact book, Benjamin was his only real friend.

But Benjamin had not just crossed a line, he'd hacked at it with a chainsaw and the damage caused by his actions had the potential to destroy both Casillas brothers. Reputations could be broken by the smallest means and businesses ruined. Luis had not been exaggerating when he'd spoken of the financial troubles he and Javier had got into seven years ago. There had been an eighteen-month period when they had struggled to find the cash to put petrol in their cars but then three projects were completed within months of each other and suddenly the money had started rolling in. Almost a decade of complete focus and hard work and suddenly they were richer than they had ever dreamed possible. Their fortune had only grown since.

He would not be poor again. He would not have his or his brother's reputation battered any more. Chloe could put a stop to all of it with two simple words: I do.

'I have explained the facts of the situation,' he said tightly. 'If you choose not to believe them then so be it but this ends now. Too much damage has been caused. Marry me and no one else need be hurt.'

'Apart from me.'

'How will marriage hurt you? You're a single woman—'

'We went on one date two months ago,' she interrupted hotly. 'You've no idea who I've seen since then.'

He mustered a smile. 'You said only an hour ago that

you were on a holiday that involved hot men. That implies you are either single or a cheat. Which is it?'

Her cheeks had turned red enough to warm his hands on them. 'I'm a grown woman. How I conduct my personal life is my business.'

He shrugged. 'Lover or not, you're an unmarried woman. Your career is in tatters… What will you be giving up to marry me and rectify the mess you helped create? It wouldn't be a permanent marriage, only one that lasts long enough to shut the wolves up and restore my and my brother's reputations. In return, I would give you everything your heart desires.'

'My heart does not desire *you*.'

'Your body does.' At the outraged widening of her eyes, his smile broadened. 'I do not forget the kiss you owe me or the way your hungry eyes looked at me.'

Somehow her cheeks managed to turn a shade darker but she tossed her hair over her shoulders defiantly. 'That was the wine talking.'

His laugh at her barefaced lie was genuine. Even now, with all the acrimony and anger between them, that undercurrent remained, thick enough to taste. 'Do you want to prove that?'

'I don't have to prove anything. I don't want to marry anyone, not even for a short time, and if I did you would be the last man on the list. I won't do it. Promise what you want, make all the threats you like, I'm not going to marry you. The end.' Her hand grabbed the handle of the door that led outside. 'This isn't the Middle Ages. Women are not chattels to be bought or traded. As fun as this conversation has been, I'm going.'

Turning her back to him, Chloe stepped out onto the deck. After the air conditioning of the sky lounge it was like stepping into a furnace, the sun high above them and beaming its rays onto her skin.

She would find a way off this yacht even if she had to row her way back to shore. She'd just have to wear a life-jacket.

All she could see to the horizon was the Caribbean Sea, shining brilliantly blue under the azure sky.

She shivered to think what creatures lay beneath the still surface.

She spotted the stairs that led to the deck below and hurried down them.

'Where are you going to go?'

Heart pounding, she paused to look up.

Luis's arms were hanging over the balustrade at the top of the stairs, his handsome, sexy face smirking down on her but that hardness still glinting in his eyes.

'I'm going to find the captain and tell him to take us back to shore,' she told him with all the defiance in her veins.

'I bought the *Marietta* from her namesake three days ago. The captain answers to me.'

'But the manager said it belonged to the owner…'

'I bribed him,' he said matter-of-factly, without an ounce of shame. 'Marietta doesn't own the complex in Lucaya.'

She stared up at him as she processed what he'd said. 'You bought a yacht to trap me on?'

'I have often considered the idea of a yacht and now I have one.'

'Just like that?'

'I had a spare two hundred million sitting in a bank account. I was going to use that money to settle with your brother…that money enabled me to make Marietta an offer she couldn't refuse.'

Her stomach cramped to imagine what other factors he had brought to the negotiating table with Marietta. If his reputation was anything to go by it was more likely to have been a negotiating bed.

Wherever he'd done his negotiations for it, knowing he'd bought this yacht with the primary purpose of trapping her almost had her struck dumb.

Seven years ago it would have thrilled her.

From the age of seventeen she'd developed an intricate fantasy in her head where Luis waited for her to become a fully mature woman then declared his undying love for her and whisked her down the aisle.

That memory, not thought of in years, lanced her.

Once upon a time she had dreamed of marrying *him*.

How idyllic she had been. And how starved for affection.

She'd woven the fantasy while living under her father's roof for the first time in her life, mourning the mother she had loved with all her heart and coping with her remaining parent's indifference. His indifference shouldn't have hurt, not after a life spent where he'd been nothing but a name, but he was her *father*. His blood ran in her veins. They shared the same nose and ears.

Once she had moved out of that awful, unloving home the fantasies about Luis had petered away. She'd had a career to embark on and she'd been determined to put the past behind her and get out there and live her life to the fullest.

It had been the biggest shock to her system to re-enter Luis's orbit and discover her old craving for him hadn't withered into nothing, just been pushed into dormancy.

It felt like poison in her veins to imagine the debauched parties he would host on this beautiful yacht.

He moved from the balustrade and put his hand on the rail as he made the slow walk down the steps. That dangerous glint remained in his eyes but there was amusement within the hazel swirl too. 'Have you not yet realised I am a man who plans everything down to the last detail?'

Her throat closed at his approach. She stepped back, off the bottom step and onto the safety of the deck.

His smile grew with every step he took closer to her. 'Your brother is good with details too. I have thought about how he was able to steal Freya and keep her under lock and key. Seclusion with only trusted employees was how he achieved it. He even got her to marry him, the clever man. I thought if such a ploy is good enough for Benjamin then it is good enough for me. All I had to do was work the details. The yacht is mine and the crew are in my employ. They obey orders directly from me and I am paying them enough to ensure their loyalty.'

She took another step back. 'Not everyone's loyalty can be bought. And don't come any closer.'

The faint amusement that had lurked in his eyes faded away as he came to a stop barely two feet from her.

For a long moment neither of them spoke. Chloe, trapped in the sudden intensity of his stare, felt her heart clench into a fist then burst into an erratic beat that echoed up her throat.

Then a tight smile formed on those sensual lips and he spread his arms out. 'Search wherever you like. Speak to whoever you like. When you are satisfied you have nowhere to escape, come and find me.'

And then he walked back up the steps, leaving her standing there, her nails digging into the palms of her hands.

She would find a way off this yacht. She would. And then she would bring the full force of the law down on him.

Luis disconnected the call from his brother and bowed his head to dig his fingers through his hair, doing his best to rub the forming headache out of his skull.

He had finally got hold of George, their Canadian partner in their venture to build the largest shopping complex in the northern hemisphere. George was one of the richest and most powerful men in North America. After much coaxing, he had agreed to a video conference. However, he had insisted it be held in the morning.

Just as they had suspected, George was seriously considering pulling out of the agreement. Without George as their partner, the permits needed would be revoked.

Unfortunately he'd insisted Javier be in attendance for the call too.

Luis swore as he thought of his brother's foul mood. His brother was like a stick of old highly temperamental dynamite ready to explode at the slightest provocation.

Even if he succeeded in getting Javier to put on a human front, Luis knew it would not be enough. Their Canadian partner was an old-school tycoon who believed in a man's word being his bond. It was the injunction he and Javier had taken out against Benjamin that would be the biggest hurdle to overcome.

That damn injunction. At the time, with Benjamin then the one behaving like a stick of temperamental dynamite, it had seemed necessary. They had rushed it through, knowing time was of the essence. Now it only served to make them look guilty over a matter in which they had broken no law.

If George pulled out of the project, the consequences were unimaginable. It wasn't the money, it was what it represented. If he pulled out he was essentially telling the world that the Casillas brothers were not men who could be trusted to do business with. It would prove fatal to their already battered reputations.

With Chloe as Luis's wife, all of George's doubts would be allayed and the dominoes would stop falling but until he got his ring on her finger he would have to play for time.

He'd known from the first look at the pictures of Freya

and Benjamin leaving the gala hand in hand how the situation would be played out in the media. He and his brother would be painted as the devils. Their parents' history would be dredged up and played to fit the media's narrative of them. The idea of marrying Chloe had floated into his mind almost immediately bringing with it a flicker of excitement through his loins. Punishment and vindication all in one neat move.

Chloe had become an itch he could not purge in more ways than one, a taunt in his dreams, and suddenly he'd been presented with the motives to scratch it all away.

He'd known her well enough to know she wouldn't agree to marriage without a fight. Chloe had been born stubborn...

The door from the deck suddenly flew open and she burst into the lounge, raven hair spraying in all directions.

In one skip of a heart his burgeoning headache and weariness disappeared and his mood lifted.

He straightened in his chair, taking in everything about her afresh.

She glared at him, her chest heaving as she struggled for breath.

Then those wonderful voluptuous lips parted. 'I *hate* you.'

CHAPTER FOUR

TWO WHOLE HOURS Chloe had wasted going from room to room, speaking with crew member after crew member, her panic growing with each brief conversation. Surely her pleas for help would be met with sympathy from *someone*? Instead she had gained the distinct impression they didn't understand what she was complaining about.

Either that or they were used to histrionics. They probably assumed she was some spoilt rich girl who'd had a fight with her boyfriend.

The worst of it was that Chloe had always prided herself on *never* having histrionics. Only once had she succumbed to it and it had ended with her moving out of her father's house and moving in with her brother. She hadn't spoken to her father since that awful argument.

Luis sat casually on a chair with his elbows resting on his thighs, his hazel eyes fixed on her with what looked like calm amusement that raised her blood pressure to critical levels.

How could he be so calm when her entire life was being pulled out from beneath her?

'When I get away I am going to make it my mission in life to destroy you.'

'I'm terrified.' He stretched his back. 'I assume you didn't find an escape route?'

How badly she hated him, his arrogance, his cruelty, his entitlement.

And how badly she despised herself for having a heart that still jolted violently just to look at him.

Why were these awful emotions for this man still inside her, after everything he had done? She could forgive her just-turned-seventeen-years-old self for blithely overlooking his reputation as a ladies' man in the dreams she had created about him but she was an adult now, with adult thoughts and responses.

She could not forgive herself for it still being him, with all his treachery and lies, evoking so *much* inside her.

'How much are you paying the crew to turn a blind eye? It must be a fortune. Not one of them is prepared to help me.'

'I hope they refused politely.'

'They are incredibly well trained and polite.'

'Good.' He smiled with satisfaction. 'Marietta assured me they were the most loyal crew on the seas.'

For some reason the name Marietta only enraged her further.

She didn't want to think about the negotiations that had taken place for Luis to take ownership of this floating prison in such super-quick time. It made her feel as if she had ants crawling all over her skin.

'Now you are back we can have something to eat.'

Chloe breathed heavily, trying her hardest to keep some semblance of control when all she wanted to do was kick and punch him into reason. She had known there was a risk in crossing Luis but she had never dreamed he would go to these lengths.

She had no means of escape until they reached land.

'I'm not hungry.'

'Yes you are. How can you hope to escape if you're faint with hunger?'

'How can you be so blasé?' she demanded angrily. 'You have *kidnapped* me.'

'Borrowed,' he corrected as his phone suddenly rang. He stretched an arm out to pick it up.

His infuriating arrogance, already burrowing under her skin like a pulse, pushed her over the edge, all her fears and panic peaking.

She could contain it no more.

Chloe charged at him, snatched the phone from his hand before he could speak into it and threw it onto the floor as hard as she could. Only two humongous arms wrapping around her waist and yanking her backwards into a solid wall of man stopped her from stamping on it.

'Let me go,' she screamed, struggling against the vice-like hold she'd been put in, but it was like fighting against a solid strait-jacket.

His hold around her tightened and then she was lifted off her feet and placed unceremoniously onto a sofa. She hardly had time to catch a breath before her arms were pinioned above her head, her wrists secured together with one of his hands and Luis was on top of her, using the strength of his legs and his free hand to stop her from bucking and kicking out at him.

She opened her mouth to scream at him again, to demand he let go of her at once but nothing came out. Her tongue had become a stranger in her own mouth, unable to form the needed words.

Far from recoiling at being trapped in his hold, she felt the fight inside her morph into something equally ferocious but of a shockingly different flavour as his scent found its way into her bloodstream. Pulses flickered to life, electricity zinging over and through her.

His dark hazel eyes hovered only inches above her own, staring down at her with an intensity that made her chest expand and her abdomen contract.

'Are you going to behave yourself now, *bonita*?' he asked with a husky timbre she'd never heard before. A fresh pulse of heat ripped through her, filling her blood and her head with the fuzziest, dreamiest of sensations.

She could not tear her eyes away...

'Make me.' Her whispered words came unbidden from a voice that belonged to someone else.

Their gazes stayed locked until she found herself staring at the sensuous mouth she had so yearned to kiss.

And then that mouth fitted against her own and claimed her in a hard, ruthless kiss that sent her head and her senses spinning.

All her defences were stripped away from the first crush of his lips. Her mind emptied of everything except this moment, the heat that engulfed her... It *filled* her, from the tips of her toes all the way up, snaking into every crevice of her being.

With a greed she hadn't known existed within her, she kissed him back, wrapping her arms around his neck and cradling his head with her hands, digging her fingers through his hair to his scalp.

She had dreamed of kissing Luis for close to eight years. On cold nights she had imagined him lying beside her and keeping her warm with that hulking, magnificent body.

She had never imagined it could be like this. Warm? Her body had become a furnace, desire running on liquid petroleum in her very core. The heat of his kisses fuelled it beyond anything fantasy could evoke. His dark, chocolatey taste, the thickness of his tongue playing against her own, the weight of his hands roaming down her sides...

those fantasies had been dull compared to this giddy, urgent reality.

Scratching her nails down the nape of his strong neck, her fingers had slipped under the collar of his T-shirt when a door into the sky lounge opened.

In the breath of a moment reality reasserted itself.

Wrenching her mouth away, she turned her face from him and saw a pair of legs exiting the room as whoever had walked in on them left abruptly.

The ignobility of the situation they had been found in was starkly apparent.

She snatched her hands away from his skin and bucked against him. 'Get *off* me.'

The sensuous lips pulled into a smile as Luis levered himself back up.

The moment he was upright, Chloe twisted herself off the sofa and fell in a graceless heap onto the floor.

She stared at him, wishing she could crawl away and hide for ever.

Chloe had been kissed before. She might be a virgin but she wasn't completely innocent. She'd experimented like everyone else but nothing she had done—which admittedly wasn't much—had been anything like this.

This was something else.

This kiss had come directly from heaven.

She had to remember it had been delivered by the devil himself.

'You did that on purpose,' she said in a breathless voice that made her wince. It was no consolation that Luis's breathing was as ragged as her own.

He arched a dark brown eyebrow. 'Kissed you?'

'You knew someone was going to walk in,' she hissed, grasping for excuses, anything to negate what she had just experienced. 'You wanted us to be caught like that to discredit me.'

What madness had taken control of her?

She imagined that within minutes their passionate embrace would be known by the entire crew, including the captain, who had locked himself in the bridge when she'd been seeking help to escape. They would all conclude that they had been right to deny her help. They would never take her entreaties seriously.

'I have many talents but mind control is not one of them.'

He could have fooled her. She would swear he'd just used a form of mind control. Something in his eyes, a magnetism, it had hypnotised her. It must have. Something that would explain the madness that had possessed her.

'I kissed you because you asked it of me.'

'I did *not*.' Scrambling to her feet, she smoothed her T-shirt over her belly, trying desperately to look composed on the outside even if on the inside she had turned into a hormonal, blubbering mess.

'What was *"make me"*, if not a challenge to kiss you?' He spread his arms across the back of the sofa in a nonchalant fashion that made her fingers itch all over again to smack him.

'It was not a challenge.' She was painfully aware her cheeks must be the colour of tomatoes.

Her lips had tingled for him. They still did.

His gaze stayed unwaveringly on hers. '*Bonita*, your eyes begged for my kiss. You kissed me back. You ran your fingers through my hair. Faking virginal outrage does not change any of that.'

'Shut up.'

'You blush like a virgin too.'

'I said, *shut up*.' Storming to the bar, Chloe grabbed the

first bottle that came to hand and poured a hefty measure into a glass.

She felt his eyes watching her every move.

'*Dios*, you're not, are you?'

'Not what?' She took a large sip hoping whatever the potent liqueur was would numb her insides.

'A virgin.'

The fiery liquid halfway down Chloe's throat spluttered back out of her.

'You *are*.'

The sudden fascination in his voice made her want to hurl the remnants of her glass at him. Instead she tipped them into her mouth and forced herself to swallow.

Oh, wow, it *burned*.

She coughed loudly and blinked back the tears produced by her burning throat, hating the amusement she found in his gaze.

'Being a virgin is nothing to be ashamed of,' he said when she had herself back under control. 'And I would go easy with that—that's Cuban rum. It's very potent.'

Staring at him insolently, she poured herself another measure. Now the burn had abated she was left with a pleasant after-taste. 'I'm not a virgin. I've slept with tons of men. Many more and I'll be on the same number of conquests as you.'

Luis ignored her gibe. Her lie was written all over her flaming-red face and trembling hands.

His heart twisted.

It had never occurred to him that Chloe was a virgin. And why would it? She was twenty-five, an age when a person would have had a number of lovers in their life. This was the twenty-first century. Women were as entitled to take lovers as men were. He had never met a woman who hadn't embraced the liberation that came with it.

Until now.

He thought of how her cheeks had always turned crimson when he saw her at the theatre, the look in her eyes when he had rubbed his nose against hers…

'It explains a lot,' he mused, shaking his head, incredulous at the turn of events since she had stormed back into the sky lounge.

Their kiss… It had exploded out of nowhere.

One moment he had been restraining her, the next their mouths were locked together, their hands burrowing hard enough to dig through flesh.

There had been no finesse. They had come together in a brief fusion of unleashed desire.

'Because I refused a nightcap?' She tossed the drink down her throat with a grimace. 'That's called having self-respect.'

'If you've had a *ton* of lovers, why refuse to sleep with me? Your self-respect would already have been out of the window if that's what you were hoping to preserve.'

'Maybe I just didn't fancy you enough to come back to your house? Maybe I didn't want to be another conquest in a long line of many.'

'If it's the former then you lie—your body language is very expressive, *bonita*.' Her blush was delicious.

She was delicious.

Her sweetness lingered on his tongue, the softness of her skin still alive on the pads of his fingers.

'If the latter, why worry about being a conquest when you have such a long list of your own?'

She poured herself some more rum. 'I do not have to explain myself.'

'I'm merely curious as to why such a sensual woman would deny herself the pleasure that makes the world turn around.'

'Pleasure—sex—counts for nothing. There are far more important things. Like loyalty,' she added pointedly.

'We are already agreed on the importance of loyalty but only someone with minimal experience would deny that sex is an important part of life, especially someone who has slept with *tons* of men.' He hooked an ankle over his knee and enjoyed the fresh batch of colour flaming her cheeks.

Her presence alone invigorated him. He'd felt a lifting of his spirits when he'd first stepped into the sky lounge and surprised her with his presence. The hammers that had pounded at his head when she'd disappeared on her quest for escape had been driven out again with one look on her return.

Their kiss had pumped something else inside him, a buzzing in his veins.

He remembered their date; that buzz had been with him throughout it then too, an electric charge in his cells that had driven out the strains of his daily life and the weight that always seemed to be pressing on his shoulders.

'If you have slept with the number of men you claim you have and can still state that sex is unimportant then that would suggest you have either been doing it wrong or have been picking the wrong partners.'

'Is this where you tell me that having sex with you will awaken me to all the things I've been missing out on?' She rolled her eyes with a snort.

Laughter bubbled up his throat. Chloe had the face of an angel, the body of a siren and a melodious voice that sang to a man's loins. It had only taken him so long to become fully aware of it because of all the years he'd seen her as a child.

He doubted there was a heterosexual man who'd met her and not felt a twinge of awareness for her.

Had she really, as he now strongly suspected, turned down every man who'd shown an interest in her?

And if so, why?

'Close your eyes, *bonita*, and let your senses guide you. What do you taste? It is the chemistry between us seeping into the air we breathe.'

If he hadn't suspected before that they had the potential to be incredible together, their brief, furious kiss had proven it.

She scowled as she poured herself more rum with a still-shaking hand. 'The only thing I can taste is the hot air you keep spouting every time you open your mouth.'

His laughter came out as a roar.

No wonder he felt so invigorated to be with her. Chloe had a zest about her that he fed off. She'd always had it.

He remembered seeing a glimpse of the woman she'd become when they'd celebrated her seventeenth birthday at the chateau mere weeks before her mother had died. She'd been a gangly teenager still growing into her face, the beauty so evident today nothing but potential back then.

She was a full decade younger than the rest of them but her indefatigable spirit during those awful months her mother had been dying before their eyes had been inspiring.

Chloe had been the one to keep everyone's spirits lifted. She had kept that smile on her face during the worst of times, never once letting her mother see the pain that had been hidden behind it, always turning the stone over to find the ruby underneath. She would speed from school to the hospital and later Benjamin's newly bought chateau where Louise had ended her days, armed with cosmetics and other feminine products, doing her mother's hair, massaging her feet, painting her nails, all the little tactile things that had shown her love. All of it conducted with a smile and that raucous laugh that had lifted everyone and pulled them all together in a web of joyous love.

Her hidden pain had only come out at the funeral.

The memory of her tears soaking into his shirt that day and the tremulous look in the baby-blue eyes staring at him now cut the laughter from Luis's lips.

Whatever mistakes he had made, he had done his best by Chloe and her family. He had loved her mother and her brother. He had loved all of them. That she could believe him capable of using that awful time for his own financial gain sliced like a dagger through his chest.

Hindsight gave him much to regret but the past was the past. It was the future he had to think of and that future involved Chloe by his side as his wife.

Sentimentality had no part in it.

She held the glass of rum to her lips. 'Does the possibility of me being a virgin not make you pause and think that what you're doing is wrong on so many levels that Dante's *Inferno* would have run out of space for you?'

'You are thinking ahead to us sharing a bed?' he asked, fresh sensation awakening in his loins as he brushed the last of the memories away.

'*Never.* I despise you.' She swallowed the rum in one hit.

'No, *bonita*, you hate that you desire me.'

'Don't tell me what I feel,' she snapped, pouring herself yet another glass. By Luis's estimate she had drunk over a third of the bottle in a very short time.

She downed it and fixed her eyes on him with a glare. 'I will *never* be yours,' she repeated, then gave a hiccup. Then another.

She reached for the bottle again.

'Are you sure that's wise?'

'Stop telling me what to...' another hiccup '...do.' Her hand went to her mouth. When she next looked at him her face had lost much of its colour.

He leaned forward, preparing to get to his feet. 'Feeling woozy?'

'No.' As if to prove her point she took two steps towards him but then stopped herself and grabbed hold of the bar.

'I did suggest you eat something. All that rum on an empty stomach...'

She swallowed then took some long, deep breaths before raising her chin and studiously walking to the nearest seat. Seated, she gripped onto the arms of the sofa she had put herself into and flashed a grimace at him. 'See? I'm fine.'

He raised a brow, torn between guilt at driving her to attacking the rum, admiration at her refusal to submit and amusement at the hangover he was certain was coming for her.

'Ready for some food now? A bread roll or some toast to soak the alcohol?'

Her beautiful, stubborn mouth opened. He could see the refusal ready to be thrown at him. But then the mouth closed and she seemed to shrink a little into the chair.

When she met his eye there was a glimpse of vulnerability in her returning stare that made his heart twist and his chest tighten.

She gave a short jerky nod. 'Just something light, please. I think I'm suffering from seasickness.'

Dios, she was amazing. Clearly inebriated as she had suddenly become, she still had the wit to try and turn it to her advantage.

'You suffer from seasickness?' he asked with faux sympathy.

She gave another nod. 'You should put me on dry land... unless you want me to vomit all over your new toy?'

'That is certainly something for me to consider,' he said gravely.

'I would consider it quickly if I were you or I won't be... hic...responsible for the consequences.'

'If it gets too bad I will get the ship's doctor to give you something. He has a supply of anti-nausea injections and pills for such an eventuality. In the meantime, I'm sure some food will help.'

Whistling, Luis strolled out of the sky lounge with the weight of Chloe's glare burning into his back.

CHAPTER FIVE

'FEELING BETTER?'

'A little.'

'Still seasick?'

'Yes. Very seasick.'

Luis's cynical laughter ringing behind her ear sounded like a hammer to Chloe's brain.

She tightened her grip on the railing and kept her gaze fixed on the clear waters surrounding her. She had been standing at the front of the yacht for almost an hour, inhaling the fresh air to clear her banging head.

She knew she wasn't fooling him with her woes of seasickness.

Faking seasickness had been better than admitting she was slightly—okay, a touch more than slightly—drunk.

The last time she'd consumed that much alcohol she'd been living in London but that had been spread over a number of hours, never in such a short space of time.

She had never drunk as much black coffee as she had since either. Cut her and she was quite sure she would bleed caffeine.

She'd needed the alcohol's numbness to smother the tortured emotions that had been engulfing her. There was nowhere to escape, nowhere to flee the heat his kiss had generated and her excruciating embarrassment at being called out as a virgin.

How had he known that? *Did* he have psychic powers? Or had he been with so many women that he could tell an innocent by one kiss?

Reaching the age of twenty-five a virgin was just something that had happened, not something intentional and not something she had been embarrassed about before.

When she'd moved to London months before turning nineteen to take on her apprenticeship with the ballet company, all the freedom in the world had suddenly been in her lap. It hadn't been that she'd been denied her freedom before then; she'd lived with her father and stepmother for the year following her mother's death and neither of them had shown the slightest concern for her whereabouts, then she'd spent a year living with her brother, who had watched her closely but never stifled her. This had been a different freedom.

Her whole life had opened itself out to her, unanswerable to anyone. She had embraced that freedom with gusto.

She had loved her life in London. Living in a shared house with three other young women had meant lots of partying and a growing number of friends. Long days and long nights, young enough to burn the candle at both ends without any ill effects...yes, she had loved her life back then but not as much as her housemates had.

Rarely a morning had gone by when Chloe would go downstairs for breakfast and not find a man or two in the kitchen, different faces on a seemingly daily basis. She'd recoiled from such casual hook-ups for herself. She'd dated though, even kissed a few of them, but nothing more. The mechanism inside her friends that allowed them to discard their inhibitions and embrace sex whenever and wherever they could seemed to be faulty in her.

'You're too choosy,' her best friend Tanya had drunkenly told her one night. And she had been right. Chloe loved her male friends but she did not trust them. There were only two men she'd trusted. One was her brother, the other had been Luis.

She hadn't deliberately sought Luis out. When she had seen his ballet company advertising for a costume maker she'd been ready for a fresh challenge.

To discover her old teenage feelings for him had been merely dormant and then to find her resurgent desire reciprocated had been both exhilarating and terrifying.

She had spent the past two months consoling herself that at least she hadn't accepted his offer of a nightcap.

Everything she had believed about Luis for her whole life had been torn asunder.

He had ripped her misplaced trust to shreds.

And now she knew her self-consolation had been pointless too. She still desired him. She'd been pinned beneath him and instead of kicking him where it hurt she had melted for him.

Worse, he knew it too.

'You will be glad to know we will be docking within the hour,' he said nonchalantly placing his hand on the railing beside her.

Chloe's heart leapt, although whether that was at his sudden closeness or his announcement she could not be sure.

She stepped to the side, away from him, not quite daring to get her hopes up. 'You're going to let me go?'

'No, *bonita*. I'm taking you to my island.'

'*Your* island?'

'*Sí*. I bought it with the yacht.'

'You bought an island to trap me on as well as a yacht?' Her leaping heart sank in dismay as that tiny glimpse of freedom disintegrated.

'They came as a package. I had intended to stay at sea a few more days so that Marietta's furniture could be moved out but necessity has brought the schedule forward. I have a video conference in the morning. This yacht, as magnificent as she is, was designed as a pleasure vessel and does not yet have business facilities.'

A swell of something hot and rabid pulsed in her chest. 'You bought the island off Marietta too?'

'I've met her a few times socially—I'd attended one of her parties on this yacht. When I learned where you were hiding and its close proximity to her island, I called her with my offer. The stars aligned for me that day, *bonita*.'

'If the stars aligned for you then God knows what torturous trick they were playing on me,' she whispered bitterly.

'What can be torturous about staying in paradise?'

'How about that I'll be staying in it against my will?'

His tone became teasing. 'At least you won't have to worry about seasickness.'

She tightened her hold on the railing and breathed in deeply. 'How long will we stay there?'

'You will stay until you agree to marry me. It really is very simple. Marry me and then we return to the real world.'

'The real world where I'll be your wife?'

'That's what marriage means, *bonita*. We marry, make some public appearances together to kill the heinous rumours and speculation being spread about me and my brother and then you go free. It will all be over. You will be free to resume your life and your brother will not have to spend *his* life watching his back for my vengeance. You can put an end to all of it. The power is in your hands.'

She stared down at Luis's hand, tanned and huge, holding the rail so loosely beside her own. *That* was a powerful hand, in more ways than one. It could swallow her own hand up.

If she didn't find a way out of this mess *he* would swallow her whole.

But this was a mess she didn't know how to resolve. She *couldn't* marry him.

Just having him there beside her, that masculine scent her nose hungered for catching in the breeze and filtering through her airways had her senses dancing with awareness.

But she couldn't stop her eyes darting back to those hands. They had pinned her wrists together without any effort at all.

Her abdomen clenched, warmth flooding her to imagine them touching her again...

She would not let that happen. Luis would never lay a finger on her body ever again and she would not allow herself to touch him either, whether she married him or not.

Suddenly it occurred to her that Luis was taking her to an island which meant new people, telephone lines—her phone had no means of communication on this yacht—and transport. Which all meant potential escape routes...

But what if he meant it about ending the feud with her brother? Her being trapped here in his power proved the lengths Luis would go to.

She could laugh at her naivety. As if she could trust a word Luis said, after everything he had done.

Gathering all the raging emotions zipping within her and squashing them into a tight ball, Chloe twisted to look him right in the eye and then immediately wished she hadn't.

She was trapped, in more ways than one.

All she could do was gaze into the dark hazel eyes staring at her with a force that made her stomach melt and her fingers itch to touch him all over again.

Those strong fingers she had only moments ago stared

at with a strange aching feeling reached out to smooth a lock of her hair behind her ear.

'Marry me, *bonita*,' he whispered, then craned his head towards her and brushed those sensuous lips over hers.

Chloe's feet were still stuck to the decking when he pulled his hand away and strode back into the sky lounge. It wasn't until the door closed behind him that the strange fog-like thing that had happened in her head filtered out to be replaced with anger, at Luis and especially at herself.

So much for never allowing him to touch her again. She had barely lasted a minute from making that vow.

In disgust, she wiped her still-tingling mouth with the back of her hand.

Must try harder, she thought grimly as she stared back out to sea with a heart still thumping madly.

Chloe came to a stop on soft golden sand upon which dreams were made. In front of her, gleaming like a Maharaja's palace under the descending sun, set in an island within the island, was a whitewashed mansion with a terracotta roof from which even more fantastical dreams were made.

They had been met off the yacht by a skinny boy of around ten, who skipped alongside her, clearly bursting with excitement. In rapid-fire English he happily told Chloe that he was the caretakers' son and had lived on the island his whole life.

His cheerful presence was a welcome respite from the turbulence she had been through that day, although did nothing to lessen the coils knotted tightly in her belly.

Luis walked some way behind them, deep in conversation with the yacht's captain. She felt his presence like a spectre.

Determined to blank him out while she could, she tried

hard to concentrate on the child's chattering while taking in everything around her.

The closer she got to the palace-like structure, the more she realised her initial thoughts were an illusion. What she'd thought was one palatial villa was a complex of interlinked homes around one huge main house nestled with high palm trees and traversed by the longest swimming pool she had ever seen, snaking the perimeter and weaving between the individual beautiful buildings. Only as she crossed a bridge over the swimming pool did she realise it was a saltwater pool filled with marine life that must feed directly from the sea.

Following the wide path, she saw what was undoubtedly a traditional pool snaking the main house like a moat, more bridges leading to the smaller homes.

Chloe sighed with pleasure then hated herself for it, immediately following her self-castigation with the thought that it was better to be locked away in paradise than in a cell.

She'd thought the complex she was staying on in Grand Bahama was paradise. This was nirvana.

'Who else lives on the island?' she asked the boy when she could get a word in.

His nose wrinkled but before he could answer, Luis got into step beside her.

'No one,' he answered cheerfully, the look in his eyes telling her clearly that her hopes of finding escape off this island were as futile as her hopes of finding help on the yacht. 'I will bring new staff in soon.'

'Jalen!' a loud, harsh voice called out. 'Come here.'

The little boy's skinny frame froze momentarily before he pulled himself together and ran off, back over the bridge they had just crossed to a scowling, weather-beaten man who'd emerged from the side of the main villa.

'Who's that?' Chloe asked, following Jalen with her eyes.

'Rodrigo. His father.'

She looked at Luis and found his gaze was also following the boy. 'The caretaker?'

He nodded, his attention still on the boy. 'He looks after the island with his wife, Sara.'

'Jalen said they've been here for a long time.'

'Sara's lived here for ever. Her parents were the caretakers before she took over.' There was a grimness to his tone.

Chloe looked back at Jalen. He'd reached his father and his head was bowed. He was obviously on the receiving end of a scolding. 'What do you think he did wrong?'

'I have no idea. I met the family three days ago when I took possession of the island. I know nothing about them.' Luis shook his head and pushed his attention away from the young boy and back to the beautiful woman at his side.

Small boys always pushed their luck. It was a parent's job to discipline them. Just because Luis's father's methods of discipline had been extreme did not mean Rodrigo used the same methods.

But when he met Chloe's gaze he saw the same concern ringing out from her as needled in his own skin.

'Where do they live?' she asked.

'In one of the staff cottages at the back of the main house.' He pushed Jalen and Rodrigo more firmly from his head. He would have plenty of time to observe them interact and, he was sure—hoped—he would find the father-son relationship that he had spent so many years wishing for.

His own history was not others' reality. That was a truth he had always been aware of.

Luis had long ago accepted that there had been something in his genetic make-up that had triggered his father's violence towards him, something dirty and rotten.

It had to be inherent otherwise Javier would have been on the receiving end of it too. He'd never bought Javier's reasoning that he'd got away with only mild chastisement and a rumpled shake of the hair because their father had looked at Javier's face and seen a mirror of himself.

There was no denying that Javier had inherited their father's looks while Luis had inherited a masculine version of their mother's, and there was no denying that only Luis had been Yuri's whipping boy, right until the day their father's drunken, jealous rage had turned on their mother.

His father had served ten years of his sentence for killing his mother. A year after his release he'd died of pancreatic cancer. Luis sincerely hoped he'd suffered every minute of his death.

Dios, would it always be like this? Would he be condemned to a life where every time he saw a father chastise his child the memories of his own childhood would smack him in the face afresh?

Would the past ever set him free?

Strolling along another bridge that led to the door of a pretty villa, he said to the woman who could kill the demons from the past affecting his future, 'This will be your villa while we're here...'

She raised a startled eyebrow. 'I get my own villa?'

'Did you want to share one with me?' he mocked, glad to be back on familiar ground with her.

'No!'

He pushed the door open and winked at her.

This was better. Flirtation and teasing. Let it flow between them. Let it warm the coldness that had settled in his veins.

'If you change your mind, I will be in the villa next door.'

'Get over yourself.'

'I'd rather have you over me but I can wait.'

'You'll be waiting a long time.'

He gazed at her flushed cheeks and smiled. 'We shall see.'

She scowled but there wasn't the force behind it that had been there throughout the day.

She had made no effort to step into her new home. 'Are you not going to live in the main house?'

'Not until Marietta's possessions have been shipped out. I'll show you around it tomorrow but, for now, I have a conference call to plan for and I need to make sure everything's set up. Tonight, *bonita*, you get to amuse yourself. Sara will be with you shortly and will go through everything. She knows the island better than I do and has arranged the villa for your arrival. If there is anything you're not happy with, take it up with her.'

'You're not scared I might try and escape?'

He laughed. 'There is no escape. And no rescue, if that's what you're thinking. This island is an unnamed dot on the map.'

'What about the ship that's coming for Marietta's stuff?'

He noticed the darkening of her eyes as she spoke Marietta's name. It was the same darkening he'd noticed earlier.

'She's in no hurry for it.'

'I can hijack the yacht.'

'I'm afraid not. Captain Brand's taken it back to the mainland. He will return in a week and then he will marry us.'

'He can't.'

'He's a recognised officiate.'

'What does that mean?'

'That he can marry us.'

'But I haven't agreed to marry you!'

'You will and the sooner you accept it and say yes, the

sooner we can marry and the sooner this nightmare will be over for the both of us.'

He could manage a week away from the business but, he had realised earlier, no longer than that. He was still in communication with those he needed to communicate with but this island, for all its beauty, was cut off from civilisation as he knew it. For this to be a true holiday home he would need to purchase a helicopter to be permanently manned there and possibly get a landing strip put in and buy a smaller version of his private jet.

He was confident he would gain Chloe's acceptance to marry him in the seven-day deadline he had imposed.

He could sense her resolve failing her. She knew there was no escape. If she wanted to leave the Caribbean she would have to marry him.

She was the reason he was having to scramble together a conference call the next morning to salvage a deal that had been in the bag and stop the business he and his brother had worked so hard for from crumbling around them.

Before she could respond, a slender, tired-looking woman with frazzled hair crossed the bridge to them.

Luis shook Sara's hand then introduced her to Chloe. 'Please see that Miss Guillem has everything she needs,' he said, then turned back to Chloe.

Was it his imagination or was that panic resonating from those beautiful blue eyes?

He reached out a hand to stroke her soft cheek.

The pupils of her eyes pulsed at his touch.

'I will find you after my conference call tomorrow,' he said. 'Until then, stay out of trouble.'

Chloe watched him walk away with the strangest desire to call him back.

She managed a small smile at Jalen's mother and was relieved to receive a warm, if tired, smile back.

The villa she was shown into was charmingly beautiful if a little old-fashioned and fitted with its own kitchen and all the amenities a woman could want. The swimming pool curled past the bottom of the pretty garden her living room opened out to.

'I hear you've always lived on the island,' Chloe said when Sara was about to leave.

Chloe *hated* being alone at the best of times but with her head so full of the day's events, so full of Luis, the thought of only her own company terrified her.

Sara nodded and put her hand on the door. 'I was born here.'

'What's Marietta like?' she couldn't resist asking.

Why she couldn't stop imagining the mystery woman she could not begin to fathom but the name had lodged itself in her head like a spike digging into it.

Luis had bought Marietta's yacht and island off her and taken possession of them both in mere days. He'd met her socially.

Chloe knew all about Luis and his sociability. His party-loving ways were legendary. She remembered the leaked photos of his thirtieth birthday party, a joint event with his twin at which her brother had, naturally, been a guest. Someone had captured pictures of Luis dancing, beer in hand, surrounded by a hive of semi-naked women, all with their attention fixed firmly on him.

A quote in the paper by an unnamed source had described it as the party of the decade. To the question of which of the beauties Luis had ended up with, the answer had been, 'Knowing Luis, it could have been all or any of them.'

Recalling that picture made her want to vomit.

Had Marietta been at that party? Had she been one of those beauties draped all over him?

Sara's face lit up into a smile that momentarily transformed her tired features into beauty. 'She's an amazing woman.'

Later, alone on her villa's veranda after a light supper eaten alone, Chloe sat under the starry night sky nursing a glass of water.

Other than the crickets chirruping madly to each other, the silence was absolute. There was no sign of life from the villa next door, no lights, no sound.

She could be the only person on this earth.

Luis must still be in the main villa preparing for his video conference.

She should be happy to be rid of him, not reliving their kiss for the fiftieth time.

Dieu, now she was alone with her thoughts it was *all* she could think about, their lips and bodies fused together and the *heat* that engulfed her.

She rubbed her eyes and breathed even more deeply.

Why did any of this have to happen?

If Luis and Javier had been straight with Benjamin all those years ago instead of luring him into a lie then she would...

Would what?

She would have gone on that second date with Luis. She would have accepted his offer of a nightcap. She would have let him kiss her. And then she would have let him make love to her.

And then he would have broken her heart.

In a way, he had broken it already through his treachery to her brother and all the memories that had been shattered as a result.

He had a ruthless streak in him she would never have guessed ran so deep.

But, as her memories continued to torture her, she thought back to his vehement denials of treachery.

Now she had a little distance from him and could think without his magnetic presence disturbing her equilibrium, she couldn't help but wonder if there was some truth in his defence of himself.

As a child Luis had been her favourite visitor to their home. She had loved it when he and Javier had come to stay, had a strong memory of climbing to the top of the fifteen-foot tree at the bottom of their garden but then losing her nerve and being too scared to climb back down.

She had sat at the top of it, crying her head off, terrified of the drop, which to her five-year-old self had looked petrifying.

Luis had been the one to haul himself up and get her down. She had clung to him like a limpet but he had got them both down safely. She had hero-worshipped him for that. His steady presence when her mother had become ill had been such a comfort to all of them. His visits had brightened her mother's mood, invigorated her brother and made her own heart lighten a little.

Had that *all* been a lie? Had twenty-five years' worth of memories all been false or distorted?

And then she thought of the social media comments he had mentioned, the sick ones that had equated Freya leaving Javier out of fear of ending up like Clara Casillas. Fear of ending up murdered at Javier's hands.

Had there been cruel comments aimed at Luis too?

The rustle of movement nearby pulled her back to the present, a door being closed softly.

Footsteps crunched and, although their individual gardens gave them privacy, she knew in her bones that Luis had stepped outside into his villa's garden.

Chloe held her breath. Her heart beat maniacally beneath

her ribs, all her senses pinging to life. The knots in her stomach had tightened to become a painful ache inside her.

Could he sense her, feet away, separated only by the hedgerow filled with an abundance of beautifully scented flowers?

A short while later she heard the distant splash of water. Luis had gone for a midnight swim.

Still holding her breath, she took that as her cue to bolt back inside.

Her head felt hot and thick when she slipped under the cool bed sheets a short while later. A riot of images flashed behind her closed eyes that no amount of trying could dispel.

Luis swimming.

Luis naked.

Luis, Luis, Luis…

CHAPTER SIX

THE IMAGE OF Luis swimming naked was the first thing Chloe saw in her mind's eye when she awoke the next morning after a turbulent night that had not involved much in the way of sleep.

Throwing the bed sheets off, she hurried into the bathroom and took a long shower, washing the images—which weren't even images, just something conjured by her pathetic imagination—away.

With a towel wrapped around her torso and another wrapped around her head, she opened the dressing-room door to see what clothes had been brought in for her. Inside she found a collection of beach and summer wear, all in a variety of sizes.

She supposed she should feel grateful that Luis had made sure there would be something that would fit her. She wasn't the easiest of women to dress. At five foot eight, she was taller than average. If not for her breasts, she would be considered slender. Her breasts had been the envy of her friends when she'd been a developing teenager. She'd always considered them to be a nuisance. Dresses were a nightmare to buy, always a compromise between fitting from the waist down or the waist up. If she wanted them to fit the rest of her without looking as if she were wearing a tent, she was forced to cut the circulation of her breasts off. The times she found a dress she liked and that fitted perfectly she would buy it in all the available colours.

She'd been wearing one of those dresses in the Madrid coffee shop the day she had seen Luis through the window, she suddenly remembered, hit afresh with the liquid sensation she had experienced as their eyes had met and, for the very first time, she had seen interest in his eyes.

The date that had followed had been the best evening of her life. She hadn't wanted it to end.

It had taken all her willpower to get into the cab and return to her apartment without him.

Inhaling deeply, she selected a blue bikini and covered it with a denim skirt that fell to mid-thigh and a black T-shirt, both of which fitted well.

She left her damp hair loose, put the coffee on as Sara had shown her and opened the front door to the glorious bright Caribbean sunshine.

As she had promised, Sara had left a tray of food there for her. Sitting next to the tray and looking straight at her was a two-inch-long gecko.

Chloe crouched down to look properly at its cuteness. 'You are adorable,' she said, smiling at the reptile that appeared unfazed to have a strange woman making cooing noises at it.

'Stay where you are,' she told it, leaving the door open as she backed into the villa.

She'd left her bag on the dining table and quickly upended the contents to find her phone.

Her intention to take a picture of the cute gecko came to nothing when she stepped back out and found it gone.

With a sigh, she carried the tray in, shoving her mess to one side to fit it on the table.

About to put her phone down and pour the coffee out, she suddenly noticed the Wi-Fi icon showing itself.

Luis must have got the Wi-Fi working for her phone had logged in to it, no password needed for access.

She had no signal to make phone calls but she could communicate with the outside world.

The first thing she did, while absently chewing on a freshly baked croissant, too intent on her potential freedom to taste her food, was search the island's co-ordinates.

A message flashed up warning her that her Internet safety settings did not allow her to search this.

She tried again but to no avail. Equally, she found herself blocked from accessing her emails and social media.

She could scream.

Foiled again.

As always, Luis was two steps ahead of her.

Luis...

Remembering his claims about malevolent comments on the Internet, she wrote his and Javier's names into the search box.

Her search engine announced there were over two hundred thousand results.

She clicked on the first news article, a gossip piece about Freya and Benjamin's 'secret' wedding. She scrolled to the comments section.

Twenty minutes later she switched her phone off and threw it onto the heap of stuff from her emptied beach bag, nauseated.

How could people write such things? And on public forums too?

She wished she could scrub her eyeballs out and cleanse them from the poison she had just subjected them to.

Had Luis read those comments?

She fervently hoped not. She hoped Javier hadn't either.

No one deserved hateful comments like that. No one should ever have to read faceless, anonymous opinions that they had evil in their eyes, were inherently bad, were secret psychopaths, were women-beaters, that they'd inherited their father's violence.

What the hell were the moderators of these news sites doing? she wondered angrily. How could they let such toxic bile onto their sites?

This was worse than she had imagined. A thousand times worse.

She closed her eyes as a memory hit her of when she'd been really young. It might have been the same summer she had got stuck in the tree. The Casillas twins and Benjamin had sat around her kitchen table playing a board game she'd been too young to join in with. She couldn't remember the game itself but vividly remembered the booming laughter that had echoed through the walls of her home, remembered stealing into the kitchen in the hope of sharing the array of snacks her mother had laid out for them. One of the boys—she wished she remembered which—had ruffled her hair and slipped her some crisps.

In her mind back then, the three had been giants fully grown in comparison to her puny self, but now she knew they'd been kids in frames their brains were trying to catch up with. Two of the three had been living with a trauma her own young brain had been unable to comprehend.

That those two vulnerable boys should have such spite aimed at them now made her heart ache.

Chloe was comfortable with the world at large questioning the Casillas brothers' business integrity but this…

This was sickening. This was personal.

She had never, would never, could never, have wanted this. Not for anyone but especially not for them.

Luis closed his laptop with an exasperated sigh.

The video conference with their Canadian partner had not gone well.

He had a bad taste in his mouth and was thankful his brother was thousands of miles away so he couldn't give in to the urge to punch him in the face.

'We do not have to explain ourselves to you,' Javier had said from his home office in Madrid. 'The litigation between ourselves and Benjamin Guillem is not a matter of gossip.'

'I am not a man who deals with gossip,' George had retorted, visibly affronted. 'But I am a man who needs to feel comfortable with who I do business with. The rumours are that you ripped Benjamin Guillem off on the Tour Mont Blanc development. If you cannot refute those rumours then I cannot be expected to put my name and money to this development with you.'

'We do not need your money,' Javier had said coldly.

'But you do need the access I can provide. Without my backing this project is dead in the water.'

That was when Luis had stepped in. 'The litigation between us is sealed for confidentiality reasons. However, I can assure you Benjamin Guillem was paid every cent owed under the terms of the contract we all signed seven years ago.'

'I'm afraid your assurances are not enough. I will need to see that contract and the full accounts for the project if I am to proceed.'

'If our word is not good enough for you then it is *us* who needs to rethink this deal,' Javier had retorted, ice seeping through every syllable. 'We will not do business with someone who takes the salacious word of the tabloid press over ours.'

And then his brother had cut himself off from the conference.

Luis had kept the deal on the table only by apologising profusely and explaining the tremendous strain his brother was under.

A huge part of him had been tempted to tell George to take a hike and pull the plug on the project himself, write off the money they'd already spent and the hours he'd spent as point man on it, but that would mean giving in.

His brother had since turned his phone off, no doubt taking himself off to pound the hell out of a punching bag as he always did when his anger got the better of him. Living with the shadow of their father's violence had affected them in different ways and it was in their own reactions to anger that they diverged the most. Javier closed himself off and showed his true emotions only to inanimate objects. Luis was as comfortable with anger as he was with pleasure. Harness it in the right way—a lesson learned by always doing the opposite of what his father would have done—and the anger could be used as fuel.

Javier might be prepared to throw in the towel but Luis was not. Why should they allow the business they had worked so hard for be destroyed? Was it not bad enough that their reputations were being destroyed, their names dragged through the mud?

He would not let it all go without a fight.

And from Chloe not the slightest bit of contrition.

He hadn't seen her since he'd shown her to the villa that would be her dwelling for the immediate future.

She had been on his mind every minute of her absence, even during that damned video conference.

Fed up of the cloying walls of the room he'd turned into an office for himself, Luis left the main villa and headed over the moat to the beach.

His beach.

This whole island, bought as an insurance policy to keep Chloe tied to his side, belonged to him.

Rolling his sleeves up, he welcomed the sun's rays onto his skin as his attention was caught by two figures on the golden beach...

Was that *music* he could hear?

He pulled his loafers off and stepped onto the soft sand, walking closer to the figures that revealed themselves to be Chloe and Jalen. They were dancing...or something that looked like dancing, the kind of moves the more drunken revellers at his parties would make as the night wore on, body popping, robot moves; the pair of them facing each other having some kind of dance-off, oblivious to his presence.

Not wanting to disturb them, he sat on the sand, enraptured with what was playing out before him and enjoying the beat of the hip-hop music.

The longer he watched, the thicker his blood ran, awareness spreading like syrup through him.

This was the Chloe he knew, joyous, enjoying a spontaneous moment, her beautiful face lit up and glowing, her raven hair spraying in all directions and...*vaya*, that body.

After a good ten minutes of frenzied dancing, Chloe stopped and doubled over to massage the side of her stomach. By the grimace on her face she was the victim of a stitch.

She twisted slightly and that was when their eyes met.

After a long moment of hesitation, she turned away and said something to Jalen, who immediately looked at Luis, grabbed what was recognisably an old-fashioned boombox and scarpered.

Slowly she trod barefoot to him, one hand holding her flip-flops, the other still massaging her side, breathing heavily, her eyes not leaving his face until she stood before him.

For a passage of time that seemed to last for ever, they stared wordlessly at each other until she took one last inhalation and sank onto the sand, lying flat on her back beside him, clearly exhausted.

'I didn't know you were into hip-hop,' he said wryly, bemusement and awareness laced together in his veins.

She gave a ragged laugh, her gaze fixed on the sky. 'Neither did I. Sara told me you were still on your conference call so I went for a walk and found Jalen.' She took a breath that turned into a groan. 'I'm shattered. I've become so unfit.'

He stared at the flat of her white stomach, exposed where her T-shirt had ridden up her midriff, and resisted the temptation to run a hand over it. 'Not from where I'm sitting.'

She followed his gaze with a flush creeping over her cheeks, then tugged the T-shirt down over her navel. 'Some ground rules. If I'm going to be your wife then no flirting.'

'My wife?' His heart jolted then set off at a thrum. 'You are agreeing to marry me?'

The breath she took before inclining her head lasted an age. *'Oui.'*

He studied the beautiful face that was no longer looking at him. 'What made you change your mind?'

The last time they had spoken Chloe had been vehement in her refusal. He'd known she would agree eventually but had been sure it would take a few more days for her to see reason.

'I read the comments you spoke of.' Her brow furrowed. When she continued, there was real anger in her voice. 'They are *vile*. How people can even think such things…it is beyond anything I have ever seen. To post them on public forums like that…? Vile, vile, vile.'

'Let me be sure I am understanding you correctly,' he said slowly. 'You are comfortable with my business and reputation suffering through your actions but take exception to mindless fools' comments on the Internet?'

Chloe turned her head to stare into the hazel eyes that

were studying her with an expression she did not understand.

'Those comments are *vile*,' she repeated fiercely. It was the only word she could think of that fitted. 'You and Javier are not your parents. Your father's crimes are not yours. You have suffered enough from what your father did, you shouldn't have to suffer in this way too.'

Because in essence that was what the cruel, ignorant commentators were saying, that the apple didn't fall far from the tree and that Yuri Abramova's violence had been inherited by his sons and that they must have used their wealth and power to cover it up.

Oh, it made her *rage*. The more she had thought about it over the morning, the greater her anger had grown, reaching a boiling point when she had bumped into Jalen walking around with his beloved boom-box on his shoulder.

The simple, uncomplicated innocence she had seen on his young face had been the exact tonic she had needed while she waited for Luis to be done with his video conference.

'You'd manipulated things so I would have been forced to marry you eventually but this made my mind up for me,' she said into the silence that had broken out, reminding herself of his actions that *were* reprehensible and deserving of her fury. She might be having doubts on whether he had intentionally ripped her brother off but that did not excuse what he had done to *her*. 'I don't want to be stuck in limbo here for the rest of my life.'

'Being forced to spend your life on these beautiful shores sounds like a real hardship.'

For some reason, the dryness of his tone tickled her funny bone. She covered her face with her hands so he couldn't see the amusement he'd induced.

She didn't want him to make her laugh. It hurt too much.

'Are you crying?'

'No, I'm holding back a scream.' A scream to purge all the torment building itself back up in her stomach.

'What was that? I can't hear you.'

Moving her hands away, she was about to repeat what she'd said when she found he'd shifted to lean over her, his face hovering above hers.

'Do you mind?' she snapped, frightened at the heavy rhythm her heart had accelerated to in the space of a moment.

'You want me to move?'

'Yes.'

A gleam pulsed in his eyes. 'Make me.'

Instead of closing her hand into a fist and aiming it at his nose as he deserved, Chloe placed it flat on his cheek.

An unwitting sigh escaped from her lips as she drank in the ruggedly handsome features she had dreamed about for so long. The texture of his skin was so different from her own, smooth but with the bristles of his stubble breaking through...had he not shaved? She had never seen him anything other than clean-shaven.

His face was close enough for her to catch the faint trace of coffee and the more potent scent of his cologne.

Luis was the cause of all this chaos rampaging through her. She hated him so much but the feelings she'd carried for him for all these years were still there, refusing to die, making her doubt herself and what she'd believed to be the truth.

Her lips tingled, yearning to feel his mouth on hers again, all her senses springing to life and waving surrender flags at her.

Just kiss him...

Closing her eyes tightly, Chloe gathered all her wits about her, wriggled out from under him and sat up.

Her lungs didn't want to work properly and she had to force air into them.

She shifted to the side, needing physical distance, suddenly terrified of what would happen if she were to brush against him or touch him in any form again.

Fighting to clear her head of the fog clouding it, she blinked rapidly and said, 'Do I have your word that your feud with Benjamin ends with our marriage?'

Things had gone far enough. For the sake of the three boys playing board games in her kitchen all those years ago, it was time to put an end to it.

'*Sí*. Marry me and it ends.'

She exhaled a long breath. '*D'accord*. If I am going to do this then there will be some ground rules. Our marriage will last as short a time as is possible.'

'Agreed.'

'And it will not be consummated.' Aware of her face going crimson again—*Dieu*, the heat she knew that was reflecting on her face was licking her everywhere—she scrambled to her feet.

A few inches of distance was not enough. Not when it came to Luis.

Two months of distance hadn't been enough.

How was she going to get through this? How was she going to cope with living with him, even if it was only for a few months, and keep her craving for him contained?

Somehow she would find a way. She could not give in to it; the dangers were too great.

This was *Luis* she was going to marry. The only man she had ever had feelings for, the man she had fallen for when she had been only seventeen, the only man other than her brother she had thought she could trust. Even if he'd spoken the truth about not deliberately betraying Benjamin, she knew it had only been the headiness of newly discovered desire that had made her want to trust him before.

She could never trust this ruthless, pleasure-seeking hedonist, not with her body and especially not with her fragile heart.

She could feel his eyes burning into her as he clarified, 'No sex?'

'Our marriage will be short and strictly platonic.' She strode away over the warm, fine sand, heading for the footpath that led back to the villas, needing to escape from him.

'Still holding on to your virginity?' he called after her.

She closed her eyes but didn't break stride.

She would not give him the satisfaction of a response.

The hairs on the back of her neck lifted as he easily caught up with her.

'Captain Brand's bringing the yacht back in six days. We will marry then. In the meantime, I'll get the pre-nuptial agreement drawn up.'

'What pre-nuptial agreement? If you think I want your money you're crazy.'

She didn't want *anything* from him.

'I am not interested in protecting my wealth, only my reputation and my future. You will sign a contract that forbids you from discussing our marriage.'

She stopped walking to stare at him in disbelief. 'You're going to put a gagging order on me?'

'I will not have you sharing with the world that you only married me because you were forced to.'

'Haven't you learned your lesson about stifling free speech from my brother?' she snapped, affronted. 'That injunction you put on him worked out so well, didn't it?' she added over her shoulder as she set off again.

The only reason she was agreeing to marry him was to

stop the cruel things being stuck all over the Internet about him, not to add fuel to the fire.

Those cruel comments had hurt as much as if they had been personally directed at her. More.

As she was about to step onto the bridge over the sea-water moat, a strong hand snatched hold of her elbow and spun her around.

Where moments ago there had been a casual, almost lazily seductive look to his eyes, now there was a hardness. 'The injunction against Benjamin was necessary. He was a loose cannon—'

'Only because he felt you took advantage of him when our mother was dying.' She grabbed hold of the outrage that filled her, negating the growing guilt at what her actions had helped lead to. 'You can shout it as loudly as you like that you were going to give him that money but where's the evidence to back it up? It's been two months since the truth came out and all you have done is fight him in the courts. One phone call could have put an end to it.'

His hold on her elbow loosened but his angry face leant right into hers. 'Your brother hit us with the lawsuit two days after our confrontation when I was still furious at his accusations. You speak of betrayal, well, what about your brother's betrayal to friendship? He turned this into war, not us, and you were happy to join in with it. The only thing Javier and I are guilty of is protecting ourselves and if you would pull those damned blinkers from your eyes you would know it too, but you won't because then you would have to accept responsibility for *your* actions and accept that it suits you to cast me as the monster in the scenario.'

'In what possible way does it *suit* me to cast you as the monster?' she demanded to know as the rest of his accusations dragged through her skin as if they were attached to barbs.

She had never been *happy* to join her brother's side. She had been heartbroken for him…

But what if Benjamin had been wrong? What if his fury at the supposed betrayal had driven his actions to the point where reason was something no longer available to him?

'Because you, *bonita*, are running scared and have been since you ran off like a frightened virgin at the end of our date. Your brother's war with me was the excuse you needed.'

'*Excuse?* Listen to yourself! Your ego is so big you should buy another island to contain it in.'

Her heart thundering and her skin feeling as if the barbs of his words were being pulled through it, Chloe marched away. There was a cramp in her stomach far sharper than the stitch she'd had on the beach.

'Chloe!' His deep voice called after her in a growl but she didn't stop, upping her pace, trying her best to keep herself together through the burn of tears growing at the backs of her eyes and the cramp that had spread into her chest.

Hearing his assured footsteps closing in on her, she broke into a run, almost skidding over the swimming-pool moat bridge that led directly to her villa's path.

That she was doing exactly what he'd just accused her of—running scared—was something she understood on a dim, hazy level of her psyche but enough to propel her faster, a desperation to escape the eyes that saw too much and the emotions brimming inside her.

She pulled the door open with Luis only a couple of strides behind her and slammed it shut.

CHAPTER SEVEN

IF LUIS HAD been one step quicker the door would have slammed in his face.

He turned the handle, had pushed it open an inch when she threw her weight against the other side.

'Stay away from me,' she screamed through the closed door.

'Let me in or I will break it down,' he said with a calmness he did not feel. Right then he felt anything but calm.

He knew he should walk away and wait for Chloe to regain her composure but reason be damned. He would not allow her to walk away. She had run enough from him.

'I don't want anything to do with you.'

'Tough. Last chance, *bonita*. Open the door.'

His ultimatum was met with a choice of rude words.

He sighed heavily. 'Don't say I didn't warn you.' And with that he used all his strength to barge the door open against the pressure Chloe exerted on the other side of it.

But he was by far the stronger of the two and in seconds he had it open.

She clearly had no intention of letting him in without a fight. As he stepped over the threshold, she hurled herself at him, pounding her fists against his chest, kicking him, her long raven hair whipping around her face as she threw curses at him.

He grabbed at her flailing arms and held her wrists

tightly as she continued to struggle against him, clearly uncaring that her height and weight against his own made it a fight she could never win.

He managed to manoeuvre her so her back was to the wall and pulled her hands up and above her head and used the strength in his legs to pin her own and stop them kicking.

'Is this how it's going to be for the next few months?' he demanded, staring hard at the beautiful face glaring at him as if condensed with all the poison in the world. 'Is every cross word going to end with you running away or fighting me?'

Those gorgeous, voluptuous lips wobbled. The eyes firing loathing at him became stark, the fight dissolving out of her like a balloon struck with a pin.

'I don't know how to deal with it,' she whispered tremulously. 'It scares me.'

She no longer struggled against him.

His chest twisted to see the starkness of her fear. 'What scares you, *bonita*?'

She inhaled deeply through her nose. Her throat moved, her eyes pulsed and darkened, her lips parted...

And then those soft lips brushed against his and he was no longer pinning her to the wall but pulling her into his arms. The hands that had been hitting at him wrapped around his neck as their bodies crushed together and their mouths parted.

Her taste hit his senses like a knocked-back shot of strong liqueur. It played on his tongue, the sweet nectar that was Chloe's kisses, a flavour like no other.

Every cell in his body caught fire. The fever caught her too; there in the crush of her lips moving greedily against his own and the digging of her nails into his scalp and the hungry way her body pressed itself against him, an instantaneous combustion trapping them in a magnetic grip.

What was it with this woman that he responded to with such primal force? Chloe lit a fire inside him, fuelling it with kisses a man could use for sustenance. It was like nothing he had ever known before, as if all others before her had pitched him to a mere simmer.

Mouths clashing and devouring, Luis swept a hand up her back and under her cropped T-shirt, headily relishing the warm softness of her skin. Such beautiful, soft, feminine skin...

He found the ties of the bikini that contained the breasts he'd fantasised about for so long and pulled it undone. The bikini rose upwards as he traced his hand around her midriff and up to the newly released swell.

She gasped into his mouth as he cupped a breast far weightier than he'd imagined but soft like her lips and her skin. Her hands burrowed under the neck of his T-shirt and grabbed at the material.

The fire condensed into his loins. It burned, a pain like nothing he had felt before.

He'd never felt *any* of this before.

When he pressed his groin against her, his arousal ground against her abdomen, they moaned into each other's mouths before she wrenched her lips from his and rubbed her mouth against his cheek and tugged even harder at his T-shirt.

Together they scrambled to pull each other's T-shirts off and fling them to the floor, and then her arms were hooked back around his neck and her hot mouth devoured him all over again.

In a frenzy of kisses, Luis tugged the ties of her bikini at the back of her neck and whipped it off fully, discarding it without thought.

A pulsing thrill ripped through him at the first press of her bare breasts against his bare chest.

He wanted to taste those breasts and all her other hidden places and burrow his face in their softness.

Everything about Chloe was soft. Everything. And so utterly, amazingly feminine, the yin to his yang, soft where he was hard, porcelain wrapped in silk.

She was a woman like no other. Feisty, stubborn, smart, funny, all contained in a body that could make a grown man weep.

And she was going to be his wife.

Chloe's breaths were coming in pants. She could hear them, could feel herself make them but they seemed to be coming from somewhere else, from someone who was not herself.

She was not herself.

Her body had become something new, a butterfly emerging from its chrysalis, coaxed into the sunlight by the only man she had ever desired or wanted. She had become a vessel of nerve-endings, and they were all straining to Luis, all her hate and rage, pain and sorrow, turned on their head in the time it took for a coin to flip from heads to tails.

She was beyond caring about yet another self-made vow being broken.

If this was what broken promises felt like then she would break a thousand of them.

For two months she had focused on her passionate hatred of him. But her passion for him was more than hate, it always had been, and to deny this part of her feelings for him was like denying herself air. If she were to walk— run—away right now she would forget how to breathe.

Even her skin felt alive. Tendrils curled around her and through her, sensation burning deep inside.

She gasped again when he squeezed her bottom roughly

and ground himself more tightly to her, the weight and size of his excitement pressed so deliciously against her loins sending newer, deeper sensations racing through her.

As he held onto her thighs and lifted her up, she wrapped her legs around him and kissed him even more deeply as he carried her to the bed in three long strides.

She had to keep kissing him. She needed the heat of his mouth on hers and that dark masculine taste firing into her senses to drive out the fears that had held her in its grip for too long.

What had there been to fear about *this*?

This was pleasure. Erotic, greedy and needy, not something to be frightened of but something to be embraced.

He placed her on the bed, her bottom on the edge, her arms still wrapped around him, Luis between her parted thighs.

He was the one to break the kiss.

She moaned her complaint and tried to resist as he put a hand on her shoulder and gently pressed her back.

Her complaints died when she saw the darkness pulsating in his eyes as he lightly circled her breasts with his fingers, sending brand-new sensation over skin she hadn't known could be so sensitive. When he put his lips there too...

She closed her eyes to this new, intoxicating pleasure as he kissed each breast, flickering her nipples with his tongue.

So intense were the sensations that she was only dimly aware of his hands working on the buttons of her skirt and tugging it down her hips with her bikini bottoms, only fully aware that she had helped shed them by kicking them off when he brought his mouth back to her lips for another of his darkly passionate kisses.

When he put a hand to the womanly heart of her, an

electric pulse charged through her, strong enough to lift her back into an involuntary arch. She drank his kisses while fresh, new pleasure assaulted her. His fingers gently but assuredly stroked and manipulated her, making her senses spin and rocket to an undiscovered dimension, and she cried a protest when his hand moved away from his heavenly doings and traced up and over her belly and covered her aching breasts.

Time slipped away and lost all meaning, thoughts dissipating to just one concrete thing: Luis.

This, here, now, was everything she had dreamed, everything she had...

Her eyes flew open.

Luis must have removed the rest of his clothing for suddenly she was conscious of a velvety thickness pressing against the apex of her thigh.

She gazed into the dark hazel eyes gazing so sensually into hers but with a question contained in them.

This is the point of no return, they said. *If you want this to stop then now is the time.*

Chloe would rather take a knife to the heart than stop. She had never wanted anything more than she did at this moment.

She placed her hand on his tightly locked jaw. It softened under her touch before he turned his face to kiss her palm.

Then she moved her arms round his back as he kissed her mouth again and put his hand between their conjoined bodies to take hold of himself and position himself at the most secret, hidden heart of her.

A hard, heavy pressure pushed against her but it was a pressure she welcomed; craved, his kisses no longer enough to satisfy the intense heat overwhelming every part of her.

Slowly he inched inside her with a careful tenderness to his movements that drove out what little fear still lived inside her. His lips brushed over her face and his hands stroked her hair, as he filled her bit by bit until he was fully inside her and their groins were locked together.

The newness of the sensation stunned her. She could feel *him*, inside her, over her, on her, two bodies fused together as one.

And then he kissed her again and began to move…and that was when she discovered the true meaning of pleasure.

Her legs wrapped around his waist, Chloe closed her eyes and let Luis guide her.

Luis.

Even with her eyes shut she could see him so clearly. The scent of his skin, a new muskiness to it, the smoothness of his skin, the bristles of the hairs of his chest brushing against her breasts…

He was her everything. Her pain, her pleasure, her desire, her hate, all blended together so there was only him.

Low in her most hidden part an intensity built, every slow thrust raising it higher and yet somehow deeper, everything inside her concentrating into one mass that finally reached a peak and exploded within her. Ripples pulsated and surged through her body with a strength that had her crying out. Pressing her cheek tightly to Luis's, she rode the waves of pleasure, the only thought echoing through her head that she didn't want this feeling to ever, ever leave her.

There was a wonderfully languid weight in Chloe's limbs she'd never experienced before, a mellow buzzing sensation in her veins. Luis's face was buried in her neck, his breath hot on her skin, fingers laced through hers.

Time seemed to have come to a stop.

She sighed when he raised himself up to stare down at her. She couldn't read the expression in his eyes but what she saw made her stomach melt and her heart clench.

His kiss was light but lingering before he climbed off the bed.

'Are you going?' she asked before she could stop herself.

A shutter came down in his eyes but his stare remained on hers. 'Do you *want* me to go?'

She hesitated before answering. She should want him to go. What they had just shared hadn't been planned—*Dieu*, had it not been planned—but the culmination of something that had fired into being months ago and been left to simmer. To tell him to leave would be an admission of regret and a denial of her own complicity.

She did not regret it. How could she? It had been the most intensely wonderful experience of her life.

And she would not be complicit in any more deceit.

There had been enough deceit between them to fill his yacht.

She swallowed. 'No.'

He inclined his head, a gleam returning in his eyes. 'Good. Because I'm not going anywhere apart from the bathroom to dispose of the condom.'

That made her blink.

When had he put that on?

She watched him stroll to the bathroom, unable to believe she hadn't noticed Luis slipping a condom on.

Wriggling under the bed sheets, she cuddled into the pillow, dazed that passion had engulfed her so acutely that it had swept her away to a place where she had lost all sense.

When Luis came back into the room in all his naked glory her heart skipped up into her mouth.

Her imagination of his naked form had not done him justice. He truly was a titan of a man, broad, muscular, bronzed, unashamed in his masculinity.

A smile curved on his lips as he strolled towards her and lifted the bed sheets to climb on top of her.

Elbows either side of her face, Luis gazed down at the face that had been like a spectre in his mind for so long, drinking in the expression in the baby-blue eyes, the flawless porcelain skin, the voluptuous lips that kissed like the softest pillow.

He dipped his head and kissed her softly. 'Do you regret making love?'

She arched a perfectly shaped brow. Her mouth had quirked with amusement but there was something in her eyes that negated it; a vulnerability. 'Is that what you call it?'

He shuffled down to kiss her neck. *Dios*, barely minutes since they'd made love and he was hard again. 'What do you prefer to call it?'

'Sex?' From the breathless way she suggested the word he sensed her own arousal sparking back to life.

'I thought the French were a romantic people?'

'We are with people we feel more than hate for.'

'You feel more than hate for me.'

'No, I don't.'

He nipped her shoulder. 'Yes, you do. And what we shared was more than sex.'

'No, it wasn't. And stop telling me what I...' he'd encircled one of her nipples with his tongue '...feel.'

'Ah, I forget you have had *tons* of lovers.'

'I might have exaggerated a little.' Now there was a sensual hitch in her voice.

'When are you going to admit you were a virgin?'

'Never.'

He moved his attention to her other breast, enraptured with its texture, its taste, its weight, the sheer feminine beauty of it... 'You didn't answer my question.'

Her hands found his head, her fingers digging through

his hair. 'Which question was that? There have been so many.'

He rested his chin on her nipple to look in her eyes. 'Do you regret us making love...having *sex*?'

The returning stare shone at him. 'I should regret it.'

'But you don't?'

'No.' She wound a lock of his hair in her fingers. 'I don't regret it. It doesn't change how I feel about you or anything else. I still think you're the devil.'

Trailing his tongue up her breast and to her neck, he pressed his mouth back to hers. 'Maybe one day you will discover I am not the devil you think I am,' he said before kissing her deeply.

No more words were spoken between them. Not verbally.

The gecko was back.

Chloe had woken early, much earlier than she usually liked to wake, and had come to an instant alertness.

That had been a man lying with his head on the pillow next to hers, an arm slung across her midriff. She had moved his arm carefully and sat up to stare at Luis's still-sleeping face.

There had been something surprisingly innocent in his sleeping form, his features smoother except for the now thick stubble around his jawline.

Resisting the urge to press a kiss to the stubbly cheek, she had torn her gaze from him and got out of bed, pausing only to put her thin robe on. Then she had made herself a coffee and slipped through the sliding door and onto the veranda, which was where her two-inch friend had found her.

Of course, it could be a different gecko. Luis's island was full of them. She was sure their parents could differentiate but they all looked the same to her, all except for this one.

This one was cute. It had perched itself on top of the seat next to hers and was staring at her with what she liked to think was interest.

'What do you want, little one?' she asked softly. 'Food? Drink? I would share but I don't think coffee is good for a little thing like you. Are there any bugs you can eat for your breakfast?'

As ridiculous as she knew it was to talk to a reptile, there was a comfort to it. Focusing on the cold-blooded creature stopped her thinking too hard about the warm-blooded creature she'd left sleeping.

This was the first time she'd left the villa's walls since Luis had barged her door open the morning before.

He'd had food brought to them at varying points with jugs of cocktails of varying strengths. She couldn't remember any of it, not what they'd eaten or drunk. The only image with any solidity to it was making love…having sex…with Luis.

The desire that had simmered between them for so long had finally been unleashed and she was in no hurry to tie it back up, not when the things he did to her felt so utterly wonderful.

Luis had taught her things her imagination had never conjured, taught her pleasure that was about so much more than the mechanics of sex.

What had surprised her the most was how fun it had all been. There had been passion—lots of passion—but there had been laughter too. Dirty jokes. A shared bath that had ended with far more water on the floor than in the tub.

She was French, she'd reminded herself many times that day. Taking a lover meant nothing. That her lover was her… fiancé—was that what she was supposed to call the black-mailing, kidnapping devil?—was irrelevant.

But she didn't feel like a kidnap victim. In truth, she'd

never felt like his victim. His pawn, yes, that was an apt description but victim, no.

She had known when she'd offered to help her brother that there would be a price to pay in putting herself up against Luis.

A shiver ran up her spine. She shook it off.

Better to have lost her virginity with a man who made her stomach melt with one skim of his finger on her skin than with...

But that was the problem. There never had been anyone else. When she and Luis were done with she still could not envisage herself with anyone else.

She couldn't reconcile her insatiable hunger for him. It was wrong on so many levels that soon she would be joining him in the special level built just for him in Dante's *Inferno*.

The patio door slid open and Luis stepped out onto the veranda, cup of coffee in hand, charcoal boxers slung low over his hips...and nothing else.

Chloe gaped, struck anew at his rugged, masculine beauty.

With the early morning sun beaming down on him he looked like a statue of a Greek god brought to life and filled with bronzed colour, albeit a Greek god with hair sticking up all over the place and eyes puffy from sleep.

For some reason, seeing him like this made her want to cry.

The smile he bestowed her with made her heart double flip on itself.

'You know that talking to yourself is the first sign of madness?' he said casually.

It took a beat for her to get what *he* was talking about.

She grinned, although it was an effort to make her lips and cheeks comply. 'I've been talking to Greta.'

'Greta?'

'Greta the Gecko.' She nodded to the chair Greta was perched on.

Luis took a step towards it and Greta fled.

'You've scared her away,' Chloe chided.

'I have that effect on women,' he teased, taking Greta's vacated seat.

He certainly did, she acknowledged with a painful twist of her heart.

Luis was a man any right-thinking woman would run a mile from.

She had run, as fast as she could.

And then she had drawn him back.

It suddenly struck her that the method she had chosen to get him out of the way for the gala had put her directly in his firing line when there must have been numerous other methods that wouldn't have pointed the finger at her as perpetrator.

But she had *wanted* him to know her part in it. She had imagined his face when he'd worked it all out and taken bitter satisfaction from it while her heart had splintered.

And why had she chosen to make out she was a damsel in distress? Because she had known he was a man who would never let a woman be alone and in potential danger when he could help her.

He'd carried her out of the tree, hadn't he, when he had been only fifteen…?

Luis's fundamental nature was, not exactly good, but selfless. He'd put his own life on the line to help a small child.

Had Benjamin got it all wrong as Luis insisted?

Before she could follow her train of thought any further, Luis put his cup on the table and opened his other hand to reveal a rectangular foil package.

CHAPTER EIGHT

LUIS WATCHED CHLOE'S REACTION, being careful to keep his own lurching emotions in check.

Her cheeks were stained red. 'Have you been going through my things?' she croaked.

'No, *bonita*. I saw them on the dining table with the rest of the contents of your bag. They caught my eye. You're on the pill?'

He thought of the trio of condoms he'd had in his wallet, which they'd used up in relatively short order, and the other ways of making love they had embraced that hadn't required actual penetration since.

She stared back at him, the same thoughts obviously going through her mind too because darker colour flooded her cheeks.

Although incredibly willing, there had been a shyness about her over all the new things they had done, a shyness not quite disguised with laughter and quips. He'd found it utterly beguiling, just as he found most things about her.

When they had run out of condoms and he hadn't wanted to break the headiness of the spell they had created together to return to his villa for more, she hadn't breathed a word that she was already protected.

He hadn't wanted to break the spell until their limbs were so heavy and sated that the only bodily command they could obey was the one demanding sleep. In the back of his mind had been the certainty that the moment he walked out of this villa, what they were sharing would be over.

The chemistry between them had in no way been a precursor to what they would be like together.

Spending the day in bed making love…it had made him forget why he had her there, her conspiracy against him and the consequences he and his brother were living through. It had been passionate and, strangely, fun, a heady combination he had never experienced before.

'I had a bad outbreak of acne when I was nineteen so my doctor put me on the pill to help,' she blurted out, cutting through the increasingly tense silence that had formed between them. 'I stayed on it because I found it helped with the monthly pain.'

Luis dragged a hand through his hair and muttered a curse under his breath, suddenly feeling like a heel.

It had been a reflex action. He'd seen the packet, recognised it, and scooped it up to examine it. It hadn't been a conscious decision to confront her over it. What was there to confront? It was *sensible* for her not to trust him or any other man to keep her safe.

Luis knew his reputation with women wasn't the greatest. There was some truth in his playboy reputation, he had to admit, but it wasn't the whole truth. He'd never hopped from one bed to the next like some of the Lotharios he knew, but didn't see the point in pretending to pine for a relationship that had run its course…although, to call these interludes relationships was pushing it a little.

Marriage or anything remotely long-term had never been on the cards for him. None of the women had wanted to be in a relationship with him, Luis, the man, just with Luis Casillas, child of the murdered Clara Casillas and her killer husband Yuri Abramova, generous host of great parties and generous giver of gifts.

The point was, he told himself firmly, he always used condoms. Always. He didn't care if his lover was on the pill *and* had an IUD fitted, he used condoms, end of discussion.

It must be sleep deprivation that made it feel like a stab in the guts that Chloe didn't trust him to keep her safe.

Their relationship was nothing to do with trust. The sex, great as it was, gave it an added piquancy but that was all.

Chloe owed him nothing but marriage.

'You don't have to explain yourself, *bonita*. I apologise for embarrassing you.'

'You haven't embarrassed me,' she insisted even though her cheeks, flaming all over again, contradicted her statement.

'*Bueno.*'

'No, really, you haven't embarrassed me.' A sudden hint of mischief flashed in her eyes. 'After all, I am a woman of great sexual experience.'

Her obvious and deliberate lie was so outrageous that he burst into laughter.

She caught his gaze and burst out laughing too.

It was only a minor moment but the tightness that had formed in his chest loosened and, with it, the tension between them defused.

She did not owe him a thing more than she had already pledged. Chloe had agreed to marry him. That she was now sharing a bed with him was a delicious bonus.

Very delicious.

Luis settled back in his chair and sipped his coffee, admiring how Chloe could look so fresh and ravishing after such little sleep, slouched back in her chair as she was. She had on only a white robe tied loosely around her waist, the V of it gaping enough for him to see the divine swell of her wonderful breasts.

He exhaled a long sigh. A part of him wanted to press her back on the table and make love to her, the other part content to merely sit there and soak in her rare, unblemished beauty.

His suspicions had been confirmed. He really had been her first.

He'd been as gentle as he could be the first time he'd possessed her and if she had suffered any pain from it she had covered it well. They had been amazing together.

It struck him then that if he was her first, it stood to reason that one day some other man would be her second.

'Are you comfortable in marrying me knowing it won't last?' he asked curiously.

She arched a brow. 'Are *you*?'

'Very comfortable. Marriage has never been on my agenda.'

'It's never been on mine, either.' Although the fresh, light stain of colour that crawled up her neck made him suspect that there was something there she was keeping from him. 'Marriage is an outdated institution. People make those vows every day without meaning them. At least there's an honesty in the vows we'll make.'

'Are you speaking of your parents' marriage?'

'Their marriage was never honest.' Her eyes held his. 'Did you know your mother and my mother deliberately planned it so they fell pregnant at the same time?'

'That has been alluded to over the years,' he said. He and Javier were only three months older than Benjamin. Whenever his mother had toured, Benjamin and his mother would go with them, Louise as his mother's costume-maker, Benjamin as their playmate.

'My father was, in essence, a sperm donor. My mother married him because she didn't want to be a single mother but she raised Benjamin *as* a single mother. My father had little involvement or say in his upbringing, which was how he liked it. He got the glory of a son without any of the work.'

'I didn't know your father.' He'd been nothing but a name to them. Benjamin had rarely mentioned him.

'Their marriage was all but dead when Maman got broody again.' She rubbed her nose and gave a sad laugh. 'He was ready to leave her but she got him drunk and seduced him. *Et voilà*, nine months later I was born. He left before I was born.'

Luis ran a hand through his hair at this revelation he had known nothing about. 'Your mother told you this?'

'*Non*, my father told me the day before I left his home. He never wanted me and he hated my mother for tricking him into being a sperm donor for a second time.'

He gazed at the beautiful elfin face staring back at him with the merest hint of defiance to counteract the wobble of her chin.

'You learned all this after your mother died?'

She gave a sharp nod.

'That must have been a hard thing to accept.'

She shrugged but her chin wobbled again. 'It explained why he'd never been in my life. I'd only met him three times before Maman died.'

He gave a low whistle. 'Obviously I was aware there wasn't much in the way of involvement from him but I didn't realise it was that bad.'

'It was good,' she insisted. 'My childhood was incredibly happy. He's the one who chose not to be a part of it.'

'So why did you move in with him? Couldn't you have lived with Benjamin?'

'It wasn't allowed. I had only just turned seventeen, I was still at school and still a minor, so that's how it had to be. One parent dies so you move in with the other even if he is a stranger to you. And at the time Benjamin was struggling to cope financially—it wouldn't have been fair to burden him with me too, not then.'

Benjamin had been struggling financially because he'd taken out a huge mortgage to buy the chateau for his mother to end her days in and then neglected his business to care for her in those last days. The savings he'd had to purchase the chateau outright had been given to Luis and Javier for the Tour Mont Blanc land.

Another unintended consequence of that damned contract that Luis was becoming sure would haunt him in the afterlife.

'But you moved in with him eventually, didn't you?' he asked, his brow furrowed. 'I remember visiting the chateau once and you were there. I remember him telling me his fears about you moving to London.'

'I stuck it out with my dad and stepmother until I completed high school then moved in with Benjamin for a while before I moved to London. When I moved back to France after I'd completed my apprenticeship I split my time between his chateau and his apartment in Paris.'

'You never went back to your father's home?'

'Non.'

'Did they treat you badly?'

She made a sound like a laugh. It was the most miserable sound Luis had ever heard from her. 'They didn't treat me like anything. They might as well have had a ghost move in for all the attention they paid me. My mother was dead and they couldn't have cared less. They clothed and fed me and made sure I attended school but that was it. They were always out, seeing friends, going on holidays, but they never included me or invited me anywhere with them. I didn't get a single embrace from either of them in the whole year I lived with them. I could understand it from my stepmother but from my father...'

Chloe blinked back the burn of tears.

She would never cry over her father again.

When she'd left her father's home she'd sworn to forget all about him. She'd survived perfectly well for the first seventeen years of her life without him; she didn't need him.

But it still hurt. It really, really hurt.

Whatever the circumstances of her conception, she had been innocent. Benjamin had been innocent. Their father hadn't just walked out on their mother but his ten-year-old son and unborn child too.

The first time he had met his daughter, Chloe had been three years old. It had been another four years before she'd seen him again.

'They didn't want me there,' she explained, trying her hardest to keep her voice factual and moderate. 'I learned when I turned eighteen that my mother had saved all her child support payments from him. It wasn't a fortune but was enough for me to live with Benjamin without being a financial burden.'

'Your father didn't object?'

She gave another miserable laugh. 'He couldn't wait to be rid of me.'

And that was what hurt the most. Deep down Chloe had wanted him to object. She'd wanted him to raise himself up and insist on being her father. She'd wanted to be important to him. She'd wanted him to love her but he didn't. He never had and never would.

She had never spoken about any of this before. Benjamin knew she'd had a hard time living with their father but she'd never confided the depth of her misery there or the enormous one-sided argument she and her father had had, scared she would come across as a spoilt, needy brat. Her stepmother, in a rare moment of interaction with Chloe, had called her exactly that.

It had been a one-sided argument because it had essentially consisted of Chloe having a complete breakdown. She had screamed at her father, all her misery and pain pouring out of her in an emotional tirade that had been met by her father's cold retelling of the past and her stepmother's cruel words.

The closest she had come to that feeling of betrayal and helplessness and that total loss of emotional control was with the man whose arms she had found such pleasure in.

She hadn't seen her father since the day she'd left.

A buzzing sound rang out.

'That will be our breakfast.' Luis jumped to his feet, grateful for the disturbance.

After defusing the tension between them things had suddenly become extremely weighty.

He admired Chloe's spirit, her beauty, her feistiness…

Her vulnerability was not something he liked to see and there had been more than a flash of it then as she'd narrated a part of her life he'd only known the basics of.

Dios, her father's treatment of his child had been as deplorable as his father's, even if their methods of abuse had differed. Chloe's father had abused her with his indifference. Luis's father had abused him with his hands.

'Stay there. I'll let them in.'

Pulling a pair of shorts on first, he opened the door to find Sara and Jalen. The little boy took one look at him and hid behind his mother.

Sara rolled her tired eyes and said apologetically. 'He was hoping to see Chloe. My son has taken quite a shine to her.'

Remembering the hip-hop dancing the boy had been doing with her, Luis quite understood why.

'I will tell her you were asking for her,' he said to the boy pretending to be invisible behind his mother's legs, before taking the breakfast tray from Sara's hands.

At some point soon he would have to employ more staff for the island. Marietta hadn't been to the island in the three years before she'd sold it to him and had let all the other permanent staff go. Sara had proved herself to be an excellent cook but she had a hundred other jobs to get on with.

He carried the tray out onto the veranda and set it on the table.

Chloe gave him a small smile.

As she helped herself to toast, he said, 'Your boyfriend was asking after you.'

Her brow furrowed in confusion. 'What?'

'The caretakers' boy.'

He did not want to go back to tales of her childhood. Listening had had the effect of a hook being wound around his stomach.

His diversion did the trick.

'Jalen?' Her face lit up. 'Oh, he's a sweet little thing.'

'He hides or runs away whenever he sees me.'

She shrugged with bemusement. 'You're three times the size of him. To his eyes you're a big scary giant.'

'You think?'

'He told me that himself.'

'It's not men in particular that he's fearful of?'

'No—why do you ask?'

'I keep thinking of his reaction when his father called him over the day we got here. He looked terrified.'

Chloe grinned. 'That's because his father had expressly forbidden him from speaking to us.'

'Why would he do that?'

'You're the new boss. They don't know you and they don't know how tolerant you are to children. They're worried for their jobs. They're scared that if you think Jalen is a nuisance you will replace them with childless caretakers.'

'Jalen told you all this?'

'He's a chatterbox without a filter.' Her pretty white teeth flashed at him again. 'I can understand why they're scared of him talking to you.'

'They have nothing to worry about. I appreciate that this is their home...you are sure that that's the only reason Jalen was afraid of his father?'

Her eyes narrowed slightly as she tilted her head. 'He wasn't afraid of his father, he was afraid of the telling-off he knew he would get from him.'

He nodded slowly. It was the way Jalen had hung his head while speaking to his father that had sent the alarm bells ringing in him. It had taken him back thirty years to how he would stand when summoned to see his father.

'I suppose all children are afraid of their father some of the time.' Luis had been one of the unlucky ones who had been afraid of his father all of the time. The only times he'd ever fully relaxed as a child was when he and Javier had gone on tour with their mother without him.

Chloe was watching him closely. He could see the questions swirling in her head, her curiosity piqued.

The tension that had filled him when he'd discovered her contraceptive pill packet and her matter-of-fact explanation on her relationship with her father crowded back into him.

He got back to his feet and leaned over to place a hard, hungry kiss to her mouth. 'I'm going to my villa. I'll be back in five,' he murmured into the silkiness of her hair before kissing her again.

When he broke away there was a dazed look in her eyes, her questions successfully driven away.

He returned to her in four minutes with his pockets stuffed with condoms and carried her to the bedroom.

CHAPTER NINE

CHLOE FINISHED HER lunch with Jalen on the beach then headed to the main villa where Luis had spent the morning working.

Butterflies rampaged through her belly, the product, she told herself, of nerves that they were going to sign their pre-nuptial agreement, not excitement at seeing him again. That was a ludicrous notion. He'd only left her bed four hours ago.

But it frightened her how much she had missed him in those four hours apart.

No, she told herself firmly, it was the sex she missed. Two days of doing nothing but making love was bound to affect her and, as a lover, although she had no one to compare him to, Luis was amazing. They were amazing together. So long as they kept things physical then everything was fine.

She still struggled to understand why she had divulged her relationship with her father to him. She'd crossed an invisible line there and had only just stopped herself from crossing it again when they had been talking about Jalen.

There had been an undercurrent running behind Luis's questions about the boy, and she'd recalled the fleeting concern she'd seen on his face when Jalen had been scolded by his father.

Scared of being alone with her thoughts, she had sought Jalen out, assuring Sara repeatedly that he was no bother at

all. She liked the little boy's company. There was no artifice to him, everything laid out in that innocent way only
a child could manage.

Sara opened the door with a welcoming smile and invited her to wait in one of the living rooms while she let
Luis know she was there.

The living room in question was an enormous elegant
space with a distinctly feminine touch to it. Chloe stared at
all the clutter and boxes filling it with awed disbelief. How
did any one person accumulate so much *stuff*?

A huge, elaborately framed portrait at the front of a
stack of frames resting against the wall caught Chloe's attention. It showed a young, strangely old-fashioned beautiful woman with thick curly black hair, posing elegantly
with an enigmatic smile.

'I'm sorry about the mess,' Sara said, slipping back into
the room. 'We are packing up Marietta's things to get them
shipped to her. It's taking us a lot longer than we thought
it would.'

Chloe smiled then pointed at the portrait. 'Is that Marietta?' The armchair the sitter had posed in was in the corner of the room.

'It is.'

Something sharp stabbed into Chloe's heart. So this was
the woman who had sold her yacht and her island to Luis
in the space of days.

Her stomach curdled again to imagine the *incentives* Luis
must have brought to the table to convince her so quickly.

The ghost of Marietta had haunted her since she had arrived at this beautiful island, a phantom reminder that, to
Luis, women were disposable.

'She was only eighteen when this was painted,' Sara
explained. 'Her father had it done to celebrate her coming of age.'

'He must adore her,' she said, unable to contain her wistfulness.

Chloe had been living with her father on her eighteenth birthday and he'd still managed to forget it. The huge row that had exploded between them the day before she had moved out of his emotionally cold, horrible house had resulted in Chloe being struck from his address book permanently. She doubted he knew she now lived in Madrid.

Sara laughed. 'I don't know about that. It was the done thing with the gentry in those days.'

'What do you mean?'

'That portrait is over seventy years old.'

Chloe's jaw dropped. 'Seriously?'

'Marietta's going to be ninety on her next birthday.'

She stepped over to look at the portrait in more detail and crouched down. Close up it was even more majestic.

Footsteps sounded behind her.

'It's incredible to think this is seventy years old,' she murmured. 'It's in remarkable condition, and the detail…'

'It's something special, yes?'

Chloe almost fell backwards onto her bottom. She hadn't heard Luis enter the room, had thought Sara had come to stand behind her.

He held out a hand to her.

Her legs wobbling in protest at her crouching position, she grabbed onto it and let him help her up.

'Thank you,' she murmured, disconcerted to find her heart racing.

His eyes sparkled. 'Pleasure.'

She felt more unsettled than ever. Her insides were a cauldron bubbling with a thousand differing emotions, all of which boiled for him.

But she would not show it. She would never let Luis

know how easily and seamlessly he had burrowed under her skin.

Smiling broadly, she pulled out the contract she'd shoved into the back pocket of her shorts. 'Shall we get this signed?'

Sara and her husband Rodrigo were going to act as their witnesses.

'You are happy with the terms?'

'What terms?' she snorted. There had been only one; the one forbidding her from speaking publicly about any part of their relationship. She would be gagged for ever from speaking about Luis in any shape or form.

It was a term she could live with.

She would never do anything to fuel the poison out there about him.

At some point she would need to speak to her brother and warn him. It would have to be done before she and Luis exchanged their vows. How Benjamin would take it she couldn't begin to predict. Her brother's hatred of both Casillas brothers ran so deep she had no way of knowing if he would listen to reason.

Surely he wouldn't have wanted all this poison for them?

But her brother was wounded. Their betrayal had cut him so deeply that his instinct had been to lash out. Chloe understood that because it had been the same for her.

Had Luis been right when he'd accused her of using it as an excuse to run away from him?

'Before we sign, let me give you a tour of the house,' he said, cutting into her thoughts. 'I need a fresh pair of eyes to help me decide how to redecorate this place.'

'Isn't that what interior designers are for?'

'And I will employ one but right now it's your opinion I'm interested in.'

Curiosity piqued, Chloe let herself be guided through

the magnificent villa that was more than a match in size for her brother's chateau. But where Benjamin's chateau was decorated and maintained to the highest possible standard, the deeper into the villa she went, the more its neglect shone through.

'Marietta inherited it from her father,' Luis explained as he took her into the library. 'It had been in the family for generations and Marietta was the end of the line.'

'Did she not have children?'

'No. She never married either. She was a socialite who preferred life on the bigger islands and in Manhattan. She used this island as her personal holiday home for her and her closest friends but she never liked living here. She found it too isolating.'

'Is that why she was happy to sell it to you?'

'She hasn't set foot on the island in three years. She lives permanently in Manhattan now. I made her an outrageous offer for the island and the yacht and she accepted on the spot. She'd kept it for so long only out of an old sense of duty. The yacht was just one of her many toys she bored of playing with.'

Chloe looked up at the faded wallpaper fraying away from the ceiling.

To think she had assumed he'd seduced Marietta into selling up...

For some reason to know she had been way off the mark made her feel lighter inside.

A burst of laughter flew from her mouth. 'I still can't believe you would spend that much money just to kidnap me.'

'To make money you have to spend money. In this case, to preserve my fortune and salvage my reputation, I had to spend a good sum. It's money well spent. And I got a yacht and an island out of it,' he added with a grin before pulling her in for one of the heady kisses she was becoming addicted to. 'I'm already thinking ahead to the parties I will host here once I've renovated the place and had a runway put in.'

She hooked her arms around his neck and gazed into his eyes. Luis had shaved since he'd left her bed. The scent of his fresh cologne danced into her senses in the dreamiest of fashions. 'Won't having a runway ruin what makes the island so special?'

'I'll keep the runway small and discreet. There won't be any jets landing here.'

'Good.'

He grinned. 'You should come to one of my parties. You can do the hip-hop dancing I saw you doing on the beach.'

'By the time you've renovated the house and sorted out a runway, you and I will be long over,' she pointed out.

Instead of the joy she expected to flush through her at the thought of the day her life became her own again, her stomach plummeted.

The gleam in his eyes made the slightest of dims before his grin regained full wattage and he tugged her arms away from his neck.

Keeping a firm hold of her hand, he led her up the winding staircase that creaked on every tread. 'You should still come. Your hip-hop dancing is very entertaining.'

She forced a laugh.

She much preferred it when they were making love and she could concentrate on the physical side of their relationship, because that was all their relationship would ever amount to and there was no point in allowing the old dreams she'd once had for him rear their head again. She wasn't a teenager any more. She'd seen enough of life to know dreams did not come true.

'I've never had much rhythm,' she told him.

'I remember when you were small. You were always wearing a tutu.'

'That's when I was young. I grew up in a house that my brother called a shrine to dance. My mother was crazy about it and had me in dance classes when I was three.'

'Did you not enjoy it?'

She hesitated before admitting, 'My dream was to dance like your mother.'

The shrine to ballet that had been her childhood home should really have been called a shrine to Clara Casillas. Pictures of her in dance had framed all the walls, along with tour posters and pictures of the two women, Clara and Chloe's mother, Louise, together. The latter had been Chloe's favourite pictures. Her absolute favourite had been one taken in Clara's dressing room in New York. Clara had been dressed in a red embellished costume, Chloe's mother on her knees making adjustments to the hem. In the background, sitting squashed together cross-legged under Clara's dressing table were three small boys all with sulky faces. Benjamin, Luis and Javier. That picture had made her smile for so many different reasons.

When their mother had died, Chloe and Benjamin had gone through all her things together. He had been happy for Chloe to have the ballet memorabilia, all except for that one picture. He'd explained that it had been taken minutes after he and the Casillas twins had been scolded for trying to set off the theatre's fire alarm. Their mothers had made them sit in silence for ten minutes, threatening the withdrawal of the promised after-show pizza for non-compliance.

Her eyes met Luis's, the middle child in that long-ago picture. A fleeting sadness passed between them that pierced straight into her heart.

'What stopped you pursuing ballet?' he asked after a sharp inhalation.

'I told you, my lack of rhythm.' Then she sighed. 'To be truthful, I lived in denial for many years. I always hoped that one day the rhythm would find me and I would turn from the ugly duckling of dance to the swan but it wasn't to be.'

'When did you give it up?'

'When I was thirteen and my breasts exploded from molehills to mountains. Have you seen a ballerina with large breasts? They don't exist, do they? I had so little talent that no one bothered suggesting breast reduction surgery for me. I used that as the excuse for giving it up but, really, everyone who had ever seen me dance knew the reason was simply that I wasn't good enough.'

'I'm sorry you had to give up your dream.'

She shrugged. 'There are worse dreams to give up...'

Like the dream of having a father who actually wanted to be a father. Living under his roof for barely a year had been the final proof that dreams really did not come true no matter how hard she wished them.

Her ballet dream had always been more of a wispy cloud than anything concrete.

Her dreams of a miracle cure suddenly appearing for her mother... Chloe had seen the cancer ravaging her mother with her own eyes and known that to focus on a cure when the present was all she had left with her would ruin the remaining time they had together. But that dream had still been there, buried deep, getting her through the nights until time had finally run out.

She'd never realised how concrete her dream of wanting her father to *be* her father had been until she'd learned that it was never going to come true. That was a dream that couldn't come true not through a lack of talent or a lack of a medical cure but because *he* didn't want it to happen.

Dreams did not come true. Chloe would never be Clara Casillas. Her mother had died. Her father would never love her. And Luis would never...

Luis would never what? Love her either?

She didn't *want* his love. All she wanted from him was her freedom.

'And I always liked watching Maman create costumes,' she continued, blinking back the sting of hot tears that had sneaked up on her without warning. 'It turned out that costume-making was a talent I did have and the good thing about it is I don't have to watch what I eat or exercise for a hundred hours a day.'

She'd realised in the first week of her apprenticeship at the London ballet company that she would not have made it as a professional ballet dancer even if she'd had the talent. To reach the top as a ballet dancer required self-discipline and a *lot* of sacrifice. She'd had the dream but it had never been matched by the needed hunger.

She liked the niche she'd carved as a costume maker, liked that she'd followed her mother's footsteps, liked the camaraderie and the creativity. She had the best job in the world...

Anger and pride had had her denying to Luis that she cared about losing her career and in that heated moment on his yacht she had meant it. But now, with tempers cooled, it chilled her skin to think how perilously close she had come to throwing it all away.

She had to hope that when this was all over with Luis she would find another ballet company to take her on.

'It does take dedication to reach the top,' he agreed, opening another door. As with all the other doors he'd opened, Chloe took only a cursory look at the room behind it, her attention on their conversation.

'Did you ever dance?' she asked. Luis was the son of

two professional dancers. The masculinity issue that prevented many boys from trying ballet would not have applied in his household.

'Me? *Dios*, no. My mother tried to encourage us but neither of us had the slightest interest in it. We just wanted to play.'

She hesitated before asking, 'What about your father?'

A hardness crept into his voice. 'What about him?'

'Did he not encourage you and Javier to follow in his footsteps?'

'Not that I remember.' He opened another door and smoothly changed the subject. 'This was Marietta's bedroom. I'm debating whether to turn it into my own bedroom. What do you think?'

She thought that she needed to respect his reluctance to speak about his father but that undercurrent was there again and, against her better judgement, she said, 'What was your father like?'

'You know what he was like. The world knows what he was like.'

'If I ever met him as a toddler I don't remember it. Benjamin never spoke of him. I know what I've read about him but I would think only a very small part of it is based on truth.'

'No, you will find the majority of it is based on truth. I hated him.'

At the widening of her eyes, Luis took a deep breath, fighting for air in his closed-up lungs.

'Was he always violent towards your mother?' she whispered.

'As far as I know—and your mother confirmed this to me—my father was never physically violent to my mother until the night he killed her.' He relayed this matter-of-factly, hiding the manic thrumming of his heart that even the mildest of allusions to that night always broke out in him. 'I took the brunt of his anger.'

'In what way?'

'In the way that involved belts across naked backsides. It was a form of corporal punishment that was accepted in those days.'

'Just you?'

He nodded curtly. 'He never touched Javier. When we got into trouble together the blame would be put on my shoulders.'

'Even if Javier was at fault?'

'In fairness to Javier, he rarely instigated any trouble. I was the ringleader. I was drawn to trouble like a magnet. When your brother toured with us he was a far more willing accomplice than Javier.' He took another long breath and put a hand to the flaking doorframe, ready to put a stop to this conversation immediately. Instead, he found himself saying, 'Our father was a bitter man. You know he defected from the Soviet Union in the early seventies?'

She nodded, wide-eyed.

'He was a star to the western world back then, another Nureyev. When he met my mother in London she was an up-and-coming ingénue fifteen years his junior. Her star was not supposed to eclipse his but eventually it did and he hated her for it. Our mother carried us twins and returned to the stage stronger than ever. As her star rose his faded. He was always a drinker and prone to outbursts of temper but when he started fighting choreographers and fellow cast members, he no longer had the star power for companies to turn a blind eye. Work dried up. His resentment towards my mother grew. There were months when we wouldn't see anything of him—those were the best times—then he would reappear on the scene and act as if he had never been away.'

'Didn't your mother mind?'

He shook his head as bile curdled up his throat. 'Theirs was a strange relationship. The power balance always tilted from one to the other. They both had lovers. They both flaunted it. But then my father found the young lovers he wanted no longer wanted him; and why would they? He was a drunken mess. He couldn't touch my mother so he took his anger out on me.'

'Didn't she stop him?'

'He was my father. To her mind it was his duty to punish me when it was deserved. She was no disciplinarian herself.' He felt the smallest of smiles break over skin that had become like marble to remember his mother trying to hide her amusement at their japes by putting on her 'stern' face. 'She never raised a finger to us. If my father's punishments went too far she would cup my cheeks and tell me to smile through the pain.'

He heard Chloe suck in a breath.

'My mother understood corporal punishment,' he said, compelled to defend the mother he had loved. 'Her own parents would often use it to punish her. To my mother it was normal and, though she couldn't bring herself to physically punish us herself, she cited it as toughening her up and giving her the tools she needed to succeed in such a competitive world. Her ballet training had taught her to smile through the pain and she wanted me to have that resilience too.'

There was a long period of silence before she asked, 'Why do you think he chose to punish only you?'

'He never liked me. There was something in me that pushed his buttons; I don't know what it was. He adored Javier.'

'That must have been hard.'

'Harder for Javier,' he dismissed. 'It hurt him to see *me*

be hurt. We are not identical but we *are* twins and we've had each other's back our entire lives. It is a bond that no one can come between. He suffered in his own way too— our mother loved us both but she doted on me. That was hard on him. He always tried to protect me. He was always trying to save me from the worst of my behaviour because he could always see what the consequences would be.'

'Couldn't you see them?'

'I could but I didn't care.' Just as he'd seen that the consequences of keeping silent about the profit share with Benjamin could be dire but had kept his mouth shut through the years rather than rock a friendship that had meant so much to him.

His relationship with his brother was like a rock, solid and impenetrable. His friendship with Benjamin, which had been stronger than Javier's and Benjamin's, had had the fun element to it. They had broken the rules together, Javier tagging along not to join in with the rule-breaking but to try and stop them going too far.

Benjamin had been his closest friend. He grieved the end of their friendship but in life you had to look forward. Always look forward. Never let the past hook you back.

But the past was hooking him back. He could feel its weight clasped around his stomach, the tentacles digging in tighter and tighter with each hour that passed.

'Maybe it was because you look so much like your mother,' she said softly.

'What was?'

'Your father… Javier looks so much like him whereas you resemble your mother. Maybe he preferred Javier because he thought of him as a miniature version of himself.'

Her words were a variant of Javier's attempts to placate him over their father's cruelty.

Luis moved his hand away from the frame to run it

through his hair then caught the flakes of paint on his palm and wiped it on his shorts instead.

The main house needed to be bulldozed and started again from the foundations upwards, he thought moodily.

Unfortunately he had made a promise to Marietta that he would keep the actual structure intact.

He looked back at Chloe, took in the compassion ringing from those beautiful eyes and suppressed a shudder.

Her experiences, different from his as they were, were similar enough that she would have an inkling of what he had felt when growing up.

He needed to keep the structure of their relationship intact too. A marriage that lasted long enough to kill the nastiness circulating about him and his brother. They would have fun and enjoy the time they had together but there would be no bonds between them other than the bonds made in the bedroom.

'No,' he denied with more ice than she deserved. 'It was nothing to do with any physical resemblance. My father disliked me because there was nothing in me for him to like.'

At the parting of her lips, he pressed a finger to them. 'Enough about my father. He's dead. The past is over.' And why he was rehashing long-past deeds with Chloe was beyond his comprehension. His past had nothing to do with their marriage. 'The future's what matters now. And now I would like your honest opinion about this room as I am thinking of making it my bedroom.'

Only his.

As she had rightly said, he and Chloe would be long over when this house was fit for purpose.

He would be the one to pull the trigger to topple the structures holding them together.

CHAPTER TEN

'ARE YOU GOING to join me?' Luis cajoled from the side of the pool.

Chloe, who'd been admiring his strong, powerful strokes from the safety of her sun lounger, shook her head.

Another day in paradise...

After spending the entire morning in bed making love, Luis had suddenly declared himself in need of exercise.

She'd raised a disbelieving eyebrow at that, which had made him laugh and plant an enormous kiss on her mouth. Then he'd strode naked from the bed, strolled through the villa and down to the bottom of the garden and dived straight into the swimming pool, still unashamedly naked.

And with that glorious body, why should he be ashamed? she'd thought dreamily as she'd spied on him from the bedroom window before slipping a bikini on and moving outside for a better view. Luis was a man made for a physical life and the more time he spent showing that physical prowess off in the most physical way with her, the better...

Her increasingly erotic thoughts about him were cut short when Luis hauled himself out of the water and scooped her into his arms.

'Into the water with you,' he said with a grin as he carried her effortlessly to the water's edge despite water dripping off him.

'Put me down,' she squealed, panic setting in instantaneously as she threw her arms around his neck and clung on tightly.

He held her over the water. 'Scared of getting your hair wet?' he teased.

'I can't swim!'

He took an immediate step back and stared down at her with a combination of bemusement and concern. 'Are you serious?'

'Yes!' she yelled. 'Now, put me down!'

Carrying her back to the sun lounger, he gently deposited her on it then grabbed the towel she'd brought down for him and rubbed it through his hair.

'You really can't swim?'

She rolled her eyes. 'I really cannot swim.'

'Why not?'

'Because I hate getting my hair wet.'

He wiped his hand over the droplets of water shining on his chest and flicked it at her hair.

'Behave.'

He laughed and helped himself to a glass of the orange juice Chloe had also brought out. He drained it, wrapped the towel around his waist and sat next to her.

'You're not vain enough to care about your hair getting wet,' he observed with a grin.

She grinned back at him. 'Benjamin tried to teach me when I was little but I hated the shock of the cold water and refused to go any deeper than my thighs.'

'So you never learned?'

'I hate the cold. And I was a stubborn thing.'

'Some would say you still are.'

She mock-glowered at him and, to better show her disdain, swung her legs round to rest on his wonderful, muscular thighs.

He shook his head mockingly and rubbed a hand on her

calf. 'The water here is the perfect temperature. I could teach you.'

She made a non-committal grunt. Chloe had managed perfectly well without swimming and didn't see that she'd missed out on anything by preferring to be on land.

'It's better to be able to swim,' he pointed out. 'You never know when it will come useful.'

'Says the man who was probably born able to swim like a world champion.' His prowess in the water was a thing of wonder.

Now he was the one to make a grunt-like noise. 'Hardly. I didn't learn until I was eight.'

'That's late, isn't it? Benjamin had given up on teaching me by then.'

'I learned on our only family sunshine holiday. Our father decided he was the man to teach us.'

The tone of his voice sent a chill up her spine.

The easy playfulness between them seemed to hover on a pair of scales between them as Chloe weighed up whether to ask anything about it.

Would this be a rare happy childhood tale of his?

It pained her to think that unlikely.

So she went with the most neutral question she could think of. 'Did you pick it up easily?'

'No. Javier did, but like you I was a stubborn thing and did everything wrong.'

'On purpose?'

He nodded. 'One day my father got so angry with me for not trying, he said that in the morning he would throw me in the deep end and it would be up to me to sink or swim.'

Nausea creeping through her, Chloe shifted forward so her arched thighs were pressed against his and stroked his damp arm.

'You believed him,' she whispered, resting her chin on

his shoulder. She did not doubt for a second eight-year-old Luis had believed his father would let him drown.

His jaw clenched. 'Javier believed it too. He dragged me to the beach with him—we'd found a cove near the resort that was really secluded and calm—and made me learn.'

'You were eight?' she clarified, stunned to think of two such small boys being allowed to go off on their own.

'It was safe,' he insisted. 'The cove was next to the resort. My parents were having one of their good spells and had gone off for what they called a siesta. We had free rein.'

Chloe knew better than to comment on this, did nothing but continue stroking his arm, making her way down to the palm of his hand and tracing circles around it.

'Javier took me out into the sea and made me lie on my back while he held an arm under me to keep me afloat. He kept telling me that if I could float I would never drown. Chloe... I cannot tell you how scared he was, much more than I. He was crying and begging me to trust him. And I did trust him. He was my twin. Who else in the world could I trust more than the boy who was always trying to save me from myself?'

Chloe closed her eyes, trying hard not to allow sympathy into her heart for the small boy Javier would have been, the boy terrified his father would let his beloved twin drown.

'You floated,' she said softly.

'*Sí*. I floated for my brother's sake. By the end of the holiday we were racing each other in the water.'

'How did your father react when you floated?'

'He didn't do it. I don't know if it was a burst of his meagre conscience or if he forgot but he never did throw me in.'

'I'm glad.'

'So was I.' He took a deep breath then carefully moved her legs from over his thighs and got to his feet.

When he looked at her she could virtually see the shutters that had come down in his eyes.

It was the same look as when he'd told her about his father's abuse. End of discussion.

After the strangest pause where he gazed at her as if seeing her for the first time, he blinked.

The shutters had gone and now he stared at her with that hungry look she knew so well.

He grinned widely and held his hand out to her. 'Come, *bonita*. If you won't get your hair wet in the pool with me then you can get wet in the shower.'

Her heart hurting for him, she let him help her to her feet then, when she was upright, wound her arms around his neck and kissed him deeply.

His fingers speared her hair as he kissed her back, his arousal undeniable despite the thick cotton towel draped around his waist.

How badly she wished she could kiss away his past and drive out the pain she knew on an instinctive level still haunted him.

But then, when he lifted her into his arms and carried her back into the villa, the moment overtook her and all thoughts were driven from her mind as she revelled in the heady pleasure they had found together.

Chloe sat on the beach digging her toes into the soft sand and stared up at the sky. There was no moon that night and the stars were in abundance, twinkling down on her like tiny dazzling jewels.

She had been unable to fall asleep. Her mind was filled with too much for it to switch off.

Her resolve over Luis was made of the same fine sand as this warm beach. She could laugh at her weakness but it frightened her too much to be funny.

In two days she would marry him.

She had lain in the bed with him breathing deeply and rhythmically beside her, her lungs getting tighter and tighter until she couldn't draw air any more.

There was a turbulence in her stomach that had grown stronger with each passing hour spent with him.

She spent *all* her time with him, laughing and making love. She would gaze into his hazel eyes and feel all the breath leave her in a soar.

And then she would recall their conversations about his childhood and her chest would cramp so tightly she couldn't breathe the air back in.

His childhood had been more violent and tempestuous than she could have imagined. The old stories about his violent father that she'd assumed had been embellished by an insatiable media had, if anything, been underplayed.

He'd come so far, both he and Javier. What they had lived through in their formative years could have destroyed lesser men. Not them. Not Luis.

And then he had shut her out. It had almost been a physical act; a blink of the eye and then shutters appeared in them. She understood it was his way of telling her, without words, to back off, to keep things between them on the loose footing they had agreed on, his way of telling her not to get too close.

There was a reason Luis had reached the age of thirty-five without a single long-term relationship under his belt and she strongly suspected it had its roots in his relationship with his father.

She shouldn't *need* telling. She didn't want their marriage to be anything other than temporary either and had no clue as to why that turbulence in her stomach felt strong enough to dislodge her heart.

This craving for him, which had grown so much more than physical, had to stop.

'Chloe?'

She turned her head to see Luis emerge from between the palm trees lining this stretch of beach.

'Hi,' she said softly, her pulse surging just to see his silhouette.

He walked to her wearing nothing but a pair of navy shorts and his deck shoes. 'I wondered where you'd got to.'

'I couldn't sleep,' she confessed.

'You should have woken me. Are you okay?'

Her heart twisted to hear the concern in his voice. In his own way, he did care about her.

She nodded. 'I just needed some air.'

He sat down beside her and stretched his long legs out. 'Something on your mind?'

She gave a hollow laugh. 'Right now it feels as if I have the whole world on my mind.'

Silence bloomed between them and then stretched, a tension in it that she soon found herself desperate to break.

'I keep thinking back to our childhoods,' she said, speaking without really thinking of what she was going to say, just aware that all the stuff that had accumulated in her head as Marietta's possessions had accumulated in the main house needed an outlet. 'Do you remember my mother's funeral? You found me crying and you comforted me. You let me cry in your arms and said things that really resonated and gave me the courage to hope that one day the pain would become bearable. You understood what I was going through. I always remembered that. I carried your words with me for so long... When Benjamin told me about the profit terms with Tour Mont Blanc I felt betrayed, not just for him but for myself and our mother too. I'd been with Benjamin at the hospital the day you made that call to him asking for the money. We'd been told barely an hour before that our mother was dying. I remember him telling you the news. I was holding his hand.'

She felt his eyes burn into her but kept her gaze out on the still sea, black and sparkling under the night sky.

Luis's heart had clenched itself into a fist.

He'd awoken alone in the bed to find Chloe missing. Intellectually he'd known she wouldn't have gone far but there had been a punch of nausea to see the indentation of her head on the pillow.

The hook that had wrapped around his stomach was now so tight it threatened to cut off his blood flow.

If not for the starkness in the way she'd spoken, he would drag her back to bed and distract her in the only way he knew how.

'Being told about your mother's diagnosis is why I have little memory of what occurred the rest of that day,' he said, recalling how Benjamin's news had lanced him.

The Guillem siblings hadn't been the only ones hoping for a miracle.

'Javier and I were fighting to save our business. To then hear your mother's condition was terminal... Chloe, it cut me to pieces.'

'Really?'

The simple hope that rang from her voice sliced through Luis as if it had a blade attached.

'When we went to Benjamin's apartment to sign it that night I barely gave the contract a second thought. I thought Javier had told him we wanted to renegotiate the terms...'

'But he hadn't.'

He breathed heavily. No. His brother hadn't done. For seven years Luis had believed it to be an oversight on his brother's part but now, as he relived that time in full, he had to wonder...

'Our lawyer and his paralegal came with us to witness it. The contracts were laid out on Benjamin's dining table. He wanted to get it signed and done with. Neither Javier nor I had any way of knowing he hadn't read it. We all signed it, Benjamin transferred the money, Javier and the lawyers left, then Benjamin and I got drunk together.'

'Didn't Javier stay with you?'

'Someone had to finalise the deal with the seller and that someone was Javier. Besides, he doesn't drink.'

His brother had never drunk alcohol. The healthy hell-raising that was a rite of passage for most young men had been left to Luis and Benjamin.

'I drowned my sorrows with your brother because, *bonita*, your mother had been a part of my life from when I was in the womb.' He breathed the salt air in deeply as even older memories hit him in a wave. 'Did you know I was named after her?'

'*Non!*' she gasped, her head turning to face him. 'You were named after my mother? No one ever told me that.'

He smiled to see how wide her eyes had gone with her disbelief. 'I always felt a bond with her because of it. I will never forget the way she broke the news of my mother's death to us and the kindness and love she showed us that night. My grandparents took good care of us when we became their wards but they were old and would never talk about my mother. They found it too painful.'

The loss of their only child had devastated his grandparents, who had been in their forties and resigned to a childless life when they had unexpectedly conceived Luis and Javier's mother. When they had taken their twin grandsons into their home they had been in their seventies, old-fashioned and set in their ways and unprepared for the mayhem bereaved teenage boys would bring to their orderly lives. When they had tried to discipline Luis in the manner they had disciplined their daughter all those decades before, he'd stood his ground and refused to accept it.

He'd vowed on the death of his mother that he would never again be a whipping boy for anyone. He would never let another person raise a hand to him or look at him with the contempt he'd always seen ringing from his father's eyes.

In Louise Guillem's home Luis had found a modicum of peace. The Guillems' suburban house was near to the Parisian apartment he and Javier had called home with their parents until their lives had been destroyed. Being under Louise's roof with his brother and his best friend, speaking the language that had come more naturally to him than his own had been the only light he had found in those years.

'Your mother found it painful to talk about her too but she was always willing. She kept my mother's memory alive for me. She became the surrogate parent my grandparents weren't capable of being. Carrying her coffin was one of the hardest things I have ever done. Saying goodbye to her was like saying goodbye to my mother all over again.'

A tear glistened on her cheek. She wiped it away and gave a deep sigh. 'I'm glad you loved her. She loved you and Javier very much.' She wiped another spilling tear. 'Can I ask you one more question?'

How could he refuse? 'Anything.'

'Did you ever see your father again, after…?'

After he'd killed Luis's mother.

'Never. I never visited him in prison and I never visited him on his deathbed.'

Their father successfully pleaded diminished responsibility and got convicted of manslaughter. He served only ten years of his sentence, nothing for extinguishing such a precious life.

It had felt fitting that he should die of pancreatic cancer less than a year after his release, alone and unloved.

Only as the years had gone by had regrets started to creep in.

'Do you regret not seeing him?'

Her question was astute.

'My mother has been dead for over twenty years and I still miss her. My father has been dead for half that and I have never missed him but now I wish I had accepted the visiting orders he sent me from prison and taken the opportunity to look him in the eye and ask him how he could have done what he did.'

Her voice was small. 'He did want to see you, then?'

He sighed heavily. 'Yes. He asked for me in the hospice too. He died a very lonely man.'

He pressed his head to hers.

There didn't seem any more need for words. In their own wildly differing ways each had suffered at the hands of their fathers. And in their own way each still suffered at them, Chloe with the indifference she lived with each day, he with the legacy of his mother's murder, a story that would not be extinguished.

Another tear rolled down her cheek. She brushed it with her thumb before lying down on the sand. 'I am so sorry, Luis.'

'Sorry for what?'

'For conspiring with Benjamin against you. I should have known it had never been a deliberate act on your part…'

He wished he could say the same for his brother.

'Hush.' Laying himself down next to her, he gently took her chin and turned her face to look at him. 'Your brother had good reason to think we ripped him off. I regret not handling it better when he confronted us about it but what's done is done. All we can do is put things right for the future.'

'But we have caused such damage, and after everything you've already...'

He put his lips to hers and slid a hand down the curve of her neck. 'Damage our marriage will repair.'

She burrowed her fingers into his hair and gazed intently at him.

The lights from the stars glittered from her tear-filled eyes, desire mingling with her pain, all there ringing at him. Another solitary drop spilled down her cheek.

Suddenly unable to bear looking into those depths any longer, he kissed the tear away then plundered that beautiful mouth with his own, taking her pain away the only way he knew how.

Her response was as passionate as it always was, their desire for each other a simmering flame that only needed the slightest coaxing to bring fully to life.

It was so easy to lose himself in her softness and her passion. There was such openness in her lovemaking; no pretence, no artifice, nothing hidden, just a celebration of the joy their lovemaking evoked, there in her every touch and moan.

As he pulled her dress off and kissed the breasts he just could not get enough of, it came to him that he'd changed as a lover. The pleasure he gave Chloe was far more intoxicating than the great pleasure she gave him, never an exercise in ticking boxes until the time was right for him to take his pleasure but an erotic, heady experience all of its own.

When it came to giving pleasure there was nothing he would not do for her.

And it was the same for her too.

Chloe was the most unselfish lover he could have dreamed of.

Trailing his tongue down her soft belly to the pretty heart of her femininity, he used his tongue in the way he knew she loved, enraptured with the melodious mews that escaped her throat and the scraping of her nails on his skull. He savoured her special, inimitable taste, the downiness of her hair, the silky texture of her skin, all unique to Chloe. Blindfold him and he would know her from the imprint of her mouth and the scent of her skin alone.

The nails scraping into his skull pulled at his hair, urging him on, her moans deepening, her breaths shallowing until she was crying out, his name spilling from her tongue and echoing through to his marrow.

Chloe sighed happily and gazed up at the stars while the stars Luis had set off in her twinkled with equal joy.

His touch alone was enough to soothe her. When he made love to her nothing else existed but them and the moment they were sharing.

So many moments. So many memories to take with her when they were over...

A pain sliced through her chest so sharp she gasped.

Luis, his wonderful mouth making its way back up her belly, must have assumed it was a gasp of pleasure for he took her breast into his mouth and encircled her nipple with his tongue in the way they had discovered she liked so much.

Fresh sensation building back up in her, Chloe closed her eyes and welcomed the pleasure, let it drown out the fleeting pain. When he reached her lips she kissed him greedily and looped her arms around him, needing to feel the solid warmth of his skin beneath her fingers.

She could have had the ton of lovers she'd once lied about but nothing would have compared to what she and Luis had. She didn't need to be experienced to know what they had was special and unique and belonged only to them.

She could drink his kisses for ever.

And, when he was finally inside her, fully sheathed, filling her completely, she wound her legs tightly around his waist and let go of everything but this most beautiful of moments.

CHAPTER ELEVEN

TINY SHARP PRICKLES dug into Chloe's cheek, as she roused into consciousness.

Absently running a hand over her face, she found sparkling grains of sand clinging to the pads of her fingers.

She smiled sleepily and rolled over, memories of Luis making love to her under the twinkling stars on the beach awakening other parts of her...

Luis shuffled in his sleep and groped for her hand.

She laced her fingers through his and stared at him. The sun had almost fully risen, its light filtering through the curtains. Luis's features were clear and strong. Thick dark stubble had broken through his skin since he'd shaved the morning before. When he had made love to her that stubble had scratched her breasts in a way that had been half pain and half pleasure.

Everything about them was like that. Half pain. Half pleasure.

So much had been revealed between them in the days they had spent on this island.

She felt wretched about the hand she had played in Benjamin's revenge.

It had been her revenge too, she had to acknowledge painfully.

Luis had never set out to cheat her brother.

He had kidnapped her and blackmailed her but that all

felt like a lifetime ago, actions done to and conducted by two different people.

The man she had once believed herself in love with *did* exist.

And if he did exist then didn't that mean...?

That their marriage could be for real...?

'You've got that look on your face that tells me you are thinking,' he whispered, his voice thick with sleep.

She blinked, reopening her eyes to find his gorgeous hazel gaze fixed on her.

You don't want to know what I'm thinking.

Or maybe he did.

Maybe it wasn't just the desire they shared.

Oh, what was she *thinking*?

She would still be entering a marriage based on revenge.

But that had been agreed before they'd made love and before they'd opened up to each other.

Before she'd accepted that she loved him.

And even if his feelings for her were as strong as hers were for him, that didn't mean they had the basis of anything that could last.

Luis was a twin. He and his brother had a bond she could not begin to understand and it pained her to know that even if she and Luis were to have a proper future together, she would always come second to Javier.

This was a dream she didn't dare hope for.

'I'm just thinking it's been a few hours since you made love to me,' she whispered back, putting her hand on his cheek.

Her brain hurt from sleep deprivation and too much conversation. Now she was hallucinating thoughts.

Love?

No, that was taking things too far.

She felt a lot towards this man, but love...?

Proper, uninterrupted sleep was needed. Then, when her brain and body were refreshed, she would be able to think properly.

But first she wanted the closeness she felt when he was deep inside her.

Snuggling into him, she welcomed his arms wrapping around her, a blanket in their own right, and closed her eyes to the heady power of his intoxicating kiss.

Sleep. Everything would look different after she'd had some.

Everything was the same.

Everything.

Chloe was lying on her back in the calm sea, Luis's arm acting as a float.

After making love and then falling into a deep, pure sleep, she had woken with the urge to swim. He hadn't questioned it—she didn't allow herself to think too deeply about it either—just led her to the section of beach where the water was calm and so clear she could see the tiny pebbles on its bed.

The most important part, he'd reiterated seriously, was being able to float. And to be able to float, she needed to relax in the water.

They had taken it slowly.

'Are you ready for me to remove my arm?' he asked.

The patience he'd shown in getting her to this stage filled her heart with the buoyancy she needed to stay afloat.

She trusted him. To not let her drown. To keep her alive.

With her heart.

For the better or the worse she did not know but loving Luis had changed something fundamental in her.

When he looked in her eyes she almost dared hope she saw the same reflected as shone from hers.

And if it wasn't there yet then she had to take the chance that one day it would be.

She had allowed her father to destroy her fragile heart for too long.

She had carried his rejection every day for seven years... No, she'd carried his rejection her entire life.

He was the reason she had kept men at arm's length, she'd come to realise. Her father had rejected her twice, the first time while she had still been in the womb. The second rejection had been the one that had destroyed her and shattered any trust she might have. She'd always told herself it was men she didn't trust but the truth, as she could now see clearly, was that her father's rejection of the almost fully grown-up Chloe had left her feeling inherently unlovable. If her own father couldn't find anything to love about her then why would anyone else?

Tomorrow she would exchange her vows with Luis. If she didn't take the chance and trust the passion and friendship that had grown between them then she would never find it with anyone else and she would grow into a lonely old woman.

There would never be anyone else for her.

She looked into Luis's eyes and smiled.

His eyes sparkled. 'Is that a yes?'

Her smile widened.

She couldn't speak. Not with words.

She loved him.

He let go.

She floated.

When Luis opened his eyes into the duskiness of early morning he thought for sure he was still sleeping. This had to be a dream. A wonderful, heady, sensuous dream.

Dreams of Chloe were nothing new. He'd woken with

erotic dreams of them simmering in his blood so many times over the past few months that it was more a surprise when he didn't have them. The intensity of them had only grown since they had become lovers.

They never felt this real though.

He closed his eyes and hooked an arm above his head with a sigh.

Dios, that felt good.

Chloe was underneath the sheets, between his legs, pleasuring him with her tongue.

He groaned as she slid him into her mouth, groaning even louder when she cupped his...

Dios.

This was incredible.

In his dreams he was always left unfulfilled but now he could feel telltale sensations tugging at his loins.

And then she stopped.

This time his groan was one of frustration that was cut off from his tongue when she pulled the sheets off him and crawled over him.

Putting her hands either side of his face, she stared down at him with a soft gleam in her eyes. 'Good morning.'

And then she sank down on his burning erection.

Luis gasped.

There had been a very real danger then that he would have come undone with one thrust.

But, *Dios*, this was like nothing he had ever felt before. This was something new.

They had never made love without a condom before.

He had never made love without a condom before.

He could not have comprehended how different it would feel being completely bare inside her or the sensations that would course through his blood and loins.

Adjusting herself so she was sitting upright with him fully inside her, she rested her hands lightly on his chest.

Luis gazed at her, now quite certain that he wasn't dreaming and that this was real, that this was Chloe waking him in such a pleasurable way, Chloe, the woman he would be marrying that day.

He raised a hand to cover one of her breasts. *Dios*, he loved her breasts. Loved her soft, rounded belly. Loved her supple thighs currently squeezing against him. Loved the raven hair falling in waves over her breasts and down her back.

And then he loved when she began to take her pleasure from him, finding a rhythm, leaning forward to stare deep into his eyes as her breasts gently swayed with the motion.

He couldn't take his eyes from her face. Her eyes had darkened in colour, becoming violet, her cheeks slashed with the colour of passion. Harder and deeper she ground against him, tiny moans flying out of those gorgeous lips that became louder when he grabbed hold of her hips to steady her and drive himself up into her.

Colour heightened on her cheeks and then he felt her orgasm build inside her as vividly as he felt his own, her muscles thickening and tightening around him as, with a loud cry, she fell against him at the exact moment he lost all control of himself.

For long moments the world went white.

'We didn't use a condom,' he said a short while later when they had finally caught their breath.

He didn't know if it was an oversight on her part or if she had meant it.

He didn't know which he hoped the answer would be.

Since they had become lovers they had only ever used condoms, which he'd armed himself with from the numerous boxes he had thrown into his suitcase on a whim before he had kidnapped her. He made sure to always have some handy wherever he went, their passion for each other often finding them making love in the most unlikely places, like on the beach in the middle of the night.

Neither of them had mentioned her being on the pill since he had confronted her with the packet.

She was still on top of him.

He was still inside her.

She nuzzled into his neck. 'I know.'

Then she raised her head and put her chin to his.

The look in her eyes was one he had never seen before. 'I trust you, Luis.'

He forced a smile to lips that had become leaden.

The euphoria of the moment died as a klaxon set off in his guts at this declaration of trust that instinct told him meant much more than had been said.

In truth, he had felt that klaxon warming up since he had taken her swimming the day before.

There had been a moment when he had been encouraging her to try and float when she had looked in his eyes and he'd felt as if she had seen right down to his soul.

The only thing that made him certain she hadn't seen right down into it was that she hadn't run away screaming.

His yacht was on its way to the island, the captain and crew preparing for the ceremony that would make him and Chloe husband and wife. The press release had been prepared, the champagne was on ice, everything that could be controlled taken care of.

And yet he felt his control over the situation slipping through his fingers and he didn't know how to claw it back.

Luis pounded along the beach, stretching his legs as he jogged, running as he hadn't run in too many years to count.

He hadn't wanted to swim. He'd needed to do something physical that didn't remind him of the woman he'd left burrowed under the covers, her lips curved in a beautiful smile as she slept.

The sun rising over the Caribbean like an enormous jewel was a glorious sight but not one he could appreciate. The knots in his stomach were too tight for him to appreciate anything at that moment.

In a few hours he would be a married man to the most beautiful woman in the world.

Their marriage was supposed to be an exercise in damage limitation.

It was not supposed to feel like this.

He was not supposed to let her get close to him.

A short, entertaining marriage that fixed all the problems she had helped create. That was all it was supposed to be.

He was not supposed to feel her presence like a pulse.

How the hell she did it he did not know but Chloe had a talent for drawing things out of himself that he'd hardly acknowledged to himself. She was better than any priest for making a man want to bear his rotten soul. Not even Benjamin knew he'd been his father's whipping boy.

He had never had to physically drag himself away from a woman before.

After running for an hour he headed back and went straight in the shower without checking in on her.

The knots in his stomach hadn't gone.

Almost ten miles of pounding his legs and he felt as out of sorts as when he'd set off.

Only when he had dried and dressed did he check his phone and find a missed call from his brother.

As if he didn't feel crap enough as it was.

Javier had ignored his calls since that disastrous video

conference with the Canadian. He'd messaged him a few times about the business but voice-to-voice conversations had been blacklisted.

His brother really could be a cold bastard when he wanted. Add injured pride—and Javier's pride had been enormously injured by Benjamin stealing his fiancée away from him and in such a deliberate and public manner—and his brother was a tinderbox primed to explode.

Luis wanted to help him but had learned through their thirty-five years together that there was no point in putting pressure on his twin to see reason. When he was in a mood like this it was best to keep his distance and wait either for Javier to open up or for the darkness to pass.

With a heavy sigh, he stepped out onto the balcony and called Javier back.

'Why are you with Chloe Guillem?' Javier asked, not even bothering with a cursory greeting.

'I am saving our backsides,' Luis informed him calmly. He had hoped to have this conversation after the deed was done. He'd known from the outset that his brother would not approve this plan of action. How he had discovered that he was with Chloe was a mystery to be solved another time.

'By getting involved with that poisonous bitch?'

'Do not speak of her in that way,' Luis cut in, his hackles rising at the insult to Chloe.

She was the least poisonous woman he knew.

'She is a Guillem. Everything they touch is poison.'

Luis counted to ten before responding.

He had to remember that it was Javier's fiancée Benjamin had stolen away with Chloe's assistance. For Javier, it ran much more deeply.

'I'm marrying her today. Having Chloe as my wife will prove to the world that the rumours of what happened between us and Benjamin are unfounded. George will be placated. It will save the Canadian project and kill the rumours flying around about us.'

'I don't care about any of that.'

'We have already invested fifty million euros in it. That's money we will never get back. Investors on other projects are asking questions too. I'm not telling you anything you don't already know.'

'The other investors won't do anything, you'll see. It will blow over and, even if it doesn't, I would rather take the financial hit than have a Guillem marry into our family.'

'Don't be so petty. I'm saving our business by doing this.' He almost added that marrying Chloe was an excellent form of revenge on Benjamin but stopped himself at the last moment.

It felt like a lifetime ago that revenge had been the driving force behind all this.

When had that motive disappeared?

He shrugged the thought away and concentrated on the conversation at hand.

'Our backsides don't need saving any more than our business does. Our fortune is safe. We might take a short-term hit but we can claw the long-term back, and we can preserve our reputations by other means.'

'*What* other means?' Luis demanded to know.

'We would have thought of something already if you hadn't gone running off on this hare-brained scheme.'

'You were not in the mood to talk,' Luis reminded him with equal venom. 'Need I remind you that your whole attitude was to sit and seethe with only yourself for company?'

'I was thinking.'

'And I was doing. Marrying Chloe is the best solution for everyone.'

'Have you lost your mind?' his brother demanded with incredulity. 'We have overcome worse than this by working together and putting on a united front. That's all we need to do. Ride it out. We don't need her and I cannot believe you would think otherwise. That woman conspired with her brother to destroy us and now you want to marry her into our family? No, you *have* lost your mind, and over a *woman…*' His disgust was clear to hear. 'Has her pretty face blinded you to her poison?'

'Do not be ridiculous,' Luis snarled, the end of his tether reached. 'Chloe regrets the part she played and wants to put things right.'

'You *defend* her?' Javier's laughter was hollow. 'Marry her if you must but do not pretend it's for our sake. We do not need her to get through this and for you to think otherwise only proves your head has been turned.'

Then the line went dead.

Anger fisting in his guts, Luis threw his phone on the floor.

How dared his own twin question his judgement in such a way? And as for saying he'd lost his mind over Chloe…

Luis accepted that he'd let her get closer than he'd ever intended but he had not lost his head. He could walk away from her right now and not feel an ounce of regret.

In an instant the anger was replaced by a wave of relief so strong he could almost see the ripples in the air as it left his shoulders, all the tension and knots that had grown in him these past few days leaving with it.

Javier was wrong about his feelings for Chloe but in one respect he *was* right.

It always had been the two of them, the Casillas brothers against the world. Everything the cruel world had thrown at them had been faced and defeated together. Why should this situation be any different?

And why had it taken so long for him to recognise it?

Whatever the reason, his relief was absolute.

He didn't have to marry Chloe.

CHAPTER TWELVE

CHLOE STEPPED OUT of the bathroom with only a towel around her. Luis was sitting on the edge of the bed.

One look at his face told her something was wrong.

'What's the matter?' She walked to her dressing table to put her watch on.

'Nothing's wrong. Quite the opposite.'

'What are you talking about?'

'Our wedding is off.'

She laughed. 'Funny. You should be a comedian.'

'Our wedding is off. I've let the captain know. I've had a helicopter flown in which will transport us to Lisa Island and...'

'Are you being *serious*?' she interrupted.

'Yes.'

She searched his face. 'But why? Is it something I've done?'

'No, *bonita*. You have done nothing wrong. *Au contraire*, as you would say. I have spoken to Javier. We are in agreement that it is unnecessary for me to marry you. We have decided to proceed as we have always done; together, putting on a united front to the world. Be happy. You can be out of my life sooner than you had hoped.'

Chloe felt the blood drain from her face. It happened so quickly she had to grab hold of the dressing table tightly as the room began to spin.

It took a few goes before she could open her throat

enough to speak and when she did, her words were croaky. 'Our marriage is no longer necessary?'

'I apologise for wasting your time.'

'Are you for real? Is this a joke?' This absolutely did not make sense. The look on his face did not make sense, a mixture of lightness and grimness, a strange combination that terrified her.

'I am for real and this is not a joke.' He got to his feet. 'The helicopter will leave here in an hour and I've arranged for a jet to take you from Lisa Island back to Grand Bahama. Let me know when you wish to fly back to Europe and I will get that arranged for you too.'

He headed out of the bedroom door, hands in pockets, as nonchalant as if he'd just told her breakfast was about to be served.

This could not be happening.

This *was* happening.

Violent storms churned in her belly, hot and cold darts bouncing in her dazed head.

Forcing her newly leaden legs to move and holding tightly to her towel, Chloe hurried out of the room behind him. 'Wait just one minute.'

He couldn't end it like this. No. This was all wrong. Not now, not after everything.

He was halfway down the corridor.

'Wait just one minute,' she repeated, raising her voice so he could not pretend to ignore her.

He stopped.

'Why are you doing this?'

'I just explained it to you.'

'No, you didn't. And please show me the courtesy of looking at me when you are speaking to me.'

He didn't move. 'I thought you would be happy.'

'Will you turn around and *look* at me?' she begged. 'Please, Luis, just look at me. *Talk* to me.'

If she had something to hand to throw at him to compel him to turn and face her she would take it gladly.

She needed to look in his eyes, really look, make sense of this grenade he had just thrown at her feet.

All she had was her towel.

He slowly turned.

When she finally got to look in his eyes she quailed.

There was nothing to read in them.

The shutters had come down and locked themselves shut.

'You only agreed to marriage because I blackmailed you,' he reminded her steadily, his frame like a statue. 'Neither of us wanted it.'

'I don't care about the marriage. I care that you're walking away from *us* without a word of discussion about it.'

'*Bonita*, there is no us. There never was.'

'Then what was the last week all about? That felt like an *us* to me.'

She had seen tenderness in his eyes. She had felt his tenderness in his kisses.

Surely, surely that hadn't all been a lie? Surely she hadn't dreamt it all up?

Her brain clouded in a steamy fog as she realised what she had done.

She had allowed herself to dream.

A fiery burn stabbed the back of her retinas and she blinked rapidly, driving the tears back, begging them not to fall, not to humiliate her.

'I am not responsible for your feelings,' he told her in that same steady voice. 'We were both very clear that our marriage would be a temporary arrangement to quell the stories and preserve my business. Javier and I...'

'Was it *him*?' Ice plunged into her spine at the mention

of that hateful man, the ripples driving out the fog in her brain and bringing her to a form of clarity.

She believed Luis had had nothing to do with her brother signing the contract under false pretences but she would bet her brother's chateau that Javier had known.

'Talking to Javier made me see that this route was unnecessary. I acted rashly in demanding marriage from you. I should have thought things through in more detail but I was angry. Your brother had declared war on us.' He shrugged, a nonchalant, dismissive gesture that had her clenching her hands into fists. 'As regretful as it is with hindsight, anger leads to impulsive actions.'

She stared at him, trying her hardest to get air into her lungs. 'So I've given you all of this for nothing?'

'All of what?'

The tears she had come so close to shedding were sucked away as fury finally cut its way through the anguish.

She dropped her towel and held her arms out. 'This! Me!'

Let him see her naked. Let him see what he had taken, what she had given him, the very thing she had never given to anyone. Let him see her heart beating so frenziedly beneath her skin and the chest struggling to get air into it.

Let him see *her*.

Finally there was a flicker of something in his eyes.

'Oh, you liked this part, didn't you?' She laughed mirthlessly. 'You couldn't get enough of it. I bet you were laughing through your teeth every time you made love to me. But there was no love in it, was there? It was all just *sex* to you—'

'Chloe,' he tried to cut in, but she was on a roll, anger and humiliation and a splintering heart too much to bear with any form of stoicism.

'Was it all a joke the pair of you dreamt up? Did I give you my virginity as part of a screwed-up *game*?'

His face contorted. 'You are making too much of this. We were never going to be for ever.'

'Of course we weren't going to be for ever. You don't do for ever, do you? Too busy hiding your feelings, scared someone will see too deeply and think the same as your father did. That's what scares you, isn't it?'

'How dare you?' The statue suddenly came to life with a roar.

'No, how dare *you*? How dare you make love to me like I mean something, how dare you comfort me, how dare you confide in me, how dare you make me dream when dreams were something I had given up?' Aware of angry tears splashing down her cheeks, she swiped them away.

'I have never lied to you,' he snarled, storming over to stand before her, as tall and as broad as she had ever seen him. 'You are the one who has made too much of what we've shared here. How would you have liked me to make love to you? With indifference?'

'I wish I'd never let you touch me in the first place!'

'But you did, didn't you?' He took hold of her chin roughly but painlessly and stared at her with eyes that spat fury. 'Do not blame me for *your* desires. We were never going to last. We've had fun together—I admit, I never expected to enjoy our time here as much as I have but now it is over. All I'm doing is bringing the end date forward and allowing us to pick up our lives.'

Chloe's open hand was inches from connecting with his hateful face before she became aware that she was on the verge of slapping him.

Even with all the hurt and fury unravelling like a nightmare kaleidoscope inside her she could not bring herself to physically harm him, not now, not with the tales of his father's violence so fresh in her mind.

What kind of a person would that make her?

She had lashed out at Luis before and he'd overpowered her easily but that meant nothing.

If she struck her hand to him that would make her as bad as the dead man she hated.

She *wanted* to hurt him. But not like that.

She would rather rip her own heart out than strike him in anger again.

Taking a deep breath, she dropped her hand and, with all the dignity she could muster in her naked state, looked him straight in the eye.

'You call what we have shared *fun*? Fun is for the parties you like to throw and for the women whose beds you hop in and out of without a care. I bared my soul to you. I confided things in you that I have never shared with anyone because I trusted you. I deserve better than to be discarded like an unwanted puppy that's outgrown its cuteness.'

But the dignity was fleeting for as soon as she had said her piece she could feel the bones in her legs begin to crumble.

Terrified he would see the depths of her pain, Chloe turned on her heel and fled back to the bedroom.

The door shut with a bang loud enough to damage the hinges.

Luis closed his eyes and blew out a long puff of air.

After taking a few moments to gather his composure and rub his forehead to lessen the forming headache, he bent down to pick up Chloe's discarded towel. Discarded as she claimed he was discarding her.

He'd known she would be shocked that he was ending things so abruptly but never had he expected her to react like that.

He hadn't expected to see the pain in those blue eyes.

Dios, his head was really hurting.

Slinging her towel over his shoulder, he headed down

the stairs to the kitchen and poured himself a glass of water and scavenged for painkillers. He found a packet stuck in the back of one drawer and popped the tablets out.

This was not his fault, he thought angrily. He was guilty of many things—kidnap, blackmail; the pain in his chest deepened just to think of it—but he had never led her on. Not by word or deed had he done anything to indicate he wanted a future with her.

She should be grateful. Better he ended it now, before she looked hard enough at him and she saw the rottenness that lay in his core. She'd alluded to it, to his father, but how she couldn't see it already was beyond him. He had kidnapped her. He had blackmailed her.

And she acted as if he'd wounded her by setting her free early.

He tossed the pills down his throat and drank the water. Maybe they would help the pain that had erupted in his chest as well as his head.

He should never have let it get this far. He should have worked harder to keep things on a purely physical level as he had always done before. Maybe then the sting of her words wouldn't feel so acute.

Hearing footsteps on the stairs, he braced himself for another onslaught.

Chloe appeared in the doorway.

She'd thrown on the shorts and red T-shirt she'd been wearing the day he had kidnapped her and had her beach bag stuffed tightly under her arm.

She walked to him, her gait stiff, stopping far enough away that there was no danger in either of them touching, accidentally or not.

'I apologise for bringing your father into it,' she said tightly. 'That was uncalled for.'

He inhaled deeply then inclined his head. His throat had closed.

But what could he say? There was nothing left *to* say. Everything that could be said had already been said.

'I would be grateful if you would allow me to travel on my own in the helicopter,' she said into the silence, no longer looking at him.

By the time his throat had opened enough for him to speak, Chloe had walked out of the front door.

He let her go.

Chloe opened the letter with a shaking hand.

The large padded envelope had the official Compania de Ballet de Casillas logo embossed on it. It had been forwarded from her shared apartment in Madrid to the house she was currently staying at in London, where she had taken sanctuary with her old friend, Tanya. She hadn't called it sanctuary, of course, had said only that she was taking a break and begged use of Tanya's spare room.

Inside the envelope was a letter of reference written by Maria, the Head of Costume.

It was a glowing reference too.

She held it to her chest and blinked back tears.

Luis had authorised this for her. He must have done. Maria, as wonderful as she was, would not dare write a reference for her without permission.

Chloe hadn't asked for a reference. She'd assumed that there was no chance of her getting one, not after she had quit without working her notice and then for her hand in stealing their principal dancer away from the co-owner. She'd assumed her name would be mud in the whole company.

A separate, smaller envelope had fallen out of the package and landed by her feet. She picked it up, opened it and pulled out a goodbye card signed by the entire costume department and many of the other backstage crew. Even a few of the dancers had scribbled their names in it. There was also a personal handwritten note from Maria wishing her all the best for the future and telling her to seek her out the next time she was in Madrid.

The postscript at the end was what got her heart truly racing.

My daughter was going to have this ticket but she can no longer attend. It's yours. Please come.

Tucked in the envelope was a ticket for the opening night of Compania de Ballet de Casillas's new theatre.

Chloe resisted the instinct to rip it in two.

Instead, she placed it on her dressing table and pinched the bridge of her nose to keep the tears at bay.

She'd cried too much in the past month.

The worst of it was that she couldn't tell anyone, not even Tanya.

How could she admit that she'd been stupid enough to fall in love with the man who'd kidnapped her and black-mailed her? They would think she was suffering a version of Stockholm syndrome.

She wished she could explain her pain away on that. That would be easier to cope with.

Easier to cope with than to accept that she, the woman who had learned the hard way that dreams did not come true, had allowed herself to dream of a future with a man incapable of returning her love.

The flash of cameras that went off as Luis stepped out of the limousine with his brother would have blinded a less practised man.

Unfazed, the Casillas brothers cut their way through the reporters all eager for a sound bite, past the chanting crowd all hoping to spot a famous face, and up the stairs and through the theatre's doors.

The new theatre that homed Compania de Ballet de Casillas was, Luis thought with satisfaction, a perfect blend of new and old. They had employed the best architect to work on it, Daniele Pellegrini, and he had produced the same magic that had won him so many awards through the years.

The fifteen-hundred-strong audience crowded inside were enjoying a drink in one of the five bars or finding their seats, excited chatter filling the magnificent bowled space. He and Javier had made the conscious decision to give only a third of the tickets to VIPs. The remaining two thirds had been sold through a form of lottery, reasonably priced so any member of the public should be able to afford it, something they both felt strongly about, that the arts should not be the domain of the rich. Every member of the audience, whether rich or poor, had made an effort with their appearance and it warmed his cold heart to see the glittering dresses, smart suits and tuxedos.

The press were out in force, not from a desire to see the theatre's grand opening or to review the performance of *The Red Shoes*—although the bona fide critics had been allocated seats—but because two of the parties of the love triangle would be under the same roof for the first time since Benjamin had stolen Freya two months ago.

It would be the first time Javier had come face to face with the woman who had dumped him so publicly.

The tension emanating from his brother's huge shoulders let Luis know the strain Javier was under. He hadn't loved Freya but his pride had suffered an enormous blow.

It would not be easy for Javier to see the woman he'd

intended to marry dancing on his stage, the star of the performance. Despite the animosity that curdled between them, Luis felt for him.

Things had been strained between the brothers since Luis had returned from the Caribbean. They continued to work together, conducted their regular meetings, nothing changed in that respect, but a coldness had developed between them, unlike anything they had been through before.

However, Javier had been correct that they would get through the bad press that had been unleashed on them. They'd written the Canadian project off—damn, that had felt great telling that sanctimonious oaf George where to go—and it had generated the expected flurry of headlines. But with all the parties in the Javier, Benjamin and Freya love triangle remaining tight-lipped, the press had run out of new angles for the story. The ever-moving news cycle had moved on to new fodder...until that evening.

Although this was an opinion he chose not to share with his brother, Luis was grateful that Freya had some loyalty left in her. She had, naturally, handed her notice in with Compania de Ballet de Casillas but had agreed to honour her commitment to this opening performance. They kept their star performer for one last night and, without actually saying a word, Freya was telling the world that they couldn't be the complete monsters the cruel Internet commentators gleefully insisted they must be.

Whenever Luis thought of those comments now, he thought of Chloe. She had been far more outraged by them than he had been. It was as if she had taken them personally.

Sometimes, alone in his bed, Luis would gaze at the ceiling and wonder where the madness had come from that had made him think marrying her would be the solution to all their problems.

His brother had been right: he *had* lost his mind.

And then he would stop thinking.

Or try to stop thinking.

He couldn't rid himself of her. Everywhere he went his mind played tricks on him. He'd walked past the coffee shop where he had first been so dazzled by her and had seen her in there, laughing, her raven hair flowing like waves around her. And then he'd blinked and she'd gone.

Drinks in hand, faking cordiality, he and Javier settled themselves in their private box, which they had chosen to share that evening with senior members of the Spanish royal family. Sitting on his other side was a ravishing princess. Four months ago he would have decided on the spot to get her into bed. Now he couldn't even muster basic interest.

There had been no one since he had left the Caribbean. Not even a twitch in his loins. There had been no one other than Chloe since their one date all those months ago...

The curtains fell back and the performance began.

Within minutes Luis experienced his usual boredom when watching the ballet. He much preferred watching an action-packed movie to this, and he found his gaze drifting over the audience.

Minutes before the interval, he saw, hidden at the back of the box on the other side of the theatre, the unmistakable dark features of Benjamin Guillem.

Putting his binoculars to his eyes, he trained them on him to confirm it.

Yes, it was Benjamin.

Luis had not expected him to be there. Indeed, if he were a gambling man he would have put his money on Benjamin staying away.

Admiration flickered in him. Benjamin had voluntarily entered the lion's den. That took balls...

And then he saw the expression on his old friend's face and moved the binoculars to the stage where Freya was dancing a solo. Then he trained them back on Benjamin and he understood, his heart suddenly thumping rapidly, why he had come.

He was there to support the woman he loved.

Luis's thoughts flashed to Chloe.

His thoughts *always* flashed to Chloe.

'What is she doing here?' Javier hissed in his ear. He too was looking through his binoculars.

'Who?' He would not mention Benjamin's presence.

'Chloe.'

Whipping his binoculars to where his brother's were trained, high up in the gods, Luis sucked in a breath as he worked on the lens's focus.

He made sure to blink before looking again, certain that his eyes were playing their familiar trick on him.

Dios, it was her, ravishing in a black lace dress, her raven hair framing her face in a sleek, coiffured style he had never seen before but which enhanced her elfin beauty.

'What is she doing here?' Javier repeated.

'I don't know.'

He had no idea where she had got a ticket from or why she had come.

Or why his heart hammered so hard his ribs vibrated with the force.

CHAPTER THIRTEEN

CHLOE WATCHED THE performance without paying any attention to what was happening on the stage. She managed to keep her frame still but emotionally she was all over the place.

She had a good view of the Casillas brothers' private box and had spotted Luis the moment he'd entered it. That one look had been enough for her heart to set off at a thrum and for her palms to become clammy.

That one look had been enough to prove she had made an enormous mistake in coming here.

On one side of him sat his hateful brother. On the other side a beautiful woman dressed in crushed velvet whispering intimately into his ear.

Chloe had put her binoculars back in her clutch bag and refused to look in his direction again.

What was she trying to prove to herself? she thought miserably as the performance went on. That she was over him?

The ticket had been sitting on her dressing table for a week when, after another terrible night's sleep, she had decided to go.

She needed to see him one last time, in circumstances over which *she* was in control.

She'd had it all planned out. She would find him during the interval or the after-show party—she knew enough people to be confident of someone helping her sneak in—and then she would graciously thank him for the reference and sweep out with all the grace she had been practising all week.

It destroyed her to know his last memory of her was as an hysterical wreck.

She hadn't even cared that coming here would mean she would see Javier or that there was the chance she would bump into her brother. She hadn't seen Benjamin since she'd returned to Europe.

Her wounds were too fresh for her to see anyone who cared enough to notice the insomnia-inflicted bruising beneath her eyes. Tanya cared but she was busy with her work and still the party animal of old. In Tanya's home, Chloe found the peace she craved but also the time she'd always shied away from that allowed her to think.

Oh, what had she come here for?

More humiliation?

Luis didn't love her. He wouldn't care that she had made a deliberate effort with her appearance or for any graceful sweep away from him. She would have been relegated to his past. She doubted he'd given her more than a fleeting thought, other than arranging her reference.

She had to do what he had always said and look to the future. She could do nothing about the past but she could pick her life up and move forward. She could complete the application form for the ballet company in New York and make a fresh start.

Another fresh start.

But this would be the last.

She wouldn't go chasing a dream; she would create her own.

Suddenly filled with determination, she straightened her spine and waited for the performance to end.

* * *

How Luis remained in his seat through the rest of the performance he would never know. He kept his binoculars trained on Chloe, willing her to look his way.

But she didn't. Her eyes stayed fixed on the drama unfolding on the stage, oblivious to his presence and oblivious to the drama unfolding in the pit of his stomach.

Dios, she looked so beautiful. The way she was holding herself too... When they'd been together she had been a great one for slouching and putting her feet up wherever she went. Tonight she looked as regal as the princess sitting beside him, who had given up her attempts to draw him into conversation.

It must have taken real guts for Chloe to come here tonight.

Which begged the question of why she had come. Was it merely that she'd procured an invitation and, being a ballet lover, had decided to use it? That was the only logical explanation he could think of. He hadn't seen or spoken to her in over a month.

Whatever her reasons, the Guillems had more guts than an ice-hockey team. Both of them had entered the lion's den.

But Benjamin had entered it to support the woman he loved.

After the way things had ended between him and Chloe he could say with one hundred per cent confidence that she was not there to support him.

But she was there.

And he couldn't take his eyes off her.

And he couldn't fight the knots in his stomach that were pulling tighter and tighter in him.

'I'm going to have a word with Security and make sure they know not to let her into the after-party,' Javier murmured as they rose to their feet at the end of the performance.

As Luis was craning his neck to keep watch over Chloe, it took a few moments to understand what his brother was saying.

He turned his attention to him. 'You will leave her alone,' he said sharply.

Javier's face darkened into something ugly. 'You still defend her? After what she did?'

'She was defending her brother, doing what either you or I would do if we felt someone had hurt us.'

Their royal guests had got to their feet.

Remembering his manners, Luis managed to exchange a few words with them as they exited the box.

Right at the last moment he turned his head for one last sight of Chloe but found her row empty.

Swallowing back the bile that had risen up his throat, he forced a smile to his lips and joined the throng in the corridor.

The after-show party was being held in one of the theatre's underground conference rooms and, trying hard to keep his attention on his honoured guests and not allow his eyes to keep darting about in the hope of catching a glimpse of a raven-haired beauty, Luis headed to it.

When the group took a left where the corridor forked, he saw, in the distance, the tall figure of Benjamin.

Not hesitating for a moment, Luis put his hand on his brother's back and steered him in the other direction, calling over his shoulder to their guests that they would join them shortly.

'What's the matter?' Javier asked, staring at him with suspicion as they walked.

'I wanted to talk to you alone.'

He hadn't realised until he said the words that he *did* want to speak to his brother.

Avoiding a confrontation with Benjamin was the impetus he needed to confront his brother with a conversation they should have had a long time ago.

'You knew we were ripping Benjamin off all those years ago, didn't you?'

It was the first time Luis had vocalised this notion.

His brother's face darkened. 'We didn't rip him off. He was the fool who signed the contract without reading it.'

'And you should have warned him the terms had changed as you'd said you would do. You didn't forget, did you?'

His brother merely glowered in response.

'I knew it.' Luis took a deep breath, trying hard to contain the nausea swirling inside him that was fighting with a swell of rage. 'All these years and I've told myself that it had been an oversight on your part when I should have accepted the truth that you never forget. In thirty-five years you have never forgotten anything or failed to do something you promised.'

'I never promised to email him.'

'Not an actual promise,' Luis conceded. 'But look me in the eye and tell me it wasn't a deliberate act on your part.'

But all he saw in his twin's eyes was a black hardness.

'For what reason would it have been deliberate?' Javier asked with a sneer.

'That is for your conscience to decide. All I know for sure is that Benjamin was our friend. I have defended you and I have fought your corner…'

'*Our* corner,' Javier corrected icily. 'I assume this burst of conscience from you is connected to that damned woman.'

His temper finally getting the better of him, Luis grabbed his brother by the collar of his shirt. 'If you ever speak about Chloe in that way again then you and I are finished. Do you hear me? Finished.'

'If you're still defending her to me then I would say we're already finished, *brother*.' He spat the last word directly into Luis's face.

Eyeball to eyeball, they glowered at each other, the venom seeping between them thick enough to taste.

Then Luis released his hold, stepped back and unclenched the fist he hadn't been aware of making.

His eyes still fixed on the man he had shared a womb with, had shared a bedroom with, had fought with, had protected, had been protected by, had grieved with, the other side of the coin that was the Casillas twins, Luis took backwards strides until he could look no more and turned his back on his brother for the last time.

With long strides, Luis walked the theatre's corridors, hardening his heart to what he had just walked away from, his focus now on one thing only: finding Chloe.

He had the rest of his life to sort out his relationship with Javier. And if they couldn't sort it out? He would handle it.

An incessant nagging in his guts told him he had only one opportunity to make things right with the woman it had taken him far too long to realise he was in love with. He did not think he could handle it if his attempts didn't work.

As he picked up his pace, scanning the crowds ahead for a tall, raven-haired woman, he collided with a much smaller blonde woman with a face he vaguely recognised.

'Sorry,' he muttered.

'My fault,' she whispered, looking over his shoulder. 'I wasn't looking where I was going.'

Forgetting all about her, he continued to scour the corridors and bars, put his head into the conference room where the after-show party was being held three times, until he had a burst of inspiration and hurried to the costume department.

By the time he reached it, he was out of breath.

He pushed the door open and there she was, chatting with Maria over a bottle of wine.

Both women looked at him, startled at his appearance.

Only Chloe turned a deep red colour to match her lipstick to see him there.

'Maria, can I have a minute alone with Chloe, please?' he asked as politely as he could.

She must have read something on his face for she shot to her feet and hurried out of the door. 'I'll be at the party,' she murmured as she closed the door behind her.

'Can I have some of that?' he asked, nodding at the bottle of white wine.

Chloe handed him her glass without a word.

He drained it and handed it back to her. 'I was thirsty,' he said in an attempt at humour that failed when her lips didn't move.

And then they did move. 'I'm here legitimately. I was given a ticket.'

'I'm not here to question your legitimacy.' He took Maria's vacated seat and rolled his shoulders.

Chloe pushed her chair back, away from him. 'Then why are you here? I assume you've been looking for me.'

'I saw you from my seat.'

'I saw you too. You looked very cosy. Have you abandoned your date?'

'I don't have a date,' he said, confused.

She raised her brow and pursed her lips.

Then he understood who she meant and gave a hollow laugh. 'The women who sat with us are members of the royal family. We invited them to share our box out of courtesy. There is nothing in it.'

'I wouldn't care if there was.'

But he recognised the look he'd seen fleetingly on her face from the times he had mentioned Marietta, before she had realised Marietta was nearly ninety years old. It was the first time he recognised that look as jealousy.

That jealousy allowed him to breathe a little more easily.

'How have you been?' he asked.

'I've been having a great time in London, thank you.'

'London?'

'Yes. I've been there since I left the Caribbean and I'm flying back there in the morning. Now, did you seek me out to make small talk or was there a purpose to it?'

'Have mercy on me, *bonita*. I know I don't deserve it but allow me the small talk. What I have to say is hard for me. I need to build up to it.'

She looked at her watch.

Was he imagining it or did it look loose on her wrist? Had she lost weight?

'My cab is collecting me in thirty minutes. I will need ten minutes to get to the front, which gives you twenty minutes to say what you need to say.'

'I can give you a lift to wherever you want to go.' Hopefully home with him.

Unmoved, she looked again at her watch and said pointedly, 'Twenty minutes.'

He nodded and took a deep breath. 'Okay. Did you get the reference?'

'Yes. Thank you for arranging that. I assume you authorised it?'

'I did. And now I would like you to rip it up and return to Madrid.'

'You want me to come back and work for you?'

'No, I want you to come back and be my wife.'

There was a moment of silence before a grin broke out

on her face. It didn't meet her eyes and there was no humour in it. 'You really are a comedian.'

He cursed under his breath. 'I am not being funny, *bonita*. I want you to marry me.'

'And I am not being funny either, but if you call me *bonita* one more time I will pour the contents of the bottle over your head.' The fake smile dropping, she got to her feet. 'Excuse me but I don't have time for any more of your games.'

He managed to take hold of her hand before she could snatch it away.

'Please, sit down. I'm not playing games. I know I am doing this all wrong but I have never told someone I love them before.'

Her eyes widened, a pulse ringing through them before she blinked all expression out of them.

Snatching her hand from his, she said, 'I thought Javier was the cruel one.'

'He is cruel,' Luis agreed sombrely. 'Our childhoods screwed with our heads. He has to live with seeing our father's reflection every time he looks in the mirror.'

'And how did it screw with yours?'

'I have to live with seeing the reflection my father hated.'

She studied him in silence then carefully sat back down. 'I have to live with seeing the reflection my father didn't want every day,' she said slowly.

He couldn't tell if she was relaying this as a fact or to empathise. Her usually melodious tones were flatter than he had ever heard them.

'I know you do. How you have turned into such a vivacious and loving woman is inspiring. You could be bitter with the world but you're not. People like you.'

'People like you too,' she pointed out.

'They like my money. They like the parties I host and the presents I give. I've had to buy my friendships.'

Something flickered in her eyes. 'That's not true. You've always been a fun person to be around.'

'I like to have fun,' he conceded. 'But I am talking of real friendship. You and Benjamin are the only people other than my brother that I have been able to let my guard down with.'

'Because you have known us all your life?'

'With Benjamin, yes. We grew up together. He knew me before the nightmare, but you were just a child then and remained a child in my eyes until you came to Madrid and I suddenly saw the beautiful, vibrant woman you had become. I looked at you with brand-new eyes and I fell in love, and I never even knew it. I ended our date filled with emotions I can't explain because I have never felt them before, and then everything blew up with your brother and you, rightly, didn't want to know me any more. Through all the litigation we were going through, you were always there in my mind. I couldn't stop thinking about you. When you called me to say you had broken down in the mountains... *Dios*, I have never driven so fast in my life. To learn it had been a trick to get me away from the gala...ah, *bonita*, I was furious—please don't pour the wine over me—but my revenge was never focused where it should have been, on your brother, but on *you*.'

He paused for breath and gave a shake of his head. 'Javier says I lost my mind insisting that you married me and now I can see that he was right. Of course, back then I didn't see it—in truth, it's only becoming clear to me now as I say it to you.'

'Truth?' she said with only the slightest hint of cynicism. 'You're saying you kidnapped me and blackmailed me because you love me? Do you have any idea how screwed up that sounds?'

He ran a hand through his hair. 'Don't you know by now that I *am* a screw-up?'

'Then explain this. If you did all that because you love me, why did you end it so cruelly?'

'I was scared,' he replied simply. 'What I felt for you was like nothing I had ever felt for anyone. It scared the hell out of me. And I was scared that you were falling in love with me, scared that if you fell much harder you would see me too clearly.'

'I did see you clearly,' she said slowly. 'I always did. Even when I hated you I understood you. I understood you more when I learned about your relationship with your father. In many ways we are kindred spirits, two children longing for love from a parent who refused to give it. I fell in love with you when I was seventeen years old. I dreamed of marrying you…and then I grew up and learned the truth of my conception and had to come to terms with my father…' She took her own deep breath. 'But you know all this. I confided it in you. I had never told a soul. No one knew. It was too raw and too personal but I entrusted it with you.'

'You were in love with me all that time?' he asked in dazed disbelief.

'All that time.' Her smile was sad. 'You were there for all of us when we most needed you. You made my mother smile on the days she was so ill and so low from her treatment that she could hardly lift her head. You brought joy to all our lives and then on the day we buried her, when I so desperately needed someone to hold onto, you were there to hold me up and give me the strength to keep going. Of course I fell in love with you. Over the years I thought my love for you had…not died but been put aside with all my other childish things. And then I saw you again in Madrid and all my old feelings for you erupted.

'When Benjamin told me about the contract it broke my heart. I couldn't understand how you could be there for us during the worst time of our lives and at the same time conspire against us. Of course, I know differently now and as soon as I accepted that I had been wrong, my love for you… Luis, it never died. It's always been with me.'

He sighed. He couldn't hide it from her, not now that he knew the truth. 'Javier did know.'

'What do you mean?'

'When he didn't warn your brother about the change in the profit terms… It was a deliberate act. He didn't forget.'

'I know that.'

Unsure if he understood her correctly, he clarified, 'You know? How?'

She shrugged. 'Benjamin was adamant he mentioned the terms of profit on the night it was signed and that nothing was said to the contrary. That's why he felt so betrayed and why I felt so betrayed. If it wasn't said to you it must have been Javier.'

'I'm sorry.'

'You are not your brother. And he's paid for his deception. I'm sorry you were dragged into it.'

'Don't be. I kept my mouth shut for seven years and ignored the nagging voice that told me Javier's actions had been deliberate.'

'I can't say I wouldn't have done the same if I had been in your shoes. What you two have lived through together…' Her sigh was heavy as she got to her feet and looked at her watch. 'He's your brother. Your loyalty is to him. I understand that. I always have.'

As she headed to the door, he suddenly realised what

she was doing and stood, kicking his chair back so force-fully it fell onto its side.

'Where are you going?'

'To my cab. I'm already running late for it.'

'You're *leaving*?'

She closed her eyes and nodded.

'But...' He groped for words, unable to comprehend this turn of events, not after the heartfelt exchange they'd just had that had alternately ripped his soul from him and cleansed it.

'I told you I would be getting a cab, Luis,' she said softly. 'I'm sorry. I can't marry you.'

She could not be serious. Please, God, do not let her be serious. 'You just told me that you love me.'

'I *do* love you but it's not enough. Don't you under-stand?'

'No,' he answered flatly, walking over to her, trying his hardest to quell the rising panic in his chest. Putting his hand on the nape of her neck, he brought his forehead to hers. 'I love you, you love me, what else is there to under-stand? You are my heart. Do you understand *that*? I have spent the past six weeks feeling as if something inside me has died and it was only when I saw you in the audience tonight that I realised what was wrong with me. *You* were what's wrong. I love you, more than anything or anyone.'

'I'm sorry,' she repeated, blinking frantically. She slipped out of his hold and wrapped her finger around the door handle. 'Please don't come any closer. I'm sorry. You hurt me too much. I've been in agony without you and have only just patched myself back together. I can't go through that again. I love you but I don't trust that you won't break my heart again. Forgive me.'

Ready to argue some more, to fight, to make every

promise that would make her see sense, Luis caught the look in her eyes and closed his mouth.

What little fight was left in him vanished.

The pain he saw reflecting back at him was too acute to argue with.

He could gift-wrap his heart for her and she wouldn't believe it.

Their eyes stayed locked together, a thousand emotions passing between them before she gave a small nod of her head, raised her shoulders and walked out of the room.

Slumping against the door, Luis listened to the click-clack of her shoes fade away to nothing.

And then he fell to the floor and buried his face in his hands, every wretched part of him feeling as if it were being pulled through every circle of Dante's hell.

Chloe walked as fast as she dared on heels she was unpractised in walking in.

She tried to text the cab driver to let her know she was on her way but her fingers were all over the place.

All she had to do was get to the front entrance, get in her cab and get to her hotel. Three simple things easily achieved, or they would be if her feet and fingers would work properly.

In the morning she would fly back to London and complete the application form for the New York ballet company.

That was all she allowed herself to focus on. She would not think of the man she had just left behind.

An usher, who was shrugging a coat on, saw her approach and stepped in front of her. 'Is everything all right, miss?'

'Everything's fine. Why do you ask?'

The usher looked embarrassed. 'You're crying.'

'I am?' Putting a hand to her face, Chloe was horrified to find it wet with tears.

'Can I get you something? A coffee? Something stronger?'

'No, no, I need to get to my cab.' As she spoke her phone buzzed. It was the cab driver telling her she had five minutes to get to her or she would have to leave for her next job.

Panic now setting in, Chloe put a hand on the usher for support and leaned down to pull her heels off.

Shoes in one hand, phone clutched in the other, she set off at a run.

Had she thought the theatre's corridors wide when she'd arrived earlier? Now they seemed to have shrunk, the sides pressing closer and closer to her.

She picked up speed as she spotted the staircase, and kept close to the side as she ran down steps that seemed to go on and on, winding and winding, the exit so near and yet so far.

As soon as she reached the bottom she sprinted, running as fast as she had ever run in her life, the people she streamed past nothing but blurs.

Everything was a blur.

But still she ran until the warm night air hit her face and she was outside.

The cab driver, the same woman who had dropped her off hours before, tooted.

Doubling over as the first signs of a stitch set in, Chloe hobbled to the car, gasping for air.

Hand on the passenger door, she went to open it but then found her fingers still refusing to work.

The driver wound the window down and said something to her. It was nothing but noise to Chloe's ears, that distant sound of interference like a car radio going through a tunnel.

She spun around and stared up at the magnificent theatre, the name 'Compania de Ballet de Casillas' proudly embossed in gold leaf around the silhouette of a dancer in motion above the entrance door.

The Casillas Ballet Company. Named after the beloved mother of two boys whose life had been so cruelly taken at the hands of their father, her own husband.

A ballet company bought to keep her memory alive, a state-of-the-art theatre, dance school and facilities created from nothing to showcase the best that ballet had to offer, all to honour the memory of the woman they had loved.

Luis had loved his mother. Twenty-two years after her death and still he loved her. Javier had loved her too. For the first time in months she allowed a wave of tenderness into her heart for a man who had also lost so much, a man who'd clamped down on his feelings so tightly and effectively that he could deliberately cheat his oldest friend.

Luis hadn't clamped down on his feelings. Luis had opened his heart and embraced them—for her.

He had laid his heart on the line for the first time since his mother had died and Chloe, out of rabid fear, had turned it down.

She had dreamed of the day he declared his love for her then learned that dreams never came true.

But what if they did?

Luis *loved* her.

That was a truth.

He had seen all the good and bad in her just as she had seen the best and worst in him and still he loved her.

If she ran away now...

She would never have this chance again.

This was her time, *their* time, if only she had the courage to accept that sometimes dreams *did* come true, even for people like her and Luis whose own fathers could not bring themselves to love them.

Working automatically, she dug her hand into her clutch bag and pulled out the cash she had ready for the cab and thrust it into the driver's hand, unable to speak, able to apologise only with her eyes.

On legs that felt drugged, she walked back up the stairs and into the theatre foyer. The tears pouring down her face were so thick she struggled to see. She sensed the concerned faces surrounding her but blocked them all out.

Oh, Luis, where are you?

He couldn't still be in the costume room. Could he?

'Chloe?'

She spun round to the sound of the voice she knew so well and loved so much, and there he was, only feet away.

She didn't need her vision to see the haggard state of him.

How had she not seen it before?

'What's wrong?' Concern laced his every syllable. 'Have you been hurt?'

She shook her head, trying desperately to stop the tears that were falling like a waterfall, trying desperately to speak through a throat that had choked.

Her limbs took control of matters for her, legs propelling her to him, arms throwing themselves around him and holding him tightly, so tightly, burying herself to him.

Only his innate strength stopped them buckling under the weight of her ambush and after a moment where he fought to keep them steady and upright, his strong arms wrapped around her as tightly as she clung to him and his face buried into her hair, his warm breath seeping through to her skin.

'Oh, Luis,' she sobbed, 'I'm sorry. I'm sorry. I love you so much it hurts. I'm sorry for hurting you and for...'

But two large hands gently cupped her face to tilt her head back. The dark hazel eyes she loved so much were gazing down at her with a tenderness dreams were made of.

'My love,' he breathed. 'Please, say no more. It is *I* who am sorry.'

She shook her head, fresh tears spilling free. 'I love you.'

'And I love you, with all my heart. I swear, I will never hurt you again. You are my life, Chloe, please believe that.'

'I do. Because it is the same for me. I don't want to live without you.'

'You won't,' he promised reverently. 'You and I will never be parted again.'

'Promise?'

'Promise.'

'For ever?'

'For ever.'

And then his lips found her and they kissed with such love and such passion that neither doubted the other's love again.

EPILOGUE

THE SUN SETTING over the Caribbean like an enormous jewel was a glorious sight and one Luis gazed at with full appreciation.

'How are the nerves holding up?'

He turned his head and smiled at Benjamin. 'No nerves.'

The Frenchman raised a brow that was a perfect imitation of his sister. 'No nerves?'

'None. This is a day I have been looking forward to for so long I think I might burst if she makes me wait any longer.' Chloe had insisted they not rush into exchanging their vows, reasoning that as they were only going to do it the once, she wanted it to be perfect for them.

Benjamin laughed. 'My sister can be very stubborn.'

'It's a family trait.'

'*Oui.*' A flash of white teeth. 'A trait I imagine will be inherited by my niece or nephew.'

'She told you?'

'She told Freya. Who told me...'

Luis burst into laughter.

Chloe had taken the pregnancy test only the week before and had made him swear not to tell anyone until the first trimester had passed.

He should have guessed she wouldn't be able to contain herself from telling Freya.

After the first heady days when they had finally declared

their love for each other, days spent in bed, surfacing only for food, all forms of contraception forgotten about, Luis had come out of the daze determined to make things right with Benjamin.

Chloe had elicited her sister-in-law's help in the matter, Freya falling under her spell enough to forgive Chloe's part in Benjamin's kidnapping of her. With his wife and sister both on his case over the matter, Benjamin had eventually given in and accepted a meeting with him, just the two men, in a neutral venue.

Naturally, that had meant Chloe and Freya had come along to the chosen hotel too, doing a terrible job of hiding behind menus at a table on the other side of the room.

Luis knew it was their presence there that had given Benjamin the impetus to hear him out. He'd refused Luis's cheque that equalled the total profit lost, plus interest, telling him to donate it to charity. But he had accepted a beer from him. And he had listened.

Three beers each later and Benjamin had apologised for his own terrible deeds.

Five beers each later and they were cracking jokes together.

And now, two months on, Benjamin was to be Luis's best man as he married the woman who had stolen his heart then given it back to him whole with her own nestled in with it.

The only fly in the ointment was Javier's absence.

His twin had cut himself off so effectively a French guillotine could not have severed it better.

Chloe kept telling him to give Javier time but Luis knew his brother better than anyone.

For Javier it was simple. By choosing Chloe, Luis had switched his loyalty. His brother could not accept or understand that it hadn't been a choice for Luis; his love for

Chloe was all encompassing, his need to be with her as necessary as breathing.

But then he forgot all about his estranged twin for the woman he loved appeared on deck, radiant in a floor-length lace white wedding dress that showed off her mountainous breasts—*Dios*, early pregnancy really suited her—and holding a posy of flowers over her non-existent bump. Her smile illuminated everyone. Even Captain Brand, officiating at the wedding, smiled broadly along with the rest of the crew.

Chloe made no attempt to walk serenely to him, bounding over like the galloping gazelle who had thrown her arms around him all those months ago.

The beaming smile didn't leave her face for a moment as they exchanged their vows. When the time came for them to share their first kiss as husband and wife she threw her arms around him and kissed him for so long they missed the first set of fireworks.

With his beautiful wife snuggled securely in his arms, Luis watched the spectacular display and reflected that he was the luckiest man to have sailed these waters.

Luis and Chloe Casillas are delighted to announce the birth of their first child, Clara Louise Casillas, born at 5.22 a.m., weighing 7lb 3oz. Both mother and daughter are doing well.

* * * * *

THE ITALIAN'S
ONE-NIGHT
CONSEQUENCE

CATHY WILLIAMS

CHAPTER ONE

FROM THE BACK seat of his chauffeur-driven car, which was parked a discreet distance away, Leo Conti took a few minutes to savour the edifice that dominated this tree-lined Dublin road. Prime location, perfect size, and with all the discernible signs of wear and tear that indicated a department store clinging to life by the skin of its teeth.

Frankly, things couldn't have been better.

This was the store his grandfather had spent a lifetime trying to acquire. It was the store that had eluded the old man's grasp for over fifty years, always just out of reach. Despite the vast property portfolio Benito Conti had built up over the decades, and the grand shopping complexes he had opened across the globe, this one department store had continued to hold sway over him.

Leo, raised by his grandparents from the age of eight, had never been able to understand why his grandfather couldn't just let it go—but then, being outmanoeuvred by someone you'd once considered your closest friend would leave a sour taste in anybody's mouth.

Which said something about the nature of trust.

Over the years Leo had witnessed his grandfather's

frustrated attempts to purchase the department store from Tommaso Gallo to no avail.

'He would rather it crumble to the ground,' Benito had grumbled, 'than sell it to me. Too damn proud! Well, if it *does* crumble—and crumble it will, because Tommaso has been drinking and gambling his money away for decades—I will be the first in line to laugh! The man has no honour.'

Honour, Leo thought now, as his sharp eyes continued to take in the outward signs of decay, was an irrational emotion that always led to unnecessary complications.

'Find yourself something to do, James,' Leo said to his chauffeur, leaning forward, eyes still on the building. 'Buy yourself a decent meal somewhere. Take a break from that fast food junk you insist on eating. I'll call you when it's time for you to swing by and collect me.'

'You plan on buying the place today, boss?'

A shadow of a smile crossed Leo's face. He caught his driver's eyes in the rearview mirror. James Cure—driver, dogsbody and rehabilitated petty thief—was one of the few people Leo would actually trust with his life.

'I plan,' Leo drawled, opening the passenger door and letting in a blast of summer heat, 'on having a little incognito tour to find out just how low I can go when it comes to putting money on the table. From what I see, the old man has died leaving a nice, healthy liability behind, and from what I understand, the new owner—whoever he is—will want to sell before the dreaded words *fire sale* start circulating in the business community.'

Leo had no idea who the new owner was. In fact he wouldn't have known that Tommaso Gallo had gone to

meet his maker a mere month previously if his grandfather hadn't summoned him back from Hong Kong to
buy the store before it went to someone else.

'Now,' Leo said, briskly winding up the conversation, 'off you go, James—and while you're finding yourself a nice, healthy salad for lunch, try and locate the
nearest pawn shop, so that you can offload that array of
jewellery you insist on wearing.' Leo grinned. 'Hasn't
anyone told you that medallions, signet rings and thick
gold chains are things of the past?'

James smiled and rolled his eyes before driving off.

Still grinning from the familiar exchange, Leo
strolled towards the bank of revolving glass doors,
joining the very small number of shoppers coming and
going—which, on what should have been a busy Saturday morning in the height of summer, pretty much said
it all about the state of the department store.

Four storeys of glass and concrete, heading for the
knacker's yard. Mentally he dropped the price he'd had
in his head by a couple of hundred thousand.

His grandfather, he thought wryly, would be pleased
as Punch. He would have found it galling to have paid
top whack for a place he privately thought should have
belonged to him fifty years ago, had Tommaso Gallo
been prepared to honour the deal he had promised.

Strolling away from the revolving doors towards the
store guide by the escalator, Leo gave some thought to
the tales about the now legendary feud that had been
part and parcel of life as he had grown up.

Two friends—both from Italy, both talented, both
seeking to make their fortunes in Ireland. One small,
dilapidated shop, up for sale at a knockdown price. But
sitting on a slice of street that both Tommaso and Benito

had fast recognised would be worth a lot in years to come. The drift of business hadn't quite reached that part of the city then, but it would.

They could have done the sensible thing and gone into business together, but instead they had tossed a coin after way too many drinks. Winner to take all. A drunken handshake had sealed the bet that would prove the unravelling of their friendship—for Benito had won the toss, fair and square, only for his one-time friend to go behind his back and snap up the property before Benito had been able to get his finances together.

Bitter, Benito had retreated to London where, over time, he had made his own vast fortune—but he had never forgiven Tommaso for his treachery. Nor had he ever stopped wanting that one department store, which he really didn't need because he had quite enough of his own.

Leo knew that he could have worked a little harder to dampen his grandfather's desire to have something that no longer mattered, all things considered, but he loved his grandfather and, much as he didn't believe in emotions overriding common sense, he had to admit that something in him could understand the need for some sort of retribution after such an act of betrayal.

And also, from a practical point of view, it would certainly work in Leo's interests to have the place. Dublin would be an excellent addition to his own massive portfolio of companies. He had already agreed with his grandfather that once the store was back in Conti hands he, Leo, would do with it as he wished, with the proviso that the name Conti replaced Gallo.

Leo had argued with his grandfather, wanting him to allow him to pay for the purchase himself. Because there was no way he intended to leave it as a cumbersome department store, however iconic it had once been.

That sort of sentimentality wasn't for him. No, Leo wanted the place because he liked the thought of finally getting his foot into Dublin—something long denied him because he had never found the perfect property to set down roots.

Along with his own start-up companies Leo had acquired a string of software and IT companies, which he had merged under one umbrella and continued to run while simultaneously overseeing Benito's empire by proxy. He had only a handful of outlets for his highly specialised merchandise, where expert advice was on hand for the elite group of medical, architectural and engineering giants who used what he had to offer.

This site would be perfect for expanding his businesses into a new market.

His thoughts far away, he was already indulging in the pleasurable exercise of planning how he would use the space to its best advantage.

Naturally it would have to be gutted. Wood, carpet and dowdy furnishings might have worked back in the day—although to be fair Leo wasn't sure *when* that day might have been—but as soon as he got his hands on the store they'd have to go. God knew, the place was probably riddled with rising damp, dry rot and termites. By the time he was through with it, and the 'Gallo' sign had been unceremoniously dumped, it would be unrecognisable.

He looked around, wondering which decrepit part of the store he should hit first—and there she was.

Standing behind one of the make-up counters, she looked as out of place as a fish in a bookstore. Despite the fact that she was surrounded by all manner of war paint, in expensive jars and shiny compact holders, she herself appeared to be devoid of any cosmetics. Frowning at an arrangement of dark burgundy pots on the glass counter, and needlessly repositioning them, she was the very picture of natural, stunningly beautiful freshness, and for a few seconds Leo actually held his breath as he stared at her.

His libido, which had been untested for the past three weeks, ever since he had broken up with his latest conquest after she'd started making unfortunate noises about permanence and commitment, sprang into enthusiastic life.

Leo was so surprised at his reaction that he was hardly aware that he was staring like a horny teenager. Not cool. Not *him*.

Especially when the leggy girl he was staring at was definitely *not* a Page Three girl and even more definitely *not* the sort of woman he was attracted to.

She was tall and willowy, from the little he could make out under the cheap store uniform, and she had the sort of wide-eyed innocence that was always accompanied in his head with the strident ringing of alarm bells. Her skin was smooth and satiny and the colour of pale caramel, as though she had been toasted in the sun. Her hair was tied back, but the bits escaping were a shade darker than her skin, toffee-coloured with strands of strawberry blonde running through it.

And her eyes…

She abruptly stopped what she was doing and looked up, gazing directly back at him.

Her eyes were green—as clear as glass washed up on a beach.

The kick of sexual attraction, a lust as raw as any-thing he'd ever felt before, shot through him like a bolt of adrenaline, and Leo felt himself harden in immedi-ate response. It was fierce enough to take his mind off everything that had hitherto been occupying it.

His stiffened shaft was painful, and he had to adjust his position to release some of the pressure. As their eyes tangled he thought that if she kept looking at him like that, making him imagine what it would be like to have that succulent full mouth circling the throbbing, rigid length of him, he would soon be desperate for release.

He began walking towards her, every hunting in-stinct inside him honing in on his prey. He'd never wanted any woman with such urgent immediacy be-fore and Leo wasn't about to ignore the pull. When it came to sex, he was a man who had always got what he wanted—and he wanted this woman with every fibre in his body.

The closer he got to her, the more stupendously pretty she was. Her huge eyes were almond-shaped, fringed with very dark lashes that seemed to contradict the colour of her hair. Her lips, parted, were sensuous and full, even though their startled-in-the-headlights expression was teasingly innocent. And her body...

The unappealing, clinical white dress, belted at the waist, should have been enough to dampen any man's ardour, but instead it sent his imagination into frantic overdrive and he caught himself wondering what her breasts would look like, what they would taste like...

'Can I help you?' Maddie's heart was beating like a sledgehammer, but her expression was studiously po-lite as she met the stranger's openly appreciative gaze.

Man sees girl. Man is attracted to girl. Man makes beeline for girl because he has one thing on his mind and that's getting her into bed with him.

Maddie was used to that response from the opposite sex. She hated it.

What was even more galling was the fact that this particular man had, just for a second, aroused something in her *other* than her usual instinct to slam down the shutters hard the minute she saw a come-on situation on the horizon.

In fact, for a second, she had felt a stirring between her thighs—a tingling, tickly *melting* that had horrified her.

'Interesting question,' the man murmured, positioning himself directly in front of her.

The look in her eyes seemed to amuse him.

'Are you looking for make-up?' Maddie asked bluntly. 'Because if so you're in the wrong department. I could always point you in the right direction.'

In response, the man randomly picked up a jar from the precarious display she had been fiddling with earlier and twirled it in his hand.

'What's this if not make-up?'

Maddie removed it from him and swivelled it so that the label was facing him. 'Regenerating night cream, targeting a woman in her sixties,' she said crisply. 'Are you interested in buying it?'

'Oh, I'm *interested*,' he said, in a tone laced with innuendo.

'Well, that's all I'm selling, so if it's not what you're *interested* in you should probably keep moving.'

Maddie folded her arms. She knew she was blushing. She also knew that her body was misbehaving. Once upon a time, it had misbehaved before, and she still had the scars to show for that. A repeat performance wasn't on the cards—especially not with some arrogant guy too good-looking for his own good.

'Are we cutting to the chase, here?' Leo purred, rising to the challenge and liking it. 'Who's to say I'm not...*interested*...in that very expensive pot of cream for my mother?'

'Oh!' Maddie flushed. She'd misread the situation.

At this rate, sampling how things worked on the shop floor was going to get her precisely nowhere—because she clearly had no idea about effective salesmanship. But then she'd never stood behind a counter selling anything in her entire life.

Yet again she wondered whether she was doing the right thing. *Was* she? Three and a half weeks ago she'd received the startling news that she was the sole beneficiary of a bequest that included a department store, a house, and various assorted paraphernalia—courtesy of a grandfather she had never seen, nor met, and never really known existed.

Having been struggling to make ends meet, and living the sort of disastrous life she had never imagined possible, she had already been asking herself what direction she needed to take to wipe away the past couple of years of her life, or at least to put it all in perspective, and *wham*—just like that, she'd received her answer.

She'd arrived in Ireland still barely able to believe her good fortune, with big plans to sell the store, the house and whatever else there was to sell, so that she could buy herself the dream that had eluded her for so many years.

An education.

With money in the bank she would be able to get to university, an ambition she had had to abandon when her mother had become ill four years previously. She would be able to throw herself into the art course she had always wanted to do without fear of finding herself begging on street corners to pay for the privilege.

She would be able to *make* something of herself— and that meant a lot, because she felt that she'd spent much of her life being buffeted by the winds of fate, carried this way and that with no discernible goal propelling her forward.

But she'd taken one look at the store and one look at the house she had inherited—full of charm despite the fact that it was practically falling down—and she'd dumped all her plans to sell faster than a rocket leaving earth. Art school could wait—the store needed her love and her help *now*.

Anthony Grey, the lawyer who had arranged to see her so that he could go over every single disadvantage of hanging on to what, apparently, was a business on its last legs and a house that was being propped up only by the ivy growing around it, had talked to her for three hours. She had listened with her head tilted to one side, hands on her knees, and had then promptly informed him that she was going to try and make a go of it.

And that, first and foremost, entailed getting to know what it was she intended making a go of. Which, in turn, necessitated her working on the shop floor so that she could see where the cracks were and also hopefully pick up what was being said by the loyal staff who suspected that their jobs might be hanging in the balance.

A couple of weeks under cover and Maddie was sure she would be able to get a feel for things.

Optimism hadn't been her companion for a very long time and she had been enjoying it.

Until now. She'd jumped to all sorts of conclusions and screwed up. She pinned a smile to her face, because the way too good-looking man staring down at her, with the most incredible navy blue eyes she had ever seen in her life, looked rich and influential, even though he was kitted out in a pair of faded black jeans and a polo shirt.

There was something about his lazy, loose-limbed stance, the way he oozed self-confidence, the latent strength of his body...

She felt it again—that treacherous quiver in the pit of her stomach and the tickling between her thighs—and she furiously stamped it down.

'Your mother...' She picked up the pot and squinted at it. 'She'd love this. It's thick, creamy, and excellent at smoothing out wrinkles.'

'Are you just reading what's written on the label?'

'I'm afraid I've only been here a short while, so I'm just getting the hang of things.'

'Shouldn't you have a supervisor working with you in that case? Showing you the ropes?'

The man looked around, as though expecting said person to materialise in front of him. He was *enjoying* himself. It was clear this stranger was so accustomed to women fawning over him that the novel experience of a woman not caring who he was or how much he was worth was tickling him pink.

He rested flattened palms on the glass counter and Maddie shifted back just a little.

'Dereliction of duty,' he murmured.

'I beg your pardon?'

'You need to tell your boss that it gives the customer a poor impression if the people working on the sales floor don't really know what they're talking about.'

Maddie stiffened at the criticism. 'You'll find that everyone else on the shop floor has worked here for a very long time. If you like, I can fetch someone over here to help you in your…your quest for the perfect face cream for your mother.'

'I'll let you in on a little secret,' the man said with a tinge of regret, his navy blue eyes never once leaving her face. 'I lied about wanting the cream for my mother. My mother died when I was a boy.' Sincere regret seeped into his voice. 'Both my parents, in actual fact,' he added in a roughened undertone.

'I'm so sorry.'

Maddie still felt the loss of her own mother, but she had had her around for a great deal longer than the man standing in front of her had had his. Her father had never been in the picture. He'd done a runner before she was old enough to walk.

Maddie knew scraps of the story that had brought her mother from Italy to the other side of the world. There had been an argument between her mother and the grandfather Maddie hadn't ever known which had never been resolved. Harsh words exchanged and then too much pride on both sides for any resolution until time took over, making reconciliation an impossibility.

Her mother had been a strong woman—someone who had planted both feet and stood her ground. Stubborn… But then she'd had to fight her way in Australia with a young baby to take care of. Maddie felt that her grandfather might have had the same traits—although she had no real idea because she'd never been told. Secretly she wondered if the grandfather she'd never met might have attempted to contact her mother, only to have his efforts spurned. Parents were often more forgiving with their children than the other way around.

Her eyes misted over and she reached out and impulsively circled the man's wrist with her fingers—and then yanked her hand back because the charge of electricity that shot through her was downright frightening.

He raised his eyebrows, and for a second she felt that he could read every thought that had flashed through her head.

'No need,' he murmured. 'Have dinner with me.'

'I beg your pardon?'

'I'll pass on the face cream. Frankly, all those wild claims can't possibly be true. But have dinner with me. Name the place, name the time...'

'You're not interested in buying anything in this store, are you?'

Maddie's voice cooled by several degrees, because he was just another example of a cocky guy who wanted to get her into bed. She'd been spot-on first time round.

'And as for a dinner date... That'll be a *no*.'

Dinner with this man? How arrogant was he?

Her eyes slid surreptitiously over him and she understood very well why he was as arrogant as he was. The guy was drop-dead gorgeous.

Lean, perfectly chiselled features, dark hair worn slightly too long, which emphasised his powerful masculinity rather than detracting from it, a tightly honed body that testified to time spent working out, even though he didn't look like the sort of man who spent much time preening in front of mirrors and flexing his muscles. And those eyes… Sexy, bedroom eyes that made her skin burn and made her thoughts wander to what a dinner date with him might be like…

She forced herself to conjure up the hateful memory of her ex—Adam. He'd been good-looking too. Plus charming, charismatic, and from the sort of family that had spent generations looking down on people like her. Well, that whole experience had been a learning curve for Maddie, and she wasn't about to put those valuable lessons to waste by succumbing to the phoney charm of the man in front of her with his sinful good looks and his *I could make your body sing* bedroom eyes.

'Should I be?'

Maddie frowned. 'What do you mean? What are you talking about?'

'*Should* I be interested in buying anything here? Look around you. This is a department store that's gone to rack and ruin. I'm staggered that you would even have contemplated working here in the first place. The job situation in Dublin must be dire for you to have settled on *this*—and you've obviously had no on-the-job training because there isn't enough money to go round for such essentials as training programmes. I'm pretty sure that if I looked I'd find an array of out-of-date merchandise and demotivated sales assistants.'

'Who *are* you?'

Maddie looked at him narrowly. Was she missing something?

Leo met her stare and held it. He'd planned on a little incognito surveillance and he was going to stick to the plan—bar this little detour which, he thought, he could very well use to his advantage. She'd turned down his dinner date but he wasn't fazed by that. Women never said no to him for very long.

Although...

He frowned, because *this* particular woman didn't seem to fit the mould.

'Just someone browsing,' Leo said smoothly, and then he added, truthfully, 'I don't get to this part of the world very often and I wanted to see this store everyone seems to know about.' He looked around him. 'I'm less than impressed.'

The woman followed his gaze and said nothing, perhaps because she'd noticed those very same signs of disrepair. She seemed to suddenly realise that he was still watching her, his eyes narrowed.

'I can see that you agree with me.'

'Like I said, I haven't been here for very long—but if you're looking for something to buy as a souvenir of the store, there's an excellent selection on the second floor. Mugs, tote bags, lots of stuff...'

Leo suppressed a shudder at the image of tackiness created in his head. Had the place moved with the times *at all*? Or had progress being quietly sidelined as Gallo's money ran out?

He had a satisfying vision of what the place would look like under his dominion. High-tech, white glossy counters and open, uncluttered spaces, glass and mirrors, ranks of computers and accessories waiting to be explored—no irritating background elevator music and salespeople who actually knew what they were talking about.

'If you have lots of money to spend, then we offer a range of leather handbags which we manufacture ourselves to the highest possible standard. They're Italian, and really beautiful quality.'

'Sadly,' Leo said, easily giving voice to the lie, 'my finances would struggle to stretch to one of your leather handbags.'

She nodded. He didn't seem like the sort of broke, wrong-side-of-the-tracks kind of guy she had encountered during her life, but it was a fact that a good-looking man could look expensive in anything.

'But I could probably stretch to one of those tote things you mentioned...'

'Second floor.'

'Take me.'

'Come again?'

'I want you to do your sales pitch on me.'

'I'll be honest with you,' she said flatly, 'if this is another way of trying to get me to have dinner with you, then you can forget it. I won't be doing that.'

Leo wondered whether she would have had a change of heart had she known his true worth. Most definitely, he thought, with his usual healthy dose of cynicism. That said, he was a man accustomed to getting what he wanted—and the more he talked to her, looked at her, felt the pleasurable race of his pulses and the hard throb of his libido, the more he wanted to rise to the challenge of breaking down whatever walls she felt she had to erect.

For once, work and the reason he was in this sad excuse of a store had been put on the back burner.

'You're very arrogant, aren't you?' he murmured, watching her carefully as the slow burn of anger turned her cheeks a healthy pink. 'Do you think that you have what it takes to make a man keep banging on a door that's been firmly shut in his face?'

'How *dare* you?'

'You forget—I'm the customer and the customer is always right.'

His grin was meant to take the sting out of his words and make her realise that he'd been teasing her.

'That's better,' Leo said as her anger appeared to fade, then glanced at his watch to find that time had flown by. 'Now, why don't you show me this souvenir section of yours?' He raised both hands in mock surrender. 'And you can breathe safe in the knowledge that there'll be no more dinner invitations. You say you're new here... You can practise your sales patter on me. I'm just passing through, so you won't have to worry that I'll be gossiping behind your back with the locals, telling them that the new girl at the big store doesn't seem to know the ropes.'

Maddie looked down, but she wanted to smile.

So far she'd made no friends. It would take time for her to integrate. This interaction almost felt like a breath of fresh air. Naturally she wasn't going to be an idiot and go on any dates with any strangers—especially good-looking ones who obviously knew how to say the right things to get a woman's pulse racing. But he had valid criticisms of the store, and she would need those—would need to find out what customers thought when they entered. Customers would look at the place through different eyes from hers. It might actually be a good idea to encourage his opinions.

So he'd asked her out... Maddie didn't spend time staring at her reflection in mirrors, but she knew that she was attractive. It was something that had dogged her, for better or for worse. Certainly for worse when it had come to Adam, but she couldn't let the memory of that determine every single response to every single guy who happened to look in her direction. Could she?

Besides, setting aside the killer looks, the man still staring at her wasn't a rich creep—like Adam had been, had she only had the wisdom to see that from the very start. This guy was more tote bags than soft Italian leather.

Maddie felt a thrilling little frisson as she breathed in deeply and said, 'Well, I guess I could get someone to cover for me just for a little while.'

Brian Walsh was in charge of the store temporarily, and he was the only one who knew who she really was. He had worked there for over twenty years and was keen to see the store become again the place it had once been, so he was fully on board with her decision to evaluate the store undercover for a short period of time while she worked out a way forward.

'My…er…my boss is just over there. I'll ask his… er…permission…'

'Your boss?' he asked, his interest clearly pricked by the knowledge.

'Mr Walsh. If you don't mind waiting…?'

'I have all the time in the world,' he said expansively, deciding on the spot to tell James to head back to the hotel, just in case he found himself staying longer than anticipated. 'I'll be right here when you return.'

CHAPTER TWO

LEO COULD HAVE taken the opportunity to probe her about her boss—the man Leo would soon be putting through the wringer—but that, he decided as he watched her heading back towards him, could wait. His grandfather wanted the store *yesterday*, but tomorrow or the day after was just fine with Leo. There was no doubt in his mind that he would secure the store—so what was the harm in letting himself be temporarily distracted?

She moved like a dancer, her body erect, looking neither right nor left as she walked gracefully across the department store floor. He suddenly realised he didn't even know her name, and he put that right the minute she was standing in front of him again, her fresh, floral scent filling his nostrils and turning him on.

'Shouldn't you be wearing a name tag? Something discreetly pinned to your nice white outfit so that I know exactly who to complain about if you sell me overpriced face cream that makes my girlfriend's skin break out in spots?'

'You have a girlfriend?'

The interest in her voice pleased him.

'Because,' she went on quickly, the flush on her cheeks betraying the fact that she'd realised her slip, 'if you do, then you should have said. I could have pointed you in the direction of a whole different selection of face products.'

Leo glanced down at her. She was tall. Much taller than the women he was fond of dating. 'Alas, that's a position that's waiting to be filled,' he murmured. 'And it has to be said that, as presents go, anti-wrinkle, anti-ageing face cream wouldn't make a good one for any of the women I've ever dated in the past. So, what *is* your name?'

'Madison.' She kept her eyes professionally forward as the escalator took them up one floor and then the next, up to the second floor, where any visible effort at revitalisation had been abandoned. Here, the décor begged to be revamped and the displays craved some sort of creative, modern overhaul.

'Madison…?'

'But everyone calls me Maddie. We're here.'

She began walking towards the back of the floor while Leo took his time strolling slightly behind her, taking in the store's rundown appearance. He was surprised spiders weren't weaving cobwebs between the dated merchandise—although he had to concede the sales assistants they passed were all wearing cheerful smiles.

Attention distracted, he glanced at the arrangement of souvenirs, all bearing the Gallo logo. Absently he toyed with a canvas bag, and then he looked at her seriously.

'You're not Irish.' He dropped the bag and it dangled forlornly on its rack.

'No. Well, not exactly.'

Maddie looked at him and felt her insides swoop.

Even standing at a respectable distance away from her, he still seemed to invade her personal space. He was so…*big*…and his presence was so…*suffocatingly powerful*. Curiosity gripped her, and she wondered who exactly he was and what he did.

Where did he live? Why would a man like this be dawdling on a Saturday morning in this particular department store?

Alarmed, she cleared her throat, but for some reason found herself unable to drag her eyes away from his stunningly beautiful face. 'Australia. I'm Australian.'

'You've come from the other side of the world to work *here*?'

'Are you always so…so *rude*… Mr…? I don't even know your name!'

'You mean just in case you want to complain about me to your boss? My name is Leo. Shall we shake hands and make the introductions formal?'

Maddie stuck her hands firmly behind her back and glowered. 'I feel I can speak on behalf of my boss when I say that it's always useful to hear constructive criticism about the store, but your criticism isn't at all constructive, Mr… Mr…'

'Leo.'

She glanced around her and winced slightly at what she saw. 'I believe,' she said carefully, 'that the owner of the store passed away a short time ago. I don't think much has been done in terms of modernisation in recent years.'

'I have some experience of the retail market,' Leo said absently, his eyes still wandering over the shelves and wares around them.

Suddenly those eyes were back on hers and a smile tugged at his lips.

'This isn't a dinner invitation, but I see that there's a coffee shop on this floor. If you'd find it helpful, I could give you a few pearls of wisdom...'

'You've run a department store in the past?'

Leo grinned, his deep blue eyes lazy and amused. 'I wouldn't quite put it like that...'

'I get it.'

Maddie knew all about doing menial jobs to earn a living. She also knew all about the way people could look at someone attractive and misconstrue their place in the great pecking order. *She* didn't look like someone who should be mopping floors in a hospital on the outskirts of Sydney. If she had, her life would never have ended up taking the unfortunate twists and turns that it had.

She met his direct gaze and smiled.

That smile knocked Leo sideways. Just like that he wanted to drag her away from the tasteless display of goods, pull her into the nearest cupboard and get underneath that prim and proper clinical white get-up that wouldn't have gone amiss on a dental assistant. He wanted to kiss her raspberry-pink lips, crush them under his mouth, feel her tongue lashing against his, and then slowly, bit by bit, he wanted to get up close and personal with her body.

He suppressed a groan. She was still smiling, and his erection was getting more rigid by the second. He had to look away to catch his breath and focus on something innocuous. A stack of Gallo-label tea towels did the trick.

'You do?'

'I can understand. I've had lots of menial jobs in the past. Trust me—it's heavenly being here.' Maddie said it with the utmost sincerity.

Somehow they were walking away from the souvenir section towards the café.

Leo turned to her, his fingers hooking in the waistband of his low slung faded jeans.

'I'm thinking you'll probably get in trouble with the boss if you take time out to have a coffee with me.'

'I expect I might.'

The fierce antagonism that had filled her when she'd thought he was after her seemed to have evaporated. Somehow he'd managed to put her at ease. And Maddie wasn't sure whether to be alarmed at that development or happy about it.

Ever since Adam she'd made a habit of practically crossing the road to the other side of the street every time she spotted a man heading in her direction. Events had conspired to turn her social life, sparse as it had been, into a no-go zone. Men had been the first casualty of her experience with Adam and friends had fast followed, because her trust had been broken down to the point where it had all but disappeared.

But should she allow those experiences to follow her all the way to the other side of the world?

This was going to be her new home, and the last thing she wanted to do was to commence life in her new home as a crazy lady recluse.

Yes, warning bells had sounded when she'd first met Leo. But he wasn't rich, and as soon as she'd told him to back off he'd backed off. He wasn't from the area. He wasn't going to be around. He was also happy to talk to her about the store, and she could use a little impartial advice—even though he wouldn't know the reasons behind her wanting to hear what he had to say.

Sometimes nomads and wanderers—people who fell in and out of jobs— picked up life lessons along the way, and the very fact that they were streetwise gave them an added insight into life. Taking the path of adventure, untethered by the ropes that held most people down, brought its own rewards.

And, my word, was the man sexy...

She looked at him, every nerve-ending in her body tingling as he settled his fabulous eyes on her and allowed the silence between them to stretch to breaking point.

'How long are you going to be in this lovely city?' Maddie asked a little breathlessly, and Leo shrugged.

'Perhaps not even overnight,' he mused, harking back to his original plan and marvelling at the speed with which it had changed course along the way. Just as well as he was a man who could think on his feet and adapt.

At any rate, he'd probably seen everything there was to see with regard to the condition of the store, short of tapping on walls and peering into cupboards. He knew enough to settle the thorny matter of how much he should offer for the place and how fast he should move. He presumed the boss was ready to throw the towel in.

But that wasn't what was putting a smile on his face at the moment.

'It might be nice to…er…to have dinner with you.' Maddie blushed and glanced away.

'May I ask what's prompted the change of heart?' Leo asked wryly. 'Five minutes ago I was the devil incarnate for suggesting any such thing.'

'I…' Maddie took a deep breath. 'I haven't been in

Ireland long, and it would be…nice to have some company for a couple of hours. I've more or less stayed in on my own for the past few weeks.'

With her looks, Leo mused, solitude would have to be her chosen option—because she'd only have to step foot out of her front door and company would be available in any direction she chose to look.

But then that probably wasn't the sort of company she had in mind. The sort of company that came with strings attached. The sort of company she had assumed *he'd* been offering— and, frankly, her assumptions had been dead-on.

Leo wasn't surprised that her looks had made her wary of the attention she got—had made her guarded and cynical about what men wanted from her. It wasn't that different from the way his vast wealth had made *him* guarded and cynical when it came to the opposite sex.

He wasn't looking for commitment and he didn't do declarations of love. He enjoyed impermanence when it came to women.

Leo didn't know whether he might have gone down the normal route of marriage, two point two kids and a house in the country—or in his case several houses in several countries—if bitter experience hadn't taught him the value of steering clear of relationships.

His grandparents had been very happily married. His parents, he had been told, had likewise been very happily married—indeed, had been on something of a second honeymoon when a lorry, going too fast in bad weather, had slammed into their little Fiat and crushed it.

He had not been blighted by poor childhood memories or affected by warring parents or evil stepmothers. Alcohol, drug abuse and infidelity had been conspicuously and thankfully absent from his life. *His* cautionary tales stemmed from an altogether different source.

He shrugged aside this lapse in concentration as well as any niggling of his conscience, by reminding himself that he was as honourable as they came, because he was always, *always* upfront in his relationships. He told it like it was.

Sex and fun, but no cosy nights in front of the telly, no meeting the parents.

That said, he was a one-woman man, and any woman he dated would have all of him—if only for a limited amount of time. Largely, he was the one who usually called it a day, but he was perfectly happy if it were the other way around. He was the least possessive man he knew and he liked it that way.

He looked at Maddie in silence for a little while. She'd rebuffed him first time around, and he was sharp enough to pick up that little comment about how it would *'be nice to have company for a couple of hours'*.

'Tell me where you live,' he drawled. 'I'll pick you up.'

'You have a car?'

'I have a fleet of them,' he said, which was the absolute truth. 'Of course they're garaged in London—which is where, incidentally, I have my penthouse apartment—but if you tell me which make you'd prefer, I'll make sure it's delivered to me in time to collect you later. So, what's it to be? Ferrari? Range Rover? BMW? Or maybe something classic like an Aston Martin...?'

Maddie burst out laughing. The guy had a sense of humour and she liked that. She hadn't laughed for a long time, but now she was laughing so hard that tears came to her eyes.

Finally, sobering up, she said, still smiling, 'I'll meet you somewhere. I think there are some cheap and cheerful restaurants we could go to...'

'I'll give you my number. Text me. I'll meet you there at...what? Seven? What time does this place close?'

'Seven would be great. Now, really, I have to go...'

'One last thing...' Leo looked at her seriously. 'You need not fear that I'll make a pest of myself. I won't.'

Maddie reddened and an errant thought flashed through her head,

What would it be like if you were to make a pest of yourself...?

'Good,' she said nonchalantly. 'Because I've a lot going on in my life at the moment and the last thing I need is...is...'

'Fending off a nuisance?'

'I was going to say that the last thing I need is a relationship.'

At which Leo was the one to burst out laughing. He looked at her with his midnight-blue eyes, 'Trust me—relationships don't ever feature on my agenda. See you later, Maddie.'

And he was gone, leaving her standing as still as a statue, even though inside her everything was weirdly mushy, as though she'd just stepped off a death-defying rollercoaster ride and was struggling to get her bearings.

She spent the remainder of the day in a state of low-level excitement. She told herself that this wasn't a date. Not really. This was dinner with someone who'd made her laugh—because the alternative was yet another night in, going through the mountains of paperwork her solicitor had left for her, trying to work out the best approach to take when she went to see the bank manager for a loan the following week.

She was twenty-four years old! Where was the harm in acting her age? She couldn't remember the last time she'd felt young, and the tall, dark, handsome stranger had made her feel young.

And he wasn't going to be sticking around.

By seven that evening, as she stood outside the cheap Italian restaurant where they'd arranged to meet, the nerves which had abated at some point during the day were back in full swing.

She smoothed down the front of her shirt. No one could accuse her of dressing to impress. She was in a pair of ripped jeans, some flat navy ballet pumps and a tee shirt that was a little tighter than she liked and a little shorter than she might have wanted, exposing a sliver of flat brown skin. It, like the jeans, was faded and worn.

She'd had a brief flirtation with designer dressing. Adam had liked to see her in expensive gear and, much against her will, he had encouraged her into wearing clothes that he'd bought for her—expensive, slinky silk outfits and high, high designer heels.

He'd enjoyed the way everyone's heads had turned whenever she'd stalked into a room and Maddie had gone along with it, albeit reluctantly, because she'd loved him and had wanted to please him.

She'd sent the entire lot back to his flash apartment when their relationship had crashed and burned, and had promptly returned to the sorts of clothes she'd always felt comfortable in.

Leo, at least, would appreciate her choice of clothing, since they came from the same side of the tracks.

Feeling more buoyant, she pushed open the door to the trattoria and looked around, hoping she'd arrived before he had because then she could have a drink to steady her nerves, and also hoping that she hadn't, because to arrive early might suggest that she was desperate for male company. More than that—desperate for *his* company.

Nursing a drink at the very back of the restaurant, Leo had spotted her immediately. How could he not? The entire restaurant had spotted her at roughly the same time. Every male head swung round. Mouths fell open. In fairness to her, she didn't seem to notice any of this as she peered around her, squinting into the semilit depths of the trattoria, which was noisy, packed and uncomfortable.

In a room full of pale faces her honeyed tan stood out, as did her hair, flowing in a wavy mane over narrow shoulders almost down to her waist. Leo half stood and she walked towards him, weaving a path through the crowds until she was right in front of him.

'Been here before?' he asked, and when she shook her head he nodded and scanned the room. 'Do you think we'll be able to have a conversation or should we resign ourselves to shouting?'

'It's cheap and cheerful. And I hear that the food's good.'

She slipped into a chair and tried not to drink in his masculine beauty. She'd just about managed to convince herself that he couldn't possibly be as striking as she remembered, but he was even more so. He radiated a dynamism that made her shiver with awareness, and his exotic colouring only added to the potent appeal of his good looks.

Very quickly Maddie had a glass of wine to calm her nerves, even though common sense told her there was nothing to be nervous about.

Certainly he was sticking to the script. If his original dinner invitation had set her antennae onto red alert, actually being here with him was doing the opposite, dispelling any misgivings she might have been harbouring about his intentions.

He was charm itself. He chatted about the many countries he had visited—which made sense because he was obviously a guy who lived for the present and absorbed whatever adventures life had to offer. It was something she really admired. He was witty and insightful, and she found herself laughing out loud at some of his anecdotes, barely noticing the antipasti he had ordered for them to share.

'I envy you,' she said truthfully as plates were cleared, glasses refilled and bowls of pasta placed in front of them. 'I've never got to travel. I would have loved to, but my mum and I barely had enough to make ends meet and we would never have been able to afford it. I guess it's a lot easier when you only have yourself to consider, and I suppose you could always pick up jobs here and there to pay your way...'

'I do try and get myself an honest day's work when I'm abroad,' he said, almost uncomfortably. 'Tell me why you've run away from Australia.'

The abrupt change in the conversation caught Maddie off-guard and she stiffened—her natural response whenever she thought about her past. What would this complete stranger think were she to tell him the truth? He might be an adventurer, living off the land and shunning responsibility, but that didn't mean that he wouldn't be judgemental if she were to share her story with him.

The *whole* of her story.

Maddie found that she didn't want him to think badly of her. 'Whoever said anything about running away?' she hedged lightly, winding long strands of spaghetti around her fork and avoiding eye contact.

Leo raised his eyebrows wryly. He sat back and gave her the benefit of his full attention, which was enough to make her blush furiously.

Her glass-green eyes drifted to his forearms, strong and muscled and sprinkled with dark hair, and she wondered what it would be like to be touched by them, to have his hands roam and explore her body. Her heart picked up speed and she licked her lips, panicked by the way her body was insisting on slipping its leash and running wild.

'Well,' Leo drawled, his voice a low murmur that made the hairs on the nape of her neck stand on end, 'looking at the facts: you're on the other side of the world, without a network of fellow travelling friends, and working in a job that can't really be classed as career-building. You haven't mentioned anything about studying, so I'm thinking that's not relevant. Which leads me to think that you're running away from something. Or someone. Or both.'

Maddie laughed, but the tide of colour in her cheeks was more vibrant now. 'My mum died,' she said, twirling the stem of her wine glass and then pausing as he filled it with more wine. 'I'd spent some time looking after her. It was very unexpected. Bad luck, really. She broke her leg, and it was a very complex break, but it should have been okay.' She blinked furiously. 'Unfortunately the operation turned out to be a fiasco. She was confined to hospital for much longer than anticipated and then she needed a great deal of further surgery. Every time she felt she was back on her feet something would go wrong and back she would have to go.'

'How old were you when all this happened?'

'Just before my twentieth birthday,' Maddie admitted.

'Must have been tough.'

'Everyone goes through tough times.' She brushed off any show of sympathy because she was close enough to tears already. But she could see sympathy in the deep navy eyes resting on her and that was weird, because her very first impression of him had been of a guy who was as hard as nails.

Something about the predatory way he moved, the cool, lazy self-assurance in his eyes, the arrogant set of his features… But then being wary of the opposite sex, suspecting the worst before the worst could happen, had become a way of life for her.

'*You* must have,' she said lightly, blushing. 'Gone through rough times, I mean? Or at least had one or two hairy encounters! Isn't that part and parcel of being a nomad? A side effect of living life as an adventurer?'

Leo was enjoying the tinge of colour staining her cheeks. *Australia*. Hence the golden hue of her skin. Next to her, the other women in the restaurant seemed pale and anaemic.

He shrugged, adept as always at evading any sort of real sharing. 'Sisters? Brothers?' he asked. 'Anyone out there for you when your mother was ill?'

'Just me.' Maddie realised that somewhere along the line food had been eaten and plates cleared away. She couldn't remember when exactly that had happened. 'My mother was from here, actually…'

'Ireland?' Startled, Leo caught her eyes.

'As a matter of fact, she was.'

Maddie wondered what he would think if she told him that she was the owner of the very store he had been busy criticising only hours before. He didn't look the type to scare easily, but men could be funny when it came to women being higher up the financial pecking order than they were.

'Hence you're returning to your motherland…?'

'I thought it made sense. I wanted to get out of Australia after…after everything…'

Leo didn't say anything, but his gaze was penetrating.

The waiter had approached, asking them what they'd thought of their meal, pressing them to sample some dessert but they both politely declined, asking only for the bill.

Maddie reached into her rucksack, withdrawing a wallet and extracting notes.

'What are you doing?' he asked with a frown.

'Paying my way.' Maddie looked at him, surprised at his reaction to what she thought was perfectly obvious.

'When I go out with a woman *I* foot the bill,' Leo asserted.

She stiffened. 'Not this woman. I pay my half. That way I'm in no one's debt.'

'The price of a cheap Italian meal doesn't put you in my *debt*.' Leo tossed a handful of euros onto the silver platter—enough to cover the meal with an overly generous tip.

'Have you never met a man who knows how to treat a woman?' he asked, rising to his feet.

Maddie thought of her ex-boyfriend. Adam had *loved* paying for things for her. Flowers, chocolates, expensive meals out—but with the lavishing of gifts had come the manacles of control, the compulsion to turn her into something he wanted. And underneath all that had been his superiority—thinking that by making her into his doll he was asserting ascendancy over her, owning her.

But she'd remained the girl from the wrong side of the tracks, and sure enough that was something that couldn't be buried under gifts and presents. Inevitably she'd learned a valuable lesson in the perils of ever thinking that someone rich and well-connected could ever be anything but condescending and manipulative.

Anyway, all those wildly expensive gifts had made her feel horribly uncomfortable, and she certainly didn't like the idea of Leo or anyone else paying for her. As she had found to her cost, there was no such thing as a free lunch.

'Are you asking me if I've ever met a man who knows how to reach for his wallet and buy me pretty baubles?' She slapped a few euros on the table. The waiter was going to be very happy indeed with the extravagant tip coming his way. 'Because if that's what you're asking then, yes, I have. And it didn't work out for me. Which is why I prefer to keep things simple and pay my way.'

She stood up, and Leo shrugged, but his deep, dark eyes were assessing and thoughtful.

'Far be it from me to tear someone away from her closely held principles,' he murmured.

They headed outside, walking in the balmy summer air in no particular direction.

Except with some surprise Maddie realised that her

legs were somehow moving towards the honeycomb of streets where her grandfather's house was. It was on the outskirts of the city centre and, whilst the location was to die for, the house was not nearly as grand as some of the others and was in a state of disrepair.

The old man, so she had been told by her solicitor, had gradually downsized over the years, more and more as his healthy income had been whittled away to next to nothing, lost in gambling dens and crates of whiskey.

Maddie had wondered whether the absence of his only child had perhaps fuelled that spiral of despair, which had made her even more motivated to accept the challenge that had been bequeathed to her.

She stole a sneaky glance at the towering, over-the-top, sex-on-legs guy next to her and suddenly felt ashamed that she had snapped at him for trying to be a gentleman when in all likelihood he couldn't afford it any more than she could.

'Sorry,' she apologised sheepishly. 'You hit a sore spot there.'

Leo paused and looked down at her, holding her eyes with his, his expression speculative.

Her body trembled as she gazed back up at him, her eyes undoubtedly betraying her want.

'I'll be on my way,' Leo murmured, breaking eye contact to stare up the road which was still as busy now as it had been hours previously. New York was not the only city, it would seem, that never slept.

'Leo…' Maddie breathed.

She wanted him. She didn't know whether it was because she was lonely or because the unexpected stirring of attraction had reminded her that she was still young after all. Maybe he had unlocked some realisation that she couldn't remain a prisoner of her past for the rest of her life.

Or maybe he was just so damned sexy that she simply couldn't resist the pull of raw, primal lust.

Two ships passing in the night, she thought…

'Do you want me to kiss you?' Leo asked on a husky murmur, still not touching her.

'No!' Thank goodness they had managed to find themselves in a quiet corner of the otherwise busy street.

'Then you need to stop looking at me like that.'

'Like what?'

'Like you want to eat me up…like you'd like *me* to eat *you* up.'

'Leo…'

'We're both adults,' Leo delivered on a rough undertone, 'so I'll be honest. You're spectacular-looking and I want you more than I can remember wanting any woman for a long time. I want to touch you. I want to taste you…*everywhere.* But I don't do long-term and in this instance we're talking a one-night stand. A one-night stand to remember, but still a one-night stand. If you don't like that, then walk away, Maddie.'

'I always promised myself that I would never have a one-night stand,' Maddie said, by rote, but her body was certainly not walking away. Indeed, it was staying very firmly put.

Leo shrugged, holding her gaze.

Confusion tore through Maddie, because she wasn't lying. She'd never been a one-night stand kind of girl. From a young age her looks had attracted attention, and she had learned very fast that attention from the opposite sex more often than not bypassed the important stuff—like getting to know her, giving her credit for having a brain and seeing beyond the fact that she was, in Leo's words, 'spectacular-looking'. Adam had only served to cement those lessons in her head.

But...

But, but, but...

'Would you like to come in for a cup of coffee?' she hazarded.

Leo's eyebrows shot up. He refused to let her hide behind the cup of coffee scenario. 'You want me. And I want you. I'll accept the offer of coffee, but I'm not interested in a push-pull game of one step forward followed by two back.'

'Nor am I.' She tiptoed forward, filled with a sense of heady daring, and brushed his perfect mouth with hers.

CHAPTER THREE

AFTER A BRISK walk away from the city centre, they found themselves in a tree-lined avenue filled with mansions.

'I don't live in one of these.'

Maddie didn't look at him as she said this but her cheeks were flaming red. She wasn't lying, but she was uncomfortably conscious of the fact that she had played fast and loose with the truth.

She consoled herself with the obvious justification that launching into a garbled, long-winded explanation about inheritances and distant relatives was not relevant, given they were not going to be in one another's lives for longer than this one night.

Which brought her full circle, questioning what she was doing. A one-night stand? Her proud, stubborn, fiercely independent mother would have had a heart attack on the spot, because she had drummed it into her only child that you had to choose carefully when it came to giving your body to someone else.

'You'll make mistakes,' Lizzie Gallo had told her daughter, 'but it's still important to go into every relationship thinking it could be the one.'

Reflecting now on that advice, Maddie had to concede that her mother might not have ended up where she had, if she'd a one-night stand with Maddie's father rather than running away with him, only to be abandoned the second he realised that the fortune he'd banked on Lizzie's father providing wasn't going to be coming his way.

Disinheritance in the name of love hadn't been his thing. He'd stuck around just long enough to determine that there was going to be no reconciliation between daughter and rich daddy, and then he'd scarpered.

'But I gave it my all,' her mother had said, in one of her rare moments of honesty—because Lizzie Gallo had never been someone to moan and look backwards. 'And, for me, that was the main thing. You climb into bed with someone for a few hours and, believe me, you won't feel great when you climb out of it so that you can do the walk of shame back home.'

Well, that, Maddie reflected, sneaking a sidelong glance at the virtual stranger who had somehow managed to ensnare her into jettisoning all her principles, had not exactly served her well when it came to Adam.

She'd thrown herself into her relationship with Adam and given it everything. She'd been so in love with the idea of being in love that she'd missed all the warning signs of a relationship that had been made anywhere but in heaven.

This time… *This time she knew what she was getting into.* No girlish fantasies and romantic daydreams about Prince Charming only for Prince Charming to turn out to be Mr Toad. She was with a guy who wasn't interested in laying down roots and who'd made it perfectly clear what he wanted.

She felt the bloom of longing between her legs and swallowed down a rush of powerful excitement.

The houses they were passing now were getting smaller and finally, at the end of the elegant road, she swung up the only drive that was unkempt.

'Not what I expected.' Leo glanced at the edifice of what must once upon a time been a rather charming cottage but now looked like something from the Land that Time Forgot.

'What did you expect?'

Maddie unlocked the front door and pushed it open into a hallway that was worn, but still carried the hallmarks of the house it had once been. A flagstone floor, an old-fashioned wooden umbrella stand, a sturdy banister leading upstairs, and worn paintwork with great big discoloured patches from where she had removed dark, lugubrious paintings.

'Something a little less…imposing…'

'Does that bother you?'

'Why should it?'

She'd turned to look at him and Leo could not resist the urge to touch, to feel the smoothness of her cheeks. He ran an exploratory finger over her striking cheekbones and then outlined the contours of her full mouth. When she shivered, he smiled with undisguised hunger.

'I don't know how you do what you do to me,' he murmured, trailing his finger down towards her tee shirt and stopping just where the shadow of her cleavage began, 'but all I want to do right now is rip those clothes off you and take you right here, right now…'

Maddie's breath caught in her throat and she unconsciously arched her body up, so that her small, high breasts pushed towards him in a bold invitation for him to touch.

It was clear she wanted him—so badly that it was a physical ache—and her whole body shuddered as he slipped his hand underneath her tee shirt and then cupped her breast briefly, before tugging the lacy bra to one side so that he could feel the softness of her skin and the tightness of her nipple.

Positioning himself in front of her, Leo reached under the shirt with both hands, pushing up her bra completely to free her breasts, all the while keeping his eyes firmly pinned to her face, because he was absolutely loving the mesmerised hot burn of desire in her bright green eyes.

He stroked her nipples with the pads of his thumbs and her lips parted on a sigh of pleasure.

'Liking it?'

'Don't stop.'

If *he* couldn't understand the primal urgency of his reaction to her, then the same must be said for her. Leo didn't need any more encouragement. He removed her tee shirt in one easy movement and for a few seconds just looked at her perfect breasts, no more than a handful, tipped with rosy buds. His erection was hard and heavy and painful, and he had to breathe in deep to control the fierce sweep of lust.

Her head was flung back, her eyes closed as he slowly backed her towards the staircase, and then she was standing, holding on to the banister, her body beautifully positioned for him to attend to her naked breasts.

Which he did.

He suckled one stiffened nipple, licking and teasing it with his tongue, while he readied the other for his ministrations with his fingers. Her soft moans were doing all sorts of wonderful things to his body and right now he couldn't get enough of her. It was remarkable.

Leaving one throbbing nipple behind, he gave a repeat performance on the other, drawing it deep into his mouth while his tongue continued to torment her.

Maddie reached down to undo the button of his jeans but Leo stopped her.

He would have liked to kid himself that this was to do with his mastering the situation and taking his time, but he had to admit wryly to himself that it was more to do with breaking things off briefly so that he could gather his crazily scattered self-control. Any more touching and he would have to fight not to explode without warning.

'What about the coffee?' he reminded her shakily, and Maddie blinked, roused from her slumberous enjoyment and clearly desperate for him to carry on touching her.

'Coffee?' she parroted weakly, which actually made Leo burst out laughing.

He kissed her on the mouth—a teasing, gentle kiss that made her squirm because it was so tender.

'You can't promise a man coffee and then renege on the offer...'

'Of course not.'

Maddie grinned and slung her arms around his neck to pull him towards her, before shuffling her heated body back into her bra and tee shirt while he watched with avid, devouring hunger. Then she reached out to pepper his sexy mouth with little, darting kisses before slipping her tongue in.

'You're a witch,' he muttered against her mouth.

In the grip of a situation he could never have predicted, Leo followed her towards the back of the house and into a kitchen which, as with the rest of what he'd seen, was in dire need of attention.

'Tell me what you're doing in a house like this,' Leo said, his eyes returning to her slender frame, her back towards him as she made them both mugs of coffee.

Maddie stilled, but only for a fraction of a second, and then she said lightly, 'I can thank a relative for the use of this house. It's not much, but it's brilliant just having a roof over my head. Even a roof that springs leaks when it rains. You should see the corridor upstairs. I've learned just where to position the buckets and pans.' She spun round to hand him his mug. 'You never told me whether it bothers you?'

'I believe I said, why should it?'

'Well,' she said, 'you might get it into your head that I'm a snob because I happen to be staying in a house like this. You might think that we're from different worlds and that wouldn't be the case.'

'Whether it's the case or not,' Leo countered smoothly, 'it doesn't really matter, does it? We're here to enjoy ourselves, not analyse one another's beliefs.'

He let her lead the way into a sitting room, where she opted for switching on one of the lamps on the table rather than the overhead light.

The sofas were deep and squashy, but there were an abnormal amount of small tables and a feeling of a place stuck in time. Leo had no idea where this helpful relative was, but he sincerely hoped he was on an urgent spending spree to replace the furnishings.

He placed his cup on one of the many tables and sat next to her on one of the sofas. Sprawled against one end, he crooked his finger and she wriggled up towards him. He swivelled her so that she was lying against him, her back pressed against his body, nicely pushing down on his hard, thick erection.

He took her coffee from her and settled them both into a more comfortable position.

If this house belonged to him, he decided on the spot, he would put a floor-to-ceiling mirror on the opposite wall for an occasion such as this, when he would have enjoyed nothing better than seeing their reflection, watching the little changes on her beautiful face as he touched her.

He removed the tee shirt once more, wondering why she had bothered to put it back on in the first place when it was always just going to come off again, and cupped her breasts in his hands, playing with them and working her up bit by bit.

Looking down at her, with the soft, flowery scent of her hair filling his nostrils, Leo could see the faint blush of her skin. She was still golden, but paler where her clothes had protected her from the sun, and against the paleness of her breasts her nipples were deep rosy discs. He badly wanted to suckle on them again but he would wait.

At least, he reflected wryly, he wasn't on the verge of coming prematurely. A temporary reprieve from the unthinkable.

She was wearing button-fly jeans and he began undoing the buttons one at a time until he could glimpse her white knickers.

'Take your jeans off,' he murmured. 'I'd do it myself, but my hands are otherwise occupied at the moment.'

He moved them back to her breasts as she wriggled

out of the jeans, leaving her underwear on. The jeans fell to the floor and then she squirmed a little, like a cat preparing to settle on a feather cushion. She reached up and began to turn around, but he stilled her with his hands, silently instructing her to stay as she was.

'I'm hanging on to my self-control by a thread,' he confided. 'Turn around and I won't be able to predict what might happen. Your eyes do something to me...'

Maddie laughed. And as his hand moved from breast to ribcage she parted her legs and whimpered with pleasure.

'I wish I could see your face,' Leo said huskily, and she laughed again.

'I'm glad you can't. I'd be embarrassed.'

Leo grunted. He was accustomed to flamboyant women who weren't easily embarrassed—and certainly not by antics between the sheets. He found her diffidence a turn-on.

Gently he slipped his hand underneath her white panties, felt the brush of downy hair against his fingers, and as he slid one long brown finger into her wetness he couldn't prevent a groan of pure sensual enjoyment.

He found the throbbing bud and she moaned as he began playing with it. She parted her legs further and he cupped her briefly before carrying on with what he'd been doing.

Maddie feverishly wriggled out of her underwear. Sensation was tearing into her and she found that she could scarcely breathe. When she looked down to see the motion of his hand as he played with her she wanted to pass out from the sheer erotic pleasure of it.

Letting go of the last of her inhibitions, she gave herself over to what he was doing to her body. The rhythmic stroke of his finger against her core was taking her higher and higher, and her breathing was staccato as she moved against his hand, bucking and arching, and then, as a low groan was wrenched out of her, she toppled over the edge and spasmed against his fingers in an orgasm that went on and on and on, an unstoppable spiral of pleasure.

Spent, Maddie lay against him, her eyes closed. And then, as she floated back to earth, she turned around and straddled him.

Strangely, she wanted him even more now, but she would have to give her body time to recover. She linked her fingers behind his neck and smiled.

'That was…wonderful…' she confessed.

Leo placed his hands on her waist. He could very nearly circle it with his hands, she was so slender.

'For me too.'

'I'm sorry. It was selfish of me to come, but I couldn't hold off.'

'I didn't want you to,' he said roughly. 'You'll come again, but next time I'll be deep inside you, and when you do I'll see your face and watch when the moment happens.'

Maddie blushed, because she had never indulged in this sort of sexual banter, and the way he was holding her gaze was such a turn-on that she could almost come again without him having to touch her.

She buried her face against the side of his neck and felt a pang, something so sharp and painful that she almost drew back—a pang of *missing*.

She swept that silly feeling aside and this time *she* was the one to touch and arouse. She stripped him of his clothing, looked in wonder at his impressive size. When she ordered him to lie back on the sofa, he laughed.

'I guess we should migrate upstairs to a bed,' she said at one point, in between licking him, teasing him with her mouth and kissing him.

'Why? This sofa does very nicely indeed...'

Was that because a sofa somehow carried on the one-night stand theme? Maddie wondered.

She lost herself in the wonder of his glorious body. He was lean and strong, and the dark hair on his chest felt like a declaration of masculinity. He was all man. Alpha male to the very core of him. And she couldn't get enough of his body, of *him*.

This time things moved at a pace that allowed them to explore one another as if they had all the time in the world.

Where his fingers had been, his mouth explored. He tasted between her thighs until she was practically crying for him to take her all the way. She tasted him as well, and his hands curled into her long hair, directing her so that she knew what felt good for him—although she quickly discovered that she seemed to have a second sense for pleasing him.

Or maybe it was simply the fact that the novelty of this situation had made him so aroused that whatever she did and wherever she touched it would have the same dramatic effect.

Leo wanted to hang on. Hell, it shouldn't be a problem. He was a master when it came to self-control in the bedroom—a guy who knew how to orchestrate sex and time it to perfection. Not so now.

He couldn't hang on. He couldn't find his self-control or *any* kind of control for that matter. He couldn't think. He just had to have her before he splintered into a million pieces.

Whatever world he had entered, it was in a different league from anything he had ever experienced in his life before. Savage want poured through his body in waves that carried the ferocity of a sledgehammer, knocking him for six and wiping out his formidable composure.

The disconnect between his head and his body had never been greater, but all that was forgotten when he thrust into her and felt her body arch up to meet his, moulding and fitting against him as smoothly as a hand fitted into a glove personally made for it.

Leo felt as though she had been fashioned for him, her body so perfectly tuned to his that the straightforward business of making love was elevated into an experience beyond description.

His climax was the most powerful he had ever had, and he only surfaced when it was over and his body was well and truly spent. Then he turned her to face him so that their naked bodies were pressed together.

'Maddie…' The self-control that had been left at the front door now made its presence known. 'We didn't… *hell…*' He groaned aloud and raked his fingers through his hair. 'It's never happened before but I didn't use protection. Are you…this is not be a question I should ever have to ask…but are you on the pill?'

Slumberous green cat's eyes focused on him and she frowned. 'No. No, I'm not.'

How could she have taken a chance like this?

But then, he thought, she'd taken it for the same reason he had. Because lust had been so much more overwhelming than common sense. Their bodies had been on fire and the notion of protection hadn't even registered.

'There's not a lot we can do now…' She sighed and squirmed, the heat of his body already scattering her thoughts and fogging her mind.

Leo was astounded at the speed with which he was prepared to immerse himself in that vague assurance, but he reminded himself that he had friends who'd taken months, and in a couple of cases years, to achieve what he'd always been scrupulous in protecting himself against.

He placed his hand on her waist and shifted. This was a one-night stand. Right about now he should be getting his act together and telling her that it was time for him to go.

'Maddie…'

'I hope you have a good trip back to…to…'

Maddie was quick to silence any little voice that wanted to promote something more than the one-night stand that was on the table.

She feathered a kiss on his mouth. 'To wherever it is you're going next.'

'London.' Leo cleared his throat. 'I'm going straight down to London from here.'

'Well, in that case I hope you have a very good trip back down to London. Say hi to Big Ben for me.' She traced an idle pattern on his hard, naked chest.

'It's possible,' Leo inserted gruffly, without batting an eyelid, 'that I could explore Dublin for a few days, however…'

It could work. He could do a few background checks on the store, fill in the blanks. It wouldn't hurt. And while he was here he could wine and dine this woman who had just made the earth move for him. Wine and dine on a budget, of course, bearing in mind that she thought that he was in the same financial bracket as she was.

The thought held a great deal of appeal for Leo. He wasn't ready to chalk this heady experience down as a one-night stand. He was a man who had always had everything he wanted—and certainly every woman he had ever wanted. Having it all, however, had definite downsides…one of which was a jaded palate. Maddie, from the other side of the world, was like a dose of pure, life-giving oxygen.

Doubtless this sense of exhilaration would wither and die after a couple of nights, because they had absolutely nothing in common and sex, however earth-moving, was just sex after all, but in the meantime…

He pulled her back towards him, wanting her all over again. The more he thought about it, the more appealing was the idea of playing truant for a couple of days, of taking time out from life as he knew it.

'Really? You might stay here for a while?'

Maddie felt as though a cloud she hadn't even realised had been there had suddenly lifted to reveal a bank of unexpected sunshine.

'There's nothing more exciting than exploring a new city.'

'That would be lovely,' Maddie said.

Leo grinned. 'Let's go for a bit more enthusiasm,' he encouraged,

Maddie hesitated. She'd geared herself up for a one-night stand, at the end of which she'd wave goodbye to this stranger who had filled her life with joy for a brief period of time. A two-or three-night stand posed a few more issues, and top of the list was the fact that she hadn't been entirely truthful with him.

'Okay.' She smiled and wriggled against him, and felt the jut of his erection against her belly. 'I'd really like that. But there's something I feel I ought to tell you...'

'Please don't tell me that you're a married woman with a jealous husband hiding in a cupboard somewhere.'

'Of course I'm not!'

'Then what?'

He gently pushed her onto her back and rose up over her, nudging her with the tip of his throbbing erection, swiping it slowly against her core until she was losing track of what she wanted to tell him.

No condoms? No problem. There were myriad ways to pleasure one another without penetration, and in the morning they could stockpile protection.

'I'm not quite who you think I am. I mean, you've got the major details, but there's one little thing... You know the store?'

'The store?' Leo nudged a little further into her moistness, clearly only half registering what she was saying because his body was already taking over and deciding where its priorities lay. *Not* in a heart-to-heart discussion.

'Where we met.'

'Ah, *that* store. What about it?'

'I'm not actually a shop assistant there.'

'No? Shoplifter?'

Maddie laughed. In the short space of time she'd known him she'd found that he had a brilliant sense of humour.

'Owner, as a matter of fact.'

Leo stilled and slowly pulled back so that he was staring down at her, scarcely believing his ears. *'Owner...?'*

Sensing the shift in atmosphere, Maddie laughed nervously. 'It doesn't matter,' she assured him. 'I haven't suddenly turned into a crashing snob.'

'Owner? Please explain. I'm all ears.'

He slung his muscular legs over the side of the sofa and began getting dressed.

Maddie didn't try to stop him—if he wanted to leave then he should leave—but she felt as though a black hole had opened up beneath her feet.

'My grandfather owned the store.'

Maddie was beginning to feel uncomfortable now, and disadvantaged because she was still naked and vulnerable. So she too began to sling on the clothes she had earlier discarded in such excited haste.

From having their bodies pressed so closely together they might have been one, they now stood awkwardly in the dimly lit living room, facing one another like sparring opponents in a ring.

Maddie had no idea why or how this had occurred. But past experience had taught her the wisdom of developing a tough outer shell, and it came into effect now, stiffening her backbone, lending defiance to her glass-green eyes.

'I'm listening,' Leo said softly.

'I never met him. He and my mother fell out before I was born and never reconciled. But when he died a short while back he left the entire store to me, along with this house.' She gestured to encompass the building in which they were standing. 'And a few other bits and pieces. I'm sorry I wasn't upfront with you, but I didn't see the point of launching into my back story.'

'I had no idea…' Leo said slowly.

Tommaso's granddaughter. This changed everything, and already the shutters were falling into place. He didn't believe in age-old enmities, and he certainly didn't believe in taking sides in a feud in which he had played no part, but something stirred in him—a sense of injustice done to his grandfather. Was this what they meant when they said that blood was thicker than water?

That aside, he intended to buy the place—whoever or whatever stood in his way—and the woman standing in front of him now was no longer the lover he wanted to keep in his bed but his adversary in a deal he intended to close.

'I don't see that it changes anything.' Maddie winced at the plea hidden behind her words.

'It changes *everything*,' Leo said softly, heading towards the door.

'Because you've found out I'm not impoverished?' Maddie threw at him, half following, but only because she was so angry and bewildered.

'You'll find out why soon enough…'

Pride held her back and killed the questions rising fast inside her, but when she heard the front door slam she sagged onto the sofa.

She didn't care. He meant nothing to her! She wasn't going to beat herself up about her decision to go to bed with him and she certainly wasn't going to waste time asking herself what he'd meant by that parting shot.

CHAPTER FOUR

MADDIE HAD HUNDREDS of steps to take and a veritable long and winding road to go before she could ever begin to return the store she had inherited to its former glory. But, despite the fact that she had no formal training in business, she discovered she had an innate talent for the work and enjoyed the straightforward process of planning a way forward.

If you could call climbing a mountain straightforward…

Certainly over the next fortnight work occupied her mind to the point where she could almost come close to forgetting about her encounter with Leo.

Almost but not quite.

In the quiet hours she spent in the house, meticulously working out how to pull it apart so that she could put it together again, he invaded her thoughts like a stealthy intruder, finding his way into all the nooks and crannies of her mind.

She had no regrets about what they had done. She had taken a risk and lived in the moment and she had enjoyed every minute of it. But she had to ask herself whether she had somehow inherited her mother's gene for always picking the wrong man. First Adam and then Leo.

With finances for moving forward with the store's

overhaul now in place, thanks to a sympathetic bank manager who was as keen as she to see the store resume its rightful place as the leading light in the city centre, there was just one hurdle left to overcome.

'There's a buyer waiting in the wings,' her lawyer, Anthony, had told her three days previously, 'and he is prepared to be hostile to get the store.'

'Over my dead body.'

The house had been remortgaged, dozens of valuable paintings and artefacts which had been bought when her grandfather had been living in boom times had been sold, and sufficient capital acquired to support the loan from the bank. Maddie had got little sleep while putting it all together, and she wasn't going to have the rug pulled from under her feet at the last minute.

But Anthony had told her that with a good enough offer on the table he would find it hard not to advise a sale. He had then gone into the complexities of the money she was being lent, and interest rates and time frames, and Maddie had zoned out, focusing only on the fight that lay ahead of her.

More than ever, as she fought to get things in order, it seemed to her that she was doing something the grandfather she had never met had intended her to do.

She'd never known what it was like to have any sort of extended family. Her mother had been tight-lipped on the subject of her own family, which had been diminished to just her father by the time she had left for Australia with the man who would eventually turn out to be precisely the fortune-hunter she had been warned against.

Maddie had always secretly felt saddened at the thought of her grandfather perhaps trying to keep in touch. Who knew? Her mother had died relatively young. Perhaps if she hadn't she would have eventually swallowed her pride and returned to England.

Just being in the house where her grandfather had lived had warmed Maddie towards the man she had never known. In her mind he had been a kindly gentleman who had been big-hearted enough to leave all his worldly goods to her.

No one was going to deprive her of her legacy and everything that was wrapped up with it. This slice of her past had completed her—filled in the dots about where she had come from. It wasn't just a business deal for her. It was a reconnection with the past she had never known, and it was giving her a sense of direction and purpose in a life that had always held a lot of unanswered questions.

Which didn't mean that she wasn't feeling sick to her stomach as she and Anthony strode into the imposing glass house on the outskirts of the city centre where a meeting of the buyer's lawyers had been arranged on neutral territory.

'Where are we?' she asked nervously as they entered the building and were faced with grey modernist splendour.

She'd dressed in her most serious outfit, bought especially for the occasion—a sober grey suit, a crisp white shirt and very high black heels that would give her the advantage over any hostile bidder because in her heels she was at least six foot tall. Provided she didn't sit down, she was sure she would appear a sufficiently commanding figure and be able to announce to the assembled crowd that she wasn't someone to be messed with.

She could tell that Anthony, who only just reached her shoulder, approved of the tactic.

She had also pinned her chaotic hair back into a neat chignon that had taken for ever to do and had almost made her late.

'We're within the hallowed walls of one of the most influential companies in the country,' Anthony adjusted his tie a little nervously. 'Mostly building and construction, but recently diversifying into electronics and smart installations in new-builds.'

'Impressive.'

'Our buyer obviously has a lot of connections if he can snap his fingers and arrange for the meeting to be held here. I've done my background research and he's made of money.'

'Well, money isn't everything. Maybe he's trying to intimidate us.'

Maddie told herself that scare tactics weren't going to work, but she was as nervous as a kitten as they were escorted along a cool marble walkway that circled an impressive courtyard, which was visible through banks of glass. When she looked down she could see a few figures dotted around a central fountain, enjoying the sunshine even though it wasn't yet lunchtime.

Then, looking ahead, she saw opaque glass, and as their escort stood aside she entered a long, brightly lit room. *Quite a few men*, was Maddie's first thought. All kitted out in regulation charcoal-grey business suits.

Except one.

One man dominated the space around him and was head and shoulders taller than every other man there. He was not wearing a suit. Black jeans and a black polo shirt, short-sleeved. The epitome of *I don't give a damn what I wear* cool.

Leo.

* * *

Leo had been expecting her, but he still felt a sizzle of something as she walked into the room, towering over the short man next to her, so strikingly pretty that every single male in the room fell silent.

His white teeth snapped together in a surge of something primitive and proprietorial.

He'd had her. She was his.

His woman.

Except, he thought as logic reasserted itself, she wasn't, was she? She was his opponent. And, as such, no time must be wasted on thinking about all her delectable, distracting assets.

His midnight-deep eyes roved broodingly over her. She was wearing the most boring outfit in the world, but even that couldn't stand in the way of his imagination which had already taken flight.

He mentally stripped her. Got rid of the dreadful suit and the prissy top. Unhooked whatever bra she was wearing and pulled down her panties. Why had she tied her hair back? The urge to see it spilling in colourful splendour over her slender shoulders was so powerful that he had to steady himself.

It had been over a fortnight.

He hadn't been braced to walk away from her but walk away he had—because, with him, business always came first. Always had, always would.

There wasn't a woman in the world who could damage that sacred pecking order.

But he knew that he was getting excited just looking at her and thinking about what she'd felt like under him and over him and touching him and inviting him to touch her everywhere.

That sign of weakness enraged him, and he broke the mental connection by stepping forward and walking straight towards her.

It took willpower she had never known she'd possessed to hold her ground and not fall back as the one man she had never expected to see again sauntered towards her.

What on earth was going on?

Maddie knew that whatever impression she was making it wasn't that of a confident businesswoman in charge of the situation. More a gaping goldfish, stranded and gasping for air.

'I don't understand…' She stared at Leo, her breathing rapid and shallow, as though she'd been running a marathon, her nostrils flaring as she inhaled the clean, woody scent of him.

She'd thought about him so much that she could scarcely believe that he was standing in front of her—especially as none of it seemed to make any sense.

Leo didn't say anything for a few seconds, and when he did speak it was to tell the assembled crowd that they could leave.

'I'll deal with this privately,' he said dismissively. 'When the transaction is agreed you can prepare the required paperwork.'

'Maddie… Ms Gallo…' Anthony approached her with an expression of concern—only to meet Leo's cool navy eyes.

'Maddie will be as safe as houses with me,' he said, addressing the much shorter man in a kindly voice that made Maddie's teeth snap together in anger because it was just so…*patronising.*

'Now, wait just a minute…er…'

'Leo. You know my name. You just don't know my surname. Conti.'

'You're…you're…' Her brain was moving at a snail's pace.

Yes, Conti was the name of the man who was planning on pulling the rug from under her feet. Maddie vaguely recalled that much sinking in when Anthony had explained the situation to her. She'd been far too wrapped up in feeling angry that someone could just swan along and try and snatch the store away from her before she'd even had a chance to do something with it.

The men in suits were quietly leaving the room. Maddie was conscious of their departure, but only just—because she was gradually putting two and two together, and by the time the door closed on the lawyers who had come to draw up a deal she had no intention of agreeing to she was fit to explode.

'You *lied* to me!' she burst out, galvanised into action and storming over to the window, then storming back towards him, hands on her hips, eyes spitting fury.

Leo stood his ground and met her tempestuous gaze head-on, without so much as flinching.

'Did I?' he drawled, moving towards the table at the back of the room to pour himself a glass of water, taking his time.

'You let me think that you were…you were… What were you doing in my store in the first place? Oh, don't bother answering that! You'd come along to have a look at what you wanted to get your hands on!'

'I like to see what I'm sinking my money into, yes.'

'I'm leaving!' She spun round, shaking, and began heading towards the door.

She didn't get there, because two strides in she was stopped by his hand on her arm.

Her whole body reacted as though a shot of high-voltage electricity had been injected straight into her bloodstream. The heat from his hand would have been enough to stop her dead in her tracks even if no pressure had been applied.

Her body remembered his and that terrified her.

'How could you have lied to me!'

Leo met her vivid eyes. 'Stop playing the crucified martyr, Maddie. Have you conveniently forgotten that you weren't exactly forthcoming about who *you* were when we were climbing into the sack together?'

'That was different!'

'How? Enlighten me?'

'I thought you might have been scared off because I happened to own the store! *Ha!*'

'Is that right? And if I'd told you who I was…would we have ended up in bed?'

'I'm getting the picture, Leo. You're rich and powerful and you were scared that a poor little salesgirl might have decided you were a promising candidate to get involved with…'

'Is that so far-fetched?'

Maddie stared stubbornly at him, too angry to give an inch on this, even though she could see that he might, conceivably, have a point.

Not that it mattered! What mattered was that he was not going to get his rich, powerful paws on the store her grandfather had left her.

'Well?' Leo pressed, his tone making it clear he felt she was equally guilty of deception to suit her own purposes.

'If you knew me *at all,*' Maddie snapped, 'then you

would know that the fact you're rich doesn't work in your favour. If you'd told me from the start who you were and what you were worth I would have run a mile! I've had enough experience of rich creeps to last me a lifetime!'

Leo's eyes narrowed.

He'd loosened his grip on her arm but he was still holding her, and the look in his eyes was saying he wanted to do so much more than just hold her.

Their eyes locked and she felt a shift in the atmosphere from blazing anger to the slow sizzle of sexual awareness.

She found that she was holding her breath.

'Don't,' Maddie whispered.

'Don't what?'

'Look at me like that.'

'You mean the way you're looking at me? As though the only thing on your mind now is the thought of my mouth on yours?'

She wrenched herself free from his grasp and took a few shaky steps back.

'Don't kid yourself!'

She wrapped her arms around her body to stop herself from shaking like a leaf. He was so big, so powerful, and she was so drawn to him that she had to make a conscious effort not to stumble back into his hypnotic radius like a zombie under the spell of a master magician.

'Like I said, I don't go for guys like you!'

Guys like him?

Leo was enraged to be categorised and written off. He was even more enraged that his body was reacting to her like a sex-starved, randy adolescent when his brain was telling him to drop any pointless back-and-forth conversation and get down to business.

'That's not what you were saying a fortnight ago, when you fell into my arms like a starving person suddenly presented with a five-course spread.'

The erection pushing against the zipper of his jeans was as hard as steel and he abruptly turned away, giving himself time to get his runaway libido under control.

'I made a mistake with a rich man,' Maddie flung at him in a trembling voice. 'I got involved with someone I thought had a conscience and a moral compass and I discovered that, actually, rich people don't operate like that. Rich people are above the law, and they don't give a damn who they step on because they know they're never going to have to pay the price for what they do!'

Leo stared at her through narrowed eyes. 'You're judging me by someone you happen to have been involved with who...*what*? Did a runner? Hit on your best friend?'

'If only,' Maddie said bitterly. 'Oh, Adam White was a lot more destructive than *that*!'

She seemed to catch herself and fell silent, breathing evenly as if to stifle the emotions which had definitely got the better of her.

'It doesn't matter,' she told him coolly. 'What matters is that I'm not going to be selling you the store and I don't care how much money you throw down on the table.'

'Sit.'

'I'm perfectly fine standing.'

'Let's put our brief liaison behind us, Maddie. What's at stake here has nothing to do with the fact that we slept together. We're both adults. It happened. Neither of us knew the full story when we climbed into bed. Or should I say when we occupied the sofa in your sitting room.'

The evocative image his words conjured did nothing

to lessen the surge of his unwanted attraction. Leo carried on without skipping a beat, but he had to divert his eyes from her face. Even the fact that she was glaring at him couldn't diminish her pulling power.

'There's no point playing the blame game. Okay, so you might have run a mile if you'd known how rich I was.' He shrugged indifferently. 'And maybe I didn't advertise my wealth because I've had experience of what it's like to be targeted by women who only have one thing on their mind.'

'Oh, please,' Maddie muttered sarcastically.

Leo raised his eyebrows to look at her. 'You think I'm lying?'

'Don't pretend that you don't know how attractive you are—with or without your stupid oversized bank balance!'

Leo shot her a slow, curling smile and the atmosphere was suddenly charged. She flicked her tongue over her upper lip and the gesture was so *sexy* that Leo found himself stepping towards her.

She didn't pull back. She couldn't, because her legs had turned to lead. She almost whimpered when he was only inches away from her, but fortunately pride kicked in and instead she drew a steadying breath and tried to clear her mind from the fog enveloping it.

'Tough, isn't it?' Leo drawled huskily, and the low, velvety timbre of his voice sent shivers racing up and down her spine.

'I don't know what you're talking about.'

But she was mesmerised by his eyes and the sheer beauty of his face. He had the most amazing lashes, she thought distractedly—so long, so thick. It was just another detail to take in and store.

She balled her hands into defensive fists and made a concerted effort to drag her wayward mind back from the brink—which was a very, *very* dangerous place for it to stray.

'Oh, you know exactly what I'm talking about, Maddie. The thing our bodies are doing right now. Don't try and pretend that you don't want me to touch you right here, right now, and damn the consequences.' Then he drew back abruptly and said, his voice brisk, 'But that's not going to do. Business before pleasure, I'm afraid.'

He grinned and her humiliation was complete.

How could she have allowed herself to forget that this was her enemy? Another rich man who had lied to her? A man who wanted to take what was hers and was willing to do so by whatever means he deemed fit? A bully, in other words.

She blinked and glared and wanted nothing more badly than to wipe the grin from his face—not least because it just ratcheted up his outrageous sex appeal.

'I suppose,' Leo drawled, stepping away and sauntering towards the window, where he proceeded to glance out before returning his full attention to her face, 'your lawyer, or your accountant, or whoever that little man was who came in with you, has explained the deal that's been put on the table?'

'I didn't pay much attention to that because I'm not interested in selling.'

'Big mistake. You should have. Sentiment is all well and good, but money is what does the talking—and I'm prepared to put however much money down on the table I have to if it gets me what I want. And believe me when I tell you that my supply of cash is bottomless.'

He'd gone into that store fully prepared to pay the

least amount of money for the place he could, but he was fast revising his original plan because she was stubborn and—for reasons that frankly confounded him—she wasn't going to roll over and play dead because he wanted her to.

He felt a sense of grudging admiration, because people, as a rule, were prone to caving in to him in the face of any show of determination, such was the range of his power and influence and the force of his personality.

She, on the other hand, looked as close to caving in as his art teacher had looked when, at the age of ten, Leo had asked to be let off detention because the dog had eaten his project.

'Maddie, you could have your dream life with the money I'm prepared to offer. Frankly, as it stands, I would be handing over far more than the place is worth. Because in case you haven't noticed it's falling apart at the seams and it's lost its customer base. One more poor season and the whole house of cards will come tumbling down.'

'I've sorted out the finances and I have a business plan to get it back up and running.'

'Impressive. I had no idea you had experience in bringing ailing companies back from the brink.'

'This is more than just a game for me, Leo. I never met my grandfather and yet he placed his faith in me to transform the store.'

'The store that *he* ran into the ground because of his fondness for the bottle and the nearest gambling den.'

Maddie stiffened. If he thought that he was going to get to her by insulting her grandfather then he was mistaken. Yes, Tommaso Gallo had drunk too much and gambled away his fortune, but she was convinced that

that was because he had lost his only daughter. That was what misery could do to a person.

'Why are you so keen to have it, Leo?' She shot him a look of helpless frustration. 'Why can't you just buy something else? Somewhere else? I mean, it's a *store*. If you're sarcastic about *my* lack of business experience, then how much experience in retail do *you* have?'

She realised that she actually had no idea what he did for a living or where his money came from.

Leo was staring at her thoughtfully. Her sentiments seemed to be skewed. Did she somehow see herself as the beneficiary of a kindly old Father Christmas figure? She'd never met the old man, and clearly had no idea of the sort of person he was.

Should he break the glad tidings that Tommaso Gallo and Father Christmas had about as much in common as a rattlesnake and a mouse?

He decided that revelations could wait until another day. He pushed himself away from the window and flexed his muscles as he prowled through the vast conference room, finally sinking into one of the leather chairs and swivelling it so that it was facing her.

'I wouldn't keep it as the same type of traditional retail store.'

Strangely, despite her high heels and the fact that, standing up, she was towering over him, he had shed nothing of his dominance. If anything, she felt awkward standing, so she in turn sat at the very end of the long, walnut table.

At least she now felt more businesslike. 'What would you do to it?'

'I want a foothold in Dublin,' Leo said flatly. 'This store is exactly where I want to be and it's exactly the right size. I have a portfolio of companies and it would continue being a store, but exclusively dealing with my targeted software, adapted high-tech computers and specialised training stations.'

'An electronics shop?'

Leo frowned. 'The retail market is saturated, Maddie. Too many people are buying too many products online. You'll never find a better offer than the one I'm prepared to give you. Take it and don't fight me.'

'Surely you can source another big store to gobble up!'

'You have your personal reasons for wanting to hang on to your white elephant. I have my own personal reasons for wanting to take it from you.'

'What are you talking about?'

'You don't know much about old Tommaso, do you?'

'You *knew* my grandfather?' Confused, Maddie stared at him in consternation. 'How *old* are you?'

Leo smiled drily. 'I'm not an eighty-year-old man rescued from looking his age thanks to plastic surgery.'

'I didn't think you were.'

'And no, to answer your first question, I never met the old man.'

'Then how do you…? I don't understand.'

'My grandfather and Tommaso were friends back in the day. Did your mother never talk about what went on between them?'

'No. No, she didn't.'

'Not a word?'

'I think that part of her life was something she walked away from, and when she walked away she made sure never to look back. I knew she'd fallen out with my grandfather over her choice of partner, and had exiled herself on the other side of the world, but beyond that I really don't know anything about either of my grandparents. *Or* their friends.'

'Well, he and my grandfather were, once upon a time, very good friends. Indeed, they landed in Ireland searching for the same thing,—their fortunes.'

'What was your father called?'

'Benito. Benito and Tommaso. Two friends as tight as thieves until a simple bet tore their friendship apart.'

'A *bet*?' Maddie shook her head. She had no idea where this was heading, but her gut instinct was telling her that wherever it was it wasn't going to be her idea of a dream destination.

'One bet over a certain small shop. The toss of a coin. My grandfather won the bet.'

'But...'

'I know,' Leo purred with an undercurrent of coolness. 'You're asking yourself how it is that Tommaso ended up with the iconic store in Dublin when he lost the bet. I'll tell you how. Your grandfather betrayed Benito. While he was planning what to do with the shop Tommaso hit the bank, secured a loan and made the deal in record time—and then he put his hands up in mock surrender so that he could take his punishment safe in the knowledge that he'd got what he wanted. So you see—you have *your* reasons for hanging on and I have *my* reasons for making sure to loosen your grip. My grandfather has wanted that store for decades. It's just about the only thing he has left to want. He's never stopped trying to get it, and I intend to make sure he gets it before he dies.'

Leo thought that technically, the store wasn't *quite* the only thing his grandfather had left to want. The pitter-patter of tiny great-grandchildren's feet was also high on the old man's wish list—but that was something that wasn't going to happen.

Not given to introspection, and certainly not given to rehashing a past he wanted to forget, Leo was suddenly reminded of the one and only catastrophe that had provided him with the most valuable learning curve he had ever experienced.

Forget about deals and money and what one power broker might be saying to another power broker in order to undermine him. In the great scheme of things, how did *that* figure? No, *his* learning curve had been at the hands of a woman.

He'd been twenty-three, cocksure and confident that he knew all there was to know about women. She'd been ten years older, and what she knew hadn't yet registered on his radar. She'd been sexy, offhand, and she'd made him work. She'd made him work all the way up the aisle into a marriage that had ended before the ink on the certificate had had time to dry.

The alluring, enigmatic sexy woman he'd married had turned out to be a wily fortune-hunter who'd known just what tricks to play on a young rich kid with too much self-confidence and too little cynicism.

After two years she'd relinquished her band of gold in exchange for financial security for the rest of her life.

Leo still kept a picture of her in his wallet—because everybody needed a reminder of their youthful folly.

Afterwards, he'd wondered whether he hadn't been subconsciously ripe for the picking because his grandmother, desperately ill at the time, had been so keen for him to settle down. He'd gone into something and it hadn't been with his eyes wide open.

Thankfully his grandmother had died before she

could witness the true horror of Leo's divorce proceedings and all mention of those pitter-pattering little feet had been dropped, but Leo knew that it was something his grandfather still secretly longed for. He still nurtured a burning desire to see his one and only grandson settled with some plump homely wife who would be there to keep the home fires burning.

Not going to happen.

But number two on the list *could* happen.

'I don't believe you.' Maddie glared at him defiantly. 'The world doesn't need another electronics store. My grandfather's place adds to the history of this city and I'm never—repeat, *never*—going to sell it to you or to anyone else. And I don't care *how* much money you throw at me!'

She was furious on so many levels that she could scarcely breathe. Furious that he had tried to destroy the image she had in her head of her grandfather. But of course he would try any low trick in the book to get what he wanted! Furious that he was so unfazed by every single thing she'd said to him. And furious that he still had that stupid, *stupid* effect on her even though she absolutely *hated* him!

'Is that the sound of a gauntlet being thrown down?' Leo drawled, enjoying the hectic colour in her cheeks and wanting more than anything else to kiss her into submission in just the sort of crazy, macho way he really should have no time for.

'Yes, it is!'

'Fine.' Leo shrugged and began sauntering towards the door. 'In that case…game on.'

CHAPTER FIVE

LEO LOOKED AT the report sitting in front of him. It was slight, but significant. Three pages at most. In the week since he'd seen Maddie he'd had time to reflect on what approach he wanted to take with regard to the store.

'I won't rest until I have it.'

That was what his grandfather had declared only days before, when Leo had presented him with the obstacle in his way in the form of one very beautiful, very stubborn and ridiculously fiery girl from the other side of the world.

'It's a matter of pride. I was fair to Tommaso when he started haemorrhaging money because of the gambling and the drinking. I knew about his wife, knew how unexpected her death was and how hard it'd hit him, and I felt sorry for what the man was going through. We'd been friends, after all. But time and bitterness and pain had turned him into a vengeful old man. He would rather have seen the store fall into rack and ruin than sell it to me—even though I offered way above market price for it—just like he sliced his daughter out of his life rather than forgive and move on. Forget what the granddaughter says about hanging on to it because it's part of the city's heritage. Rubbish! Tommaso couldn't have given a damn about heritage! He refused to sell through sheer spite. He never forgave me because I refused to accept what he had done—refused to accept that he had betrayed me and I'd called him a dishonourable cheat!'

Leo was quietly pleased that his grandfather had still insisted on the purchase. Had he not insisted it was possible that he, Leo, would have shrugged and walked away because he couldn't be bothered with the fight. He would have simply bided his time, waited a couple of years until the place was collapsing—because how successful was it going to be, really, when Maddie hadn't the first idea about running a business—and moved in for the kill.

But she'd thrown down a gauntlet. That was something Leo had never been able to resist.

And more than that... The thought of Maddie being the instigator of the challenge frankly thrilled him.

He hadn't been able to dislodge the woman from his head, where she seemed to have taken up semi-permanent residence. Walking away from her might just have been more frustrating than walking away from the purchase.

And now, in front of him, he had just what he needed to get what he wanted. The trump card, in a manner of speaking. The ace of spades.

To play it or not to play it...?

He would see how their meeting went.

This time he had invited her to his own offices in London. No accountants would be present...no high-powered lawyers.

'We need to talk,' he had drawled when he had called

her two evenings previously. 'I have some information you might find of interest…'

He had heard the hesitation in her voice when she had demanded to know what he could possibly have of interest when she had already said all there was to say on the matter.

He'd had his doubts that she would show up, in which case he would be prepared to simply go and get her, but to his surprise she had texted him only a few hours ago to confirm the meeting and added,

I have something to tell you as well.

When he had tried calling her she had failed to pick up.

And now here he was, and he hadn't been so invigorated in as long as he could remember.

When his PA buzzed to tell him that his visitor had arrived and was waiting in the foyer downstairs, he relaxed back into his chair and smiled to himself, savouring the tingle of anticipation.

'Show her up in fifteen minutes.'

After all, a little bit of mind-games never went amiss…

Downstairs, Maddie was trying hard to squash the painful sensation of nausea rippling through her in little waves. It was like seasickness except far, far worse.

What did Leo want to see her about? What did he have to say that he thought might be of interest? Would he offer more money?

As things stood, Anthony was already getting cold feet about her plan to keep the store, and she'd had to endure a long, meaningful chat about the importance of at least *considering* the very generous offer Leo had made. There was only so far the very loyal investors would agree to it, he had said. In the end they were only human, and if enough money was thrown at them, they would start leaving the sinking ship in droves.

Maddie knew that she would have to be as cool as a cucumber and stand her ground. Except…

She felt another wave of nausea and knew it had nothing to do with the financial discussions ahead of her. Feeling faint now, she closed her eyes briefly and tried not to relive the shock of finding out that she was pregnant.

How *could* she have been so reckless? She'd thought the chances were slim when they'd made love, but the possibility of pregnancy had begun nibbling away at the edges of her mind. Beneath all the angst over the store, and her even greater angst at her chaotic feelings towards Leo, there had been a dragging fear that that one slip-up might have had repercussions.

Even so, she'd been convinced when she'd done a test that she couldn't be *that* unlucky. Wasn't there a limit to how much bad luck one person could have in a lifetime? Surely she'd used up her allowance?

Seemingly not.

Little did he know, but one more euro on the table and she would have to relinquish her dream of resurrecting the store and carrying on the legacy her grandfather had left her.

How could she gamble on making a success of something she had never done before when, with a baby inside her, taking a gamble was the one thing she couldn't afford to do now?

But Maddie wasn't going to think of worst-case scenarios. Not yet.

She sat.

She waited.

And she grew more and more nervous with each passing second.

If he'd wanted to intimidate her he'd chosen his venue well, because this was luxury on a scale that was practically unimaginable. Looking around her, she could tell that even the tiniest of details, like the potted plant on the smoked glass table in front of her, was pricey.

The *people* looked pricey! All young and beautiful in sharp suits, scuttling to and from the bank of elevators on a mission to make more and more money.

She jumped when someone suddenly stood in front of her and told her to follow.

She'd been sitting around for over a quarter of an hour, but instead of the delay giving time for her nerves to settle it had had the opposite effect.

'Mr Conti apologises for the delay in seeing you,' said the forty-something woman with the severe hair cut but kindly face as she preceded Maddie to one of the elevators.

Maddie very much doubted that, but she remained silent, too overawed by her surroundings and too wrapped up with what she was going to say to Leo to say anything at all.

But even in her distraught, anxious daze she couldn't help but notice the details of his vast offices—the smell and feel of money beyond most people's wildest imaginations.

The lift was a deep walnut with smoked glass, and

when it stopped they were disgorged into a huge glass space where workstations were separated by glass partitions and exotic plants. It was predominantly white, and there were a lot of sleek, wafer-thin computers on desks where everyone was hard at work. In fact, no one even glanced across as they walked away from what almost looked like a greenhouse with industrious worker bees towards a more intimate area.

The offices of the CEO were private, and concealed behind walnut and chrome doors. Nerves building to a peak, Maddic nearly turned tail and ran when they finally paused in front of them, closed at the very end of the plush, wide corridor.

'Don't be nervous.' The PA turned to her with a smile and a wink. 'Deep down, he's a lamb.' She paused. 'Well, perhaps *lamb* isn't quite the word I'm looking for, but he's scrupulously fair.'

'I'm not nervous,' Maddie lied, her teeth all but chattering.

Her stomach was in knots as she was propelled through a vast outer office—grey, white and glass—through an interconnecting door and then she was there. Standing in front of him while behind her the door quietly clicked shut.

Maddie stared. She couldn't help herself. The real-life Leo Conti was so much more powerful, so much more breathtaking than the two-dimensional one who had dominated her thoughts for the past couple of weeks since she had seen him.

Her mouth went dry and every single coherent thought vanished from her head, zapped into the ether by the devastating effect he had on her.

'Why don't you have a seat?' Leo said politely.

He wondered whether she was looking at him like that on purpose. Was she trying to turn him on?

Just like that his thoughts veered off at a tantalising tangent.

She wanted the store and, as she'd said, that *want* was wrapped up in all sorts of motivations that had nothing to do with money.

What if she'd decided that stubborn refusal and a fight was the wrong approach to get what she wanted? What if she'd decided that a more powerful weapon was sex?

The drab outfit, a replica of the one she had worn at the last meeting she had attended, certainly didn't advertise a woman prepared to bare her all as a means to an end, but strangely it was even more provocative than if she'd worn a mini-skirt and stilettoes.

Leo toyed with that pleasurable notion in the space of the few seconds it took for her to sink into a chair which was strategically slightly lower than the one in which he was sitting.

He imagined her coming on to him, offering herself to him. He pictured that interconnecting door being locked and his PA dispatched while he stripped her, very, very slowly, and took her even more slowly on his desk...on the sofa in his outer chamber...on the floor...

Sudden craving surged through him and he had to breathe evenly and focus—although even focussing he still found himself overly absorbed at a scenario he had not once considered.

Would he back off the deal in exchange for that luscious body at his disposal?

Sex and women had never—not once—come ahead of business for him, but in this instance Leo found himself giving serious consideration to breaking that sacred principle.

Angry with himself, he shook his head and looked at her coolly from under lowered lashes. 'You seem to be having a problem accepting the deal I've offered you.'

'Is that why you called me in? To go over all this? Do you think you can intimidate me if there isn't an army of lawyers and accountants around?'

Maddie wanted to sound firm and in control, and she wondered whether he could detect the nervous wobble in her voice.

She'd spent ages wondering when she should break the news of her pregnancy to him. Or even if she should tell him at all! Not only had he been a fleeting visitor in her life but he had entered it under false pretences. Was that the sort of man she wanted as an influence on any child of hers?

He might do crazy things to her body, but wasn't he just another mega-wealthy guy who believed that life was his for the taking? Arrogant? Superior? Not above stamping on other people if it suited them? Hadn't she had too much experience of men like that to invite one into her life simply because she'd happened to fall pregnant by him?

She had had enough of a shock—was now facing enough of an altered future. Did she want to further compound the situation by telling Leo?

Of course there was a chance that he might just shrug and walk away from the whole situation, but what if he didn't?

He would be around *for ever*.

The pros and cons had gone round and round in her head in the space of a handful of hours, but the reality was that she had known from the very second she had seen that pink line that there was no way she could keep the pregnancy from him.

She knew what it felt like to grow up without a father. It was not something she would recommend. Not unless she had very good reason to go down that route.

Her mother had made her choices and Maddie had known that those choices had been difficult and irretrievable. Her own father had been a bastard—a coward and a fortune-hunter.

Leo, whatever else he might be, was none of those things.

So, as she waited to hear what he had to say, for his conversation to play out before hers could begin, she knew that her nerves stemmed from her own revelations to come rather than whatever it was he had summoned her into his office to impart.

'You should have a look at his.' Leo reached towards a slender file and pushed it across the desk to her.

Business was business. That had always been his mantra. Even if she *had* agreed to see him so that she could somehow seduce him into doing what she wanted, there was no way he would succumb to the temptation. At any rate, the defiant tilt of her head was *not* the body language of a woman gearing up to use her feminine wiles on him, and Leo knew that, however pleasurable it had been to play with that tantalising thought, he would have thought a great deal less of her had she chosen to go down that road.

So what choice did he have but to play the cards in his hand?

He watched carefully as she took the file and opened it. He noted the pallor in her cheeks, followed by hot colour as she read and then re-read the report he had received a couple of days ago.

When she'd finished reading it, her head remained lowered, even though she'd quietly closed the file and kept it on her lap.

Deep-seated unease coursed through him, unfamiliar and disconcerting. Leo had no idea what to do with those feelings because he'd never had them before.

This wasn't playing dirty. This information hadn't come into his possession via bribery or blackmail. It was documented, and it had been sourced in five seconds flat by the man he'd instructed.

So why did he now feel like a cad? Why was that lowered head doing all sorts of things to his conscience?

Leo scowled. 'Well?'

'Well, what?' Maddie looked at him. Her eyes were filled with unshed tears. 'Is this why you summoned me to come and see you? I'm surprised you aren't surrounded by your army of lawyers so that they can pick me apart and then spit me out. Because that's why you've got this, isn't it? So that you can use it against me. So that you can force me to sell to you under the threat of making this information public. How *could* you, Leo?'

Leo flushed darkly. 'This information is in the public domain, Maddie.'

'That doesn't mean that you should use it to scare me into doing as you say.'

Suddenly restless, Leo rose to his feet in one easy movement and began pacing his office, finally returning to his desk, perching on the edge of it right in front of her.

'Tell me what happened.'

'Why?' Her green eyes flashed.

'Because I want to hear.'

Leo sighed and raked his fingers through his hair. It felt as though life had been a lot more straightforward before this woman had entered it. Under normal circumstances, with ammunition available, he certainly wouldn't be hanging around asking for back stories.

But he could see that she was trying hard not to cry and that cut him to the quick. The report was simply factual. There would be more to it than was written in black and white.

Maddie glared at him and hesitated. Inside, anger warred with pride. He looked as though he really wanted to hear what she had to say, but how could she trust him? This was the guy who had pretended to be a pauper because it had suited his purpose at the time.

'Please, Maddie.' Leo surprised himself but he meant it. 'What's there is the skeleton of a story. Fill it out for me.'

'How did you know what to look for?'

'I didn't. But I always do very thorough background checks on people and companies before I put money on the table and start signing papers.'

'And if you come across something dodgy you use it against them? Is that it?'

'It's standard business practice to make sure all the facts are on the table. Any fresh-faced accounts manager might have a gambling problem, and that's something that would require close scrutiny of the books. I'm not a big, bad wolf. I'm doing what anyone else would do in my situation.'

Maddie looked down at her fingers and then met his hooded gaze. 'When my mother died,' she began, avoiding sentiment and keeping strictly to the facts, 'I was all over the place. I'd had to abandon my university dreams to look after her, as I think I told you. I therefore left school with a lot of dreams but not much hope of realising any of them, or even of getting a halfway decent job.'

She drew in a deep, steadying breath and detached herself from the remembered emotion. Leo was gazing at her levelly, his expression neither sympathetic nor unsympathetic, merely interested.

'I made money doing menial stuff, and eventually found a well-paid job working for a lovely elderly lady in one of the most expensive suburbs in Sydney. I lived in—which suited me because I saved on rent. In return I took care of her, and I also helped her with an autobiography she was writing. Through her I met Adam, her grandson. He was handsome and charming and... Well, the whole package, really. Or so I thought. We began dating. I was cautious at first. I've had experience with boys wanting to go out with me because of the way...'

She blushed and he looked at her with amusement, as if he'd never heard any woman so obviously wanting to play down her attractiveness.

'Because of the way you look?' he inserted smoothly, and she gave a jerky nod.

'I really thought we had something good,' she said bitterly. 'I really believed that life was being kind to me after all I'd been through with my mum. Anyway, that's by the by.'

She gathered herself, told herself that this wasn't a confessional in front of someone who was going to give her a big bear hug before telling her that everything was going to be all right. This was a story that she wanted to relate because she refused to be defined by the cold, harsh facts without him hearing what was behind those facts.

They might be on opposite sides of the fence now, but they'd also been as intimate as it was possible for two people to get. Something inside her didn't want him to be left with the wrong impression of her.

At which thought, she firmed her soft mouth and ploughed on. 'Lacey—the lady I worked for—started getting forgetful shortly after I started with her. Small things at first, and I didn't think anything of it. Not enough for alarm bells to start ringing. But then it seemed to progress quite fast—although it's possible that I just didn't notice anything to begin with because I was in recovery from Mum's death.'

She sneaked a glance at him. Was he bored? Maybe trying to sift through the information so that he could find her weak spot? She recalled what his PA had said about him being fair and realised that, however angry she was with him, she *did* think that he was fair.

'And then?' But Leo had some idea of what was going to come, and he knew that it would all be wrapped up with the ex she had fled from.

'A very valuable necklace went missing. It was worth…well, more than I can say. Adam and his sister blamed me. I tried to tell them… I couldn't believe that the guy I'd thought I had a future with could turn on me—could believe that I was nothing more than a common thief and a liar.'

She broke eye contact and stared without blinking for a few seconds, gathering herself.

Angry at a man he'd never met in his life, and held captive by the strangest surge of protectiveness, Leo thrust a box of tissues from his drawer towards her. She snatched a few without tearing her eyes away from the wall.

She sucked in some air and crumpled the tissues in her hand, then looked at Leo levelly.

'No one believed me,' she said simply, 'and Lacey was so forgetful that no one took much notice of her at all. There was a missing necklace, and I was a poor girl from the wrong side of the tracks, so therefore there was no question that I was guilty. The police were called in and I was formally charged with theft.

'I was staring a prison sentence in the face, or at least the threat of one, when one of the police officers, having chatted to Lacey, brought in a medic. She was diagnosed with Alzheimer's. Shortly after that, by a stroke of luck, the necklace resurfaced. It had been in the pocket of one of her skirts. She must have removed it and stuck it in there when she was out in the garden. I was unconditionally cleared of all charges—but mud sticks and all I wanted to do was run away. The whole episode… I felt dirty, disgraced, even though I'd done nothing wrong. The questions…the suspicions…and then the horror of what could have happened if that diagnosis hadn't been made—if one person hadn't noticed what no one else had… It was all too much.'

She laughed shortly.

'So you were right when you said that I must have been running away from something.'

'And the ex?'

'What about him?'

'Did he come crawling back to apologise, clutching flowers and the engagement ring you were hoping he would eventually put on your finger?'

Maddie stiffened with pride. 'I broke off all contact with his entire family and with him. He got the message loud and clear that I wanted nothing more to do with him.'

'But he hurt you?'

'What do you think?'

'Then suddenly, out of the blue, you discover that you're the sole beneficiary of old Tommaso's dwindling fortune...'

'It's my chance to do something with my life, to move on, and I'm going to take it.'

Did she mean that even now that circumstances had changed? Leo had detected the shadow of a hesitation in that declaration. She said she wasn't going to cave in and sell to him. She'd shouted that from the rooftops. But there was an inflection in her voice that made him wonder just how adamant she was about that.

He'd increased his offer. The diminutive lawyer who had traipsed along in her wake must have opened her eyes to the advantages of taking what had been put on the table.

He looked at the folder, still resting on her lap, his dark eyes lazy, thoughtful, speculative.

Maddie followed that lazy gaze. It didn't take a genius to figure out that he knew just what he had to do to get her where he wanted her. She'd been exonerated of all charges, her name fully cleared, but any brush with the law would be enough to have bankers and shareholders running to the table to snatch at the deal Leo had thrown down—even if she *had* emerged as pure as driven snow from the unfortunate episode.

'You're going to use this information against me, aren't you?' she said quietly.

Leo, who had decided to do no such thing, allowed a telling silence to develop between them.

'Do you think it would be fair for all parties involved in this deal—all the people who stand to gain or lose by the decision you and I make—that they remain in ignorance of what's taken place?'

It was a valid enough question as far as Leo was concerned, even though he knew without a shadow of a doubt, as he watched the emotions flicker across her beautiful face, that he would bury the report—bury it so well that it would never see the light of day.

'I see.' Maddie stood up. 'I wonder why I expected anything different.'

'Sit down!'

'Don't you *dare* tell me what to do! I should have guessed that all rich men are exactly the same. They may talk differently and walk differently, but in the end they're all the same. They're all prepared to go the extra mile when it comes to getting what they want.'

'That is outrageous!'

'Is it? Okay, Leo, you win. I'll take whatever deal it is you want to offer. I'll accept the money and I'll go away—because the last thing I need is to start a new life over here with my past following behind me like a bad smell!'

'Stop being hysterical and *sit down*! Whoever said anything about my using this information? I admit under normal circumstances I wouldn't hesitate, but in this instance...'

Maddie barely heard a word he was saying. Her heart was beating as fast and as hard as a sledgehammer and she was breathing so rapidly that she thought she might hyperventilate.

Which was the last thing she needed in her condition.

And suddenly the whole point of this meeting surged back to her consciousness and she stared at him.

'Are you going to sit down?' Leo demanded, vaulting upright and swinging round his desk so that he was staring down at her. 'And before we go any further let's get one thing straight—I am *nothing* like that scumbag you got mixed up with! I don't lead women up any garden paths and I damn well would *never* shout guilty until proved innocent!'

'But you *would* drag my name through the mud even though I *am* innocent!'

'Have you heard *a word* I've said to you?'

Maddie stared fiercely at him. Without even realising what she was doing, she rested the flat of her hand against his chest, warding him off but wanting badly to draw him towards her.

She sprang away, shocked at how he could scramble her brains even when she was in the midst of a ferocious argument.

'I am *not* going to use any information against you, Maddie, so you can relax on that score. It doesn't mean that I won't get the store from you, because I will, but I won't be making any of this sorry business public knowledge in order to further my intentions.'

Maddie stared. Her hand still burned from where she had rested it against his chest. *She was turned on by him.* There was no ignoring the hot dampness between her thighs and the pinching of her nipples.

Maybe it was her hormones, she thought wildly. Her responses were going every which way. She had come here planning on being cool and contained, but very quickly all those good intentions had unravelled and now here she was, screaming at him and not listening to a word he was saying.

He wasn't going to use the information he had uncovered. That didn't matter, however. This meeting had disclosed something very important—something she couldn't just look away from in the hope that she might be wrong.

She still wanted Leo more than she'd ever wanted anything or anyone in her life before.

No matter what she thought of him personally, her body still craved his touch and that terrified her.

So the fighting would end.

She would hand over the store to him and she would tell him about the baby.

But once the store was his, contact would be effectively broken. She would take the money and she would sell her grandfather's house and leave Ireland for good.

Maddie didn't think that a fully paid up member of the successful bachelor club would travel far and wide to see a child he had never committed to having in the first place. She would be able to step back from something that felt a lot like fire. The life she would build would not hold the legacy she had inherited, but it would have something else—something equally important. A child. Plus, she would have more than enough money to support them both.

'You don't have to fight me for the store, Leo. I told you. It's yours for the taking. You can get your lawyers to talk to Anthony and they can sort out the sale.'

Leo took a step back and tilted his head to one side, as though listening for a noise he couldn't quite hear. Yet.

'And your change of heart stems from…?'

Maddie backed towards the door until she was pressed against it. 'I have more on my plate now than just the store.'

'Explain.' Leo took two steps towards her, the depth of his navy eyes skewering her temporarily to the spot.

'I'm pregnant, Leo.'

She stared at him and watched the colour drain away from his face. He was a man who'd been slammed by a train at full speed and was finding it hard to breathe.

The outer office was empty. Maddie could tell that much. She realised Leo must have dismissed the PA, knowing that his chat with her was going to be highly personal, involving sensitive information about her past.

'I don't believe you.'

'I'm pregnant. So you can have the damned store! I'm going now. I'll give you a chance to digest what I've said. But the store is yours and that's the main thing. Isn't it?'

With which parting shot she pulled open the door and shot out of his office, walking briskly without a backward glance towards the elevator that had earlier whooshed her up to his office.

CHAPTER SIX

MADDIE DIDN'T MAKE IT. Not quite. As he followed her into the elevator she spun round, the look on her face evidence that she hadn't heard him behind her.

'Leo...'

'You don't get to do this, Maddie.'

'Do what?'

'Detonate a bomb in my life and then make a run for it.'

'I wasn't making a run for it.'

'We're going back to my apartment and you're going to tell me in words of one syllable what the hell is going on!'

But Leo knew what was going on. He'd taken an appalling chance and now the chickens had come home to roost. She wasn't lying. She wasn't the sort. He was going to be a father, and it was a nightmare so all-encompassing that he had to absorb it in stages.

After all the lessons he'd learnt from the five-second marriage that should never have happened, and which had ended up costing him an arm and a leg and certainly a great deal of pride, he'd blithely had unprotected sex with a woman because he hadn't been able to resist.

After a decade of playing it safe, never taking

chances and avoiding anything that smelled like a honey trap, he'd blown it all with a woman he'd known for less than a day.

But, by God, the sex had been amazing.

Leo was infuriated that that ridiculous thought had the nerve even to cross his mind when what he had to deal with was the fact that life as he knew it was over.

He wondered, briefly, whether she had engineered the whole bloody mess—but that suspicion barely lasted a second. Somehow, however cynical he was on the subject of women and what they would do when it came to getting their hands on pots of gold, there was something fundamentally honest about Maddie.

His mouth twisted as he followed that thought through to its logical conclusion.

She was bone-deep honest, and while he would happily have said the same for himself—despite his ruthlessness when it came to business dealings—he knew that she distrusted him. He'd ferreted out information about her, and even though he'd told her that he wasn't going to use it, the fact that it was out there, in his possession, had awakened that distrust of him.

Added to that was the small technicality of him keeping his true identity under wraps when they'd first met, and it was little wonder that she was desperate to find the nearest exit.

Tough.

He hadn't banked on this, but he wasn't a man who dodged any bullet.

He looked at her with brooding intensity. Never had he felt so restless, and yet, confined in their ten-by-ten metal box, he had no choice but to deal with the riptide of emotions flooding through him without moving a muscle.

She was keeping her eyes studiously averted. She looked as though she would break in two if he so much as reached out and touched her.

'I'm not going to your apartment with you,' Maddie said as the elevator doors opened, disgorging them back into the foyer where she had sat earlier, awash with nerves.

'Well, sorry to be a party-pooper, but if you think you're escaping back to Dublin before we can talk about this…this…*situation* then you've got another think coming.'

'You need time to mull it over,' she said, and her voice held an urgent, panicky undertone. 'You need time to digest.'

Leo didn't bother to dignify that suggestion with an answer. Walking out of the building, he was simultaneously calling his driver and keeping an extremely watchful eye on the bombshell dragging her feet alongside him. If she was searching for the most effective way of vanishing, then she was out of luck.

To his satisfaction, he saw that James, on the ball as always, was pulling to a stop in the black Jag. Leo opened the back door and propelled Maddie in without skipping a beat.

Maddie barely knew what was happening. One minute she was racking her brains to try and think of a way of avoiding Leo and his crazy suggestion that they go to his apartment to talk, and the next minute she was somehow in the back seat of a car, which was being driven by a young man with curly dark hair and lots of gold jewellery.

She was almost distracted enough by the sight to forget *why* she was in the back seat of Leo's car. Then it slammed back into her with force and she turned to him and hissed, 'You can't do this. You can't just… just…*kidnap me*…'

'Kidnap you? Stop over-dramatising, Maddie. And instead of wasting your energy trying to fight me, just accept that I intend to have this conversation you're obviously desperate to avoid.'

'I'm not *desperate* to avoid anything! I just thought that you might need time to…to…'

'Get to grips with the grenade you've just detonated in my life?'

Maddie looked at him furiously. Conscious of the strange driver at the wheel, Maddie resorted to resentful silence—which Leo did not attempt to break.

She wished she could read what was going on in his head. What was he thinking? She'd imagined that when she broke the news he would be furious. Shocked to start with, but then furious.

She had pictured herself backing out of his office, leaving him to plot how he could get rid of her and a baby he hadn't asked for as quietly and efficiently as possible. She hadn't envisaged a scenario in which she was being driven to his apartment.

In silence.

The drive took half an hour, and then she was treated to the splendour of London at its finest as the car pulled up outside a redbrick Victorian mansion, with very precise black railings and a row of perfectly groomed shaped shrubs edging the shallow bank of steps that led up to a pristine black door.

It turned out that his penthouse apartment ranged

across the top two floors. In a daze, she followed him into a wide, ornate hallway, where a porter made sure uninvited riff-raff were kept out, into a mirrored lift and then straight up into his apartment.

The lift was obviously for his use only.

Inside, greys and creams blended with wood and dull chrome. On the walls, impressive abstract art provided splashes of colour. It was all very open-plan, and configured in such a way that the most was made of the soaring ceilings and the two floors were connected by a glass and iron staircase.

Leo was walking towards a sitting area dominated by two oversized white leather sofas and Maddie followed him.

'When did you find out?' he asked without preamble. 'And there's no point perching on the edge of the sofa as though you're about to turn tail and run. You won't be going anywhere until we've discussed this... this...nightmare.'

'It's not a *nightmare*...'

'Well, it's certainly not a dream come true. When did you find out?'

'Yesterday.'

'And your plan was to show up in my office, hand me the keys to the store, inform me that you were carrying my child and then what? Head for the hills? Disappear under cover of darkness?'

Maddie reddened because, roughly speaking, he wasn't too far from the truth.

Eyes narrowed, Leo said coolly. 'It's not going to happen.'

'Which part?' Maddie asked faintly.

'The trade-off. I get the store, you get to run away. *Not* going to happen.'

'Leo...' Maddie breathed in deeply. 'We had a few hours of fun. Neither of us planned on having to deal with any consequences...'

A few hours of fun? Leo was inexplicably outraged to hear himself dismissed as *a few hours of fun*. He knew, rationally, that this was exactly how *he* would have categorised most of his exploits with women. Maybe slightly more than just the few hours, but essentially the same sentiment. Fun on the run.

That didn't make it any more acceptable.

'You didn't bank on my getting pregnant,' Maddie said, ignoring his glowering expression and ploughing on, 'and I get it that you're a bachelor through and through. The last thing you need or want is the sort of lifelong commitment that a child brings—especially when you didn't ask for this situation. No one wants to find that their nicely ordered perfect life has suddenly turned into a *nightmare.*'

Leo knew that she made sense. He was a committed bachelor. She wasn't to know why that was so deeply ingrained in him, but she had hit the nail on the head anyway. She had also been right when she'd said that the last thing he'd ever have asked for would be the lifelong commitment of a child—a duty of care stretching into infinity.

'I *didn't* ask for this,' he grated, 'but I'm honest enough to admit that no one held a gun to my head and forced me into having unprotected sex with you.'

'It doesn't matter. It's happened, and I'm not going to be responsible for lumbering you with a burden you didn't ask for.' She angled her head stubbornly and firmed her mouth. 'Well?' she pressed into the silence between them. 'You're not saying anything,'

'I'm waiting for you to finish what *you* want to say.'

Maddie breathed out a sigh. 'That's good.'

She cleared her throat to move on to stage two of the speech she had prepared in her head. It was a rough outline of the only solution she could think of, bearing in mind that she, herself, was still coming to terms with the fundamental change to her life looming on the not too distant horizon.

'If I sell the store to you then I will have more than sufficient money to make a life for myself and the baby. You won't have to take on any lifelong financial commitment. In fact you won't have to take on any commitment at all. In this day and age, single parent families are the norm.'

'I'm touched by your thoughtfulness and generosity,' Leo drawled. 'I can't think of a single other woman who, given the same circumstances, would be so overjoyed to see me walk scot-free.'

'Well…'

'Maybe it's because of your father.'

'What do you mean?'

'The stupendously low opinion you have of men.'

Maddie reddened. 'I'm giving you the option of not having your life ruined—'

'That's a very emotive word. *Ruined.*'

'So is *nightmare*,' Maddie countered, without batting an eye.

'Well, we won't be using either, because I won't be walking away scot-free. You're assuming that I'm the type of guy who's so self-interested that he's happy to get a woman pregnant and then leave her in the lurch.'

Maddie stiffened. 'What are you saying?'

'I may not have asked for this situation, but now that it's arisen walking away from it isn't going to be the solution I'll be taking.'

'You want the store.'

'It's bricks and mortar. I'm prepared to put that particular want on the back burner.'

'But I can't handle the responsibility of turning the place around when I'm going to have to deal with pregnancy and a newborn!'

'You can't handle it *alone*…'

'Even with help from a team of managers and workers…'

'Of course we'll have to discuss what the way forward with the store should be,' Leo mused, rising to his feet in one lithe, graceful movement to stroll towards the high-tech open-plan kitchen, where he proceeded to get them both something cold to drink.

Bewildered, Maddie twisted round to follow him. The accoutrements of a businessman had been shed along his way. The sleeves of his shirt were rolled to the elbow, and she hadn't noticed but he had slipped off his leather shoes and socks and was barefoot. He looked so stunning, so sophisticated…*so completely out of her league.*

She thought of Adam and her foolishness in falling for someone else who had been out of her league. She thought of the way he had stood back, siding with his family, accusing her of theft and not caring that her whole life was unravelling.

She thought of Leo, accessing that private information. Even if he had decided to withhold using it against her to get what he wanted she knew that he would have considered that option because that was the kind of man that he was.

She didn't know what was going on, but she felt a shiver of apprehension slither down her spine.

'Leo, I have no idea what you're talking about,' she confessed, having accepted the mineral water he had poured for her only to place it on the glass coffee table next to her.

'Don't you?'

'*What* way forward with the store?'

'Like I mentioned to you before, the day of the dinosaur department store, jack of all trades and master of none, is coming to an end.'

He was covering the room in ever-diminishing circles and finally he was standing directly in front of her, navy eyes unreadable, oozing just the sort of unfair sex appeal that made a nonsense of her attempts to get her brain in working order.

Maddie frowned. 'I don't know where you're going with this. Yes, I would have loved to have held on to the store, kept it as it was, but if you have it then what you do with it is no longer my concern.'

'You haven't *listened* to me, have you, Maddie?'

'I...'

'I'm not buying the store. Neither am I going anywhere. You're pregnant, and this completely changes the basis of our relationship.'

'But, Leo, we don't *have* a relationship.'

'You're the mother of my unborn baby. What do you call *that*?'

Faced with this direct question, which seemed to beg a sensible answer she was struggling to provide, Maddie could only stare at him speechlessly.

'Believe me,' Leo said heavily, moving to sit on the chair adjacent to her, stretching out his long legs at an angle and then relaxing back with his fingers linked on his stomach. 'I hadn't banked on any of this happening. But happen it has, and as far as I can see there's only one sensible solution that's going to work. I will have to marry you and legitimise my child.'

Maddie's mouth fell open. Before she could say anything he held up one assured hand, as though to stop her before she could interrupt. Which she wasn't about to do because her vocal cords had seized up.

'I won't lie to you, Maddie, marriage has not been on my radar. I'm a red-blooded male and I've had my fun, but I haven't been tempted to turn fun into anything more serious. You have your past, and that's shaped you. I have mine.'

'What? What past? This is exactly what I'm talking about. I don't know anything about you! How can you sit there and start talking about marriage when we don't know one another? It's crazy.'

'Crazy it may be, but we're in the most intimate situation it's possible for two people to be in.'

'And, as you've just said, you've never considered marriage! So how on earth do you expect me to react when you sit there now, telling me that's the only solution to this situation?'

'You're looking at this in the wrong way—putting an unnecessarily negative spin on it.'

'What do you mean?'

'Marriage in the conventional sense of the word isn't something I believe in, and there's no point in my pretending otherwise.'

'"The conventional sense of the word"? Would that

be the convention of two people being together because they're in love?'

'The world is littered with kids who end up in therapy because of parents who got married because they thought they were *in love*. Your mother,' he inserted shrewdly, 'thought *she* was in love, and absconded to the other side of the world in complete defiance of common sense only for the marriage to end in tears.'

Maddie flushed. 'That's not the point.'

'It's precisely the point. You had all contact with this country and your grandfather severed because of your mother's headstrong pursuit of *love*.'

Maddie didn't answer because he had a point. 'You're twisting everything to suit your argument,' she muttered, shooting him a fulminating look from under her lashes. 'I didn't see this side of you when we…when I…'

'When you were overwhelmed with lust and jumped into bed with me?'

'You're *so* arrogant. I should have known that you couldn't be a carefree wanderer. Someone like that would have been a lot more humble, a lot more down-to-earth. He wouldn't have had an ego the size of a cruise liner.'

Leo grinned, because in spite of the tenseness of the situation he was enjoying her dry sense of humour and the way she wasn't caving in to him. *Yet.*

'One of those humble, down-to-earth, carefree wandering souls would have hit the high seas the minute you told him you were pregnant. Generally speaking, perpetual Peter Pans don't cope well with the thought of being tied down. Which brings us back to the matter in hand. What I'm proposing is a union for the sake of our child. A practical solution. Something that makes sense.'

'Oh, wow, Leo. You're *really* selling it to me,' Maddie said acidly. 'I always dreamed of love and marriage and then the pitter-patter of tiny feet. Now you're presenting me with marriage, the pitter-patter of tiny feet, and forget about love because love doesn't count for anything.'

'You thought you'd found love with a loser who turned on you because he thought you were a thief. So much for the myth that love can survive through thick and thin. Convince me that love is all that matters when your mother learnt the hard way and so did you. Love is all a crock of—'

'Stop!' Maddie stood up to pace the room. 'Look…' She breathed in deeply. 'I know you mean well, and you have good intentions, and your offer is very generous, but I can't think of anything worse than being stuck with someone with whom I have no emotional connection.'

Stuck with? Was she actually *trying* to enrage him?

'But this isn't about *you,* is it?'

'Not entirely.' Maddie reddened. 'But it's not all about our child either. Yes, every child deserves two parents—but only if those parents are happy and committed to one another.'

Leo could no longer contain his impatience. 'Strip back the jargon and how many couples tick all the boxes?' Restless, he stood up to prowl the room, just as she was, until they were facing one another like opponents in a ring.

'I don't care about how many couples tick the boxes or don't,' Maddie muttered stubbornly, tearing her eyes away from his ridiculously beautiful face. 'I care about whether *I* would be able to tick the boxes with my partner.'

'Oh, bring on the violin music!' Leo fought down the urge to thump something in sheer frustration. How was it that he was having to wage war in an effort to persuade someone to share a life of obscene wealth and privilege?

'I couldn't bear the thought of being married to someone because he felt responsible for a situation he hadn't banked on.'

'Are you telling me that you would rather jeopardise the well-being of a child for your own selfish concerns?'

'It's not selfish.'

'You of all people should be able to understand the limitations of a life with only one parent. Yes, it's common. Yes, single parent families are a statistic. But you are turning down the option of *two* parents. Do you think our child will thank you for that in the years to come?'

Maddie glared, buffeted by the pull of his arguments, all of which made perfect sense in a way, but...

'We don't *love* one another,' she cried in protest.

She thought of those moments they'd shared and was embarrassed at how powerful her instinct was to read into them a bonding and a meeting of minds that hadn't been there. There had been something about that brief time they'd spent together that had made her feel as though she'd found her soulmate.

'What happens when we get bored with one another? What happens when you start resenting the fact that you're tied to someone you don't want to be with?'

'I don't see the point of conjecture. We have to deal with the here and now.'

'How can you be so...*practical*?'

'Because one of us needs to be.'

'I can't marry you. Yes, I *know* I should be hardened and cynical—but I'm not.'

Leo could recognise defeat as well as the next man. He'd approached the situation from the only perspective that made sense and had automatically assumed that she would fall in line—because, frankly, what woman wouldn't? He'd failed to take into account the fact that it was fair to say in the short space of time he'd known her she had been nothing like any of the women he had ever gone out with. So why should she react with any degree of predictability?

Too late he was recognising that she was as headstrong and stubborn as a mule, and as capable of digging her heels in as strenuously as he was.

'Are you telling me that you'd like to spread your net and see what you can catch while you're pregnant with my baby?'

'Of course not! What man is going to look twice at a woman who's having someone else's child?'

'You'd be shocked,' he muttered in a driven undertone.

When he thought of her putting herself out there, finding some loser who was only interested in spinning her some line so that he could crawl all over her body, he saw red. But he was quick enough to realise that any show of anger wasn't going to cut it. The more he tried to cajole and badger her into seeing things from his point of view, the more she was going to backpedal and see him as the bad guy, trying to force her into a loathsome life of undiluted luxury.

'Okay.' He held his hand up in a gesture of surrender

that made Maddie narrow her eyes suspiciously. 'Let's move on to another pragmatic approach to the situation. One that excludes what I still maintain is the most desirable solution. You don't want marriage? Well, I can't frogmarch you up the aisle, bound and tied. But we're going to have to approach this calmly.'

He patted the space on the sofa next to him and she sat down and twisted to look at him.

His dark, dark blue eyes immediately made Maddie feel hot and bothered, but when she looked away all she could see was the taut pull of his trousers over his muscular thighs, the bronzed forearms liberally sprinkled with dark hair, the way that dark hair curled round the matt gold of his watch strap... She felt faint.

'Go on,' she managed to croak, noting that he had dumped the marriage solution faster than the speed of light when she'd provided him with a get-out clause.

'I will want to be actively involved in everything from this point onwards. And I certainly will not risk you doing a runner by buying the store from you. You want it. It's yours. That way I am assured that you won't be leaving the place any time soon.'

'But you live here...in London...'

'And naturally I'll continue to oversee things here. But I can run my empire from anywhere in the world, such is the nature of communications these days. And Dublin seems to be an extremely charming place in which to settle... Nice restaurants, spectacular scenery, friendly locals...'

Leo thought that he could usefully live there for a few months and use that time to source an alternative location for his business... Or he might just explore the outskirts of the city and put in place the makings of a golf complex which he had been toying with for some time. It would be a little holiday, in a manner of speaking.

Naturally his grandfather would be curious as to his sudden change of location from London to Dublin, and the absence of a deal on the store, and in due course Leo would explain all. If Maddie was wary of *him*, then being confronted by his grandfather, whose thoughts about children being born out of wedlock were firmly rooted somewhere in the Victorian era, would have her running for the hills.

And, up close and personal, he would be able to keep an eye on her. She had dug her heels in and refused the marriage solution, but there was more than one way to skin a cat, and Leo was in little doubt that she would see the wisdom of that solution once she began to struggle with the technicalities of running a store…when the difficulties of being a single parent loomed all the more glaringly.

Because he would be there right next to her—a constant alternative waiting in the wings. He would get the girl, he thought, even if he had to play the waiting game for a bit.

'But you don't… You don't have anywhere to live here…'

Maddie wondered what it would be like to live with him, to wake up next to him every morning and go to sleep with the warmth of his body against hers. And then she immediately killed that stupid fantasy, because nothing could be further from reality.

This was never going to be a love story with a happy ending.

'That won't be a problem.' Leo shrugged. 'I'll buy somewhere.'

'*Buy* somewhere?'

'You'd be surprised how fast a house can change hands when enough money is put on the table,' Leo said drily. 'I don't foresee a problem.'

'I won't do a runner. How can I when I'll have a store to oversee? There's no need for you to decamp to Ireland.'

Leo spread his arms wide in a gesture of magnanimity which made her think of a predatory shark, trying to convince a school of minnows that, no, it wasn't *in the least bit* interested in gobbling them up.

'Like I said, whether you do a runner or not, I intend to be here for you every step of the way.' He shot her a slow, curling smile. 'You'll have me around twenty-four-seven—without the inconvenience of a wedding ring on your finger...'

CHAPTER SEVEN

MADDIE LOOKED AT the half-finished building work which she had tentatively begun on her house six weeks previously. It was just another aggravating headache added to the pile of aggravating headaches which had been slowly but steadily mounting ever since she had confidently declared to Leo that if he didn't want to buy the store from her then she was overjoyed, because she would be able to rebuild her family's legacy and return it to its former glory.

Niggling problems had arisen at the store. Missing stock, inadequate paperwork for suppliers which had only just come to light, a persistent leak in one of the departments on the top floor, which the plumbing team had ominously told her *'looked bad'*… After that she had dismissed them, so that she could consider her options.

Several members of staff had also chosen to quit, following the announcement of her ownership, and replacing them was proving another headache because everyone seemed to think that there was no chance the store was a viable employer—even though she had personally sat in at all the interviews and done her best to persuade them otherwise.

And now this.

Maddie sighed and contemplated the exposed plasterboard and the flooring which had been ripped up—but not in its entirety. Which meant that half the kitchen floor was comprised of the original tired tiles and the other half of bare brick and wood, with enough gaps to let in several families of rodents.

The fridge had been disconnected, and now the builder had phoned to say that he wasn't going to be around for the next week because of a 'personal emergency'.

Maddie looked at her phone.

Leo.

She didn't want to think of him but she did. She couldn't help herself. True to his word, he had been around a lot. Phoning her. Arranging to meet her for lunch. Insisting on doing the occasional grocery shop with her because he wanted to make sure she was buying food that was nutritious.

She refused to invite him back to her house, just as she discouraged his visits to the store. She wanted and needed her independence. She'd turned him down and for good reason. The last thing she wanted was to drift into a state where she found herself depending on him, and she knew that was a real danger because he was just so damned *present.* The perfect gentleman.

There had been no mention of marriage, nothing that could be construed as being remotely sexual... He was just strong, reliable, and annoyingly, infuriatingly *helpful.*

Maddie knew that she should be grateful that he'd never overstepped the mark.

She didn't want him in the house? He shrugged and took the hint with alacrity.

She was vague about him visiting the store? He acquiesced with another of those non-committal shrugs of his.

He treated her as though she was made of porcelain, and the only time she'd sensed that he was having trouble backing down was when she had absolutely refused to see his private doctor on a weekly basis because it was 'better safe than sorry'.

All in all, he had treated her with tact, consideration and a detached courtesy. And, however much she told herself that that was a *good* thing, she hated it.

On the spur of the moment she dialled the hotline number. For the first time since he had given it to her weeks ago.

In the middle of a high-level meeting, attended by a select handful of people who had come to see him because he had no intention of spreading himself thin by going to see *them*, Leo raised one imperious hand, at which all conversation stopped.

Maddie's name had flashed up on his screen, and since it was the first time she had deigned to call him he had no intention of ignoring the call.

Frankly, he'd grown tired of waiting. To start with he'd expected her to phone him within a few days—if only because *he* called *her* with tiresome regularity, and whatever had happened to good manners and meeting halfway on the effort front?

Then, when no phone call had materialised, he'd banked on that changing just as soon as she'd unearthed all the problems at the store. Hadn't he volunteered to help her often enough?

Several weeks later and he'd all but given up.

'Leo,' he said now, without preamble.

'Sorry, I'm disturbing you,' Maddie apologised, the reluctance in her voice making it clear how uncomfortable she was having given in to the temptation of calling him.

Leo looked at the room full of important people who had gathered there for his convenience. 'Not in the slightest.'

'It's just that...'

'Tell me what's wrong.' He half turned, making a motion with one hand to inform the gathering that they were to continue without him and indicating that his second-in-command would host.

'Nothing's wrong... It's just that...well... I'm here at home...' Maddie gazed with despair at the half-finished kitchen, in which cooking no halfway decent meal had been possible for the past two weeks. 'And I'm having one or two little problems... It's nothing, really... I shouldn't have bothered you.'

'I'm on my way.'

Leo killed the phone call before she could launch into a long-winded monologue of apology.

For the first time in his life he knew what it felt like to be worried. He was worried now. He'd never met anyone as stubbornly determined to be self-sufficient as Maddie, and the fact that she had confessed to having 'one or two problems' was a source of high-voltage concern—because *'one or two problems'* could range from a chipped nail to the sky falling down.

No, he thought, scrap the chipped nail and go straight to the sky falling down.

His Ferrari was equipped to deliver him to her house in record time, and he rang the doorbell and kept his finger there, already planning on breaking the door down if she didn't answer it within ten seconds.

She answered it before brute force became necessary.

'What's wrong?' were his opening words as he strode past her into the hall and then spun round on his heel, eyes narrowed, inspecting her from head to toe for visible signs of distress.

She was as stunning as she always was. Very slightly showing her pregnancy now, but it was hardly noticeable under the jogging bottoms and the baggy top.

Distractedly, Leo marvelled that she could take the most unfortunate of outfits and turn it into something intensely sexy.

He shifted impatiently as his body began to undermine his common sense. As it was wont to do with predictable regularity. She'd laid down her parameters six weeks ago—turned his marriage proposal down and all but said that she deserved someone better than him, someone more suitable, someone who came with the full package.

Forced into a corner, and obliged to bide his time, Leo knew that he couldn't risk undermining his own objectives by giving in to the temptation to put that will power of hers to the test.

He focused on her face, but there was no reprieve there because the connection that lured him in wasn't just about the way she looked or the way his body reacted to hers. Something ran deeper, like a powerful underwater current, and that pull operated on a completely different level.

Leo frowned, as he always did when this kind of thinking ambushed him, not quite knowing what to do with the confused jumble of feelings he couldn't seem to pin down and box up. He spoke to her on the phone and her voice did something to him. It was bizarre, a little perplexing. He didn't care to dwell on it.

Instead, he thought about those sidelong glances when she'd thought he wasn't looking. He could have done something about that, but he'd backed away. Push her even a little at the wrong time, he'd reasoned, and she would be off. And he wasn't going to risk that happening just for the sake of staunching the painful ache of desire that took him over whenever he was around her.

For someone as accustomed as he was to the transitory nature of lust, Leo was a little shocked at how much he still wanted to touch Maddie. Even when she wasn't around she was in his head like a burr. Was it because she had been elevated to a position never previously occupied by any other woman? Mother of his unborn baby. Or was it because the physical side of their relationship had not been allowed to follow its natural course and wind down to its inevitable conclusion?

Maybe it was a mixture of both. Leo didn't know. He just knew that he seemed to be engaged in a permanent battle to keep his hands off her.

Maddie chewed her lip—and then she did the absolute unthinkable. She burst into tears.

Panicked, Leo pulled her to him and held her close. He smoothed her hair and mumbled softly. Just when he needed a handkerchief he discovered that he didn't have one, so he wiped her cheek with his knuckle and listened to her tell him that nothing was wrong, that she didn't know why she was crying and that it could only be hormones—and actually she shouldn't have called him.

'Talk to me,' was his response to all that.

'I feel overwhelmed,' Maddie confessed in a small voice, getting her crazy crying jag under control but not pulling out of his embrace 'The store… The house…'

Since Leo had only heard about developments at the store second-hand, and hadn't been to the house at all, he took a chance to look around him, then beyond her, to the open door through which he glimpsed the chaos of what remained of the kitchen.

Swearing softly under his breath, he edged her away from him. 'Why didn't you tell me?'

He wanted to sweep her off her feet and carry her to the scene of the crime, but rather than spook her with caveman antics he shuffled, still holding her, until they were both in the kitchen. He settled her into one of the chairs that hadn't been rehomed somewhere else while work was being carried out.

Or not, judging from the state of things.

He inspected the shoddy, half-finished mess.

An unusable kitchen.

Leo looked around for another chair and then, not finding one handy, did the caveman thing after all and swept her off her feet as though she weighed nothing. He carried her into the living room, which contained most of the displaced contents of the kitchen.

'I repeat,' he said, gently depositing her on the sofa and then dragging a chair over so that he could pin her to the spot without any room for manoeuvre, 'why didn't you tell me about this sooner?'

'They said it would only take two weeks.'

'Name of the company?'

'Well…'

'Maddie, just tell me who you employed to do this job.'

She fumbled with her cell phone and passed it to him, so that he could see the details of the company she'd used, and then, silencing her with one hand while he phoned them, she listened as he let rip.

No shouting, no bellowing and no threats. His voice was soft—dangerously soft—and the threat was implicit. 'One week,' he said, 'and don't make me regret giving you that long…'

And then he made her tell him, leaving nothing out, what was going on both in the store and the rest of the house.

The store would come together. At least he had a foothold of sorts there, and could make sure no disasters occurred. The house, on the other hand…

'The kitchen is effectively out of bounds?' he said finally, and Maddie nodded sheepishly.

'So how have you been able to eat?'

'I… Well…'

'You're pregnant, Maddie. I don't want to hear any evasive non-answers. Yes, I have taken you out for dinners and the occasional lunch, but in between… Tell me what your diet has been. Because from the looks of it there have been no cooking facilities here for some time.'

Leo had never thought that being the Great Protector could feel so good.

'A little over two weeks...'

'That's plenty long enough when you're supposed to be putting nutrients into your body.'

'I've been eating,' she mumbled sheepishly, but he read in her eyes that it had been a long time since she had seen a homecooked meal.

'This isn't going to do,' Leo said flatly. 'I can't stop you jeopardising your *own* well-being by living off preservative-stuffed junk food, but I *can* and *will* prevent you from damaging the baby you're carrying!'

She pulled herself together and said primly, 'Once everything's in place my eating habits will return to normal. I love cooking. I would never not eat, and you don't have to tell me that this isn't a good time to have an erratic diet. I'm not an idiot.'

'Again, you should have told me sooner.'

'I didn't think the builders would just up and disappear.'

'You're stressed, and stress is the last thing you need right now.'

And, he thought, she couldn't accuse *him* of contributing to the source of her stress, considering he had done nothing but kick his heels for the past few weeks, gritting his teeth in silent frustration as she became more and more entrenched in her determination to prove how self-sufficient she was.

There were times when she seriously made him want to tear his hair out.

'Let's go upstairs,' he said abruptly, coming to a decision and not giving himself time to have any rethink.

Maddie's eyes widened. 'For what?'

Leo looked at her in silence for a few seconds. 'What

would you like it to be for?' he couldn't resist asking, his voice as soft as silk.

He lowered his eyes, annoyed with himself and with the prompt response of his libido to the thought of having her. More than anything he would like to see her changing body...ripening with his child.

'You're going to pack your bags,' he said gruffly, 'because you're leaving here today. With me.'

'What?'

'You recall I mentioned that my grandfather is cruising in the Caribbean and had stopped off to stay on one of the smaller islands? Well, the villa on that island belongs to me, and I intend on taking you there. Unfortunately there will be no meet-and-greet with him, as he's now enjoying the splendours of the open seas, but it's a great place to unwind—and you need to unwind.'

Leo couldn't disguise a certain amount of relief that Benito had left the island. In due course he would meet the woman who would become his future granddaughter-in-law, as far as he was concerned, and Leo hadn't disillusioned him. It was a bridge to be crossed when he got to it. But he would certainly be thrilled to think that they would be going to the villa together—as a couple.

'Leo, that's ridiculous! I can't just...just leave for a holiday while everything here is in disarray!'

But the thought of doing that dangled like a carrot in front of her.

'Leave everything to me,' Leo said, rising to his feet and heading out towards the hall and the staircase while Maddie shot up and tripped along behind him.

'I can manage just fine on my own,' she said, dutifully registering a protest vote.

He spun round to stare at her with incredulity.

'No, Maddie, you can't. The house is a mess. You haven't been eating. You've hired a team of builders who have obviously got the message that they can do as they please because you're too stressed out to stand your ground. You're too proud to ask for help. Whether you like it or not, you're going to pack two bags of summer clothes and we're going to fly out to my house first thing in the morning. Now, I can either pack those bags for you, or you can pack them yourself. When the bags are packed you're going to come back with me to my place, spend the night, and forget every single worry that's been dragging you down.'

'Since when did you become so bossy?'

Leo dealt her an amused, crooked smile.

'Sometimes being bossy is the only thing that works when you're dealing with a woman who digs her heels in so far that she refuses to ask for help even when she discovers she can't pull them out. Now, the bags…?'

Maddie gazed out of the window on the plane to the bank of clouds below. Everything had happened so fast that her head was still spinning. Put simply, Leo had taken over and, like a juggernaut, had bulldozed every single obstacle until she had left behind a trusted foreman who was going to supervise the work on the house with a rod of steel. And as far as the store was concerned he had moved in some of his own people.

'The store is yours,' he had told her before she'd been able to object, 'but you need the right resources to run it. I'll make sure you have them.'

Maddie had accepted without hesitation. Pride was one thing, but other people's livelihoods depended on her doing what she had set out to do with the store, and it had been proving more time-consuming and difficult than she had imagined. Pregnant, and with her head not entirely focused on the store, she had been distracted. And in the evenings she was very, very tired. Too tired to commit to the gruelling hours necessary at this stage in the process of taking the store out of the doldrums. And there was a limit to how much she could ask her trusted employees to do.

Leo would not take advantage. She knew that. She'd spent the past few weeks coming to terms with the fact that he was a man who was true to his word—a completely different species from Adam, with whom she had first so rashly compared him.

Leo was honourable to a fault. His proposal to her had been the ultimate act of selflessness, because he didn't love her, had never planned on having any sort of relationship with her after that one heady night of sex, and had never factored marriage to any woman into his agenda. He had his reasons, and she was guessing that he'd been hurt just as she had, but that aside she'd always known that he was not a guy in it for the long term. Yet, he'd bitten the bullet and proposed because he'd felt it was the right thing to do.

Not once over the past few weeks had he tried to bully her into marrying him either. He had obeyed all the *Do Not Trespass* signs she had posted without complaint. And that was pretty amazing, because she had thought that there was something fundamentally restless and impatient about him that would have had him crashing through any signs that didn't suit him.

She would not come back to find that the store had been converted into an electronics shop. Not that there was any chance of that anyway, because they would only be away for ten days.

She sneaked a sidelong glance at him. He was working, frowning slightly as he read through whatever was on his screen. He was perfectly still and yet he exuded the sort of energy that made her think of a resting tiger.

Ten days in his company…

How on earth was she going to cope?

Her heart picked up speed. Being in his company was a balancing act, and only now, with all the usual distractions removed, was she recognising that balancing act for what it was. A breathless mixture of excitement and apprehension, a forbidden longing that defied logic, and a need to get close to the fire even though it was dangerous.

It was okay when she was only seeing him now and again, only hearing that dark, velvety voice a couple of times a day. It was okay when there were other people around to dilute the force of his personality. But she quailed at the thought of being with him in an empty house.

'You never said…' She cleared her throat. 'Does anyone live in the…er…villa?'

Leo saved what he had been reading with the press of a key and angled his big body towards her in the first-class seat, which was generous but still somehow felt cramped to him.

'Anyone like who?' he drawled, amused by the delicate flush that had spread across her high cheekbones.

He'd expected her to fight him when it came to this trip because she seemed to want to fight him on everything, but she had conceded quickly and with a hint of relief.

Life was tough when you had no experience of the big, bad world of business—and when you'd made it your mission not to ask for help from the one person who could help you. Maddie was finding that out for herself and, whilst he was furious that she had allowed the situation to get out of hand before coming to him, he knew that he had finally found a way in to her.

He'd played the waiting game and he'd soon got fed up with it. It wasn't his style. Now that waiting game was over. He would show her just how good her life could be with him in it.

There was no way he was going to let her go down any road that saw him being pushed into second place in the parent stakes—arranging visits and watching from the sidelines while some other guy took the reins.

But any threat of a custody battle wouldn't do him any favours. Leo was very realistic about that. He worked long hours and, whilst he might have bottomless funds when it came to providing financial security, it would be crazy to think that a live-in nanny would be any match for Maddie. No sane judge would rule in his favour. He wouldn't contemplate any such course of action. Because if he did, and subsequently lost, the price he would end up paying would be high.

Time had not been his friend. But he intended to make sure that it would be from now on, and being with her, a little voice said, wasn't exactly going to be a hardship. She had the oddest talent when it came to lifting his spirits, even though *accommodating* and *acquiescent* were two words that could never be used to describe her. and he'd always plumped for those two things when it came to the opposite sex.

'Staff?' Maddie ventured, wondering what sort of

staff manned a villa that was empty most of the year. 'You haven't really said much about it. How big is it? And why on earth do you have a villa on an island in the Caribbean if you hardly ever go there?'

'Investment,' Leo said succinctly. 'I tend to use it as a company retreat. Occasionally as a bonus holiday for high achievers. So, yes, there's staff. When it's empty they come in twice weekly, to air the place and make sure nothing's amiss, but it's used fairly frequently so they're kept busy much of the time. They're all on hefty retainers, so they're there whenever I need them.'

'Wow. Sometimes...'

'Sometimes?'

'Sometimes when you say stuff like that—like when you said that you would stay in Ireland and buy a house and it wouldn't be a problem because you could throw money at it—I realise just how *different* we are from one another.'

'Different doesn't necessarily mean incompatible.'

'Leo, before I went to work for Lacey I scrubbed floors. My mum worked all the hours God gave to make ends meet. She didn't get a penny from my grandfather...'

No surprise there, Leo thought. Old Tommaso, if his own grandfather could be believed, had forgotten how to spend money unless it was on drink or horses. He certainly wouldn't have been sending any to the daughter he'd excommunicated because of her lifestyle choices.

He'd made it quite clear—and indeed Leo had read the letter sent to his grandfather years ago, after his last purchase attempt of the store had hit a brick wall—that selling the store was as pie in the sky as welcoming back his wayward daughter.

'Too proud to ask, I'll bet...' Maddie said sadly.

'Really?'

'She could be stubborn.'

'The family resemblance is duly noted,' Leo remarked wryly.

Maddie blushed. 'I've never had a holiday, and when I came over here it was the first time I'd been on a plane.'

'We grew up in very different backgrounds,' Leo conceded, 'but we share some very similar traits. I've never known any woman as bloody stubborn as me, or as determined to set a course and stick to it.' He looked at her narrowly. 'Occasionally a person has to dig beneath the surface.'

'You're only saying that because I'm pregnant with your baby and you have to find *some* positives.'

'If that bastard ex of yours was around,' Leo said grimly, 'I'd flatten him.'

Maddie pinkened with pleasure at the possessiveness in Leo's voice. 'He did me a favour. He made me careful about trusting people.'

'He took away your confidence, and for that he deserves to be ripped apart limb by limb.'

'I'm just being realistic. Anyway... You haven't said... Will the house be staffed?'

'There will just be the two of us.' He shrugged, 'So there won't be any need to have the place swamped with staff. There will be a discreet service—a skeleton staff—and they, naturally, will not live in. No need for you to do anything at all on the domestic front, and I feel we're perfectly capable of taking care of our own breakfasts,'

'Of course,' Maddie said faintly. 'I've been doing that

all my life. I think I've got my technique well-honed when it comes to putting some cereal in a bowl or boiling an egg and making some toast.'

Leo's mouth twitched with amusement. 'I find it tiresome if there are people hovering when I want privacy...'

Maddie wondered what sort of privacy Leo had in mind, and had to soothe herself with the timely reminder that he was no longer interested in her as a sexual being. She was carrying his child and had now entered a different category. He'd gone from wanting her to wanting to make sure she was okay—which was a completely different thing.

But she wanted him to care because of *her* and not just because of the fact that she was carrying his baby. She wanted to crawl into his arms and have him hold her because he wanted to—not because he was concerned about her stress levels because of the baby...

She pushed the thought away.

'You won't have to think about anything while you're out there, Maddie,' he continued.

'That's a big promise, Leo.' She laughed, surprised at how relaxed she felt in his company—but then, when she'd first met him she'd felt relaxed as well.

For a moment he wasn't Leo the billionaire, who'd wanted her store and was now stuck with her because of the pregnancy, but the Leo who had charmed her with his wit and humour and mind-blowing sex appeal.

'I've never been in a situation where I haven't had to think about *something*, so I'm not sure how I would cope with that.'

She blushed when he fixed his amazing eyes on her with thoughtful, speculative intensity.

'You haven't had an easy life,' he conceded, 'but now you're pregnant, and your days of having to stress and worry are over.'

'I'm not a piece of china.' But the protest was half-hearted.

'You are to me.'

Maddie blushed a little more, rattled because there was something intimate about what he was saying—even though she knew that he was just reiterating what he'd said from the beginning, which was that she was his responsibility now that she was pregnant, whether she liked it or not.

She cleared her throat but couldn't quite meet his gaze. 'I shouldn't complain anyway. I have a lot to be thankful for, thanks to my grandfather's legacy. I have the store, and a roof over my head, and sufficient money to have secured the bank loan. I just wish,' she confessed, 'that I could have met him.'

'Tommaso?' Leo looked at her, startled. 'Why?'

'What do you mean *why*?' Maddie asked. 'I never knew my dad. My mum ran away from her family—precious little of it as there was—and severed all ties. There was always just me and my mum. And, yes, she used to say that we were two against the world, but I would really have liked it to have been *lots* of us against the world. Two is such a lonely number… I knew I was never going to meet my father, and I never wanted to, but I would have loved to have met my grandfather—especially as I think that he probably wanted to meet me, to have Mum relent…'

'What gives you *that* idea?'

'He left everything to me,' Maddie said flatly. 'Why else would he have done that?'

'Because it's the Italian way,' Leo said drily.

'You're so cynical, Leo.'

'He was never going to leave his dwindling fortune to the local cat sanctuary.'

She looked away, her chin at a defiant angle, heated colour still tingeing her cheeks.

Leo could see that Maddie wanted to believe the best of Tommaso—was desperate to forge a link with the grandfather she'd never known—and taking care of the store was part of that. She obviously had no idea what the wily fox had really been like, and on the spot Leo decided that that was something he would never reveal. Let her keep her dreams.

Besides, instigating show-downs and arguments wasn't part of his agenda.

He relaxed and said soothingly, 'To the best of my knowledge, he was no animal lover. And perhaps you're right—perhaps it was his way of reaching out to you from beyond the grave...'

'You think so?'

The urge to burst out laughing died on his lips as he took in the earnestness of her expression, the *hope*. Not for the first time, he cursed the old bastard who had stubbornly refused to make amends with his only child—and with the grandchild he had never seen.

'I'm sure that's exactly how it was,' he said gravely.

Leo had always wanted the store—had promised his grandfather he'd get it—but he knew that he wasn't going to stamp out Maddie's curiously romanticised dreams to get his way, and knew that his grandfather would understand. Frankly, the prospect of a great-grandchild would be a heck of a lot more exciting to the old man.

'Mum never talked about any of it. She was way too proud. I sometimes wonder whether I should have pressed her more for answers.'

'Why didn't you?'

'I knew it would upset her.'

'Understandable,' Leo said in a low, roughened undertone. 'And of course it's only when we're older that we have the confidence to tackle our parents on an adult footing. Respect often gets in the way of interrogation, and I guess by the time you came of age you were wrapped up in having to deal with much bigger issues because your mother was ill.'

Maddie looked astounded at his understanding of just where she was coming from.

'Don't beat yourself up over that,' he said, more briskly. 'I find it never pays to dwell on the past. In less than four hours you're going to be at my villa, without a care in the world. I have everything at the store under control, and my team will be reporting daily on work to your house.'

Returning to his laptop—because there was such a thing as too much touchy-feely, *let's get the tissues out and have a good old cry* bonding—he glanced at her out of the corner of his eye and saw, with great satisfaction, that when she lay back and closed her eyes all traces of anxiety had been wiped clean from her face.

CHAPTER EIGHT

MADDIE HAD NO real idea what to expect at the end of
the nine-hour trip—mostly by plane, but for the final
leg on the small speedboat which had been waiting for
them at the marina. But any awkwardness at being so
far removed from her comfort zone with Leo was dis-
pelled in her speechless wonderment at the stunning
island on which they finally found themselves.

Evening was fast approaching, and as they were
taken from one marina on the main island to be deposited at another marina on its much smaller sister, she
could just about appreciate the scenery as it was gradually absorbed into darkness. Burnt orange skies turned
to violet, then finally to star-pricked black, and she saw
lush vegetation, soft, rounded hills, a main road that
was just big enough for two cars to pass side by side,
and banks upon banks of gently swaying coconut trees,
tall and spindly and graceful.

'It's stunning,' she breathed, her head swinging
from left to right as the car which had been waiting for
them, and which Leo was now handling like an expert,
bounced along the uneven road.

There was virtually no traffic at all. But lights from
occupied houses could be glimpsed as they went along.

This was the enclave of the super-rich—an island on which they could relax without fear of paparazzi or nosy neighbours with binoculars.

Somewhere close to the marina they had left behind was a small but functioning town, where the essentials could be purchased and where several high-end restaurants catered for the island's wealthy visitors, and for anyone else who wanted to travel by boat from the main island and enjoy the top-rated cuisine.

Leo explained all this as they drove towards his villa. His voice was low and soothing, and the melodious background noise of the sea was achieving the impossible and making her forget all about the stress she had left behind in Ireland.

Leo had promised her complete rest and relaxation and he was already delivering on that promise big-time. She hadn't felt this rested in a long, long time.

Sneaking a sideways glance at his strong profile as he concentrated on driving, she felt her body respond in the way she had tried so hard to train it not to do. Her breathing slowed and her eyelids fluttered and she was assailed by total recall of how those strong hands had felt roaming all over her body.

She pushed those thoughts away to the back of her mind because they were inappropriate. She and Leo had to grope their way to a new and different footing, and getting turned on by him had no place in that scenario.

They would share a child and have a cordial but detached relationship. There could be nothing else for them. Because she could never and *would* never marry anyone who had to be dragged up the aisle like a prisoner in handcuffs. She deserved better—no matter what he said about two parents being better than one. She *knew* that two parents were better than one! But only if those parents had married for the right reasons.

What if *her* parents had decided to stick together because of *her*? Would her childhood have been picture-perfect with a disillusioned and bitter mother and a father manacled against his will? He would only have wanted marriage for the fortune he'd anticipated getting out of her mother, and would have suddenly found himself anchored down because of a child on the way.

Needless to say that was a fairly impossible scenario to imagine, because her father hadn't had an ounce of responsibility running through his veins, but still…

And yet for all that sensible reasoning, with the balmy night air outside and the foreign sight of a velvety black sky dotted with stars, Maddie *was* turned on—as though a dimmer switch had been buzzing in the background and had suddenly been turned to full beam.

She shifted, and was alarmed at the suffocating sense of *want*.

It was almost a relief when the car rounded a bend and there was the villa, lit up on the outside. It was ranch-style, with a massive outer veranda that seemed to circle the whole impressive building like a necklace. They drove into the courtyard, with Leo making innocuous conversation about the island and what she might expect by way of entertainment.

Which was very little from the sounds of it.

'I hate clubs anyway,' Maddie said distractedly as she stared at the villa and tried to get her head around how much her life had changed in the space of a few months.

She rested her hand on her stomach and for a few seconds wished that the perfect life she'd always dreamed of had materialised. With a baby on the way and financial security, and finally feeling well and truly over her stupid, ill-advised ex, things should have been so good—but what promised so much on the outside was riddled with rot on the inside, and she couldn't get away from that.

Leo didn't care about her. He was doing all this because of the baby. If it weren't for the new life she was carrying he would have waged a no-holds-barred attack on her in order to get the store, and the single night they had shared would have been a distant memory.

He didn't care about her.

But she cared about him.

She shivered and tried to unravel that thought so that she could pick it apart and make a nonsense of it. But it had formed and it refused to budge.

She cared about him.

She might have thrown caution to the wind and slept with him for all the right reasons, but she had remained connected to him after sex, even though she'd barely been aware of it.

And then finding out she was pregnant... That had opened a door and allowed all sorts of things to enter—all sorts of emotions that she hadn't been able to staunch. She'd seen beyond the billionaire. And once that had happened she'd been seduced by all the complex sides of him that showed him to be honourable, decent, fair...

She'd fallen for those traits.

She'd fallen for the guy who had stepped up to the plate when it had mattered and had backed off when she had told him to.

Maddie had to remind herself strenuously of all the reasons she had told him to back off, because in a moment of weakness, as he drew to a stop and then turned to look at her, his beautiful face all shadows and angles, she wondered what she had done.

He'd proposed marriage and she'd turned him down flat. Why? Had he been right? Had she been selfish?

She could do a lot worse than marry someone who was *not* the sort of ruthless money-making machine she had written him off as being. And who knew? He could come to love her. Couldn't he?

Maddie hated having those thoughts, because she knew how dangerous they were.

'Hello?' Leo interrupted drily. 'I've lost you. Please don't tell me that you've suddenly decided to get cold feet because you're going to be sharing a villa with me.'

'Huh?' Maddie blinked.

Leo contained his impatience. 'Separate quarters,' he told her abruptly, swinging out of the car and feeling the blast of late-evening humidity, hearing the orchestra of insects which was so much part and parcel of this part of the world.

Never had he had to curtail his energy and his driving need to act as much as over the past few hours. It was frustrating. He was the father of her child and prepared to do the decent thing. He was ready to sacrifice his freedom for the greater good. He couldn't understand why it was so damned hard for her to see that and accept it.

He prided himself on being a pretty unemotional guy, but now he was having to deal with irrational mood swings. One minute he was optimistic, determined to work his way into any cracks he could see, to find a foothold and frankly exploit it. The next minute he could smell her retreat and was at a loss as to whether to push forward or stand still. There was a helplessness to this situation that he found maddening, and it took all he had to tame his urge to *do something*.

His work was suffering. For the first time in his life he wasn't able to focus with the level of intensity he was so accustomed to. He was, for once, impotent. Unable to stamp his authority and get what he wanted, what he *knew* was right. And he *thought* about her. Without warning he would think about the sound of her laughter, or the way she sometimes looked at him out of the corner of her eye, or the things she said that could make him laugh out loud because her sense of humour so often mirrored his.

It was doing his head in.

'Separate quarters?' Maddie parroted.

'You needn't worry that your privacy is going to be invaded in any way,' Leo gritted, not looking at her but heaving the suitcases out of the car and preceding her into the villa. 'Although I should warn you in advance that there's no one here at the moment. We're both adults, and I didn't think it was necessary to have members of staff hovering here past their bedtime because we need chaperones.'

Maddie flushed, clearly apprehensive that he might not be able to restrain himself around her. Where would she have got that idea? Considering he'd backed right off and hadn't shown the slightest interest in her since she'd turned him down.

'Absolutely!' She smiled brightly and changed the subject. 'The villa is gorgeous, Leo. I'm surprised you don't want to retire here permanently!'

'Sun, sea and stars has never been my thing for longer than five minutes.'

Leo grinned that sexy grin that made her quiver inside.

'You're more wine, women and song?' Maddie quipped, following him into the villa and doing a complete turn as she absorbed her surroundings.

Cool shades of cream complemented wood and the bold silkscreen paintings on the walls. White shutters would keep the glare of the sun out. And as she wandered, agog, towards an expanse of glass towards the back of the villa, she glimpsed manicured lawns, lit up just as the front was.

When she turned around it was to find Leo looking at her—although he looked away as soon as their eyes met.

'Hungry?' he asked.

'A bit.'

'Kitchen's through here. Food will have been prepared and there will be no shortage of anything.'

'This is the most amazing house I've ever been in,' Maddie breathed, frankly awestruck and working hard to remember every socialist tendency that should be fighting to play down the shameless splendour of the villa.

Leo paused to look at her again, head tilted to one side. 'Funny, but I no longer notice my surroundings,' he mused truthfully.

'That's because you've always had far too much money,' she said sternly, and he burst out laughing, his navy eyes appreciative.

'I never thought I'd ever hear those words leave any woman's mouth.'

'Then you've been mixing with the wrong type of woman.'

She wasn't looking at him as she said this. She was

shamelessly peering out through the glass doors, squinting into the darkness, intrigued by the glimpse of an illuminated infinity pool.

'What sort of women do you think I *should* have been mixing with?'

Maddie started, because he had come up behind her and she could see his reflection in the glass—a towering, impossibly forceful presence that gave her goosebumps. The urge to sink back against that hard body was so overpowering that she inhaled deeply and stared blindly, trying hard to block him from her line of vision.

'Well?'

Leo stepped closer towards her. He had managed to angle the conversation into a place that felt highly personal, and suddenly he seemed determined to explore all those places she was trying to keep hidden from him—places where desire and lust were locked away.

'I—I don't know,' she stammered.

When she turned round it was to discover that he was even closer to her than she'd thought. But if she stepped back she'd bump into the glass. She was trapped with only inches between them.

Maddie could feel the heat emanating from his body in waves, and like a dose of incense it went to her head and made her feel giddy. She licked her lips and tried to think straight.

'Tut-tut,' Leo chided softly. 'You can't just make sweeping statements and then refuse to back them up. Do you think I should have been going out with earnest young women who like nothing better than to spend an evening discussing books?'

Maddie shifted and blushed. She tried to imagine Leo with a woman fitting that description and honestly couldn't think of *any* woman who wouldn't want to rip his clothes off within five seconds of occupying the same sofa as him.

'Well, they would have been better than women who like you for your money.'

'What makes you think that earnest young women who like discussing books wouldn't want me for my money? Wouldn't be impressed by all of this?' He spread his arms in an all-encompassing gesture, but his fabulous eyes remained firmly fixed to Maddie's face. 'After all, *you* are.'

Maddie glared at him and Leo laughed.

'But I do know that you weren't attracted to me because of my bank balance,' he murmured with satisfaction. 'Were you?'

Maddie muttered something inaudible. He was pinning her into a corner, standing just a fraction too close to her and looking at her just a little too intently and with slightly too much sexy humour for her to be comfortable.

Sex was off the menu!

But then she mentally kicked herself for even thinking that that would be going through his head. Leo was good at making her think all sorts of forbidden thoughts just by doing what he was doing now—getting just a little too much under her skin. He probably didn't even realise what he was doing!

Restless in her own skin, Maddie stared down for a few seconds and fidgeted.

'I really like that about you…'

Leo placed one finger under her chin in a barely there touch and Maddie immediately looked up, bright green eyes meeting deepest blue.

Suddenly she had somehow managed to turn into a swooning Victorian maiden—the same swooning maiden who had been bowled over by him, enough to leap into bed with him before he'd even finished asking. And as far as impulse decisions went, how clever had *that* one been? Considering she was standing here now, pregnant with his baby?

And yet...

When Maddie went through those 'sliding doors' and thought about the other road she might have gone down, she knew that she preferred this one.

What if he hadn't been after her store? What if he had genuinely been who he'd said he was? Or *implied* he was? A sexy guy just passing through—another rolling stone looking for adventure?

One night of passion and that would have been it. She would never have lain eyes on him again. She couldn't get her head around the enormity of that, because he had managed to become such a huge part of her life— always there in her thoughts in one way or another.

With the less attractive option—and the reason why she had to stand firm against the pulsing tide of craving that threatened to breach her defences the second she took her eye off the ball—came the realisation that under normal circumstances, and without a baby on the way, she *would* have met him again.

They would have had their one night and then she would have met the real Leo—the billionaire who wanted what she had and would stop at nothing to get his hands on it. He wouldn't have been toting her off to this fabulous villa in a tropical paradise. He would have been sitting, steely eyed, on the opposite side of a boardroom table while his team of lawyers tried to prise the store away from her. He wouldn't have given a damn about the sentiment wrapped up in her need to do something with her legacy. She would have been disposable.

Unfortunately nothing could stop the ache inside her when their eyes locked. It was as if he had somehow programmed her brain to ignore common sense. She could give herself a thousand bracing lectures about why she couldn't afford to let her body do the talking, but the second he did what he was doing now—looking at her *like that*—she was all lust and craving and weak-kneed desire.

'You bucked the trend,' Leo continued in the same musing low voice, as rich and as silky as the finest chocolate. 'You thought I had nothing and you weren't bothered. In fact what bothered you was thinking that you might have more than me...'

'I'm suspicious of rich guys after Adam,' Maddie breathed. 'And besides, I was raised not to place too much importance on money. I guess, when I look back, that was my mother's response to being disinherited. She'd given up everything for love. She couldn't start telling me that the only thing that mattered was money. But she must have found it so hard—especially in the beginning, when she could still remember what it was like to have everything she wanted at the snap of a finger.'

'Like I said...you bucked the trend...'

Maddie was mesmerised by his eyes, weakly unable to tear her gaze away. She blinked and gathered herself against the riptide pulling her under. 'Poor Leo. What a daily strain it must be, having to beat back women who want nothing more than to do whatever you want and fall into bed with you.'

Leo laughed and stepped back—which at least meant that she could breathe without fear that her airways would start closing up.

'Fortunately,' he drawled, 'I'm made of stern stuff, and I've found that I can handle that thorny dilemma reasonably well. Now, shall I show you to your quarters? You can shower and then join me for something to eat. It's late, but you need to fatten up.'

Wrenched out of her heated torpor, Maddie took a few seconds to establish that Leo was back to his usual self—casual and courteous and practically whistling a merry tune as he spun round and began sauntering off into the bowels of the sprawling villa.

She tripped along, soon catching up with him. She'd packed only one suitcase, which he'd retrieved from the airy hallway. When she reached for her carry-on he tut-tutted in a fashion that made her teeth snap together in frustration and took it from her.

'I'm not completely helpless, Leo,' she said, her mouth downturned and resentful because she knew that, however appropriate it was, this was not how she wished to be treated by him.

'In my eyes you are,' he purred, ignoring her tight-lipped expression and favouring her with a smile that was an annoying combination of ruefulness and pure charm. 'I hope this will do…'

He pushed open a door that led to the most wonderful bedroom Maddie had ever seen. The white wooden shutters were closed, but she knew that when they were open the light would flood in, because they covered the expanse of one entire wall. The king-sized bed was draped in the finest of mosquito nets, and the room was cooled by air-conditioning that was virtually silent. The décor, like in the rest of the villa, was pale. Cream walls, light bamboo furniture and an oversized squashy pale lemon sofa next to a door that led directly out onto the veranda that circled the house.

Leo was striding to another door, which he pushed open in the manner of an estate agent keen to show a prospective buyer all the home comforts.

'En-suite bathroom,' he said, and Maddie walked towards him and peered into a room the size of the apartment she had shared with her mother in Sydney.

Through an archway leading from the bedroom was a spacious sitting area, complete with a giant flat screen television and all the accoutrements of an office—which was the only indicator that the villa was used for work purposes much of the time.

He returned to the bedroom and stood to one side of the huge bed. 'Think you'll be comfortable?'

Maddie stared at him, mouth dry, and tried to get her wayward thoughts back in order—because seeing him there next to the bed was resurrecting all sorts of unfortunate memories.

She half closed her eyes and pictured his lean, muscular body splayed across the puffy white duvet, bronzed and hard and *naked*.

'It's perfect,' she croaked, jerkily heading to her suitcase and flipping it open so that he would get the message that it was time for him to leave.

Which he did.

'If you need anything…' Leo pointed to a bell which she hadn't noticed on the table next to the bed '…summon me…'

'Really?' Maddie almost smiled at his use of the expression. Without thinking, she added, half to herself,

'And what would you do?' Then she realised what she'd said and reddened.

'*You're* here to do nothing,' Leo told her, straight-faced, 'so basically I'll do whatever you want.'

The quiet charge of electricity thrummed between them.

'Oh? You'd cook and clean for me?' Maddie quipped, perversely tempted to keep him in the bedroom now that he was clearly itching to leave. 'Somehow I can't picture you doing *any* of that stuff, Leo.'

'Cleaning might be a problem,' he conceded with amusement. 'But I could definitely rise to the challenge of cooking—although there will be no need for that, bearing in mind I have round-the-clock staff who are paid to take care of those duties.'

For the first time in living memory he didn't flinch at the vision of domesticity that presented itself to him. He had a strangely satisfying vision of her resting on the sofa in his living room, heavy with his child, while he brought her home-cooked food.

He'd never cooked anything that hadn't come with printed instructions on the packet in which it was wrapped, but he was sure he could rustle up something and he rather enjoyed playing with that thought. Maybe in due course he would invest in a recipe book. Who knew? His life was changing, and it was going to change even more dramatically after the baby was born. Could he say with any certainty that he *wouldn't* be spending evenings in, wearing an apron and brandishing a spatula in front of the stove?

He grinned. The faster you accepted the inevitable, the better off you were. *Fact.*

He was pro-active, creative, solution-orientated, and

he seldom wasted energy pushing boulders up hills when they were very likely to come rolling right back down.

If you worked with what you'd got, however troublesome, you usually ended up coming out the victor. And, since Leo intended to come out the victor in this scenario, he was proud of the unusual tramline his thoughts were travelling along.

'Of course,' Maddie said politely.

'Although,' he mused, 'I might relieve them of some of their culinary duties.'

He wondered where the pots and pans were kept. It was an area of the kitchen he'd never felt the need to explore.

'Why would you do that?'

'Necessity,' Leo said succinctly. He lowered his eyes and looked at her lazily, each syllable leaving his mouth replete with intent. 'You will find that I'm a man who doesn't take shortcuts when it comes to the things that matter to me. My child will top that list. Having someone else prepare food will naturally work occasionally, but I'll do much of that myself.'

'You will?'

'What sort of father do you think I will be?'

'I—I haven't really given it much thought,' Maddie stammered, caught on the back foot at this unexpected tangent.

'I'm sure you have,' Leo responded wryly. 'Just as I'm sure that I don't emerge in those thoughts with flying colours. You think I would be an unsuitable rich husband who fails to live up to the storybook image in your head, and a likewise unsuitable rich father who thinks that money can take the place of time.'

'I've never thought anything of the sort!'

'Of course you did. At the risk of disillusioning you, I intend to be a hands-on father. My work life will be tailored to accommodate my child. I didn't envisage myself in the role of a father until it was sprung on me, but now that I am I will be giving it everything I have.'

He patiently waited for her to pounce. He almost felt that he knew her better than she knew herself.

Maddie shuffled as she sifted through what he was saying. Okay, so maybe she *had* been guilty of type-casting him as the wealthy but absent parent—but was that her fault? Workaholics were never interested in the small stuff, were they? Since when could she have expected the most eligible bachelor on the planet to willingly immerse himself in nappy-changing duties?

Was he just saying that to make a good impression?

No, why should he?

'So cooking practice might be just the thing.' Leo paused and looked at her after a moment's silence. 'And of course,' he continued, 'it would carry on, I imagine, even after I have found someone…'

'Found someone?' Maddie looked at him, disorientated. 'What are you talking about?'

'Well,' Leo said crisply, all business now, wrapping up their little *tête-à-tête* just at the point when she was hanging on to his every word, her heart beating like a crazy, caged bird inside her chest, 'you don't think that while you're roaming the streets in search of Prince Charming I'm going to be sitting in my apartment keeping the home fires burning as I pine for the marriage that never was, do you?'

Leo let the silence settle between them like a piece of lead dropping into still water, only to send concentric ripples across the surface, turning the stillness into a frenzy of motion.

He was by the bedroom door now, and he lounged against the doorframe, his lean, rangy body relaxed and at ease.

'Of course not!' Maddie was aware of her voice sounding a little less stable than usual and she cleared her throat.

'Good!' he said brightly. 'Because I won't be.'

'Although I really don't think it's acceptable for any child to be exposed to a constant carousel of women coming and going,' she protested stoutly, and Leo raised his eyebrows with an expression she understood completely. She was quick to clarify. 'I have no intention of entertaining a series of men in front of any child of mine!'

'And you have my word that I will likewise be extremely discreet in all *my* relationships.'

He watched as she fidgeted and stared at him. For a few seconds he was distracted by the lushness of her parted mouth and the soft little breaths coming from her. It surprised him how many of her mannerisms he had absorbed over time—right down to the way she had just tossed her hair back in a gesture that was proud, feisty and unconsciously sexy.

He had no intention of stressing her out. He had brought her here so that she could *de*-stress. But neither was he going to spend this valuable one-on-one time tiptoeing around her and waiting patiently for her to come to her senses.

When they returned to London and Benito was back from his cruise, he would condescend to meet the mother of his much longed-for grandchild, and Leo intended the picture to be complete, with wedding bells chiming in the not too distant future if not immediately imminent. He knew that Benito Conti would be bitterly disappointed to be presented with a complicated scenario of joint custody and visiting rights.

'The only woman our child will meet will be the woman who will become his or her stepmother.'

A dull pain spread through Maddie, making her limbs heavy. She suddenly wanted to be sick, because this very likely possibility was one she had not considered in much detail. She'd been far too wrapped up in standing her ground and refusing to compromise on her principles.

'I know you'll agree with me that our child would benefit from that.'

'So you wouldn't object if *I* found someone else?'

'What could I do?'

Leo gritted his teeth and controlled the insane thought that he would be tempted to pummel whoever she happened to find, which had to be double standards at their very worst.

'As you pointed out, isn't that the way of the world these days? Split families and children being ferried from one set of parents to the other? Half-brothers and stepsisters and stepfathers and Christmas celebrated ten times a year so that everyone can get a look-in?'

Maddie didn't reply, because she was busy wondering what this wife-to-be of his would look like. It was galling, but true, that whilst as a single mother her ranking on the eligibility scale would plummet, he, as a single father, would discover that his had hit the stratosphere.

There was nothing a woman loved more than a guy

with a baby. It brought out every maternal instinct in them. Throw *rich beyond belief* and *sinfully sexy* into the mix and Leo would be lucky if he could get two steps out of his penthouse apartment before finding a queue of eager candidates waiting to interview for the job of perfect stepmother to his child. *Her* child!

'But enough of this,' he concluded. 'Towels should be in the bathroom, and there are more beauty products in the cupboard than on the beauty counter at the store. I gave very precise instructions as to the stocking of essentials while we were here.'

'Okay...' Maddie said, in a daze.

'No routine out here. I will continue working for much of the day, but I'm sure I can find time to show you around the island. Primarily, though, you're to do as you please. Come and go as you want. You may have spotted the swimming pool? You'll find it quite stunning. It overlooks the ocean. If you need anything at all, there's the bell...'

He grinned and gave her a little half-salute, but she was too distracted to respond in kind. Instead she nodded, and found that she actually needed to force herself to breathe when the bedroom door had closed quietly behind him.

CHAPTER NINE

'I'VE MADE A SCHEDULE,' Leo said, brandishing a printed sheet of paper as Maddie walked into the kitchen the following morning at a little after nine.

'You should have woken me up,' she said, sniffing and clearly detecting the smell of bacon. 'I never get up this late.'

'It's important that you get your rest.' He ushered her to a chair and sat her down. 'Sleep well?'

'Have you…*cooked*?'

'"Cooked" is a big word. I prefer to say *dabbled*. I thought I'd give the staff some time off while we're here. After all, in my role of *father* I'm going to have to function without a team of people picking up the pieces behind me all the time.'

Leo had had time to think. She disliked the notion of marriage as a business transaction. She wanted romance. She wanted to be swept off her feet by the perfect guy. He wasn't the perfect guy for her, and he wasn't going to pretend that he was. He wasn't going to wax lyrical about love. But he *was* going to show her what he was made of when it came to fulfilling his responsibilities.

As a bonus, he would also be showing her what another woman might find appealing. Goodbye Leo the womaniser and hello Leo the dutiful dad with apron and spatula. And, of course, the baby…

All's fair in love and war, he thought and finding solutions to problems was his forte, whatever the problem might be.

This was his solution and he was going to bring everything to the table.

'So what did you…er…*dabble* in?' Maddie asked.

'Bacon. Eggs. Bread.' He brought two plates to the table and continued doing whatever he was doing with his back to her, a tea towel slung over one shoulder.

He looked drop-dead gorgeous, and Maddie had to stare. He was wearing low-slung khaki shorts and a faded tee shirt and he was barefoot. With his back to her, she could appreciate the long lines of his lean body, the strength of his muscular legs, the width of his broad shoulders.

It didn't seem fair that a man in old clothes with a tea towel over his shoulder should look so mouthwatering.

Any woman looking at him right now wouldn't be able to resist.

Stick a baby in a high chair next to him and he'd have to beat them away with sticks.

She felt queasy thinking about it.

'Have you ever done anything this…ambitious… before?'

Leo produced a big white plate on which some charred bacon sat, spread across four fried eggs.

'Timing may have been an issue,' Leo declared, fetching a heaping mound of toast, 'but practice will make perfect. Eat up. You need to get nutrients into you after the fiasco with your kitchen. By the way, I got an email this morning. Things are already moving on that front.'

'Really?' Maddie helped herself to a slice of toast and then to one of the less dangerously overcooked rashers of bacon. 'But it's only been a matter of a day...'

'I said I'd sort it, and it'll be sorted in record time. I snap my fingers and people jump. Now, about this schedule.'

'Schedule?'

'I don't want you feeling bored while you're here.'

'Leo, I don't think it would be possible to feel bored here. There's the pool and the wonderful gardens to explore, and I'm very happy to wander into town and have a look around. I don't want you to think that you have to put yourself out for me.'

Leo paused, fork raised to his mouth, and looked at her. 'Wander into town?' In that little flowered sundress that made her look as pure as the driven snow and as sexy as the hottest siren? Over his dead body. No one would guess that she was pregnant. She'd be knee-deep in lecherous men within seconds.

'A tour of the island.' He swept aside her contribution and carried on eating. 'I have a boat docked in one of the sheltered bays. Nothing fancy.'

'You keep a boat here? Whatever for, when you hardly use the villa?'

'Guests at the villa are welcome to use it. It gets used. How are you on the swimming front?'

'I'm not exactly a fish...'

'I thought Australia was all about the outdoor life...?'

'Swimming lessons are pricey. I'm a self-taught swimmer. I get by, but I wouldn't put money on my chances of surviving in a riptide.'

'Then it's just as well,' Leo said smugly, 'that I'll be there every step of the way to keep an eye on you. Fortunately I'm a first-class swimmer.'

Maddie rolled her eyes. He was determined to treat her like an invalid. She should protest, but there was a warm, cosy feeling inside her created by the attention and she was rather enjoying it.

She'd never had attention—not really. Her mother had loved her, but she had been so busy working to make ends meet that there hadn't been time for lots of bonding sessions, and for the last few years of her life *she* had been the one requiring attention.

Then Maddie had gone into the business of caring for Lacey. And when Adam had come along, she had basked in the glow of thinking that she was loved. But, looking back, she could see that Adam had dressed her like a doll to be showcased, and had never shown that he loved her for who she was when she wasn't draped in the latest fashions and expensive jewellery. She could see now that he had been so conscious of the disparity in their status that cossetting her had never even occurred to him. She'd been arm candy. Nothing more.

There had been no other relatives in her life to lean on—no siblings, no doting grandparents, no aunts or uncles or cousins.

So what was the harm in accepting a little pampering from Leo?

'So, if you get your swimsuit…' He stood up briskly. 'I'll meet you in the hall in say…half an hour?'

'We should tidy the kitchen.'

'Leave all that.' Leo removed the plate from her hand. 'I'll deal with it later, once we're back from our day's activities.'

'We're going for *the day*?'

'Unless you have an unavoidable appointment?'

'No, but…'

Don't do this, don't be so nice that I start regretting my decision.

'What about work?'

'I can't remember the last time I had a holiday. A few days off isn't going to kill me. And, anyway, I'm keeping on top of things via email.'

Maddie was amused and a little relieved to find out that there would be no burnt offerings for lunch, because forty minutes later they were swinging by one of the few restaurants in the town, where he collected a picnic hamper and a cooler bag of drinks.

It was hot, the sun beating down from a cloudless turquoise sky, and the island was so small that it was possible to see the distant strip of sea from either side of the car as it bumped along away from the town.

Fringes of coconut trees lined the small ribbon of road, stretching into the distance—banks of them like upright soldiers on parade.

Every so often she would see a flash of deep blue sea, and then, after twenty minutes of driving, they were ploughing down a rocky incline and pulling into a cove.

It was a private beach, small but perfectly formed. Backed into the shrubbery among the coconut trees was a small cabin, and moored to one side was the boat he had told her about.

'How many properties like these do you own?' she asked as he swung round to help her out of the Jeep.

'A handful. All investment places. Some used slightly more than others.'

'Don't you get tired of London? Want to escape to some place like this?'

'I've never been good at escaping,' Leo confessed. He looked at her and then brushed some of her hair away from her face.

'If you were born into money...'

She bent down to pull off her sandals and Leo drew in a sharp breath, causing her to look up, catch his eyes on her cleavage and the black swimsuit holding in her pouting breasts, which were bigger and fuller now with her new pregnant figure. She looked away and quickly straightened, hopping a little because the sand was hot.

'Then surely you must have had loads of opportunity to do whatever you wanted...'

'I must have been born with an over-developed responsibility gene. That sand's hot.' He swept her off her feet and carried her to the cabin. 'Make sure you apply lots of sunblock. I'm going to fetch the hamper and we can relax for a while before we take the boat out.'

Maddie looked at him for a while, silent and speculative. He *did* that. He only told her what he wanted her to know. He never spoke about anything personal and she wished she could get into his head and prise out his secrets. He knew all hers!

'Okay.'

She shrugged. She was going to enjoy the day and enjoy being away from the chaos of the house and the weight of running the store.

The cabin was small but exquisite, as lovely as anything money could buy. She opened the few doors and peered into two bedrooms and two bathrooms, a bedroom and another bathroom on either side of a wooden-floored sitting area and an open-plan kitchen. Lots of squashy sofas and low tables.

She replaced her dress with a sarong and rubbed sun-block all over. She was used to the sun, having lived in Australia, and knew that taking chances was never a good idea, even though she tanned easily.

She looked in the full-length mirror and saw a girl who looked radiant. Her skin had deepened over the summer to the colour of a latte—her Italian ancestry shining through. Her hair was almost down to her waist. When she turned to the side she could see the small but definite bump of her tummy.

The biggest change to her appearance, though, was that the misery of the past few years and the horror of what had happened to her before she'd left Australia were no longer etched on her face.

She looked...*happy*. She was pregnant after a one-night stand, the house she had inherited had been all but dismantled the last time she'd set eyes on it, and the responsibility of running the store was a weight that couldn't be underestimated because other people's live-lihoods were at stake, and yet she was *happy*.

Happy to be right here, right now, with a man who wasn't in love with her and never would be. Just happy to be around him.

It was a frightening thought, and it made her heart beat fast—because there could only be one reason why she felt so content, despite the many things that should be concerning her.

Leo didn't love her, but that didn't mean *she* hadn't fallen for *him*—because she had. He'd got under her skin, and now that he had lodged there she couldn't prise him away.

Ever since she'd become pregnant he'd been a rock, and never more so than now. He was determined to prove just how solid he could be and it was a seductive tactic—because it was making her rethink the decision she had made.

Still pensive, she went out to find that he had set up camp under a canopy of coconut trees. She took a few seconds to absorb the setting. Powdery white sand sloping down to crystal-clear water as blue as the sky above it…rocks and coconut trees embracing the cove…the brightly painted boat now bobbing in the water to one side…and Leo, hunky and sexy and willing to cook her breakfast because he felt she needed looking after.

Had she been seeing everything from a skewed perspective? Instead of bemoaning the fact that he was protective because of the baby she was carrying and not because of *her*, should she instead just be seeing his drive to be protective as something to be lauded? As an indication of his strength of character and his fundamental decency?

Her formative experience with men had come in the form of her father, who had jumped ship and bailed on wedlock the second he'd discovered that her mother came without the dowry he'd banked on. And then Adam, who had treated her like a mannequin and then dumped her when she'd been accused of theft because he'd thought that someone who didn't come from his class couldn't possibly have principles.

And yet, despite her experiences, she realised she'd put a lot of faith in love. Heck, she'd dug her heels in and turned down Leo's marriage proposal because he didn't love her.

But what she'd failed to appreciate was that there

were all sorts of counter-arguments for the deal he'd proposed that made a lot of sense. Including the fact that not marrying him meant she'd have to face the idea of him not being in her life after the baby was born.

Leo glanced across and saw her standing there, looking at him pensively. She quickly looked away, out towards the water, but she wasn't fast enough to miss the appreciative glance he cast over her rounded stomach, which he was seeing for the first time. She suddenly realised how little the wisp of floaty fabric tied around her waist did to cover her.

'Have you remembered the sunblock?' he asked, with a hint of some deeper thought in his voice.

Maddie remembered that her feeling resentful because his concern was solely directed with the baby in mind should not be on the cards, and so she smiled and nodded.

'It's practically a criminal offence to go out without sunblock in Australia. You're really well prepared for a day at the beach, Leo.' She eyed the picture-perfect oversized towel, the hamper, the fluffy beach towels rolled into sausage shapes.

'I'm going to put the food inside,' he responded. 'Then what about a bit of sailing?'

'Are you sure…'

'That I'm a master sailor? Yes.' He grinned. 'You'll be safe with me.'

But my heart won't be, she thought as he disappeared into the cabin, and reappeared almost immediately, hand outstretched to lead her to the boat.

She felt a frisson as their fingers linked and then as he helped her in, settling her under the canopy and taking the wheel.

Maddie leaned back and closed her eyes, and as the boat chugged off in a very sedate manner she smiled, letting the wind blow her hair all round her face.

It was too noisy with the engine running to talk, and she liked that because she needed to think. She needed to do something with the churning in her head. She needed to sift through the tangle of confused thoughts and put them into some kind of order.

She needed to ask herself whether she had made the right decision in turning him down and whether it was too late to reverse that decision.

She half opened her eyes and drank him in. He'd unbuttoned his shirt and it whipped behind him, exposing the bronzed perfection of his torso. His swimming trunks were baggy, riding low on his lean hips, and he was steering with one hand, dark sunglasses in place.

He took her breath away.

He would take any woman's breath away.

If they were married, though, she wouldn't have to deal with the pain of watching him take those other women's breath away.

She walked towards him and stood right next to him, slinging her arm casually around his waist.

Leo stiffened, but didn't glance down at her.

'I'll anchor in a couple of minutes,' he said roughly. 'If you're not confident in the water you can stick to the side of the boat. The ladder will be down. You can climb up any time you get nervous. Or you don't have to come in at all. Although…' He breathed in the scent of her and felt a rush of desire. 'I hope you do. The water here is warm. If you're feeling brave, we can grab a couple of snorkels and see what's there.'

'Should I be scared?'

'Never with me around.'

He killed the engine and it spluttered into silence. When he drew back to look at her she was shading her eyes against the glare, her face upturned to his.

'You *do* make me feel safe,' she confided truthfully. 'And I know I haven't said this before, but I really appreciate everything you're doing for me now that I'm pregnant.'

Leo wondered whether she knew what that arm round his waist had done to him and how those glass-green eyes were affecting him.

'Good!' he said heartily. 'Swim?'

He turned away before his arousal became overpowering and paused on the edge of the boat, desperate for some cold water to kill his rampant libido.

'Definitely!' Maddie laughed and untied her sarong, and then faced him, still smiling.

She was the most beautiful thing he'd ever seen, and Leo dived into the sea before he let loose a groan of desire. He swam underwater, his powerful body sleek and brown as he sliced through the water and surfaced wiping his face.

She was tentatively taking the steps down and he swam towards her to help.

'I can manage!' Maddie laughed, but she did curve round and link her fingers behind his neck briefly before letting go and doggy-paddling by the ladder. 'This is as good as it gets with me. I can swim *a bit*...'

'Hang on to the ladder. I'm going to get the snorkels. There's a lifesaver ring you can hold, to make sure you don't feel out of your depth.'

'I won't need that,' Maddie teased breathlessly, 'Not when you're here and you've said that I can trust you.'

Hell, she was doing it again...turning him on when she obviously didn't mean to...

Five minutes later they were snorkelling, and Maddie was clearly having the time of her life.

It was strange that she'd never done anything like this before, especially as she'd lived in a country famed for its Great Barrier Reef and its exotic underwater life.

She got a bit braver the longer they were in the water, venturing further out holding on to Leo. She only reluctantly returned to the boat when he tapped her and told her how long they'd been swimming.

'That was amazing,' she confessed excitedly, removing the snorkel and shaking her hair, before flipping it into a makeshift braid that hung like a wet burnished gold rope down her back. 'I could do that every day!'

Leo grinned. 'Then we'll have to do something about that,' he drawled, towelling himself dry and slinging the damp towel across his shoulders.

Their eyes met and he didn't look away. Nor did she.

When she walked towards him—carefully, because a boat was not the steadiest surface in the world—he didn't move a muscle. He waited. As still and as watchful as a jungle animal on high alert.

He was picking up all sorts of signals and he didn't know what to believe and what not to believe. But when she stopped right in front of him and looked up at him he knew exactly what to believe.

'You shouldn't,' he said roughly.

'Shouldn't what?'

'Stand there looking at me as though you want me

to strip you bare and make love to you right here on this boat.'

Maddie looked down, suddenly shy. She was pregnant with his baby, and yet here she was *shy*?

'Is that what you want, *cara*?'

He tilted her chin and met her apple-green eyes steadily.

'Do you want me to do this?'

He trailed one long brown finger along her cleavage and she shuddered and let loose a stifled little gasp.

'What about this?'

He reached to the straps of her swimsuit and hooked his fingers under before he slowly began pulling them down, watching her carefully, getting more and more worked up with every passing second.

It was his turn to stifle a groan of pure pleasure as her breasts were exposed, pale orbs with those delectable rosy nipples, bigger and darker now, just as her breasts were fuller and heavier. He was startled to see that his hands were shaking as he rubbed the tips of her nipples with the pads of his thumbs. The swimsuit had bunched up at her waist and he badly wanted to take it off completely, but he hesitated.

'Is this what you want?' he demanded unsteadily. 'Because it's what *I* want…'

Maddie nodded, and Leo did what he wanted to do. He pulled off her swimsuit and then devoted himself to her body, tasting it, working his way down while she remained standing, holding on to the steel pole supporting the canopy. Her head was flung back and her mouth was half open as she moaned, a low, guttural sound as his mouth found the patch between her legs and he burrowed there, nuzzling before gently parting the folds of her womanhood so that he could slide his tongue into her slick groove.

Maddie plunged her fingers into his springy hair, arched her back and *enjoyed*. She opened her legs wider, sank against his tongue, bucked as it teased her and came explosively against his mouth, twisting and crying out while the sea breeze blew strands of hair across her open mouth and warmed her breasts.

'I can't stop wanting you,' she gasped, finally collapsing against him and letting him carry her down the stunted row of stairs that led to the small living area on the boat. There was no bed, but there was a long, upholstered bench seat, and he lay her down and stood up to look at her nakedness.

'And I you,' he growled.

Leo couldn't get his shirt off fast enough, and then the swimming trunks. And he couldn't take his eyes off her rosy flushed face. He was captivated by the way she lay there, idly stroking her breast with one hand, mesmerised by her swollen stomach.

'Is this safe?' he asked, sinking onto the bench seat alongside her and wishing he'd had the wit to install something more accommodating.

'Of course it is!' Maddie laughed and kissed him. 'I just need you, Leo. I need you to come inside me…'

Leo needed no further encouragement. Some foreplay? *Yes*. He suckled her breasts and idly played between her thighs. He wanted to devote more time to both, but he couldn't because his animal cravings were too intense.

This was his woman—ripe with his child. A surge of possessiveness and fierce pride rushed through him as he pushed into her, taking her in long, hard strokes, only just holding on for her to reach her peak before coming inside her, pouring himself into her and crying out with the pleasure and satisfaction of it.

He'd never experienced anything like it in his life before. He couldn't let this woman go. He couldn't let any other man hold the child she was carrying. The only man who would ever hold this baby would be him.

He was obviously a lot less New Age than he'd imagined.

'Marry me, Maddie.'

The silence was the length of a heartbeat and then Maddie nodded, still flushed from lovemaking.

'Okay.'

Leo dealt her a slow, slashing smile that took her breath away. 'You changed your mind?' he said, knowing he should leave well alone but needing to hear why she had come round to his way of thinking.

A post-coital rush of heated acquiescence would inevitably lead to a sober rethink in the cold light of day.

'I changed my mind,' Maddie said. 'In an ideal world, this isn't how I saw my life going—marrying a man for the sake of a baby. But it's not an ideal world and you were right. I should be the first to recognise that. I've seen how attentive you can be, Leo. You would make a great dad. That's enough for me.'

It would never really be enough, but it would have to do. And in time, who knew…? Perhaps he would come to love her the way she loved him.

'Are you sure?' His navy blue eyes were thoughtful. 'Sure you can do without the fairy tale? I'm not built for the business of falling in love, Maddie.'

Maddie didn't skip a beat, because she'd made her decision and she was going to stand by it. She adored this man, and she would always nurture the hope that his heart would open up to her, but she would never let him see that. He wanted a business transaction, and that was what he was going to get.

'I know,' she said, and shrugged. 'Maybe I'm not either. Now, let's not talk any more. Have I told you that I can't seem to get enough of you…?'

Maddie swept up the trail of clothes on the floor. On the bed, Leo was half dozing, half looking at her, sated after a bout of extremely satisfying early-morning sex.

'You're very untidy, Leo. Is that one of the bad habits of coming from a wealthy background? You're so used to people tidying up behind you that you've forgotten how to do it yourself?'

But her voice was light and teasing. The past three days had been the best three days of her entire life. He made her feel so safe, so secure, so *cherished*. Maddie knew that it was dangerous, but she could just *feel* something between them. He said he didn't 'do' love, but surely he wouldn't be so attentive and tender if he didn't feel at least *some* of what she was feeling. Surely!

He had never spoken about what had turned him off all the things that propelled most normal people into marriage, for better or for worse, and she hadn't asked. They had their pact and she wasn't going to start rocking any boats. She was going to play the long game.

She picked up his shorts, tutting, and shook them, dislodging his wallet from the pocket. It flew open, discharging its contents. Platinum cards, business cards, cash and…

Maddie frowned and stooped to retrieve the picture

that had fallen out along with everything else. She held it up to the light.

Staring back at her was a fair-haired woman with full lips and bright blue laughing eyes. There was something knowing about those eyes. And an undeniable sensuality. The woman was looking down at whoever was taking the picture and her lips were parted...teasing, tempting.

Maddie shivered—because now she *knew*. She walked over to Leo, who had sat up, and showed him the picture.

'Who's this?' she asked lightly.

Leo stilled. He reached for the photo without bothering to look at it and stuck it on the bedside table.

She'd hoped he would say it was no one of any importance, but a steely resolve had washed over his features when he turned back to her.

'That is my ex-wife.'

CHAPTER TEN

'YOUR EX-*WIFE*,' MADDIE said woodenly, folding her arms, colour draining from her face faster than water going down a drain. 'You were *married*. And you didn't think that it was important enough to tell me?'

Suddenly restless, Leo vaulted upright, gloriously and unashamedly naked. He grabbed the nearest item of clothing, which happened to be his boxers, and stepped into them.

'How is it something that impacts on us?' His voice was cool and toneless, and that said more than words alone could ever say.

That woman in the picture was his wife, who had meant so much to him that he couldn't even let her name pass his lips. *This* was the mysterious reason why he wasn't interested in love. Because he'd been there before. He'd given his heart to someone else and he no longer possessed one to give to anyone who followed.

All Maddie's dreams and hopes about time working its magic and building the sort of love in him for her that she felt for him had been castles in the sand, now washed away by grim reality.

'"How is it something that impacts on us?"'

Maddie stared at him with incredulity and Leo had the grace to flush.

'It's in the past.'

'But don't you think it's a past you should have *told* me about? I mean, you know all about mine...'

'You chose to tell me,' Leo pointed out, with the sort of remorseless logic that set her teeth on edge. Caught on the back foot, Leo always fell back on his automatic instinct to defend himself.

'I chose to share my past with you.'

'The implication being that I should return the favour?'

'Most normal people would.'

'Haven't you deduced by now that I don't play by the same rules?'

Yes, Maddie thought miserably, yes, she had. She had just opted to ignore it.

She flung on her dressing gown and stared down at her bare feet, at the pale pink of the polish she had put on her toenails the evening before.

'Where is she now?' she asked stiffly, wondering if she should be on the lookout for the sexy blonde he had loved popping out from the nearest wardrobe or lurking behind the bushes wearing nothing but that sexy, *sexy* smile.

'Things didn't work out.'

'"Things didn't work out"? But you still keep a picture of her in your wallet?'

What sort of response *was that*? What did *things didn't work out* even *mean*? Obviously whatever had happened he had been bitterly hurt and fatally scarred.

'Where are you going with this, Maddie? That part of my past has nothing to do with us. You have to trust me.'

Maddie swallowed back her hurt. She had agreed to marry this man and she loved him. He had his past, just as she had hers, and marrying him would mean living with that and dealing with it, but she couldn't live without him.

She knew what would happen if she got into a flaming row with him over this. He would vanish. To his office or out in the Jeep to a beach, or into the garden… Anywhere just as long as she wasn't there, because he wasn't going to deal with her hysterics.

Dealing with her hysterics and her jealousy wasn't part of their business transaction.

'I'm going to have a bath,' she said, turning away.

Leo nodded and said nothing. What was there to say? He had closed the door on that slice of his past and he wasn't going to re-open it. What would be the good in that? Maddie would have to trust him.

But he had glimpsed that shattered expression on her face as she had turned away and something inside him had twisted painfully.

He didn't wait for her to emerge. Instead he flung on some clothes, headed down to the pool and washed away his restlessness by swimming lap after lap after lap until every muscle in his body was aching.

When he returned to the villa it was to find her in the kitchen, seemingly back to normal.

'Where were you?' she asked from where she was standing by the stove, putting on a saucepan with some butter, ready for the eggs that stood on the counter nearby.

It must have taken so much for her to act as though nothing had happened, but she managed it.

She also managed to smile at him.

'I'm making us some of those eggs we bought at the market this morning.'

Leo looked at her, trying to gauge her mood and feeling a little disconcerted that there was nothing to gauge. If she'd been hurt by his silence then she'd recovered fast. He frowned, not knowing how that speedy recovery made him feel.

'Okay. Great. I was in the pool.'

He hovered, for once indecisive. Should he revive the subject of Claire? He frowned, because it wasn't like him to backtrack on any decision once that decision had been made—and he'd made the decision not to start babbling on about his past, on which the door had been shut.

'It looks lovely out there,' Maddie said gaily, a broad smile pinned to her face.

She sounded like a Stepford Wife. All that was missing was the gingham apron.

'Anyway, breakfast will be ready in about five minutes. Does that give you enough time to change?'

Leo grunted and disappeared, duly reappearing in under five minutes in a pair of faded blue Bermuda shorts and a white tee shirt, barefoot as always. He couldn't see the point of wearing shoes in the villa when the floor was so warm.

He gritted his teeth and wondered how it was that he was about to bring up a subject he had only minutes before sworn to avoid.

'About Claire...'

Maddie looked at him seriously. Really? He wanted to talk about his ex? Did he think that she actually *wanted* to hear about how much he had given himself to a relationship that hadn't worked out? Did she need an explanation as to why he could never give again?

No way. That would not only be a dagger to her heart, but a dagger twisting and swivelling and causing maximum damage. *Thanks, but no thanks.*

'No,' she said.

'No?'

'I don't want to talk about her. Like you said, that's your past and this is the present. We both know why we're going into this…er…arrangement. We both know that it's not the sort of marriage that most people dream about. But it's the right thing for us to do. I know that. Like I said, I've seen for myself what a good dad you would make, and we might not be a traditional couple, with all the traditional hopes and dreams, but we get along all right and that's the main thing.'

Said out loud, it sounded like a poor excuse for a union. But then she thought of her life without Leo, and the horror that image conjured up reaffirmed why she was doing what she was. He would never love her. He hadn't been lying when he'd said that he just didn't have it in him. But she would always love *him*.

She was surprised to see that Leo didn't look relieved and elated that they were on the same page. The look on his face was more…*dissatisfaction.*

He swept aside her response. 'We have something else going for us.'

'What's that?'

'This.'

He pulled her towards him and kissed her. Kissed her until she was drugged with wanting him and on fire to have him touch her the way only he could.

When he did this—kissed her and held her and let

his body do the talking—she forgot everything. Forgot the fact that she was in love with a man who'd given his heart away to someone else. Forgot that she felt like a hypocrite, hiding her aching heart under a cheery smile.

She grunted with pleasure as he pushed down her shorts so that he could caress her swollen belly.

Her pregnancy fascinated him, and his fascination thrilled her. He slid his fingers lower, taking his time to caress her intimately with slow, rhythmic movements that left her panting with pleasure.

He whispered in her ear what he wanted to do to her, where he wanted to touch and feel and taste, until Maddie was giddy with desire. Then, still taking his time, he sat her on the edge of the table and she supported herself, hands stretched out behind her, palms flat on the smooth, polished wood.

He tugged off the shorts, taking her knickers at the same time, and pushed up her tee shirt so that he could see her breasts. Then he undid his zipper and dropped his shorts to the ground.

Her eyes were closed and she sighed and moaned softly as he slid into her, angling her body so that he could take her in a few thrusts. Quick, hot sex that swept away everything in its path.

'I can't get enough of you…' he growled, when they were both sated and normal business had resumed—although the eggs were burned and had had to be chucked.

Enough of the sex, Maddie completed in her head. But she couldn't get enough of that either. And that, if she was going through the *pros* checklist, counted for a lot.

'Well, you'll have to make do for the moment,' she told him lightly. 'We've made plans for today. I'm looking forward to seeing that cove you were telling me about.'

Another bright smile. Her jaw was beginning to ache from the effort of those bright smiles.

Leo kissed the tip of her nose.

'And then back to Dublin,' Maddie said, tidying up, thinking of the house she'd left behind, which she knew was now in great order because Leo had been showing her daily updates of the work that was being done. Only the attic needed a bit of sprucing up.

'But not like before,' Leo reminded her. 'This time back to Dublin as a couple.'

Maddie choked down a painful lump. 'Yes,' she mumbled, looking away, 'as a couple…'

It was another two and a half weeks before Maddie finally made it up to the attic—the final thing on her to-do list. With Leo's support, everything that had seemed difficult and daunting had become manageable. He had helped in ways that he had said were small and incidental, but when she examined them later she saw they were huge and fundamental.

The house was near completion and new staff had been hired at the store and renovations had begun. The cobwebby elegance of a past era was being replaced by a modernist vision, but it was going to stay as the store it was meant to be.

The attic was her final as yet unexplored territory, which was why now, at a little after six in the evening, with Leo due to come over in an hour, Maddie was sitting on the ground surrounded by…*stuff*.

Boxes of old bills, receipts, random scraps of paper with names on them, which she deciphered as being the names of horses or dogs or whatever it was her grand-father had been wont to bet on. And then there were the pictures. These Maddie took her time with, look-ing at them one by one. Pictures of her grandmother, her mother—photos dating back decades.

She was barely aware of Leo, padding up the wind-ing narrow staircase that led off from one of the top bedrooms to the enormous attic.

'You can help,' she announced, pausing to look at him and then struggling to tear her eyes away, as al-ways happened.

He'd come straight from work. He'd already located premises for his offices, and magically everything had been completed with supersonic speed. His faith in the power of money had not been misplaced.

'Okay. I'll arrange for a clearance company. They can come in and remove the entire lot. I've never been in such an unmitigated disaster zone in my entire life.'

'I've got some photos here, Leo.' She shuffled over to where he had taken up residence on the floor and sat next to him, going through the pictures, marvelling at the past unfolding in front of her. Her mother had been quite remarkable-looking—as had her grandparents.

'He went bad after your grandmother died,' Leo said neutrally.

'Your grandfather told you that?'

'There was bad blood between them before that, with the acquisition of the store premises, but I believe there was some scattered correspondence between them for a while after. When your grandmother died the old man went down a different road.'

'You've not mentioned any of that before,' Maddie murmured absently, sifting through the photos and at the bottom finding a slender stack of envelopes. Maybe five.

Her mother's handwriting was on them, and Leo reached out to take them from her.

'Maddie…'

But she was already opening the first letter and Leo's jaw clenched as he read it over her shoulder—read the pleading note from Lizzie Gallo to her unforgiving father, and knew that the other letters would be along the same lines.

'Leo…' Maddie whispered, turning to look at him. 'I thought…'

'You did,' Leo said gravely.

He stroked her hair away from her face, noted the way her eyes had glazed over, the quiver of her mouth. If the old bastard had been around he wouldn't have seen the light of another day.

'You knew?'

He nodded on a sigh. 'Yes,' he confessed. 'There were words between Tommaso and my grandfather a long time ago. Probably shortly after your mother had decamped to Australia. Who knows whether she did that to get away from the toxic atmosphere in the house? Tommaso never recovered from Susan's death. My grandfather got in touch about buying the store. He got a letter back. I won't bother to tell you what it said. I imagine you can guess the gist.'

'That he would never sell the store—just like he would never forgive my mother, even though she'd begged for forgiveness. She had it so hard in Australia. Worked her fingers to the bone to earn money for both of us. And he refused to give her anything.'

'He was a bastard.'

'You never said…'

'You had your dreams and I wasn't going to shatter them,' Leo told her.

'I don't want the store,' Maddie whispered. 'It was never a legacy of love.'

'You don't know that.' Leo sighed. 'Things change when you're facing the grim reaper. Who knows what was going through the old man's head when he made that will?'

'You think?'

'I do think. Your mother was stubborn, and so was he. He couldn't bring himself to forgive, but he must have lived a life of regret—hence the gambling and the alcohol.'

'Why didn't you say anything?'

'I couldn't hurt you, Maddie.' He drew his breath in. 'I could never hurt you,' he continued in a roughened undertone.

He shifted so that he was looking directly at her. The lighting in the attic was dim—just shafts of watery sunshine filtering through the glass of the four Velux windows on the slanting roof.

'I need to tell you about my ex-wife. About Claire.'

'Please don't, Leo. I… I… No, please don't. I understand how you feel. Things didn't work out and it hurt you so much that you still can't bear to talk about it. You loved and you lost and, lest you forget, you keep her photo in your wallet. I get it. I just don't want the details.' She smiled weakly. 'There's such a thing as too much information.'

'Silly fool,' Leo said tenderly. 'Is that what you think?'

'What else? No one hangs on to a photo of someone they couldn't give a hoot about.'

'I keep that photo as a reminder of the biggest mistake I ever made,' he said heavily, and Maddie's eyebrows shot up in surprise. 'I was young and cocky and I fell for an older woman.' He grinned crookedly. 'I was a cliché, in other words. Except I was rich, so I could *get* the older woman. But she turned out to be a fortune-hunter who had spotted in me the perfect opportunity to feather her nest. And, rich young buck that I was, I fell for it hook, line and sinker. I married her and it lasted about two seconds. It was the most expensive mistake I ever made. She took the money and vanished as a wealthy divorcee, and after that...'

'You threw away the key to your heart?'

Maddie wanted to keep grounded, but inside she was taking flight, heady with the realisation that her assumptions had been unfounded.

'I threw away the key to my heart,' Leo concurred. 'And I thought that it was for the best. No love and no pretending that I was capable of it. I never banked on *you* coming along.'

'Say that again?' Maddie held her breath and tried hard to look puzzled and yet empathetic when inside her heart was racing and her mouth was dry.

'I never banked on you coming along. I never banked on falling in love. *Really* in love. In love so that I can't think of life without you in it, Maddie. In love so that if anyone tries to hurt you, I will kill them.'

'Leo...' Slowly, she smiled, heady and deliriously happy. 'You're saying all the right things.'

She reached out and ran a dusty finger across his cheek.

'I love you so much. I knew that you wanted a pragmatic relationship, and I knew that was the last thing

I wanted, but I also knew that I would rather have that with you than have anything else with anybody else. I never thought I would fall in love with you—not after everything I'd been through—but I did. Bit by bit I came to see you for the wonderful man you are. Thoughtful, kind, considerate, funny...'

'Scintillating...sexy...'

'Egotistical...untidy...terrible at cooking... The memory of that steak you cooked for me last week will live on in my head for ever...'

'Hey! That last one's going too far!' Leo burst out laughing. When he'd sobered up, he said, seriously, 'I would get down on one knee, Maddie, but I'm already sitting. Will you marry me? For the *right* reasons? Because I love you and need you and can't live without you?'

'Just try and stop me!'

Maddie flung her arms round his neck. She was living her own fairy tale. Whoever said that they couldn't come true?

The wedding was low-key. They both wanted to exchange vows before the baby was born, so less than three months later a very pregnant Maddie walked up the aisle in a picturesque church on the outskirts of Dublin.

Leo's grandfather, beaming with pride, was in attendance, accompanied by a female friend whom, he confided to Maddie, he had been seeing 'off and on' for over a year and a half.

'I've never mentioned it to Leo,' he said, 'because I'm an old fool, and you know how matter-of-fact that grandson of mine can be. Didn't want him pooh-poohing the whole thing. But all that's changed, thanks to you, my dear. The minute I met you I knew that you were the one who was going to change him for the better. No, maybe *better* isn't the word I'm looking for—because no one could ever accuse Leo of being anything but an honourable man. Maybe change him for the *softer*, if that makes any sense.'

Maddie didn't tell him that there hadn't been that much to change after all, because there had been a softie buried deep down all the time.

By now she had made friends in Dublin. Other mums-to-be, several members of staff at the store, who were all now energised as the store finally began to pay dividends.

It had been a two-pronged effort—one that had been shared between her and Leo. She had listened to his ideas for introducing a dedicated electronics department, which was loosely based on his original idea for what he had intended to do with the store, but scaled down considerably. In time, he would source a suitable location and expand operations there. He had given way to her with the rest. She had laughed when he'd suggested lending a hand when it came to choosing sexy lingerie for the women's department.

'It would definitely work,' he had murmured one evening, when they'd both been warm and sated and wrapped round one another in bed after some very satisfying lovemaking, 'if you try on each sample piece for me to inspect...'

The store had brought them together and now, for Maddie, it was something special—something more than just concrete and stone—and it would be for ever. She quietly hoped, and so did Leo, that it would be a legacy they would be able to pass down to their children, and their children's children, that its story would be told over and over until it became the backdrop to their lives. A very happy and wonderful story, despite its inauspicious beginnings.

There were no relatives for her at the small wedding—no brothers or sisters or aunts or uncles—but Maddie didn't mind. She had the most important person in the world there. She was marrying the man who had spotted her once upon a time in a store she had been battling to hang on to, and the rest, as he fondly told her, was history.

After the wedding they went on a flying honeymoon to a five-star hotel in Cornwall, and they had a wonderful time in driving rain and under heavy grey skies, wrapped up in woollens, as happy holding hands there as if they'd been on the most expensive trip to the Maldives.

'When the baby comes and you can travel comfortably,' Leo promised, 'we're going to go sailing down the Grenadines. Until then…' he looked up at the leaden skies and grinned '…we're going to enjoy the wonderful English countryside in typical English weather. It'll stand me in good stead for when we move out to the country.'

Having done up her grandfather's house to the highest possible standard, Maddie found herself reluctant to live there.

'I can forgive my grandfather for the sin of pride,' she'd admitted, 'but I can't forget. And I'll always wonder what life would have been like for me and Mum if he'd just relented and forgiven her for running away.'

'Too arrogant and too stubborn,' Leo had murmured.

'Those were traits he had even as a young man, according to my grandfather, and they probably became out of control the older he got and the lonelier he became. And don't forget he was gambling and drinking heavily. Those two things would have turned his brain to mush and wreaked havoc on his ability to think clearly.'

So they'd found a lovely little house, close to the very church where they'd married. And, of course, there was Leo's London place, which was every bit as luxurious as she remembered. But Dublin, he confessed, had grown on him.

Flora Madison Conti was born three days after her due date with no fuss at all.

Dark-haired and green-eyed, she was sweet-natured and, within hours of coming into the world, already the apple of her father's eye.

Their real honeymoon, taken when Flora was a little over three months old, was as perfect as anything Maddie could have hoped for, and made all the better when she received news that the store, for the first time in over a decade, had shown a profit.

Maddie thought that if only her mother could have seen her she would have been bursting with pride that her daughter had married for love—and also highly amused that Maddie was now in charge of the very store from which she had once been exiled.

Now, with Flora asleep, Maddie was in the kitchen in their beautiful little house, with her very domesticated alpha male husband due back at any second.

She heard the key in the lock and the sound of the door opening and her heart skipped a beat. Leo never failed to command her attention.

He strode in and smiled as his dark eyes rested on

her. Sitting there, with her long toffee-coloured hair swept over one shoulder and her golden skin glowing, she was the very picture of everything any man could ever hope for.

He was lucky, and he knew that he was. He had resigned himself to a life without love and he couldn't believe how naïve he had been in thinking that he could ever have been happy in a union that was devoid of it.

'Flora asleep, my darling?'

'She is…' Maddie stood up and walked towards him, and with every step closer her pulse raced faster and her pupils dilated. She felt the push of her breasts against her bra. 'And I've cooked us something special.'

'Tell me I haven't forgotten a special day… The anniversary of the first time you thought I was a wandering explorer…? Or maybe of the first time you realised that you were head over heels in love with the only man you'll ever need…?'

He grinned and pulled her to him, kissed her with lingering thoroughness.

'Sweet,' he murmured. 'Like nectar. Now, this special meal…will it wait?'

'Leo…!'

But Maddie giggled and tingled as he unhooked her bra and cupped her breast in his hand as though weighing it.

'Is that a plea for sex? Because if it is, then your wish is my command.'

'Is that *all* you think about?'

'It's all I've been thinking about since about…oh… three this afternoon. Highly inappropriate, given that I was in a high-level meeting at the time.' He stood back and looked at her, his beautiful eyes tender and serious.

'But I think about other things too. I think about how much I love being married to you and how bloody happy you make me. I think about how much I'm looking forward to growing old with you and sharing my life with you. And I think about my stunning little baby girl.'

'That's a lot of thinking for a top businessman like you,' Maddie said, and laughed.

'And that's not all I've been thinking about…' Leo murmured as they headed up the stairs to their bedroom suite, which was next to the nursery where Flora was fast asleep.

'No?' She was breathless as they entered the bedroom and he quietly shut the door behind them, not bothering to switch on the lights.

She began undoing the buttons of his shirt until it was open, and then she rubbed his flat brown nipple with the pad of her thumb, making him shudder at the delicate touch. When she rested her hand on the bulging erection pushing against his trousers, he stifled a moan.

'Tell me what else you've been thinking about…' She guided his hand to her loose skirt and then encouraged him to explore further, to touch her under the floaty fabric, through her lacy underwear, to feel her wetness on his fingers.

'You mean aside from what you want me to do to you right now?'

On cue, he slipped his big hand under her knickers and began rubbing between her legs with the flat of his hand. He wasn't in any rush to take things faster just yet. He kept on rubbing, before slipping a finger deep into her, loving the way her muscles contracted at the intimate contact.

'Keep that up and I won't remember what it is we're talking about,' Maddie panted unevenly.

'Okay...' Leo slid his finger to find the nub of her core and transferred his attention there. 'Here's what I've been thinking. What about making another baby, my darling? Right now?'

Maddie giggled and sighed and looked at him from under her lashes, her whole body on fire as he continued to devastate her senses with his finger.

'And that's why I adore you,' she breathed. 'You can read my mind...'

* * * * *

COMING SOON!

We really hope you enjoyed reading this book. If you're looking for more romance, be sure to head to the shops when new books are available on

Thursday
23rd August

MILLS & BOON

MILLS & BOON

Coming next month

THE HEIR THE PRINCE SECURES
Jennie Lucas

He eyed the baby in the stroller, who looked back at him with dark eyes exactly like his own. He said simply, 'I need you and Esme with me.'

'In London?'

Leaning forward, he whispered, 'Everywhere.'

She felt the warmth of his breath against her skin, and her heartbeat quickened. For so long, Tess would have done anything to hear Stefano speak those words.

But she'd suffered too much shock and grief today. He couldn't tempt her to forget so easily how badly he'd treated her. She pulled away.

'Why would I come with you?'

Stefano's eyes widened. She saw she'd surprised him.

Giving her a crooked grin, he said, 'I can think of a few reasons.'

'If you want to spend time with Esme, I will be happy to arrange that. But if you think I'll give up my family and friends and home—' she lifted her chin '—and come with you to Europe as some kind of paid nanny—'

'No. Not my nanny.' Stefano's thumb lightly traced her tender lower lip. 'I have something else in mind.'

Unwilling desire shot down her body, making her nipples taut as tension coiled low in her belly. Her pride was screaming for her to push him away but it was difficult to hear her pride over the rising pleas of her body.

'I—I won't be your mistress, either,' she stammered, shivering, searching his gaze.

'No.' With a smile that made his dark eyes gleam, Stefano shook his head. 'Not my mistress.'

'Then…then what?' Tess stammered, feeling foolish for even suggesting a handsome billionaire prince like Stefano would want a regular girl like her as his mistress. Her cheeks were hot. 'You don't want me as your nanny, not as your mistress, so—what? You just want me to come to London as someone who watches your baby for free?' Her voice shook. 'Some kind of…p-poor relation?'

'No.' Taking her in his arms, Stefano said quietly, 'Tess. Look at me.'

Although she didn't want to obey, she could not resist. She opened her eyes, and the intensity of his glittering eyes scared her.

'I don't want you to be my mistress, Tess. I don't want you to be my nanny.' His dark eyes burned through her. 'I want you to be my wife.'

Continue reading
THE HEIR THE PRINCE SECURES
Jennie Lucas

Available next month
www.millsandboon.co.uk

LET'S TALK
Romance

For exclusive extracts, competitions
and special offers, find us online:

- f facebook.com/millsandboon
- @millsandboonuk
- @millsandboon

Or get in touch on 0844 844 1351*

For all the latest titles coming soon, visit
millsandboon.co.uk/nextmonth

Calls cost 7p per minute plus your phone company's price per minute access charge